Postcolonial Writers in the Global Literary Marketplace

THE UNIVERSITY OF
WINCHESTER

Martial Rose Library
Tel: 01962 827306

'A remarkable book, bold and consequential, whose implications for the trajectory of postcolonial studies are significant and wide-ranging. Brouilette's narrow concern is with the mechanics underlying "postcolonial" writers' presentation of themselves in and through their books, their "troubled attempts at deliberate self-construction", as she puts it. Her broader concerns are to promote a form of scholarship alert to the idea that the writing of books is profoundly impacted by their production and reception as commodity objects for specific markets. These concerns are addressed here in nuanced and intricate readings of Salman Rushdie, J. M. Coetzee and Zulfikar Ghose, which serve simultaneously as substantive critical commentaries and as methodological forays into a post-Bourdieusian "sociology of literature". Original, illuminating, and compelling.'

— **Professor Neil Lazarus**, *University of Warwick, UK*

'This is a first-rate, controversial book by a young and alert scholar working at the cutting edge of a fast evolving field. Brouillette's writing is cogent and original. It covers acres of ground while drawing on incisive case studies. It is graceful, provocative and interesting. It is the real McCoy.'

— **Robert Fraser**, *Open University, UK*

Postcolonial Writers in the Global Literary Marketplace

Sarah Brouillette
Associate Professor, Department of English,
Carleton University, Canada

First published 2007
Published in paperback 2011 by
PALGRAVE MACMILLAN

Palgrave Macmillan in the UK is an imprint of Macmillan Publishers Limited, registered in England, company number 785998, of Houndmills, Basingstoke, Hampshire RG21 6XS.

Palgrave Macmillan in the US is a division of St Martin's Press LLC, 175 Fifth Avenue, New York, NY 10010.

Palgrave Macmillan is the global academic imprint of the above companies and has companies and representatives throughout the world.

Palgrave® and Macmillan® are registered trademarks in the United States, the United Kingdom, Europe and other countries

ISBN: 978–0–230–50784–5 hardback
ISBN: 978–0–230–34643–7 paperback

This book is printed on paper suitable for recycling and made from fully managed and sustained forest sources. Logging, pulping and manufacturing processes are expected to conform to the environmental regulations of the country of origin.

A catalogue record for this book is available from the British Library.

Library of Congress Cataloging-in-Publication Data
Brouillette, Sarah, 1977–
    Postcolonial writers in the global literary marketplace / by Sarah Brouillette.
        p. cm.
    Includes bibliographical references and index.
    ISBN 978–0–230–50784–5   (cloth)
    ISBN 978–0–230–34643–7 (paperback)
    1. Commonwealth literature (English)–History and criticism. 2. Authorship –Economic aspects–History–20th century. 3. Literature publishing–History– 20th century. 4. Literature and globalization–Commonwealth countries. 5. Book industries and trade–History–20th century. 6. Postcolonialism in literature. I. Title.

    PR9080.5.B76 2007
    820.9–dc22   2007060019

10   9   8   7   6   5   4   3   2   1
20   19   18   17   16   15   14   13   12   11

Printed and bound in Great Britain by
Antony Rowe Ltd, Chippenham and Eastbourne

Contents

Preface to the Paperback Edition

In Daljit Nagra's poem 'Kabba Questions the Ontology of Representation, the Catch 22 for "Black" Writers,' the speaker rails against teachers who assign a General Certificate of Secondary Education (GCSE) 'antology,' which treats 'us / as a bunch of Gunga Dins ju group *"Poems from Udder Cultures and Traditions"*.' He concludes by turning on the poet 'Daljit-Bulram':

> [...] too shy to uze
>
> his voice, he plot me
> as 'funny', or a type, even vurse –
>   so hee is used in British antologies –
>   he hide in dis whitey 'fantum' English, blacked
>
>   to make me sound 'poreign'!!¹

According to Kabba, this 'Dalgit-Bulram' uses a 'blacked' English in order to garner the kind of recognition that inclusion in the GSCE curriculum would signify. He charges that within this English the poet buries his own difference, while making 'poreign' those for whom standard GSCE fare would itself be 'udder.' The lines thus knowingly implicate themselves in the same racialized separation between self and 'udder,' the same limited apprehension of people as 'types,' and the same hunger for mainstream consecration, that they appear to attack. The poet critiques the very language in which his self-criticism is embedded.

Evident here is Nagra's self-conscious interest in the institutions that evaluate and consecrate literature, and in the relationship between the writer and the community to which he is fitfully connected. These same interests motivated the research for this book, as I sought to look at postcolonial literature through a materialist lens. The book's final form and argumentation, constrained like all writing by the author's particular competence and by time and materials, only begin to answer the questions with which I started.

Why and how are certain texts extensively circulated and celebrated, and others not? What larger social, cultural and economic forces does the highlighting of certain writers reflect and help constitute? How do the dissemination and reception of postcolonial texts shape new works formally and thematically? In asking these questions I drew on the sociology of literature – especially Pierre Bourdieu's theory of the literary field – and on book history and print culture studies, with its attention to the production, circulation, reception and valuation of texts, and its interest in how social, economic, cultural and legal contexts impinge upon and are shaped by texts in turn. Finding, however, that book history had little to say about postcolonial topics or the contemporary moment, I also referenced a small body of research on postcolonial literature's social and economic underpinnings: in particular, I turned to Aijaz Ahmad's *In Theory: Classes, Nations, Literatures*, Graham Huggan's *The Postcolonial Exotic: Marketing the Margins* and Timothy Brennan's *Salman Rushdie and the Third World: Myths of the Nation*.[2]

Motivated by this research, I attempted to uncover the relationship between the mainstreaming of English-language postcolonial literature and the processes of transnationalization, corporatization and conglomeration in the publishing industry. They appeared to be broadly coeval. Could a precise correlation be pinpointed, or was it simply a matter of a coincidence between the concentration and spread of global capital and the movement across borders of people and texts from the newly decolonized nations? I concluded that branding a postcolonial niche could be seen as one of the ways that an Anglo-American publishing industry facilitated the motivation and capture of new readerships both at home and in far-flung markets, and that this work was energized by the commercial pressures publishers faced after their incorporation into transnational media corporations or conglomerates. I stress that this is an available interpretation because, while the resources were too disparate and scant – and the original question probably too broad – for this lone researcher to glean some gospel archival truth, it matters to my study that this is a narrative that some influential critics and reviewers, along with other participants in the postcolonial literary field, at once circulated and expressed concern about.

I considered then how this particular broad narrative, which is attended by a series of sub-narratives about the tensions amongst authors' experiences, personae, texts, and markets, shapes literary form. From here I arrived at my book's focus, which is the way writers associated with particular locations deploy, worry about and deflect those associations when they enter an increasingly globalized literary marketplace and see their texts and their personae circulating there. I argue that the writers I consider, who are simply suggestive examples of broader trends, use their works both to theorize the literary field and to articulate self-criticism or self-defence (or, perhaps, defensive self-criticism). I emphasize as well that the world of circulation and reception evident in their works is decidedly imagined: never a bare reflection of a real world of consumers and producers, it is instead an always interested construction coloured by the writer's attempt to negotiate a liveable identity and career.

Some related conclusions follow. The evidence that writers naively exoticize themselves and their communities in order to sell their work to a complacently touristic readership – a readership which comfortably consumes a widening array of 'diverse' texts – is unconvincing. I argue instead that writers' relationships to their ostensible communities are as likely to be agonized and alienated as they are to be opportunistic; and I suggest, as Graham Huggan suggests, that postcolonial literature evinces a complicated process of indulging, resisting and critiquing its imagined consumption, and will distinguish between readers worthy of applause and those in need of some re-education. I conclude as well that it is likely that many participants in the postcolonial literary field, readers included, apprehend cannily or even guiltily their political complicities and responsibilities, and that the shape of the field – what it prizes, celebrates, denigrates or just ignores – reflects participants' concerns about what they consume and why. This does not mean that there is no reason to critique writers, or the industry of postcoloniality, or transnational media conglomerates. On the contrary – and this is a point I would now make more explicit – it means that a cannily self-critical cultural field is not necessarily one with a progressive politics, nor one that wishes to, can, or will oppose corporate power and the cultural dominance perpetuated by the metro-centric concentration of English-language media in London and New York.

Since this book was first published, materialist study of postcolonial books and print culture has flourished. Andrew van der Vlies' *South African Textual Cultures: White, Black, Read All Over*, Ruvani Ranasinha's *South Asian Writers in Twentieth-Century Britain: Culture in Translation*, Robert Fraser's *Book History through Postcolonial Eyes: Rewriting the Script*, Peter McDonald's *The Literature Police: Apartheid Censorship and its Cultural Consequences*, and Gail Low's *Publishing the Postcolonial: Anglophone West African and Caribbean Writing in the UK* confirm that the material forces at work within the postcolonial literary field are always more than mere context.[3] They are the productive constraints that shape what is available to our imaginations and how meaning and value are formed and crystallized.

As new research emerges, avenues for further research proliferate. Little has been said about how gender and class matter to the history of postcolonial books and print culture. Elite literature and a concern with literariness have overshadowed attention to more popular genres. The role of small and independent publishers has been studied, but not as much as that of major firms and mainstream markets. The relevance of new media has not been much examined. Nor has much attention been paid to the role that the state plays in regulating and deregulating cultural markets, or that NGOs play in funding culture and fostering its consumption. These are just a few examples. So much research is left to be conceived and undertaken, it forms an exciting but also a daunting prospect.

Finally, I should note that in the time between this book's initial publication and its appearance in paperback I have been able to discuss this work, and to continue to research and write on related topics, because of material and intellectual support I received from the Literature Faculty at MIT and from the Department of English at Carleton University. I thank in particular James Buzard, Shankar Raman, Diana Henderson, Arthur Bahr, Mary Fuller, Alisa Braithwaite, Sandy Alexandre, Noel Jackson, Joshua Green, Paul Keen, Travis DeCook, and Brian Greenspan.

Notes

1 Daljit Nagra, 'Kabba Questions the Ontology of Representation, the Catch 22 for "Black" Writers', in *Look We Have Coming to Dover!* (London: Faber and Faber, 2007), 42–3.

2 Timothy Brennan, *Salman Rushdie and the Third World: Myths of the Nation* (New York: St Martin's Press, 1989); Aijaz Ahmad, *In Theory: Classes, Nations, Literatures* (London: Verso, 2002); Graham Huggan, *The Postcolonial Exotic: Marketing the Margins* (London: Routledge, 2001).

3 Andrew van der Vlies, *South African Textual Cultures: White, Black Read All Over* (Manchester: Manchester University Press, 2007); Ruvani Ranasinha, *South Asian Writers in Twentieth-Century Britain: Culture in Translation* (Oxford: Clarendon Press, 2007); Robert Fraser, *Book History through Postcolonial Eyes: Rewriting the Script* (London: Routledge, 2008); Peter McDonald, *The Literature Police: Apartheid Censorship and its Cultural Consequences* (Oxford University Press, 2009); Gail Low, *Publishing the Postcolonial: Anglophone West African and Caribbean Writing in the UK 1948–1968* (London: Routledge, 2010).

Acknowledgements

Initial research for this study was supported generously by the Social Sciences and Humanities Research Council of Canada, and by my mentors and peers at the University of Toronto, in the Department of English and in the Collaborative Program in Book History and Print Culture. Additional writing and research took place during my invaluable time at Syracuse University, and in my early days at the Massachusetts Institute of Technology. As I formulated my ideas I developed particular debts to various readers and listeners; these include Chelva Kanaganayakam, Neil ten Kortenaar, Heather Murray, Don Moggridge, Chris Bongie, Mike Goode, and Sara Malton.

I extend thanks and love to that larger network of people whose conversation helped me decide what is worth thinking about: Zach Pickard, Archana Rampure, Kulpreet Sasan, Babur Ansari, Jenny Godfrey, and Jeet Heer; and to my family, Craig, Susan, Robert, and Scott Brouillette; and to Travis DeCook, to whom I say, 'Semper fi, Esposito. Semper fi.'

A version of Chapter 3 – shorter, and making a different argument – appeared in the March 2005 issue of the *Journal of Commonwealth Literature*. A more substantial portion of Chapter 5 appears in *Modern Fiction Studies* in March 2007. I acknowledge these journals for permission to reprint and rework some material here.

Introduction

A notable aspect of recent postcolonial writing is the way authors use their texts to register anxiety about the political parameters of the literary marketplace. Indeed expressions of self-consciousness, whether ultimately self-exempting or self-implicating, are a constitutive feature of the postcolonial field, at once eminently saleable and productive of the patterns of taste through which postcolonial literature is consumed and understood. Attending to the changing nature of current publishing, and to the position of postcolonial authors within literary markets, thus assumes a compelling relevance for meaningful interpretative practice. Situating and understanding writers' troubled attempts at deliberate self-construction is the focus of this book. In the process I recuperate the controversial author-figure for literary interpretation.

The figural strategies I consider here arise largely from political qualms that attend English-language literature's increasingly global reach. Though it has as yet said little about postcolonial contexts or about contemporary culture more generally, recent book history has nevertheless done much to reinforce the relevance of questions of media and market to literary study. Variously labeled the history of the book, *histoire du livre*, the history of texts, or print culture studies, book history develops from a lengthy tradition of close attention to the material conditions of textual production, transmission, and reception, evident in everything from historical bibliography and the French *annales* school of history to British cultural studies. Its interests are those processes and institutions that mediate literary production and consumption, as influenced by economic systems, political frameworks, and legal institutions. One of the key insights of book history, perhaps best formulated in Jerome McGann's *The Textual Condition* (1991) and in D.F. McKenzie's *Bibliography and the Sociology of Texts*

(1986), is that the material aspects of a text, including its format, cover, packaging, and typography, as well as the general field in which it is situated, comprised of the institutions of literary production, dissemination, and reception, are more than merely context for the work's conception and realization.[1] Instead they are *textual* in their own right. This works in a few ways. Most obviously, there is a relationship between the material aspects of a book's construction and the meaning any reader might glean from it. In addition, the seemingly extratextual world surrounding books, a world which includes, for example, the institutions and circumstances that make up the field of postcolonial literature, is also material for the construction of specific kinds of meaning. As Pierre Bourdieu often noted, and as my own work will show, the social production of literature often translates into literature itself. In this vein, I reveal some of the ways that the field of production specific to postcoloniality is manifest in identifiable literary and critical strategies.

An important insight that research like Bourdieu's enables is that literary production is influenced by the development of authorship as a profession and by the process through which writers consume images of themselves and reinterpret those images in order to negotiate and circulate different ones. In connecting this process to McGann's and McKenzie's insights, one could point to Gerard Genette's theory of paratextuality.[2] Like them, Genette emphasizes the connections between things like prefaces, titles, formats, interviews, reviews, and blurbs, and the 'text itself' that those elements accompany. A work's overall paratext is a key constraint on how it will be read and understood. He also emphasizes that the construction and use of authors' identities is not something that happens independently of the products those authors participate in creating. Each moment in an author's marketing instead becomes a part of the paratext for his subsequent works' reception. In turn those works become opportunities for a writer to engage in acts of self-construction and critique, and to explore the significance of authorship itself in contemporary literary culture. In outlining his influential communications circuit Robert Darnton explains:

> A writer may respond in his writing to criticisms of his previous work or anticipate reactions that his text will elicit. He addresses implicit readers and hears from explicit reviewers. So the circuit runs full cycle. It transmits messages, transforming them en route, as they pass from thought to writing to printed characters and back to thought again.[3]

One of the implications of this cycle is that authorship cannot be analyzed without reference to the general circuit through which texts pass. The separate personae attached to writers take on meaning as they circulate through it. Authors then act as consumers of their own images as they react to their own personae in their literary works, often through attempts at theorizing the process itself, whether thought of as the communications circuit, the field of cultural production, or more recently, and with more relevance here, the field of postcolonial production.[4]

In short, authors' careers are key paratexts for reception and reproduction, and the writers I consider have all used literature to interact with their own paratextual histories. But because my focus is postcolonial writers, my analysis necessarily updates the established material history of literary authorship, which I outline in my second chapter. Specifically, it refines Bourdieu's important argument, central to *The Field of Cultural Production* (1993) and to much of *The Rules of Art* (1996), that the rise of a large-scale literary marketplace that made it possible for authors to make a living by writing occurred in tandem with the development of an ideology of artistic purity and separation from economic concerns. This ideology supported the emergence of the charismatic author as a romantic creator, one who disavowed a market that relied on large-scale production as a means of capitalist accumulation. A growing body of scholarship on the history of authorship supports Bourdieu's claims.

What I argue is that anxiety about commercialization takes on a different aspect in postcolonial writers' authorial self-consciousness. While always problematic, talk of saving literature from 'reduction' to commodity status is now scarcely possible. As a niche developed in tandem with general market expansion in the publishing industry, postcolonial literature is especially compromised, and this is a situation with significant implications for the writers I discuss. While their authorship is by all means irrevocably implicated in the expanding global market for English-language literary texts, it is not threatened in any straightforward way by association with commercial expansion and mass production.

Instead the current market positioning of postcolonial writing is an aspect of – and a contributing factor in – a shift away from any sense of the writer as a being with resolute autonomy from the commercial sphere. The postcolonial author has emerged as a profoundly complicit and compromised figure whose authority rests, however uncomfortably, in the nature of his connection to the specificity of a given political location. In ways I describe throughout, writers' anxiety tends to stem from the dissemination of their texts to reading communities accessing privileged metropolitan markets that are often (though not exclusively) Anglo-American in location and orientation. Writers are compelled to resist, justify, or celebrate precisely this aspect of the postcolonial field's arrangement, in accordance with their own circumstances.

For example, they often complain that their agency is subsumed or undermined by the association of their works with overly determined local political affiliations, whether national or otherwise. Any sanctioned and saleable 'authentic' identity associated with their texts hardly grants them significant control, after all, as what is marketed as a personal biographical connection actually masks – and is designed to mask – writers' larger detachment from the relevant processes of production, distribution, and consumption. As their books reach a variety of audiences with conflicting tendencies and interests, writers are unable to determine how exactly the attachment between authorial persona and text is constructed or received.

Thus, though a publisher's emphasis on local biographical affiliation may work through a basic celebration of the representation of some 'other' region, it may result at the same time in readers' hostility toward (or praise for) the writer's problematic negation of (or triumph over) the same identified local circumstances. In fact, in a characteristic divide between the dictates of the market and the demands of a critical readership, the allure of a text's locality, authenticity, or biographical specificity, already perhaps an obfuscation of the writer's experience, is often taken as immediately undermined by its even having attained a position within an essentially compromised global culture industry. I develop this argument in Part I, explaining that due to some definitive tensions between saleable local subject matter and uncontrolled global dissemination, postcolonial authors will express apprehension about the political locations and prerogatives of their discrepant readerships. In essence, I suggest, whereas the romantic author-figure once lamented a commercial compromise in attaining widespread acclaim, for the postcolonial writer the problem is the politicization of incorporation into a discredited global sphere. This politicization is something they face and acknowledge, but do not necessarily sanction.

Still, if writers attempt to rectify a marked absence of self-authorization by figuring their career experiences in their works, the story doesn't end there. As I've noted, authors' gestures of self-consciousness, spanning the spectrum from abject self-critique to triumphant self-authorization, arise in market conditions that are defined by significant political strain. It is precisely such conditions that make declarations of self-awareness so pressing, but also largely inadequate, or at least problematic. In a recurring tension, self-constructing gestures are challenged by the same circumstances that encourage their emergence, as writers will themselves readily admit, and so a cycle of critique and response typically ensues.

On the one hand, persistent solipsism or self-consciousness is rather easily dismissed as a protective gesture of self-preservation, and as one that finesses the inadequacy of claims to self-knowledge. The willing admission of what has been taken to be one's political compromises and ethical flaws may be simply a disguise, a way of situating and critiquing those who might otherwise judge you. While the author can preempt criticism in precisely this way, he cannot necessarily weaken it thereby, as the forms of critique that writers face are typically not solved by their having been admitted to, countered, or displayed for their respective readerships.

On the other hand, since the circumstances that contribute to producing authors' self-consciousness are general to late capitalist post-coloniality, and include all those radical insecurities of the subject, of identity, of rational thought, and of the clearly bounded community, self-conscious gestures are highly saleable to the audiences that arise within this same milieu. My opening chapter is largely devoted to a consideration of this question of the marketability of postcolonial self-consciousness. Much of Graham Huggan's *The Postcolonial Exotic* (2001), a groundbreaking materialist study of 'the industry of postcoloniality,' is dependent upon faith in the existence of a global reader figure who exoticizes literature in the same way that a tourist ostensibly exoticizes 'foreign' cultures. It is in this light that Huggan identifies a certain 'strategic exoticism' that pervades postcolonial writing, as authors attempt to show that they understand the ways in which they are being asked to present the Third World or global South to a presumably apolitical metropolitan audience. I suggest that Huggan's theory of strategic exoticism both admits and deflects some of the political questioning that postcolonial writers and critics have faced. If, as I argue, the industry of postcoloniality can be thought of as having a touristic conscience, a conscience which often fuels the way authors respond to their own reception and market positioning, then Huggan's global reader figure is one correlate to a pervasive guilt about the consumption of postcolonial cultural products. His critique of an unspecified global reader in pursuit of exotic access to what is culturally 'other' is what allows him to identify, and identify with, an elite group of distinguished consumers said to apprehend texts in a more responsible way.

In turn, by pointing to a few moments in Derek Walcott's career – specifically, the moments of publication of 'What the Twilight Says' (1971) and of *The Fortunate Traveller* (1982) – I also begin to reposition the general function of authors' strategic exoticism and self-consciousness. While Walcott has been a literary celebrity since the early 1980s, having been consecrated by major literary foundations and a new life and professorships in the American Northeast, authorship constitutes a source of anxiety in 'The Fortunate Traveller.' This anxiety does not arise from interaction with a commercial sphere of commodity consumption that has Walcott imagining his own separation from the world of large-scale production. Instead his work is made analogous to a task of pleading before an international monetary agency and is as such always implicated in economic exchange. What produces anxiety within the poem is the speaker's position as spokesperson for a beleaguered polity, a group of sufferers 'What the Twilight Says' depicts as attached to him by birth but separated by acculturation. Walcott worries about his own position as a poet writing about the Caribbean, or indeed the underdeveloped world *in toto*, and dependent on that material for much of the *frisson*, acclaim, and canonization granted him within his new metropolitan location. He presents himself as anxiously responsible for that same material in an explicitly ethical way, and as critical of an imagined privileged readership that turns suffering into 'compassionate fodder for the travel book.'[5]

As they are engaged in attempts at constructing their own reception, the authors I consider all construe their career histories in ways that have as much to do with figures of readership as with fictions or configurations of self-conscious authorship. Like Walcott, they figure their careers by identifying and critiquing imagined niche audiences or communities of interest. I call this readership 'imagined' not because it corresponds with no real audience, but because its reality is less important than the author's expressed faith in its existence and in its power to constrain the political significance and repercussions of his career and writings. Writers may project or idealize their authorship and address an imagined readership, but their resulting constructions are hardly baseless. Instead they arise from often troubling real-world circumstances and experiences of labour, aspiration, fear, and guilt. Throughout Chapter 1, I suggest some of the ways these constructions take shape, by highlighting notable homologies between a series of postcolonial consumer figures – for example, the 'market reader,'[6] the ethnographer, the cosmopolitan, and the tourist. These figures reappear in altered states in the case studies that make up Part II.

Indeed reading 'The Fortunate Traveller' in light of Walcott's position in relation to a literary economy with decidedly political boundaries and implications allows me to introduce the cases that follow. Insofar as he negotiates a fraught cosmopolitan identity that has him navigating between a site of representation (the Caribbean) and a locus of reception (metropolitan London and New York), Walcott is emblematic. His will to express his self-consciousness about his position as an author working within an extended literary marketplace for postcolonial products is something he shares with the other writers I discuss. His effort to engage in specific acts of self-construction based on that positioning is also typical. And yet much though his texts might construct a reader figure in need of some amount of reeducation, I point to the problems that arise from thinking of his – or anyone's – strategic exoticism as something designed to teach a reader about her own exoticizing tendencies. Instead I find it more fruitful to understand strategic exoticism, and likewise general postcolonial authorial self-consciousness, as comprised of a set of literary strategies that operate through assumptions shared between the author and the reader, as both producer and consumer work to negotiate with, if not absolve themselves of, postcoloniality's touristic guilt. Like the business of tourism, any postcoloniality industry depends upon the very marketability of self-consciousness about the production and consumption of what circulates within it. It is in this sense that I understand postcolonial authorship as in part a generative and saleable feature of the industry that it aims to assess.

Though in quite different ways, the cases in Part II each support this larger argument. Informed by the analysis of the postcolonial literary field and by the material history of authorship offered in Part I, my readings of works by Salman Rushdie, J.M. Coetzee, and Zulfikar Ghose are supplemented by reference to the reception of each writer and to the material circumstances relevant to his work's production and circulation. Each chapter features an author whose works configure his own career and reception history, yet each also makes a unique case within my larger conception of postcolonial authorship. Though I selected these writers for reasons I will elaborate in a moment, my readings are meant to be illustrative rather than exhaustive, and countless others could be understood through a similar interpretative framework.

In each of my cases the author's locality – whether ethnic, national, or otherwise, whether fictional, real, or both – has been subject to significant market appropriation and critical attention. Each belongs to that community that Biodun Jeyifo identifies as possessed of a notably metropolitan or 'hybrid' consciousness that produces an interstitial or liminal writing. To elaborate, much postcolonial literary scholarship has been focused on the characteristics of fiction produced by migrant writers exploring aspects of life within a cosmopolitan culture, or concerned with a migrant or expatriate life away from the place of one's birth.

However, lest this scholarship continue to 'display an excessive interest in the fiction of migrants,'[7] making postcolonial critics liable to E. San Juan Jr.'s charge that they 'valorize their own dilemma as paradigmatic,'[8] it is equally important to see how the Anglo-American publishing industry, which in turn feeds global markets with literary products, includes writers who continue to remain on the periphery and who exist within local publishing structures as well as within the larger international market. These writers, too, face the expectation that their fiction will comment on their own locales for a larger, more diffuse audience. Especially given the way literary markets have recently been globalized, it is the collection of these authors, when added to those migrants or descendants of migrants inhabiting the Northern metropoles, who form an international community unified by the publishing industry for postcolonial literature's audiences.

Jeyifo's positing of the embattled coexistence of a normative literature of nationalist or culturalist 'proleptic designation' and a more 'interstitial' writing associated with metropolitan aesthetics is useful in this respect. For Jeyifo the former proleptic category applies when 'the writer or critic speaks to, for, or in the name of the postindependence nation-state, the regional or continental community, the pan-ethnic, racial or cultural agglomeration of homelands and diasporas.' Yet it is those in the interstitial category – still attached to specific locales, though less contentedly – who 'enjoy far greater visibility and acclaim in the academies, journals and media of the metropolitan First World countries than the post-coloniality of the more nationalistic, counter-hegemonic expression.'[9] In brief, in ways I describe further in Chapter 2, it is these interstitial writers who have largely comprised successful postcolonial literature for a market and academic readership, and it is their work that I situate and examine. That said, this is a broad designation, and I read each author's case as a response to his own unique position as a producer subject to forms of reception constrained by the current market.

For instance, as a South African novelist who remained in that country throughout the apartheid period and recent reconciliation process, J.M. Coetzee has positioned himself as someone made to deal with two distinct audiences. He tends to understand these audiences as having instituted radically different definitions of literary value. Under conditions of apartheid, a local audience asked that he express opposition to the South African political situation rather than write in the poststructuralist tradition he usually engaged; in contrast, his global consumers often took his work to be precisely the interpretation and representation of national politics, though necessarily and properly refracted through the lens of aesthetic distance, that the local community thought lacking. Coetzee is not alone in crediting this binary. Attending to his sense of his own fraught reception allows me to show how his recent novels – *The Master of Petersburg* (1994), *Disgrace* (1999), and *Elizabeth Costello* (2003) – engage the conditions of authorship in one particular political locale. Mainly, they represent a series of judgements, trails, and confessions in a way that critiques the naïve requirement, ostensibly obtaining for the more politicized component of his perceived readership, that writers express a sincere political commitment. In the process they construct a particular local reader figure – generally, the reader as censor – in order to subject that figure to stark contestation. This is the official state censor who polices what the larger public is allowed to read, but also, significantly, the censoring voice within the state's political opposition, which Coetzee works to align with the same silencing prerogative characteristic of its seeming foes.

Alternatively, for Zulfikar Ghose, the reader figure at the heart of his authorial self-construction is that of the cosmopolitan academic or intellectual. Ghose is a somewhat peripheral writer, and he understands his own status as owing to his refusal to write about any locale that can be identified with his South Asian origins in any straightforward way. In Ghose's experience the postcolonial authors who most often find success are those available for biographical positioning within a locality clearly aligned to their literary interests. The fact that he has attempted to establish a career that resists this positioning has become a routine concern for those who have shown interest in his work. Ghose's is a clear case of a writer who would rather not have to be positioned biographically or regionally; yet, in one of those tensions I mention above, he can only dramatize his opposition to the continued relevance of biography in literary works that emerge from and figure a personal experience of authorial crisis. He draws himself back into consideration while insisting he would rather be irrelevant to it. My own interest is in his understanding of the required coincidence between authenticating origins and literary material. *The Triple Mirror of the Self* (1992) explores the question of the validity or authenticity of assumed origins, and attributes calls for such validation to a cosmopolitan intellectual figure derived from Ghose's perception of his own readership. It at once addresses and redresses Ghose's marginal status through a dramatic debunking of those appeals to authentic location that seem to have limited his career success.

It matters to my readings that Coetzee is a Nobel Prize winning author simultaneously situated within South African and Anglo-American milieus, that Ghose has made it impossible to associate his work with one definitive location or niche, and that Salman Rushdie is in many ways the exemplary postcolonial author and the consummate literary celebrity. Currently Rushdie's equally powerful agent and publishers ensure that his works reach the largest possible market share throughout the English-speaking world, as well as a large non-English audience through numerous lucrative translation contracts. It is not incidental to his success that he writes English-language novels from within the publishing nexus formed by New York and London, in a way that both references and refracts his own identity as a one-time migrant from the colonial periphery, and then as an internationally recognized author or global icon. *Fury* (2001) features a protagonist who, like Rushdie, recently left his family in England to move to New York. Malik creates content for television, producing cultural products that escape his control in a way that evokes precisely the sort of political appropriation of cultural texts that has defined Rushdie's career.

Reviewers criticized the novel as an obvious and self-serving memoir about the author's own recent experiences, as well as for its haphazard critique of a capitalist culture in which it is entirely complicit. I suggest that attention to Rushdie's career development, coupled with a focus on his investment in the theme of the 'politico-exotic' in his non-fiction travel narrative *The Jaguar Smile* (1987), reveals *Fury* to be all of those things, but also something more. It is a novel that laments the demise of the importance of authorial will, a demise that is constructed as facilitating culture's appropriation by militant factions of combating ideologues. If in Coetzee's work the reader is figured as a kind of censor, in Ghose's as a cosmopolitan intellectual, and in Walcott's as a tourist-cum-depoliticizing cosmopolitan, in Rushdie's case self-construction works through depictions of the consumer in the guise of the politico – the nationalist or subnationalist ideologue who uses the author's works as ammunition within a larger political struggle.

*

The nature of my interest in each writer's career, as I demonstrate links between its development, the author's general biography, and the meaning of his texts, is something that rarely goes unchallenged within literary studies. Book historians have on occasion been maligned for what is perceived as a naïve interest in the intentions and prerogatives of empirical authors. The importance of authors to literary analysis has after all been systemically undermined by two dominant trends in twentieth-century literary criticism. First in the 1940s and 50s the work of W.K. Wimsatt and Monroe C. Beardsley formalized the New Critical doctrine that 'the design or intention of the author is neither available nor desirable as a standard for judging the success of a work of literary art.'[10] Later poststructuralist work, most clearly formalized in Roland Barthes' 'The Death of the Author,' relegated the role of the author to that of a function of discourse, a fiction we impose on texts in order to stem our fears of endlessly pro-liferating meanings and as an answer to a number of related psycho-logical and institutional necessities.[11] While for the former, insisting on the author's irrelevance is part of an attempt to redefine the prior-ities of effective literary evaluation, for the latter, anti-authorialism develops from more sweeping ontological claims about the place of subjectivity in discourse.[12]

In turn, speaking for the empirical interests of publishing historians, Juliet Gardiner argues that statements about the death of the author are 'at odds with the realities of archival research, empirical practice, and particularly contemporary observation, where the author-figure grows ever more ubiquitously represented.'[13] In this sense the author as a figure we attach to literary production seems to be experiencing something of an identity crisis. On the one hand, he is being exces-sively biographized by the publishing industry circulating his name; on the other hand, he is disappearing continuously as ideas like Barthes' continue to hold sway within literary study. I complicate the validity of this seeming tension by pointing to the ways in which poststructuralism and the market present surprisingly similar chal-lenges to significant authorial agency. The author's demise may well be effectively orchestrated by a critical practice bent toward the death of subjectivity in general, but it is only in a superficial way that the process is slowed by the market function of the name of the post-colonial author, a name put to work to help establish the expansive circulation of postcolonial narratives.

Further, in Gardiner's view there is an implied author inherent in any text as a Barthesian function of discourse, and this differs from the extra-textual figure of the author that is of interest to historians. These two senses of authorship are often confused, and Gardiner laments this fact because for her there remains a necessary division between analysis of a text's literary elements and attention to its existence in an economic circuit observable through empirical examination. Recuperating biographical authorship is not something done in the service of making sense of literature's meaning; what interests her are author figures 'not as a cue to an interpretive textual practice but as genre branding, promotional supplement, and marketing strategy.'[14] In contrast, finally, it is my sense that this separation between any text's meaning and the circumstances of its existence as a marketed commodity is largely incomplete. Just as the proliferating ways in which authorial identities are marketed involves the construction of biographical fictions that audiences are asked to understand and respond to, recuperation of the careers of author-figures makes potentially fruitful material for literary interpretation in general. While the 'genre branding' of the author is undoubtedly important, and central to my own concerns, recuperating authors' identities can and should be what some have claimed it is definitively not – that is, an interpretive practice that aims at insight into literature itself.

Part I

1
The Industry of Postcoloniality

> Like a telescope reversed, the traveller's eye
> swiftly screws down the individual sorrow
> to an oval nest of antic numerals,
> and the iris, interlocking with this globe,
> condenses it to zero, then a cloud.[1]

Postcoloniality's touristic conscience

According to Graham Huggan's innovative materialist assessment, postcoloniality entails a form of industrial commodification that serves the interests of certain privileged audiences; the 'postcolonial field of production' turns out 'translated products for metropolitan consumers in places like London and New York.'[2] Huggan's description of this field involves frequent reference to a global market reader, a figure with indistinct identity and agency. Indeed this cosmopolitan consumer figure is one basis upon which Huggan's analysis depends, so it seems odd that she is subject to little of the materialist examination so crucial to his study's overall project. I begin this project by determining some of what is behind this neglect.

Two of Huggan's major claims can serve as initial illustrations of my concerns. First, a set of celebrated cosmopolitan writers is said to achieve success in the market due to commodity fetishism, which operates through all of the following: 'mystification (or levelling-out) of historical experience; imagined access to the cultural other through the process of consumption; [and] reification of people and places into exchangeable aesthetic objects' (19). Here, fetishism is a consumer behaviour characterized by a reading community's desire to achieve 'access to the cultural other,' as well as by its complicity in the

15

mystification and reification of that same other's seemingly authentic experiences. Second, Huggan's definition of the exotic in its newly global guise – in essence, the foreign fitfully translated into the unthreatening and familiar – rests on the notion that, now, 'difference is appreciated, but only in the terms of the beholder; diversity is translated and given a reassuringly familiar aesthetic cast' (27). The exotic is not a quality inherent to a given text but is instead the product of a specific mode of mass-market consumption. He writes, 'exoticism describes [...] a particular mode of aesthetic *perception* – one which renders people, objects and places strange even as it domesticates them, and which effectively manufactures otherness even as it claims to surrender to its immanent mystery' (13). In short, exoticism is a willful activity in which the 'beholder' is the major participant; exotic products are *manufactured* by a form of consumption characterized most notably by aestheticization and dehistoricization.

In establishing this definition one of the key distinctions that Huggan makes is between the pursuit of real knowledge and the desire for identification or escape. Huggan's central elaboration of a separation between postcolonial*ism* and postcolonial*ity* partakes of this divide. For him postcolonialism is largely an academic discipline, 'an anti-colonial intellectualism that reads and valorises the signs of social struggle in the faultlines of literary and cultural texts.' Meanwhile postcoloniality is a 'value-regulating mechanism within the global late-capitalist system of commodity exchange' (6). So, similarly, between 'the progressiveness of postcolonial thinking,' and 'the rearguard myths and stereotypes that are used to promote and sell "non-Western" cultural products in and to the West,' there exists 'a remarkable discrepancy' (25). It is 'myths and stereotypes' that drive forms of consumption premised on the 'urge to identify' – an urge essential to exoticism – which 'often comes at the expense of *knowledge* of cultures/cultural groups other than one's own' (17). It is in deference to such urges that *some* readers – as I say, largely unspecified, but of a predictable class and metropolitan location – choose genres like ethnic autobiographies or travel writing about 'other' places 'to expand their own cultural horizons' (12). Such reading is said to privilege the aesthetics of identification over more laudable forms of theoretical and historical understanding.

Moreover, and importantly, the postcolonial writer knows about this consumer as well, and incorporates a critique of her tendencies into the text, deploying a strategic exoticism designed to interrogate the reader's own constructions. 'Postcolonial writers/thinkers,' Huggan writes, 'are both aware of and resistant to their interpellation as marginal spokespersons, institutionalised cultural commentators and representative (iconic) figures. What is more, they make their *readers* aware of the constructedness of such cultural categories' (26). In this sense it is *only* the market reader who is insufficiently canny about her complicity in postcoloniality's suspect forms of market colonization.

In just this way a great deal of *The Postcolonial Exotic* works as a kind of accusation, identifying readers as guilty of exoticizing, aestheticizing, and/or dehistoricizing what might otherwise be subject to more legitimate forms of knowledge production. It is then no coincidence that the idea of the exotic also plays a central role in Huggan's analysis of the 'tourist gaze' in recent literature; his critique of the logic of tourism can be read as a formative background to his work as a whole, infecting the way he understands consumption in general.[3] For him market exoticism and tourism are close bedfellows, dependent on a similar overarching system of authentication. Echoing his introductory statements about the consumption of postcolonial texts, Huggan writes that 'Exoticist aesthetics, and the exoticist mythologies from which the tourist industry derives its profits, disguise the real differences they help to cause by appealing to ones of their own imagining' (178). Huggan and his cohort of critics apprehend and assess 'the real differences,' while the tourist sees only their 'disguise' by the industry's 'imagining.'

That said, Huggan also points out that tourists are constantly involved in the process of distinguishing themselves from other tourists. This is a process they can never perfect, and one which therefore drives the logic of the industry itself, as it derives profits from encouraging people to see themselves as involved in ever more unusual cultural experiences. In Dean MacCannell's terms, there is 'a long-standing touristic attitude, a pronounced dislike, bordering on hatred, for other tourists, an attitude that turns man against man in a *they are the tourists, I am not* equation.'[4] Travellers and anti-tourists, Huggan writes, 'look down on "superficial" tourists, whom they see as having little or no interest in the countries they visit; as contributing irresponsibly to the despoliation of their environment; and as seeking maximum enjoyment with a minimum of effort' (179). So, tourist practice is premised on denying one's own position as a tourist, and Huggan rightly calls the distinction upon which such denial rests a 'highly profitable myth' (179).

I emphasize this 'myth' here because the process behind it mirrors Huggan's characterization of the surely equally mythic cosmopolitan consumer. Huggan's distancing of critical 'knowledge' from market

exoticism is analogous to what MacCannell calls 'touristic consciousness,' in which the traveller or anti-tourist claims access to knowledge
of the 'truth' of what she 'beholds,' while the basic tourist, like the
market reader, glories in her own ignorance of the reality behind the
exotic image. In both cases – Huggan separating the activities of 'postcolonial writers/thinkers' from those of the market reader, and tourists'
elitist scorn for other tourists – the elusive promise of legitimate and
authenticated access to the reality of lived experience forms the basis
on which such distinctions are made. Being 'one of them' requires
access to what Erving Goffman termed the 'back regions' behind the
façade of business practice, and the goal of tourism is often exactly this
kind of entrée into a rare solidarity with the visited culture.[5] The fact
that Huggan cannot avoid attributing moral authority to the idea of
some deeper truth hidden behind what is fronted in tourism experience – a truth materialist research can then work to reveal – in large
part proves MacCannell's argument, that just as we become alienated
from the realities to which they refer, a certain functional primacy is
accorded to ideas like closeness, community, intimacy, and solidarity.
Access to what's 'real' can require the valuing of forms of identification
with what is 'morally superior to rationality and distance in social
relationships.'[6]

Of course the search for unmediated access always fails, and has to
fail, since establishing the final impenetrability of the back regions –
that is, establishing their inaccessibility to outsiders – is part of the fundamental logic of tourism.[7] The kind of tourism experience that is set
up as ideal, and as distinct from the norm that is subject to critique, is
'an *authentic* and *demystified* experience of an aspect of some society or
other person.' It must make continual appeals to the actual, legitimate,
or authentic back region that 'motivates touristic consciousness.'[8] Part
of what makes such appeals necessary is the fact that an authentic back
regions experience cannot be marked off as such. Its authenticity is
precisely premised on the absence of those markers that would make it
available to other potential consumers as an experience. Yet the
absence of markers is also an anxiety-inducing problem, because those
with access to the back regions need signs that what they are viewing is
authentic, in part because they need to indicate their *in-the-know insid-
erness* to those without the same privileges. Culler calls this 'the
dilemma of authenticity.' For something to be experienced as authentic, he writes, 'it must be marked as authentic, but when it is marked as
authentic it is mediated [...] and hence lacks the authenticity of what is
truly unspoiled, untouched by mediating cultural codes.'[9]

In the same way, I think, critiquing an unnamed cosmopolitan consumer who seeks mythic access to exotic experience is premised on the notion that there exists a group of educated, elite, distinguished consumers who actually have access to the reality that the *other* consumer can only ever wish to possess. Huggan is hardly alone in this; critiquing a reader who exoticizes texts and the others they represent is actually a major plank of one strand of materialist work on postcolonial literature.[10] It is in this sense that Huggan's study is a version of what it analyzes, subscribing to a logic that separates the authentic from the inauthentic, the insider from the outsider, in an endless cycle of hierarchical distinction and counter-distinction.

It is important to recognize that as a group academic readers, most often in the guise of literary critics, have been subject to serious ethical scrutiny in debates about postcolonial studies. Since its inception Marxist critics have isolated and challenged postcolonial literary scholarship's tendency to be swayed by poststructuralism, making the reading of literature central to critical understandings of colonial and postcolonial power relations. Arif Dirlik famously claimed that postcoloniality 'is the condition of the intelligentsia of global capitalism,' and argued that critics have been 'silent on the relationship of the idea of postcolonialism to its context in contemporary capitalism'; and Aijaz Ahmad argued that the very category of Third World literature, which quickly became the major literature for postcolonial thought, is produced by the process of capitalist accumulation in the culture industries, and owes much of its currency to patterns of immigration through which the metropolitan university comes to control knowledge of its peripheries. Supporting Roman de la Campa's statement that '"postcoloniality" is postmodernism's wedge to colonise literatures outside Europe and its North American offshoots,' Ahmad wrote that as 'the governing theoretical framework shifts from Third World nationalism to postmodernism,' something called Third World literature starts to be analyzed as explicitly postcolonial.[11]

Developing this longstanding materialist challenge, postcolonial literary studies has recently focused its attention on the question of the intersections between literature and globalization. Setting out to discuss how knowledge of globalization might influence or update postcolonial scholarship, Simon Gikandi summarizes the challenges raised by critics like Ahmad and Dirlik, historically situating postcolonial literary work as follows: 'the discourse of postcolonialism [...] emerged in the 1980s when the centers of knowledge production about the "Third World" shifted from the periphery to the center, when many leading "Third World" intellectuals became transformed, for political and economic reasons, into émigré native informants.' The interests of these intellectuals have been resolutely oriented toward interpretation of texts, having emerged simultaneously with a general consensus that the global order after World War II, in its movement toward late capitalism, was defined by the proliferation of media images that could be subject to reading practices, leading in turn to the 'rule of the literary.'[12]

It is largely in response to such charges that a few critics have recently attempted to revive postcolonialism's legitimacy by constructing for it a different history, one that emphasizes its roots not within late capitalism or patterns of immigration, but rather within what Robert J.C. Young calls 'the historical legacy of Marxist critique' embodied both in decolonization movements and in the continuing legacy of challenges to neo-colonialism and imperialism.[13] In fact, a comprehensive narrative of the development and institutionalization of postcolonial studies has been emerging in recent years, in notable connection with critical opposition to triumphalist tendencies to ignore the perils of cultural and economic globalization. This narrative suggests that postcolonial scholarship has been radically diverted from its initial impetus in political decolonization, enshrined as an academic discipline woefully tied to the epistemological uncertainty characteristic of postmodernism, poststructuralism, and, most importantly, late capitalism. Current consensus holds that postcolonialism signifies a myriad of things. It is a pattern of resistance that emerges in every colonial milieu. It is a critical practice that challenges colonial discourse. It is a term that designates the world political situation after decolonization. It is an ontological deconstruction of the European power/knowledge matrix. It is a form of concern with Eurocentrism that too rarely gives way to critique of the power manifest in capitalism. It is a space for the privileging of the kind of ambivalence manifest in metaphors of migrancy or nomadism. It is a form of epistemological doubt.[14]

What has been less often acknowledged, though, is the commodity function of postcolonial texts. Postcoloniality is also a culture industry, and one with empirical parameters that have not been subject to consistent scrutiny. If postcolonial and now globalization scholarship is primarily the practice of academics situated within the literary sphere, and if all signs indicate that the discussion of the literary will remain a key interest for those working at the intersections between contemporary politics and culture, attention to the global workings of the publishing industry can lead to precisely the sort of materially-oriented scholarship critics have long deemed necessary. This is what Graham Huggan begins to perform with *The Postcolonial Exotic*, and it is why his work is so groundbreaking and so important. If the *idea* of the market, as a metonym for the late capitalist economy and its intrusions into every global locale, makes a dramatic appearance in the theoretical positions of Dirlik and Ahmad, for Huggan that same market is the real space of production and dissemination of actual literary works.

A major distinguishing feature of Huggan's analysis is that his focus is more the mass market for the products of a postcoloniality industry than it is the role of the postcolonial within the academy. The problem is that in his desire to distance his work from the Marxist formulations I've just cited (much though some of his rhetoric accords with theirs), he also seeks to distance a whole set of 'writers/thinkers' from the market impetus he outlines. This is what the image of the market reader does for him. She becomes the guilty party in the market transactions that plague the postcolonial field, protecting the position of a more educated, elite class of thinkers and readers. The latter have legitimate access to the products of postcoloniality because they understand the market's ethical and political boundaries and implications.

In this way, in Huggan's analysis the figure of the cosmopolitan reader necessarily serves a primarily rhetorical function, rather than a historical one. That reader, ceaselessly ingesting a variety of 'carefully managed products,' designed with her own easy pleasure in mind, is the shadow self of the academic critic, acting to protect him from his own proximity to the kinds of reading practices he sets aside for others. In other words, Huggan's work is a form of negative interpellation, in which positing the consumer habits of a debased global readership is in fact a way of distinguishing oneself from the habits so described. Much though Huggan himself critiques the notion of authenticity that is key to the posturing of travellers as anti-tourists, in a sense he constructs his own reading practices – and as I say he is hardly alone – as more authentic, because they are less commodified. They are more postcolonia*list* than they are the product of postcolonia*lity*. Indeed I think it is not too much to say that the image of the market reader, like the image of the ignorant and obnoxious tourist, is one inevitable product of postcolonial guilt, a guilt which is one correlate of the ethical challenges presented by analyses of postcolonial cultural markets. As MacCannell and Culler each suggests, such guilt is not a form of opposition to the system it assesses. It is instead one of its constitutive and legitimating features.

Acknowledging this kind of exemplary guilt and interpellation is potentially very useful as a means of explaining some of what is privileged in postcolonial literature's production in general. For example, it may help us to situate the incessant triumph of the notion of 'complexity.' Like access, like sophistication, like 'thick description' of history and context, 'complexity' is a virtue that is typically beyond scrutiny. Timothy Brennan has made this point as well, while writing against a cosmopolitism that castigates deeply resistant political writing as possessing too little of what's necessary for literary distinction. Brennan states that arguments against the 'monolithic' and the 'univocal' go out looking for something that rarely exists (namely, what's 'obvious'), because finding it makes it possible 'to demonstrate one's subtlety, complexity, and dialogism.'[15] In turn, of course, arguments in favour of the latter virtues become their own kind of monolithic edifice, treated for the most part to instant academic consent. Complexity is a useful trope, in that sense. It is a code the way that the markers of the legitimacy or authenticity of an experience are codes. The most apparently authentic or complex reading experience – the most exclusively (or snobbishly) accessed, say – is a form of involvement in the same signifying system it abhors, even while it marks itself off as somehow more 'recondite.'[16]

It is likely clear by now that I see Huggan's work as a *symptom* of postcoloniality even while it is an assessment of it. In the simplest sense, I am affirming MacCannell's claim that the idea of the tourist often serves a 'metasociological' function, making travel a mode of cultural experience that is quintessential to the sociology of modern life rather than one discrete process or industry within it. MacCannell himself could hardly avoid implication in this same experience. Just as *The Tourist* reveals the functionality of distinctions between surface and depth in tourists' own anti-tourism, the various incarnations of phrases like 'upon closer examination' that one finds within it *also* make claim to a conceptual space behind the hackneyed duality between exploitation and authentic access. There is always another back regions story that only MacCannell's own 'metasociology' and educated acumen can reveal. In that sense, even calls for straightforward ethnographic study of tourist behaviour (for participant observation, for example) add weight to the notion that there is a realm of truer experience and perception that can be accessed by those with certain sensitivities or abilities. The circularity is potentially endless, and certainly encompasses my own work, as I fault other approaches to the postcolonial field as overly focused on the front region appearance that masks deeper motivations and contexts.

As further illustration, think of the general figure of the cosmopolitan as another who establishes his special 'competence' and expertise through appeals to distance from standard tourism. Unlike tourists, or exiles, or oftentimes immigrants, cosmopolitans have been said to claim a desire 'to immerse themselves in other cultures.' They want to be active participants in their multiple locations; they want to seem at home with the 'locals in their home territory.' Yet the cosmopolitan's position is precarious and self-conscious, insofar as it is dependent on the belated acquisition of knowledge or competence. His forms of competence are meant to seem untied to any particular cultural formation; his theories and practices travel, and he repeatedly faces the prospect of being taken for a tourist by those whose ties are less belated. It follows that the cosmopolitan's 'sense of self' is constantly under threat. In turn cosmopolitans tend to express routine loathing for tourists, as well as for being mistaken for tourists.[17]

Think, in addition, of the ethnographer as a figure whose modes of visitation share some figural terrain with those of the cosmopolitan-cum-anti-tourist. Ethnography gained prominence as a disciplined mode of observation around the same time that tourism became a popular pastime. When understood as 'a study of a people's way of life centering on the method of immersion in extensive fieldwork and raising the issue of how, and how far, the outsider can become a kind of honorary insider in other cultures,'[18] is ethnography simply one particularly privileged form of travel? Can the ethnographer then serve as a model for the perfect traveller in anti-tourism discourse, a position which depends upon the ethnographer's claim to a privileged 'register' that allows for interpretation of others' practices?[19] Traditional ethnography was premised on the notion that the indigenous peoples studied by the 'participant observer' do not themselves 'travel.' They do so neither literally, in the sense that they do not leave the space in which their 'culture' takes shape, nor metaphorically, since they cannot transcend the epistemological apparatus that defines their distinction. In a parallel way, as I have suggested above, tourists may range widely across the globe, but do they really travel? Elite assessments tend to position them as unable to visit those back region sites that would mark them as 'real' travellers; nor can they achieve the transcendence of their particular cultural formation that would be necessary for proper analysis of it.

If we further define ethnography as, first, 'simply diverse ways of thinking and writing about culture from a standpoint of participant observation,'[20] and, second, as the study of those who cannot know themselves, but who are available as knowable to the outsider who situates their practices, then isn't it the case that anti-tourists (or cosmopolitans, or intellectuals) *pose* as ethnographers of tourism? They see how it operates as a 'culture'; they understand its overall functionality; and they try to gain intimate knowledge of what isn't obvious or immediately apparent. Moreover, could Huggan's mode of analysis be understood as placing him in an ethnographic relationship to the global consumer, or, more rightly given my critique, as exhibiting a kind of ethnographic logic without actually engaging in close observation of the subjects of his gaze? Like the traveller, the 'good' critic is the ethnographer who seeks limitless, 'thick,' and intimate access to what she studies. Travel is an infinitely complex and varied activity and the figure of the ethnographer is simply one available identity, inhabiting 'partially overlapping ideological spaces' with foreign soldiers, itinerant workers, transnational managers, as well as with the missionaries and colonists of earlier times.[21] Traveller, anti-tourist, cosmopolitan, or ethnographer: each can claim a privileged position of analysis through the identification and attribution of the characteristics of some 'other' 'culture.' In Huggan's case, what's subject to analysis is the culture of the market reader.

This aside, my point here is that it is definitively *not* a particular mode of exoticizing consumption that makes the tourism industry comparable or analogous to the global publishing industry, which verifiably expands through the promotion of those who can be marketed as postcolonial, colonizing audience niches through the incorporation of difference – a process my next chapter outlines. The suggestion that postcolonial literature, as it circulates in the Anglo-American marketplace, exists only as evidence of Western fetishization of the rest of human experience, or that reception of postcolonial texts is always or only a kind of market colonization, ignores a number of factors. Attention to the material organization of the current literary marketplace does not reveal a single market, but rather a fragmenting and proliferating set of niche audiences, which are admittedly united by a set of general rules dictated by the major transnational corporations. Moreover, scholarly attention to the postcolonial history of the book is in its infancy, and few researchers have performed the detailed analyses of reading practices that might justify the identification of a characteristic mode of cosmopolitan consumption that is dehistoricizing and depoliticizing.[22]

Instead, the way that the postcolonial publishing industry *is* like global tourism is that those observably reading and writing its products are constantly engaged in distinguishing their practices from those of other participants. The observable field is made up of those postcolonial 'writers/thinkers,' whether critics or creative writers; it is they who have a developed and well-earned sense of guilt about their own practices, and belong to professions that entail leaving those traces of their engagement with texts that non-academic, non-producing readers rarely can.

If, as Culler emphasizes, there is a 'touristic code' that unites what we might call the touring classes, so that they share a set of values that indicates where they should go and what they should think about where they've been,[23] there is a similar code within the postcolonial field of production. Due to the existence of transnational media corporations like Bertelsmann and Pearson PLC, for example, which umbrella Random House and Penguin respectively, readers of postcolonial literary fiction are spread across the globe, consumers of a truly global commodity which needs little alteration for local consumption. Yet as with the touring classes, united by experience of the industry, those readers do not experience any kind of consensus based on what is common to them. Self-conscious scrutiny and dissension are instead the norms, and more elite readers often seem to believe that there is a general public engaged in a similar activity (reading), but who practise it *badly*. Tweaking slightly Culler's argument that 'each wishes the other tourists were not there,'[24] it seems to me that any key initial revulsion soon gives way to relief, since the presumed presence of others gives one a foil against which to define what is right (such as 'complexity') in one's own position.

It might be useful to think of postcoloniality's conscience as fundamentally touristic. At the very least, Huggan's work demonstrates tourism's exemplarity, as it is situated within an academic field that attributes significant importance to the problem of access to the cultural other by the touring classes. Who is allowed access to the cultural other, which forms of access are legitimate, and who may judge whether access is legitimate? More importantly for my purposes, how do postcolonial 'writers/thinkers' establish themselves as gatekeepers to any presumed authentic access, or, alternately, disavow the very requirement that they take on such roles? As I've suggested, the touring classes can include everyone from literal tourists and ethnographers to those who metaphorically travel by reading 'other' literatures. Divisions abound between inside and outside, between a culture's visitors and its authentic members, between the complex and the debased or commodified. Each binary has been ruthlessly scrutinized since its moment of inception and solidification, such that it may seem surprising that these terms still prove useful at all. I think these binaries continue to hold because the very ability to engage in dismantling them has become a defining trait for those with the privilege to travel inside and outside at once and in tandem, always participant enough to find intimacy and community, but possessing the breadth of vision that being ultimately outside of a particular cultural formation is conventionally thought to allow.

Refiguring strategic exoticism: Derek Walcott

In Huggan's critique of postcoloniality, somebody somewhere is engaged in consuming postcolonial texts in ways that are meant to concern an academic reading audience. I have suggested that this audience may derive comfort rather than misgivings from the image of this same (safely and necessarily elsewhere) somebody. As I noted, Huggan is hardly alone in deploying the figure of the general global consumer as a means of absolving or legitimating certain other modes of cultural apprehension. Recall his argument that in many cases postcolonial writers in fact deploy strategic exoticism; they are, he writes, 'both aware of and resistant to their interpellation as marginal spokespersons, institutionalized cultural commentators and representative (iconic) figures. What is more, they make their *readers* aware of the constructedness of such cultural categories' (26). This is no doubt true, and what interests me is how much the key gesture of making 'aware' is premised on the notion that readers are actually doing what the more 'strategic' exoticizers are trying to prevent – that is, in this case, unwittingly reifying constructed categories. The strategies and techniques of some postcolonial texts are thus taken as designed to respond to the existence of a certain kind of consumer, and their very material is comprised of attempts to reorient and reeducate an unsophisticated reader.

I turn now to a writer who has often deployed the techniques of strategic exoticism. Derek Walcott's self-consciousness about his authorial position has two major aspects. On the one hand, he is consistently worried about his relationship with the people of the Caribbean, the region he comes from and about which he often writes. On the other hand, he frequently takes up the subject of his earned access to a privileged metropolitan audience, an audience educated in modernist poetics but also interested in the Caribbean as novel literary material. In each case Walcott's self-consciousness is worked out through his appeal to travel motifs; these involve him carefully illustrating the insights produced by the simultaneity of his insider–outsider positioning.

When engaging with his relationship with the people of the Caribbean, he tends to depict his own location of relative privilege as analogous to an anti-tourist's. He is always concerned to show that as someone who is *partly* a member of the culture that he *partly* experiences as a visitor, he is conscious of the underbelly machinations and incongruities that an actual outsider might not acknowledge. In turn, in a related way, when considering his metropolitan readers he will depict himself as a reluctant native guide, suspicious of the tourist-reader's exoticizing tendencies. Each of these strategies ultimately deexoticizes, and relates to the ironic posturing common to what some analysts describe as posttourism, a subject I return to below. For now, looking at some of Walcott's work clarifies what I think strategic exoticism can be said to perform. It also lends weight to my larger argument that we might think of postcoloniality as having a generative touristic conscience that is evident in many authors' defensive constructions of figures of reading that are by turns self-exempting or self-implicating.

*

The 1970 essay 'What the Twilight Says' takes up one primary subject: the conflicted and paradoxical nature of Walcott's relationship with the people of the West Indies – a category he constantly puts under erasure, but to which he cannot help but refer. Though what actually defines 'the people' remains vague by necessity, it seems clear that for Walcott it indicates a group that is at least black, and poor, and romanticized in a way that ensures their destitution's longevity.

Walcott argues that the idea of 'the people' has powerful currency in the region because it serves a number of identifiable interests that can be divided into three categories. First, there is the tourism industry, with its commercial investment in marketing a distinct local culture to foreign visitors. Second, there is the state, which colludes with the tourism industry insofar as it shares some of its profits, but which also has its own reasons for establishing an essentially apolitical folk art as *the* regional culture. 'The folk arts,' Walcott writes, 'have become the symbol of a carefree, accommodating culture, an adjunct to tourism, since the state is impatient with anything which it cannot trade.' Due to the dual demands of 'the anthropologist's tape-recorder' and 'the folk archives of departments of culture,' those things which might have otherwise been discarded – the 'old gods' are his example – are resurrected, because they are expedient.[25] In turn folk 'forms' have become entirely non-threatening, such that even poverty is mere scenery, 'part of the climate, the art of the brochure' (37). Third, there is that group of unnamed intellectuals – most notably those associated with the Black Power movement – who depend upon a romanticized national populace in articulating their own political program. Walcott's characterization of these intellectuals is a harsh one. They make 'culture' something static, condemning the islands to artistic and material poverty. They need the poor to remain poor (since materialism and individualism are imposed colonial ideals), but meanwhile, 'their wives were white, their children brown, their jobs inviolate' (35).

In sum, the idea of a unified authentic 'culture' – made up most notably by folk arts or performance – is a fiction the state constructs in collusion with commercial interests in order to make money, but also, it seems, to control the possible political implications of a truer art. In turn, those intellectuals who ingenuously refer to an authentic 'folk' culture are in this way aligned with tourism and the state: each group invests in the idea of 'the people' because it is economically or politically expedient. Dramatically drawing these three strands together, Walcott says that the descendants of the enslaved 'have gone both flaccid and colourful, covering their suffering with artificial rage or commercial elation' (27).

Walcott does not separate himself from such imperatives in any simple way. Instead he calls himself out as well, as someone privileged enough to experience the West Indies – in particular its suffering – as a tourist might. 'What the Twilight Says' is full of self-consciously voyeuristic and poetic descriptions of 'ramshackle hoardings of wood and rusting iron' (3), or of folk choirs and dancers in 'the standard imitation frippery of Mexican or Venezuelan peasants' (28). Walcott admits that at one time he had a propensity to romanticize poverty and view it as 'lyrical' (3): 'one sought out the poor as an adventure, an illumination' (14); 'nothing is lovelier than the allotments of the poor, no theatre as vivid, voluble and cheap' (4). He recalls watching the 'ragged barefooted crowd' as a child peering through a window from on high, when he and his brother would lament that they could not join in because 'they were not black and poor' (22). He describes being drawn to the island's fisherman as a sect with its own 'signs', 'a vocation which excluded the stranger.' He had yearned for what 'smelled strong and true' in their world, not to actually experience their life as his own, but to 'enter' as a tourist would, to witness a picturesque des-

titution but have the promise of escaping its pain (16).[26] 'One worked
to have the "feel" of the island' (15), he claims.

In this way, much of 'What the Twilight Says' registers Walcott's
desire for identification with the West Indies' 'people,' just as it calls
their existence into question. Walcott's wish to complicate the
notion of the 'folk' is part of what distinguishes him from regular
tourists and from consumers of the products of the region's culture
industries. It is also what makes him an artist, casting him in a role
that ensures he is even more distant from the people he already feels
at once drawn to and separate from. As a mulatto living in relative
privilege, he records that he once felt that he lacked something
that they had, and becoming an artist – not a fabricator of state-
sanctioned artifacts, but a 'real' artist – made that lack even more
apparent, entrenching an unbridgeable divide.

Walcott's self-reported alienation is central to the very way the essay
takes shape. When describing his early life – a time which includes his
indulgent voyeurism and investment in a folk mythology – he is reluctant to claim his own experiences, using third person perspective
('one,' 'he,' 'the colonial artist,' 'the brothers') or second ('you despise,'
'you rehearse'). Even the famous phrase 'the mulatto of style' appears
here not as triumphant self-definition (as it tends to be cited in studies
of Walcott's *oeuvre*), but in the guise of a general description of the
island artist: 'He is the mulatto of style. The traitor. The assimilator'
(9). It is only when he starts to describe his attempts at establishing a
viable local theatre that Walcott begins to use first person narration
more consistently, a switch that suggests the degree to which he finds
an alternative solidarity and community in artistic production.

In a sense, the distinction of being relatively well-off, light-skinned,
and half-white is what ushers Walcott into his later, artist's alienation.
If to be black and poor is to be of the 'folk' or 'the people,' then
Walcott's early identity and later art are each articulated in opposition
to those same categories. After all, the championing of the folk culture
Walcott denigrates was clearly a problem for his early career, since it
meant his own work would always face a contentious reception, and
would not be afforded the kind of audience his ambition and desire for
fame demanded. Walcott himself describes his artistic output as constantly under attack precisely because it is incompatible with the
demands that the West Indies' culture industries institute.

In this way, what's 'folk' in Walcott's analysis are all those things
that he had himself been accused of ignoring or abandoning. For
example, in his view a notable correlate of the multifaceted reliance on

a mythic 'folk' essence is the demand that West Indian cultural products be easily consumable. Walcott writes that the West Indies has
become a region 'where the folk art, the language, the music, like the
economy, will accommodate itself to the centre of power which is
foreign, where people will simplify themselves to be clear, to be immediately apprehensible to the transient' (26). Tourists and visitors – 'the
transient' – are those appeased by simplicity, because it requires no
engagement with the islands' history and complexity, and local art is
merely 'goods placed on shelves' for their pleasure (8). Thus where the
people's culture is simplified, Walcott's work is formally complex, at
this stage often absurdist, and schooled in various European traditions.
Where the people's culture is expressed through the popular cadences
of patois and other local argots, Walcott's work frames those within a
commanding and often demanding English. Where the people's
culture is amenable to Black Power appropriation, Walcott's work is
critical of the epistemological underpinnings of any nationalism. So
when Walcott argues that there is no 'people' and no 'culture' but only
'strangers' (10), who are neither attached to the earth for living there,
nor possessed of folk authenticity because they wear it as 'costume,' he
also dismantles the assumptions behind his own contentious reception. The enemy is not 'the people,' but 'those who had elected themselves protectors of the people' (35), and those 'protectors' also happen
to be Walcott's critics. So, according to the essay's argument, that 'jetti-
soning of "culture"' (17) which Walcott had himself stood multiply
accused of is actually an impossibility, since there is no essence to
betray.

Further, Walcott suggests that his rejection of the demand that he
use more demotic language and simpler forms of expression is actually
the opposite of a lack of desire to engage with 'the people.' He is canny
about his outsider status and his complicity in certain legacies of privilege, and he also admits and diagnoses a tendency to engage in the
tourist-voyeur's transformation of poverty into a romantic condition
producing authentic folk culture. For these reasons, within the text
Walcott's is the more legitimate way of taking on the necessary burden
of the people's interests. His relationship with the region's people is
the only honest kind, precisely insofar as it is self-aware.

To elaborate, as a 'migratory' West Indian, 'rootless on his own
earth' (21), Walcott can see 'the people' for what they really are –
namely, an expedient fiction. They exist not as reality but as rhetoric,
as a functional category for local construction and contestation; this is
how Walcott purports to see the 'folk' in general, and how he uses

them in 'What the Twilight Says.' The predicament of the arts in the West Indies can only be worked out if 'the people' are appealed to as just this kind of rhetorical trope, rather than as an essence. In this sense, while being an outsider in terms of race, class, and artistic sensibility is harrowing for Walcott, it also allows him something. It allows him to perceive and construct his own position as paradigmatic. It is not just that he is a 'stranger,' but that everyone is, and in that sense he can claim to see some deeper truth about art and life in the West Indies. Walcott is distinctly capable of a 'real' art only because he has the benefit and curse of seeing that any notion of a 'true' culture is a lie. Ironically, then, the revelation of that lie is the artist's truth.

*

By the late 1970s and early 1980s, Walcott was one of the several Third World cosmopolitan writers Timothy Brennan later identified as having made substantial claims to large portions of existing metropolitan markets.[27] As 'What the Twilight Says' recounts, his early career was regionally based, having evolved within a general West Indian artistic culture. His first collection, *25 Poems*, was published there in 1948-9. Walcott was not schooled abroad, but rather attended the new University of the West Indies in Jamaica, which has been called a 'product and an inculcator of West Indian cultural nationalism.'[28] Early on he lived in St. Lucia, Jamaica, and Trinidad, working as a journalist for a number of small magazines, publishing his early poetry within those same pages, and working with and initiating a number of regional theatre groups. However, though the theatre did provide an important social network, at that time there was no paying West Indian market for Walcott's literary work. He was instead dependent on the Anglo-American market for money.[29] As early as 1949 his poetry was read on the BBC's 'Caribbean Voices'; in 1952 his *Henri Christophe* was produced in London; and his work was included in the 1956 *New World Writing* collection published in New York in the New American Library Series. In the late 1950s he travelled to New York for the first time on a Rockefeller Foundation Fellowship, and in 1962 Jonathan Cape published *In a Green Night: Poems 1948-1960*, his first collection with an initial appearance outside of the Caribbean.

The stage was then set for more mainstream career success. Walcott continued to live in the Caribbean throughout the 1960s and 70s, working as a journalist and pursuing his writing as both playwright and poet, often in reaction to the general politicization of culture in the region and registering specific concerns about, for example, the Black Power revolt that took place in Trinidad in 1970.[30] In 1961 he won the Guinness Award for Poetry. Ten years later he was made a Member of the Order of the British Empire, and in 1979 he became an Honorary Member of the American Academy and Institute of Arts and Letters.[31] By the early 1980s his career was decidedly focused in the United States (US) rather than England, his works published first by New York's Farrar, Straus and Giroux (and then Faber and Faber in London), rather than by London's Jonathan Cape, his first English publisher. After being awarded a five-year MacArthur Foundation Fellowship worth US$248,000 in June 1981, he moved to the US semi-permanently. The move was facilitated by the ease with which he moved into teaching positions at Harvard, Yale, and Brown Universities, and by the general acclaim with which his work was received. Consecration in the US – in turn the path to a canonical status in the Caribbean, as well as internationally – was Walcott's major purpose during this critical phase in his career. Befriending in particular Joseph Brodsky and Seamus Heaney, two poets also expatriate from politically volatile regions and living in the American Northeast, he began to think of himself less as a Caribbean or even a Commonwealth writer, and more as an international one.

Walcott by no means left the Caribbean behind in order to embrace a new American life as a canonized poet. He has never taken American citizenship, and since moving into international poetic circles his work has elaborated an expansive theory of Caribbean nationality that allows for travel across borders.[32] Moreover, Walcott has repeatedly stated his commitment to the Caribbean, publishing *Omeros* as the region's epic in 1990, and claiming in 1993, after winning the Nobel Prize and returning to St. Lucia, 'All my work has been about this island.'[33]

That said, in the early 1980s, with *The Fortunate Traveller*, which is generally considered the transitional collection, Walcott did begin to incorporate wider cultural and political references. Non-Caribbean settings became more common in his work, and he moved toward 'a more liminal, cosmopolitan conception of his identity.'[34] Between 1979 and 1981 all but two of the poems published in the collection appeared in major metropolitan magazines. Eight were in the *New Yorker*, five in *Antaeus*, and three in the *Kenyon Review*.[35] While a version of the title poem did appear in the *London Magazine* in 1981, it was the last of Walcott's poems to do so for some time, as New York became his career's center. Farrar, Straus and Giroux and Faber and

Faber each published the complete monograph in 1982, and its very dedications – to Joseph Brodsky, Susan Sontag, and Robert Giroux, among others – show 'how much Walcott's career, especially his literary friendships in New York, had become his life.'[36] When Paul Breslin wrote to Bruce King to request specific details about the poet's whereabouts during the early 1980s, King's reply revealed much about the life of a newly cosmopolitan poet:

> Unsettled and flying non-stop all over, not possible to do a summary really. Ex. Jan 1980 Trinida[d], Feb 1980 NY, March Virgin[i]a, April Trinidad and NY, May NY, June Trinidad, September NY, Fall 1980 living in NY teaching at NYU and Columbia, Poetry Olympics in London late September, then NY, then back to UK for Welsh Prize in October, NY, back to Trinidad at x-mas. 1981: NYU and Columbia next semester, mostly, late April 1981 Trinidad for Beef, back to USA (NY base, but commuting between Chicago and Washington for productions), late May Trinidad, June MacArthur, July St. Thomas, Fall 1981, part-time at Columbia and Harvard, became assist prof at Boston in Jan 1982. The main point is that he was really a NYer at this period and still trying to make it in the USA until the MacArthur and Boston U (mid-1981/Jan 1982) changed his life.[37]

In short, Stewart Brown's 1991 statement that Walcott's work is 'now, part of [an] International Hyperculture' because the poet 'takes jets between continents as easily as he once took the row-boat ferry across Castries harbour,'[38] could be applied just as well to the early 1980s, when Walcott definitively joined the glitterati in New York and published *The Fortunate Traveller*, the first of his collections to appear while he was no longer primarily resident in the Caribbean. It is important to note that his move to the US took place despite his 'much publicized' previous commitment to remaining in the Caribbean throughout his life. This commitment evolved regardless of the detriment to his literary career, and despite what Walcott called the 'pardonable desertions' inevitable to 'all island artists.'[39]

The interconnecting aesthetic and political issues raised by Walcott's move, and by the increasing recognition of Walcott's work within Anglo-American literary culture – or, more largely, within the 'world cultural market' for 'the new national literatures'[40] – are by no means lost on Walcott himself. They inform the subject matter of *The Fortunate Traveller*'s title poem.

The poem's topic is a famine and the structures of Northern power doing all too little to alleviate it, its inspiration the starvation plaguing areas of Ethiopia and Somalia in 1979–80. The poem's speaker is a bureaucrat, a functionary of the neocolonial world we meet in his travels. He acts as an intermediary between the Third World's citizens and Northern institutions of geopolitical power in order to plead for the resources that will help alleviate the starvation. 'The Fortunate Traveller' presents considerable challenges to any straightforward explication, but its general trajectory is as follows: we meet the speaker in a European city (named as Bonn in the poem's *London Magazine* version), fresh from a visit to the World Bank.[41] We witness his pained confrontation with some French-speaking men who have an active interest in the success of his search for funding for farming equipment. We then track his return to Bristol and, finally, St. Lucia, where he is pursued by guilt, as well as by some henchmen punishing him for a task unfulfilled. The poem's frequent geographical switching is interspersed with the speaker's reflections on his past, on his task as intermediary between the structures of Northern power and the poor of the South in both Africa and the Caribbean, and on the relationship between a Western aesthetic tradition and what Paula Burnett calls 'a culture of tragedy.'[42]

Throughout, the speaker refers to himself and those like him as outsiders, invaders of a sort, bearing images their audience does not want to see:

> We are roaches,
> riddling the state cabinets, entering the dark holes
> of power. (90)

He and his cohorts are said to appeal to the members of those state 'cabinets' with a narrative of development and modernization (after all, they are asking for funds to improve farming efficiency): 'we infect with optimism,' he claims (90). 'In the square coffin manacled to my wrist,' he says:

> small countries pleaded through the mesh of graphs,
> [...] Xeroxed forms to the World Bank
> on which I had scrawled one word, MERCY. (88)

In turn, in the context of what the poem as a whole represents as a deepening crisis of starvation and poverty in areas of underdevelopment, it becomes clear that this 'fortunate traveller' – 'One flies first-class, one is so fortunate' (89) – can also be read as a figure for Walcott himself, who is, analogously, a literary intermediary between his Third World subjects and the privileged audience that reads about their plight.

For example, we are given some insight into the traveller's history. It is a typical lineage for a neocolonial bureaucrat, but it is conveyed in a way that emphasizes the coincidence between the education of a class of clerks and an author who takes his material from the political scene. A former student of history and literature, the speaker was a 'Sussex don,' an expert in 'the Jacobean anxieties.' 'My field was a dank acre' (91), he claims, suggesting both the 'dank acre' of a literary 'field' made up of the macabre plays of John Webster (the speaker mentions both *The Duchess of Malfi* and *The White Devil*, a title with other implications in this context), as well as the daily agricultural toil that necessitates his current travels.[43] The poem connects aesthetic and political narratives in just this way throughout, often through intertextual allusions that would be obscure to one not thoroughly schooled in Western literary and aesthetic traditions. The poem's epigraph is from Revelation, the New Testament Book of the Apocalypse. This biblical passage on tribulation, plight, and famine is suited to the poem's general political material:

> And I heard a voice in the midst of the four beasts say,
> A measure of wheat for a penny,
> and three measures of barley for a penny;
> and see thou hurt not the oil and the wine. (88)

Taking the epigraph from the Book of the Apocalypse also foreshadows the guilt that will plague the poem's speaker. The beasts reappear as the poem's final lines move towards an act of retribution aimed at both the poem's speaker and its readers.

Among numerous other allusions are: Joseph Conrad's *Heart of Darkness*, evoked as the speaker's travels from London to Europe and then into a realm of poverty and famine suggest parallels with Marlow's geographical movement, in turn making neocolonial poverty analogous to colonial domination, and clarifying Conrad's suggestion that the heart of darkness resides in Europe; and Chinua Achebe's 'An Image of Africa: Racism in Conrad's *Heart of Darkness*,' which references Albert Schweitzer and Arthur Rimbaud, the former as a musician, doctor, and ostensibly benign racist who reappears in Walcott's poem

as a fascist, and the latter as a man who gave up poetry and became a coffee trader and arms dealer in the region of the upper Nile colonized by the British.

More generally, the poem compares the famine at issue to the holocaust, alluding to theories of the death of God after Auschwitz, or the beginning of an apocalyptic history during the tragedies of World War II, while indicting the blindness of European intellectuals to the ongoing plight of many underdeveloped populations. It is in this spirit as well that the poem's title alludes to Thomas Nashe's *The Unfortunate Traveller*. Nashe's protagonist, the itinerant Jack Wilton, is engaged in a tour of the continent in which he encounters war and brutality of all kinds, described in a kind of startling detail that titillates while it satirizes readers' penchant for the macabre. A privileged traveller who fraternizes with the aristocracy, Jack continually laments his wretched state despite the fact that throughout his picaresque journey it is his own pranks that most often cause others' misfortunes. For Burnett the poem's allusions, not least to Nashe's work, collectively contribute to the way that 'Walcott displays how the Western elite has for at least four centuries appropriated the rest of the world as cultural tour and has indulged in self-pity when it should have been showing pity to others.'[44] In particular, in aestheticizing tragedy – a process Webster's plays and the 'dank acre' of Jacobean literature perhaps best represent – the Western tradition encourages the 'glorification' of suffering.[45]

The poem's speaker claims there is 'no sea as restless as [his] mind' (95). He laments that those consumed by the famine that the poem depicts have so obviously been abandoned by both god and by intellectuals, to become 'compassionate fodder for the travel book' (96). Importantly, wherever there is starvation it is said to be attended by an aestheticization:

> everywhere that earth shows its rib cage
> and the moon goggles with the eyes of children,
> we turn away to read. (96)

The speaker thus implicates us as readers of Walcott's poetry, calling our attention to the perverse privileging of reading practices – whether involving a 'travel book' or poetry – over an alternative alleviation of real suffering. It is in this context that he imagines Rimbaud reclined in a boat, a poet enjoying his leisure, moving through 'the blinding coinage of the river,' an effort to shroud 'an ordinary secret.' We are told that Rimbaud, unaffected by human suffering despite his work as a poet, 'knew that we cared less for one human face / than for the scrolls of Alexandria's ashes.' The implication is that Rimbaud's legacy, a legacy the poem aligns with a literary 'coinage,' will continue until the 'ordinary secret' is revealed and 'until we pay one debt' (96). The word 'debt' is carefully chosen here, given the poem's engagement with the political context of international monetary agencies. That 'debt' reappears as the humanitarian one that we as readers owe to the people the poem depicts, a debt both of money and mercy that we owe because we make of that material, at best, fodder for our own political convictions, and at worst a kind of entertainment. That debt is what we owe the subjects of literary 'coinage,' who, despite what the word might imply, are not so much invented, but have instead been made into 'coin,' into a literary currency, and also a real currency as their stories are sold to a marketplace that traffics in an aesthetics of suffering.

The poetic act is thus figured as a complex *calculation* of empathetic expression, a form of pleading for the residents of a certain area of the world at a kind of moral bank. Evidently that pleading generates no guaranteed political response. The bureaucrat-speaker does not fulfil his contract nor, it seems, his ethical duty, since the funding he requires is denied him. The men that the contract seemed to serve then become figures for a kind of poetic guilty conscience, haunting the speaker until the poem's bitter and paranoid end.

The language throughout 'The Fortunate Traveller' is that of self-incrimination. The speaker is disgusted by his own reliance on all those things meant to distance and measure. The world of the bureaucrat is full of counting, statistics, charts, and graphs. From inside a hotel room in Haiti, the hands of a child who begs, 'Mercy, monsieur. Mercy,' can become the 'white palms' of a 'gekko pressed against the hotel glass' (89). In the epigraph to this chapter I cite the lines depicting the speaker looking down at the earth from a plane, as its surface loses meaning:

> Like a telescope reversed, the traveller's eye
> swiftly screws down the individual sorrow
> to an oval nest of antic numerals,
> and the iris, interlocking with this globe,
> condenses it to zero, then a cloud. (89–90)

The world becomes a cipher or a vapour; the cloud that passes before the passenger's eyes, obscuring his view, is not a disruption but a continuation of a distancing process that turns the earth to nothing.

In the final section of the poem we return with the speaker to the place of blight and disease, where his employers are figured as 'the leather-helmed locust' and the 'third horseman' (97) assigned to bring down a punishment upon the head of the failed bureaucrat. In biblical tradition, the third of the four horsemen represents famine and rides on a black horse with scales both for grain and for justice, thus, as Burnett claims, 'combining the twin concerns of the poem, material and ethical.'[46] In the end the feeling of guilt that permeates the poem dominates, as the speaker's inability to convince his audience is deemed to be a result of his own failings. That audience is of course in a literal sense the board of the World Bank and analogous organizations. But according to a reading of the poem that recognizes how it figures Walcott's authorship, that audience is also us, its current readers, just as the speaker is in part the poet himself, who, assuming he has failed to produce some desired reaction, holds himself accountable. Despite his literary education and his 'fortunate' position, despite his appeals to compassion, despite his 'coinage' of comparisons between the current famine and the holocaust, despite his reference to the familiar category of biblical apocalypse, despite all his charts and graphs and his pleading for mercy, the speaker fails. The poet accuses himself of a critical lack, having, perhaps, insufficiently imagined his subjects. The poem's ending is thus profoundly didactic, as we are all implicated in the speaker's failure, somehow unable to do what is required, to translate the words on the page into something that might alter the situation they depict. Burnett argues, similarly, that the poet's challenge is 'to make the self-absorbed act of reading so moving an experience that it returns the reader to reality with a new commitment to respond to such "tragedy" as the Third World's starving.'[47]

In this way, 'The Fortunate Traveller' registers an imbalance between the locus of reception of postcolonial texts (the global North) and the subjects those texts represent, refract, consider, or critique (the global South). This imbalance is a recurring concern in Walcott's work.[48] To review, though hailing from St. Lucia, Walcott is typically read as a self-styled 'mulatto of style' with divided roots, interpreting specifically Caribbean experience through a very European literary tradition. His works often express a conflict between loyalty to the people of St. Lucia and those who might celebrate or consecrate the specific culture of the Caribbean on the one hand, and a sense of separation or even alienation from those people and their voices on the other. All along there have been those critics who take Walcott's references to classical Western mythology and European art as evidence of his translating of a certain native experience for a Western audience and literary culture. Thematically his work expresses significant ambiguity about politics, about colonialism and its aftermath, and about the culture native to his region. Such ambiguity, associable with a vaguely anti-imperialist and anti-colonial but resolutely 'complex' political liberalism, has been recognized as one of the major legitimizing features that sanction literary success for postcolonial writers in the current market. Walcott's work is critically appreciated, one could argue, precisely because it is 'neither complicitous nor adversarial.'[49]

'The Fortunate Traveller' is itself run through with the hallowed complexity and allusions to European art and aesthetics arguably requisite for success within Anglo-American poetic circles. Indeed, as Burnett points out, there is a tendency to think that within the poem Walcott's intertextual method is tested 'to destruction.'[50] Early reviews of the full collection fault Walcott for over-reliance on his influences and forebears. In fact, though, Walcott's intensely intertextual method is something that this particular poem deploys strategically, as a way of reckoning with the process the poet was then undergoing – namely, the process of cosmopolitan authorization and authentication. 'The Fortunate Traveller' illustrates the political valence of this process by registering the poet's alienated and often tragic relationship with the subjects of his writing, and thus with his own origins. Walcott expresses an ambiguous commitment to the underdeveloped world at a moment in his career when he might be thought to have abandoned it. Said differently, though Walcott's future poetic and dramatic works would make crucial returns to the Caribbean, 'The Fortunate Traveller' seems to express a commitment to the region as subject matter in order to negotiate a kind of leave-taking, or to arrange the terms on which he could live in the US and decidedly focus on his own career consecration. The poem expresses the complexity of Walcott's allegiances. Its speaker represents the writer's anxiety about acting as a mediator between the global South and the Anglo-American literary marketplace.

For all these reasons, the poem turns on the implication that readers do not come to Derek Walcott's work looking for a guide to action. Instead we are that somebody somewhere engaged in the consumption of exotic images of starvation and suffering as 'compassionate fodder' or for aesthetic pleasure. We come to read 'The Fortunate Traveller' to enjoy the act of interpretation of a poem that has perplexed commentators and that demands serious attention and countless rereadings. It is only through this interpretive effort that we can access the poem's message. Ironically, then, that message turns on the poem itself or, rather, the poem's content critiques its own form, and more importantly, its own imagined readership, in critiquing the critical effort that lets us arrive at understanding. The poem's strategies – available to 'cultural insiders' only[51] – would seem to undermine its thematic resonance, but in fact those strategies target the audience that presumably needs to hear Walcott's message. This is 'strategic exoticism' *par excellence*. Walcott uses the formal procedures of complexity and allusion, those that had characterized his career already, in order to deliver a political message to his own new community, the poetic and literary circles of the American Northeast. In the late 1970s and early 1980s that audience was made up of a certain class of highly educated, cultured readers of complicated poetry usually written by others like themselves, but occasionally penned by formerly Third World writers self-consciously injecting a certain novelty into the aesthetic sphere. Within that world, political subject matter must be arranged for a specific aesthetic disposition.

Like much contemporary poetry, 'The Fortunate Traveller' is thus significantly self-conscious about the act of poetic composition. Beyond that, though, what is especially interesting is the way it is self-conscious about the field in which it is situated as a piece of poetry, a field in which Derek Walcott finds significant fame by employing devices similar to those of his bureaucrat. He reimagines his career as an act of poetic calculus or 'coinage,' figuring literary work as bureaucratic negotiation. In making this kind of figural connection, Walcott constructs himself as someone torn between a desire to speak *on behalf* of his poetic subjects and Southern compatriots, and a wish to pursue the interests of his own fame or canonization. Walcott suggests he will inhabit the role of mediator of or tour guide to the South's suffering, but he will do so only ironically and with constant and considerable self-scrutiny.

*

When compiling his sociology of contemporary tourism, John Urry notes that the phenomenon of 'post-tourism' involves an admission, acceptance, and sometimes glorification of the lack of authenticity in tourism experiences. It entails a willingness to put on the guise of the tourist as a role, in a kind of outsider's game or strategy.[52] While this process can sometimes entail a kind of ecstatic play, it can also involve a more somber detachment that results from the recognition that no experience is fully authentic or meaningful, as everything everywhere yields to 'promiscuity and aimlessness [...]. There is no going back, no essence to redeem.'[53] Posttourism is a kind of elegiac performance. In this it shares some ideological terrain with strategic exoticism.

'What the Twilight Says' constructs the author's right to take up the subject of the West Indian people as predicated on the travelling perspective of the insider–outsider figure. Walcott points to his own early tendency to experience the region as a tourist, and emphasizes his efforts to overcome that tendency in order to look through a posttourist's eyes instead. In a way analogous to what the ideal island artist might do, the posttourist sees the corruption and destitution beneath a surface cogency and beauty in the region's arts, and apprehends the state, corporate, and political interests involved in the construction of the mythic 'folk.' His wariness about the existence of the 'authentic' by no means halts all self-exempting procedures involving one kind of traveller indicting others for missing what is 'true' about a given culture, landscape, or location. Instead the terms are simply negated, and inauthenticity becomes the ideal object of perception. That is, it is the recognition of inauthenticity that guarantees access to self-distinction – in this case, the self-distinction of the island artist, who exoticizes only strategically, while others continue to play it 'straight.'[54] The straight-players are that way not because they necessarily believe in the authentic (though they might, since self-delusion or lack of insight are always possible), but because they have expedient economic reasons to disguise what they know to be true. In this way, as one who deploys a strategic exoticism – or, as a variety of posttourist – Walcott's challenge to the premises of the exotic's appeal is indistinguishable from his self-exempting construction of his authorial self.

After all, Walcott's ironic assumption of a variety of traveller roles has been a recurring and self-consciously elaborated theme in his work, and this theme is much noted by academic critics, as well as by those same reviewers who might be seen as members of the glitterati that 'The Fortunate Traveller' addresses. In the *London Review of Books* Blake Morrison enacts the conventional contrast of Walcott with Edward Kamau Brathwaite, a writer thought to be more accessible, more directly political, and more attached to the culture he was born into. Morrison claims, 'Walcott's are sophisticated poems versed in the Anglo-American tradition, dedicated to the likes of Mark Strand, Anthony Hecht and Susan Sontag, and aimed primarily at a circle of readers in London and New York,' and he notes that in 'The Fortunate Traveller' itself Walcott 'explores self-accusingly the relationship between travel and betrayal.'[55] Helen Vendler, then poetry's doyenne at the *New York Review of Books*, writes of 'an often unhappy disjunction between his explosive subject ['the black colonial predicament'], as yet relatively new in English poetry, and his harmonious pentameters.'[56] She laments that at times Walcott still seems conflicted about the fact that 'not politics, and not opinions, but an inner dynamic, holds an artwork together,' as soon writing 'an essay in pentameters' as a poem. The description of his situation that she gives when reviewing *The Fortunate Traveller* aptly echoes Walcott's own self-construction in 'What the Twilight Says':

> he will remain for this century one of its most candid narrators of the complicated and even desperate destiny of the man of great sensibility and talent born in a small colonial outpost, educated far beyond the standard of his countrymen, and pitched – by sensibility, talent, and education – into an isolation that deepens with every word he writes (regardless of the multitude by whom he is read).[57]

So while Walcott may be the 'best diagnostician of his own case,' as Vendler says, he is by no means the only one. As major gatekeepers of the poetic establishment, Vendler and Morrison each note the tension that arises between the poet's loyalty to a set of political concerns related to 'his own culture,' and his commitment to a form of modernist poetics that can only be accessed by those with significant amounts of elite cultural capital. In that sense Walcott's strategic exoticism is not something that he effectively deploys against this particular set of readers. It is instead a trope knowingly acknowledged by the participants in the literary field who make up any conceivable audience for Walcott's work. They recognize Walcott self-consciously constructing a duality in which his artistic aspirations and his political commitments become irreconcilable, and they accept that duality's terms.

That is, if Walcott is the most critically lauded Caribbean poet, by all accounts a key figure in the canons of postcoloniality, his status has accrued to him not despite his articulated discomfort with the aesthetic (touristic) bent of a particular consuming audience, but instead because of it. The angst involved in having literal and metaphorical travel as a means of existence and a way of life, of being too apolitical for one (Southern) audience and too invested in 'the real' for another (Northern) one, of being between cultural formations in a way that clarifies their impermanence and porousness: all of this is central to Walcott's *oeuvre*, and its being so has been a path to the poet's success rather than a detriment to it. Simply put, Walcott's conflicted hesitation about his relationship to his material *is* in many cases his material. The literary gestures that attend this hesitation are at the foundation of Walcott's considerable critical success. His incorporation into his work of a specific figure of an expected or imagined reader is inseparable from how he creates his persona as an author. This is perhaps true of all forms of strategic exoticism, and is certainly true of the other writers I consider in this study.

Likewise, posttourism is not something that only some members of the touring classes experience. Instead it is a term that reflects a general structural change in the organization of the industry itself. Tourism proper – this includes everyone from management professionals, to hotel employees, to researchers and theorists, not to mention actual tourists, or the way these categories can at times overlap – is in a posttourist phase. Posttourism is basic to the industry's structure, rather than a singular position one might inhabit within it (though it is that too). It is in this light that strategic exoticism is not something a writer deploys to teach a reader about the errors in her conceptions about other cultures, much though it depends upon a construction of a figure in need of such instruction. Instead it indicates a set of textual strategies that communicates at all because the author and the *actual* reader likely share assumptions about the way culture operates, and concur in their desire to exempt themselves from certain undesirable practices. As an industry postcoloniality depends upon precisely this self-consciousness. Indeed it is being self-conscious and canny, being always only *strategically* exotic, that is at the generative heart of the field's flourishing. This is precisely what I mean by postcoloniality's touristic conscience. The touring classes of readers and travellers do not necessarily experience some ludic potential in saying 'Yes, I'm a tourist, I admit it, isn't it fun?' Instead postcoloniality has as a key feature the welcome liquidation of tourism's – or exoticism's – fun.

2
Postcolonial Writers and the Global Literary Marketplace

'I feel as if I have been concealed behind a *false self*, as if a shadow has become substance while I have been relegated to the shadows.'[1]

I have just made a series of connections between Derek Walcott's aesthetic concerns, his established authorial tendencies, and the multiple social and political locations within which his career has developed. The case studies in Part II work in a similar way. My attention to writers' biographies and their relationships to the literary marketplace is at odds with the notion, common throughout much of the twentieth century, and even now possessing some nostalgic power, that successful literature should register the absence of the author as its most apparent creator. As R. Jackson Wilson points out, through multiple influences from *fin de siècle* art for art's sake ideology to New Critical formalism, from semiotics to poststructuralism, the 'true artist' has often been thought to operate as though 'the cost of his success was a kind of self-denial, a successful *withholding* of the self from the work.'[2]

Yet, in part due to renewed interest in materialist methodologies like book history, support for such thinking has been undermined radically over the course of the last few decades. Wilson's own study of the antebellum American scene is part of a growing body of work that shows that attention to authorial self-construction need not be based in naively conceived readings that treat texts as though they have clearly intending, expressive authors in full control of their own meanings. Like my own, the goal of this scholarship is patently not to revive a thoroughly discredited biographical criticism in an effort to exhume a text's intending intelligence. Instead the author in the text is resolutely, purposefully *figural*, based in a set of significations that mediate between the writer in the world and the world of the work, so much so that interpretation often identifies aspects of an author's posturing that the writer in question would most likely discredit.

In fact part of the project of establishing a material history of authorship is showing that the notion of the intending author is in itself the product of changeable and contingent conditions that alter in conjunction with the status of texts within economic markets, the legal sphere, and the general cultural milieu. Broadly speaking, it was during the romantic period that the emergence of the kind of authorship that still maintains a residual hold over readers' imaginations occurred. It is important to emphasize that in any given context or era conceptions of authorship are never static or monolithic. After all, the mythic originating and controlling genius of romantic lore was typically a man and a poet, and challenges to his reign were posed continually by authors whose self-conceptions remained more socially oriented. What concerns me here is precisely that part of the legacy of romanticism that eventually attained an ascendant position, in the process effectively delimiting both the author's role and our *understanding* of that role in relation to the market and to the wider social sphere. Accounts of the surfacing of this romantic author – succinctly, the writer as creative, expressive, originating genius – tend to relate economy to subjectivity, such that the gradual commercialization and professionalization of the author's work is said to have emerged alongside 'a crisis of self-understanding'[3] involving elaborate forms of economic disavowal and claims to aesthetic autonomy.

The modern author is in part another product of the industrial revolution. For centuries after the invention of print substantial commercial publishing was limited by small reading audiences and by inefficient printing and production techniques. The publishing industry was notoriously undercapitalized. It was difficult at best to accumulate the savings necessary to expand or develop new technologies, and most firms could rarely afford to produce in large quantities and wait to have the money recuperated through sales. Early print shops required expensive manual labour and materials, and distribution across wide expanses to disparate communities was also costly. More wide-scale commercial publishing only arose when new technologies were invented and implemented. These included mechanized typesetting, paper-making, and later binding machines; coal- and steam-powered presses; the railway and its distribution networks; and more efficient communications infrastructure comprising everything from telegraphy to an improved postal system.

The history of improvements in production and distribution is inseparable from the development of a sizeable literate reading public, as a
whole series of social changes brought about by industrial development ushered in the late eighteenth-century's more modest 'reading
revolution' and the grander 'reading explosion' of a truer mass literacy
in the second half of the nineteenth century. As agrarian economics
gave way to urbanism, and as white-collar, literacy-based commercial,
trade, and manufacturing jobs became more common, traditional
'intensive' reading practices lost out to the penny press and the mass-
market book trades. Regular 'extensive' reading became at once a
social, occupational, and commercial necessity, as well as a widely
available common pastime. It was only then, with the coming of what
Michael T. Gilmore calls 'the era of the marketplace,' that the 'gentle-
manly author who wrote for a like-minded group of equals gave way to
the professional who depended for a livelihood on sales of his books to
an impersonal public.'[4]

An expanded, impersonal reading public, improved printing technologies, and increased opportunities for marketing and distribution
were all accompanied by changes in copyright law as ownership of
literary property quickly became a considerable issue for the first generation of professional writers. In fact it is here in the sphere of property
ownership and legal statute that the emergence of romanticism's
originating genius-author is often located. For example, Martha Woodmansee has accounted for the way late eighteenth-century theorists
of writing in both England and Germany 'minimized the element of
craftsmanship' involved in composition, 'in favor of the element of
inspiration,' which 'came to be explicated in terms of *original genius*,
with the consequence that the inspired work was made peculiarly and
distinctively the product – and the property – of the writer.'[5] This new
conception of writing is linked to the romantics' privileging of originality and organic unity. Rephrasing Edward Young, she writes '[o]riginal
works are the product of a more organic process: they are *vital, grow
spontaneously* from a *root*, and by implication, unfold their original form
from within.'[6] Rather than situating them solely within the aesthetic
tradition where they also reside, Woodmansee establishes that writings
like Young's, along with the kind of authorship that they supported, are
best understood as emerging in relation to the legal and economic constraints of the changing literary marketplace. Thus the transforming
epistemology of literary acts, evinced in the German and English aesthetic theory of that era, seems to parallel the movement from a literary
economy peopled by writers to one controlled by professional authors,

a group Woodmansee identifies as made up of those 'who sought to earn their livelihood from the sale of their writings to the new and rapidly expanding reading public.'[7] Establishing the inspired originality of the literary work – one part of the writer's heroic self-inflation – was an important strategy in authors' efforts to reform copyright law and gain proper compensation for their labour. For the romantics, then, '*genuine* authorship is *originary* in the sense that it results not in a variation, an imitation, or an adaptation, but in an utterly new, unique – in a word, "original" – work which, accordingly, may be said to be the property of its creator and to merit the law's protection as such.'[8]

In sum, the author that emerged during the romantic period faced a new set of material circumstances for literary production; he developed aesthetic strategies and theoretical understandings of creativity as alternately direct or refracted forms of engagement with those circumstances. Whereas medieval or premodern conceptions of authorship emphasized the public force of written texts and the role of divine revelation in textual production, with the romantic era the modern view of authorship becomes firmly one of individual, original expression.[9] The gradual movement toward such formulations was never only an aesthetic process, but instead accompanied changes in the general structure of the literary marketplace as it became a space of overwhelming commodification. Crucial within this was a transformed legal field that began to reflect the centrality to the book industries of questions of ownership over the text-as-commodity.

In turn, if there is a traceable relationship between copyright law and conceptions of authorship within romantic literary epistemology, an aspect of the residue of this connection is a marked tendency toward economic disavowal within authors' various self-constructions. In agreement with Woodmansee, Mark Rose shows that 'the representation of the author as a creator who is entitled to profit from his labour came into being through a blending of literary and legal discourses in the context of the contest over perpetual copyright.'[10] As Rose emphasizes that faith in expressive aesthetic objects needs 'a system of cultural production and regulation based on property,'[11] he also points out that the 'sense of the commercial' is the negative subtext for a variety of romantic-era works. In fact romantic-era literature is thought to have been the first to express a systematic denial of the economic motivations for authorship, not to mention substantial opposition to any material impetus for literary production in general, as writers strove to 'elaborate a conception of the writing career in a world of exchange.'[12]

In this way, as the writer strained to attach himself to the category of genius, part of the work of authorship came to involve negotiating a separation between 'the ordinary workaday world' and that of the writer's ostensibly non-alienated form of labour.[13] Given the democratization of readership that Raymond Williams assigns a central place within 'the long revolution,' just as the writer becomes more distant from his now unknown and dispersed audience, the process of literary production comes to be conceived of less as one of social reformation or communication and more as fundamentally lacking any function or utility, as a leisure activity or as an individual, creative, aesthetic pursuit.[14]

It is this striving for separation that I am ultimately interested in, as it has come virtually to define the aesthetic in some circles, and has had a remarkable longevity throughout the last century, influencing to varying degrees the way literary labour is understood by creative writers, literary journalists, reviewers, and academic critics. Consider, for example, that however much writers like Marcel Proust and T.S. Eliot criticized romanticism's tendency toward personal expression and effusive emotion, their ideology of artistic impersonality nevertheless strongly evoked the romantic 'shamanic figure' that gained status 'in proportion to its radical alienation from the empirical world.'[15] Or, further, consider the abhorrence for the everyday that Wimsatt and Beardsley express when lending their support to a critical practice that aims to evaluate the success of the text as a distinctly sustained piece of artistry: 'There is *a gross body of life, of sensory and mental experience*, which lies behind and in some sense causes every poem, but can never be and need not be known in the verbal and hence intellectual composition which is the poem.'[16] In this light, the new critical school of anti-authorialism with which Wimsatt and Beardsley are typically associated hardly radically absented the author in one fell swoop. Instead, as Donald Pease argues, it 'completed a movement' initiated much earlier, when the realities of a commercial market and of wide-scale production alienated the author from the source of his own income, and 'when the word "genius" separated the author's work from the socioeconomic world.'[17]

With this general outline drawn, what I turn to now are the challenges that the newly expansive global publishing industry presents to any emphasis on denial of the 'socioeconomic world' as an approach to the emerging conditions of authorship's development and articulation. It is my sense that there arises within the contemporary literary field, and in particular within the postcolonial field of production, vari-

eties of authorial crisis which, while certainly responsive to it, nevertheless revise in some significant ways our romantic legacy's focus on
the author's unique expressivity and separability from media and
market.

The global literary field and market postcolonialism

What *kind* of commodity is a book? The average novel is not a commodity in the way that, say, Coke is a commodity, because the word
'book' implies a variety of distinct products – there are currently several
million separate titles in print – whereas Coke implies uniformity. With
a book, too, there is presumably more room between articulation and
reception, more space for the consumer to construct meaning, and each
book product contains a distinct symbolic content. 'Books' are not just
books; the word stands in for an assemblage of separate entities, and
variety in content leads to complexity of ordering and distribution, and
in turn to special technologies for stock control and consumer profiling.
Moreover, books cannot move easily across borders due to linguistic
and cultural differences that impede easy dissemination. Coke is Coke
wherever it goes. Barring a few basic changes to its packaging and
design, the content is the same, whereas books require translation
and what Eva Hemmungs Wirtén has termed 'transediting.'[18] Notwith-
standing all this, isn't Coke itself a complex carrier of different symbolic
material, and isn't its meaning as a product something that varies with
consumption? And can't the ambiguities of a literary work be reduced
to insignificance in certain circumstances, its meaning turned into the
embodiment of a singular ideology? Moreover, isn't there a global
network of readers of English-language literary works that makes
transediting largely unnecessary, as communities across the globe access
the newest Salman Rushdie title with relative ease?

In 2004, at the time of publication of *The New Media Monopoly*, the
seventh update of the most cited study of contemporary media concentration, Ben Bagdikian could declare that five 'global-dimensions
firms' controlled all mass media on a global scale. These are 'Time
Warner, by 2003 the largest media firm in the world; The Walt Disney
Company; Murdoch's News Corporation, based in Australia; Viacom;
and Bertelsmann, based in Germany.' Even a number as small as five,
though, understates these firms' collective power, since despite some
obvious competition each is intertwined with the other. They 'have
similar boards of directors, they jointly invest in the same ventures,
and they even go through motions that, in effect, lend each other

money and swap properties when it is mutually advantageous.'[19] Book publishing, the mass media's key predecessor, arguably the first global information system, and 'a less flamboyant branch of the cultural industries,'[20] is not exempt from this concentration.

Bertelsmann, for example, is the largest book publisher, with 10 per cent of all English language book sales worldwide. It is in general the world's third largest media conglomerate, with major shares in both AOL and barnesandnoble.com. In 1998 it acquired Random House, one of the largest publishers of literary fiction, with upwards of 100 houses in 13 countries under its umbrella, including Alfred A. Knopf, Pantheon, Fawcett, Vintage and Doubleday.[21] Random House is in fact a good indicator of the changing dimensions of the publishing landscape during the twentieth century. Established in 1927 when Horace Liveright sold the Modern Library to Bennett Cerf, and originally thriving due to the booming paperback fiction market, it went on to acquire Knopf, Vintage, and other imprints in 1960–1, before being sold to RCA in 1965. In 1980 RCA sold the company to Newhouse, then Newhouse to Advance Publications, and in 1998 it became a part of Bertelsmann. In 2000 Random House's US$2 billion sales accounted for about 12 per cent of Bertelsmann's total revenues.[22] It remains a German company, but throughout the 1990s a third of its global sales revenue was earned in the US. It owns media companies producing magazines, books, and newspapers, as well as radio stations and television networks, and also printing and paper plants worldwide, including Offset Paperback Mfrs. in Pennsylvania, where one out of every five paperbacks produced in the US is printed.[23]

Corporatization in the publishing industry has occurred in a few key phases, and was in its early stages primarily a British and American phenomenon.[24] In the 1960s book publishing companies were bought by firms that did not specialize in media; they were particularly attractive to the electronics and defense industries (GE, IBM, RCA), which hoped to make inroads in textbook publishing, and wanted access to information for distribution in the new electronic formats. These 'electronic invaders' purchased existing firms, but also caused other anxious publishing houses to merge. Most of these initial acquisitions failed, and major industries divested themselves of publishing houses soon after acquiring them. In the 1980s the same houses were merged frequently with the film and video industries, until they were finally primarily concentrated in communications firms (like Bertelsmann), with a few absorbed within conglomerates (such as Pearson, which continues to do business in oil and banking, for example, while operating newspapers like *The Financial Times* of London and magazines like *The Economist*, as well as Penguin, and therein the New American Library and Viking, to name but two). These communications firms, alternately called TNMCs (Transnational Media Corporations), or 'the media' in popular parlance, commonly see themselves as existing to use all available formats, or all available media vehicles, to disseminate 'information, education, and entertainment.'[25] Getting under way in the European industry later in the 1970s, the concentration process then became significantly international, as the Traditional Market Agreement between the US and the UK collapsed, and European firms made inroads into lucrative markets where 'common ownership of the English language' had long made British and American publishers 'each other's largest customers.'[26]

Accounts of the process of corporatization have for the most part been articulated by people with direct experience in the book industries, who tend to depict a past of idyllic cultural work untainted by the pursuit of wealth. Jason Epstein, an early Doubleday editor and one of the founders of the *New York Review of Books*, is one such industry insider. He depicts recent developments in media concentration as a betrayal of publishing's 'true nature,' as it gradually, and 'under duress from unfavorable market conditions and the misconceptions of remote managers,' assumed the characteristics of a standard business. Epstein maintains the fairly conventional belief that publishing was and should be more like 'a vocation or an amateur sport in which the primary goal is the activity itself rather than its financial outcome.'[27] His condemnation of changes in the industry is characterized most notably by his avowedly urban insistence that the source of the general plight of contemporary culture is the very existence of the suburbs. The urban represents a 'natural diversity' that has been undermined by 'an increasingly homogenous suburban marketplace, demanding ever more uniform products.'[28] Whereas books 'have always needed the complex cultures of great cities in which to reverberate,' in the suburbs culture is not so much defective as overwhelmed by 'morally neutral market conditions.'[29] Ideas like these have much currency within the industry itself, and are best understood as a more recent version of a long-standing generative trope that has for centuries pitted economic considerations against what is 'truly' literary. They are also somewhat misconceived.

Books are a major industry, and concentration has by no means meant that fewer cultural products are finding their way to the market. Instead, as Herb Schiller has argued, if we have witnessed a marked 'acceleration in the decline of nonmarket-controlled creative work and symbolic output,' there has still been major growth in the 'commercial production' of culture.[30] Despite fears about the demise of reading, in the face of pressures from competing media the number of titles published worldwide every year in fact continues to grow. A number of factors have contributed to the continued presence of books as a competitive media. Media synergy has meant that publishing houses, operating within larger corporations, have been guaranteed promotion through tie-ins with television, film, and the internet. Technologies like offset lithography, film-setting, and later computer-setting have replaced metal or rubber plates, making smaller print runs economically viable. Management of distribution systems has vastly improved since International Standard Book Numbers (ISBNs) were introduced globally in 1967–8, allowing for barcoding and making it easier for bookstores to control stock. Efficient stock control has been further encouraged by the narrowing range of available publishers, as well as by the tele- and then electronic ordering taking precedence since the late 1970s.[31] These technological developments have made it possible for publishers and bookstores to cater successfully to smaller and smaller portions of the reading public, and the synergies of corporatization have provided more venues and opportunities for niche marketing. So while some feared that minority readers, for example, would be abandoned or ignored as media concentration became more prevalent, in fact, as Randall Stevenson argues, publishers recognized that they could not afford to ignore any segment of the reading public, and in response they have continually sought ways to access readers as members of specific and identifiable reading communities.[32]

In short, in recent years corporatization has often gone hand in hand with a trend toward greater diversity, as concentration has been significantly offset by a parallel formation of new companies. In turn, as Elizabeth Long points out, growing levels of affluence and education for the generations coming of age since World War II have guaranteed a 'much more diverse and sophisticated set of reading publics' than a 'massification model' might allow.[33] Critiques of the concentration or commercialization process often overlook this fact, in favour of expressing what Long describes as an anxiety that 'cultural diversity and innovation, serious literature and critical ideas, may be suppressed just as effectively by the mechanisms of mass marketing as by more visible forms of censorship.' Critics may agree that conglomerates demand rationalization and 'editorial accountability to the corporate hierarchy,' but publishing has always been a blend of or balance between commercial and other interests, and there is no sense in which the commercialization process can be considered strictly a phenomenon of the postWorld War II era.[34]

Moreover, if 'multinational' simply defines any company with partner divisions in two or more countries, then the British and American publishing industries have long operated multinationally, whether through mutual trade with one another or through the establishment of branch offices in diverse areas of the world. In addition, it is wise to distinguish between globalization and internationalization in publishing. In a globalization model, markets for 'already produced media products' are 'extended from certain centres in developed countries to other developed and developing countries.'[35] Global operations are facilitated by acceptance of the doctrine that information should flow freely across borders, by laws that allow for foreign ownership and control of media systems, by non-restrictive banking laws 'facilitating currency conversion and capital movement,' as well as by aspects of copyright law.[36] In contrast, internationalization involves significantly more reciprocal trade in products, and for real success requires the existence of a stable domestic industry which includes numerous indigenous producers. This often entails an agency system through which major publishing companies deal with offices on a local level. The parent company may retain control but profits circulate within the local market. A major firm that deals with a variety of local agents may see the feasibility of setting up, alternatively, their own local branch, thus rerouting profits to the parent company, a procedure which leads to true globalization. Scrutiny of the globalization process requires understanding the various ways companies deal with international partners, if they do at all; it should also entail analysis of how what counts as local content relies on and is marketed through the global cultural industries, and vice versa.

Granted, corporatization has changed the way publishers think about the task they perform, by changing the way manuscripts are acquired, turned into books, and marketed and sold. Though there may continue to be a growing number of publishing houses in general – *Books in Print* lists over 73,000 in 2003[37] – if more than 50 per cent of the publishing industry is run by between five and seven encompassing firms that on average make US$500 million each year, that leaves almost no income for those thousands remaining.[38] The consequence of this concentration is not so much that there are no alternative or smaller successful companies, but that the conglomerates control the rules of the game, having access to those aspects of publishing and marketing that require significant capital. As Bagdikian points out, it is the big conglomerates that have the power to acquire 'credit from big banks for expansion and acquisitions, bidding for manuscripts, negotiating and paying for shelf space and window displays in book shops which increasingly are owned by national chains, mounting national sales staffs, buying advertising, and arranging for author interviews in the broadcast media.'[39] Publishing firms that traditionally aimed for a profit margin between 1 and 4 per cent are now forced to achieve 12 to 15 per cent to keep pace with the other media companies belonging to the larger conglomerates in which they are situated. The major conglomerates, moreover, have distribution firms under their umbrellas. These firms often negotiate directly with the monster bookstore chains, selling print runs of a size inconceivable to smaller publishing houses and independent bookstores alike, and negotiating 'co-op' deals to advertise potential bestselling titles in specific key merchandising areas.[40]

This parallel process of concentration and diversification within the publishing industry, a characteristic tension within most forms of media conglomeration, has a number of possible implications. First, in ways I return to at length below, Jason Epstein is not alone in imagining that he is a part of a process that has fundamentally changed the status of books as cultural products. Despite the specific nuances of emerging corporate structures, the dominant narrative within the industry itself is one in which corporatization has significantly changed the way literature is marketed, and has contributed to the 'blockbuster' phenomenon through which particular authors become central to the imaginations of readers. Regardless of its purchase on reality, authors have imbibed this narrative as well, in part because they are now thoroughly organized as a self-conscious class of quasi-professionals. Those whose works are published in the Anglo-American marketplace have little choice but to belong to major organizations that advocate for authors' rights and express their concerns in publications like *The Author*. These organizations, such as the Society of Authors and its sister groups outside the UK, work to keep authors abreast of developments in the industry, and in recent years they have raised significant political questions about industry corporatization.

Second, if the dissemination of a specifically literary tradition remains a goal for the dominant firms, it is largely because a niche audience exists to make that tradition financially viable. Its characteristics are easily gleaned through rationalized sales systems, and then appealed to through strategic target marketing. Long speculates that

'high culture [...] is now being dealt with in publishing as one specialized aspect of a less hierarchical and more fragmentary cultural total-
ity.'[41] That is, what Robert Escarpit called the 'cultured circuit,' made
up of 'persons having received an intellectual training and an esthetic
education [...], having sufficient time to read, and having enough
money to buy books with regularity,'[42] has clearly become a niche
within the larger publishing industry. That niche is one that can be
reached through specifically global corporate operations. Indeed one
way to combat fears about corporatization in the publishing industry is
to point to the market triumph of 'serious' literary fiction as a distinct
publishing category. Since the 1970s increasing amounts of such
fiction have managed to reach bestseller or even 'fastseller' status, and
by the middle of the 1990s more than 100 literary titles per year were
selling at least 100,000 copies in the UK. Commercial viability has
been encouraged and accompanied by a number of phenomena,
including the spread of major chain bookstores and the emergence of
the trade paperback format that 'contrived to enhance the consumer
profile' of 'serious' work.[43] Publishers often divide their lists into lead
and non-lead titles, promoting only the former with any seriousness,
circulating bound proofs to reviewers up to six months in advance of a
new publication, and developing promotional portfolios that include
biographical information about their respective authors and sales
figures for their other works. It is now quite common to treat literary
works as blockbuster lead titles in just this way. In Britain there are
abundant media available for promotion or review, including the
Times Literary Supplement, the *London Review of Books*, W.H. Smith's
Bookcase, and the *Bookseller*, as well as a variety of literary weeklies and
book review pages in various daily and Sunday papers, not to mention
book-related programming on the BBC and Radio 4. Equivalents in the
US include the *New York Review of Books*, the *New York Times Book
Review*, and pages in papers like the *Boston Globe* and the *Village Voice*.
Online, both the *Guardian Unlimited* (www.guardian.co.uk) and *Salon*
(www.salon.com) are extremely popular with market readers of literary
fiction and with industry professionals.

Within this niche of literary fiction for a cultured audience, further
divisions exist. With methods previously exclusive to specialist publishing, trade fiction houses have registered the value of perceiving
readers as belonging to particular communities of interest which can
be segmented and targeted with specific marketing. Gardiner notes
that publishers' catalogues and display spaces in bookstores are now
more likely to feature generic subdivisions categorizing literary titles

('chick lit' is a commonly cited example). She also notes that these genres are established across publishing houses through bibliographic codes that unite disparate titles with, for example, similar features of format and cover design.[44]

It is with this in mind that the proliferation of postcolonial literatures within the Anglo-American market can be explained in part as an aspect of the twinned processes of niche fragmentation and market expansion in the global publishing industry. There remains some truth in a claim made by executives at Bertelsmann that their German communications megalith is less a global company than an international 'network' of national firms, in the sense that a truly global commodity 'must be able to travel easily around the world with only the most modest cosmetic retouching to appeal to local customers.'[45] However in recent years it has become possible to speak of the cosmopolitan, elite readers of English-language literary fiction as consumers of a truly global commodity in need of little alteration for local consumption. Postcolonial literatures have had something to do with this. They facilitate the sort of incorporation of niche audiences that allows for global market expansion within transnational publishing, much though that extension keeps the locus of production in a few key cities in the developed world.

This works in a number of ways. In 2004 'In Full Colour' appeared as a supplement in *The Bookseller*, the journal of the UK book trades, and presented the results of a survey of minority representation in the English publishing industry. Though its first lines state that the subject is a 'moral issue' as well, the emphasis of the remaining pages is undoubtedly the commercial implications of neglecting diversity. Researched and produced in association with *decibel*, an Arts Council of England initiative to promote cultural diversity, the report makes a few major claims based on a survey distributed to publishing industry employees. One is that the industry's workforce and manuscript acquisition trends remain 'unrepresentative' of ethnic communities in England, and especially of metropolitan London's 29 per cent minority population. In turn, those minority writers whose works have made up a growing percentage of the lists of the major publishers are said to feel the effects of a certain ghettoization, as a largely white industry forces them 'to write about multicultural issues.'[46] The other is that the industry has a commercial responsibility to correct these imbalances. In fact the publishing professionals who make up *The Bookseller*'s major readership are appealed to through continual reference to the market implications of any neglect of the necessity of significant improvements in representing diversity. It is said that there are minority markets for literature that publishers will certainly fail to reach if they continue to lack the staff 'who have an inside knowledge of those markets.'[47] In fact ethnic groups are taken to be more appealing potential markets for publishers than the white majority. Arts Council of England surveying has shown that minorities do more than average amounts of creative writing and visit libraries at rates higher than the overall national average. It is noted in particular that the South Asian population exceeds all norms in mobile phone and personal computer ownership and in internet access, modes of consumption considered indicative of a generally elevated level of investment in 'lifestyle commodities' like books and films.

The report promotes Race for Opportunity as a potential corrective. A network of 'over 180 UK organizations working on race and diversity as a business agenda,' to which W.H. Smith, the BBC, the Guardian Media Group, and 'education' conglomerate Pearson PLC all belong, Race for Opportunity encourages the business community to recognize the commercial value of managing diversity. In chairman Allan Leighton's words, 'communities equal customers and potential employees.'[48] It is the larger publishers that are meant to form the vanguard of this activity, since they have the resources to engage in the kind of market research and employee diversification that will ensure their success within a changing market. The report cites Random House and Penguin Books as two publishers making notable efforts to access minority markets, at least in part through actively recruiting employees from minority populations. For example, Penguin's 'diversity project' actively seeks participants for its work experience program at schools with a high percentage of minority ethnic students. Penguin director Helen Fraser explains, 'A workforce that mirrors the population, especially urban populations where the majority of books are sold, will be able to tap into the whole market.'[49]

As *The Bookseller's* report suggests, publishers now recognize the commercial necessity of attracting minority ethnic writers within metropolitan locations. Companies solidify their dominant positions by incorporating postcolonial writers for global distribution, and also by opening branch offices in the regions from which their authors emerge. These offices attract local authors who would likely seek publication abroad in any case, and they distribute them at the local level while also arranging international publishing contracts for global release. A good example is Penguin Books, which is incorporated within Pearson PLC. Penguin opened branch offices in India in 1985, where it represents Vikram Seth, Arundhati Roy, Vikram Chandra, and Upamanyu Chatterjee, amongst others; in Ireland in 2002, where it aims to take advantage of the popularity of 'local interest' titles in the region, and to 'harness the talent of the authors to a professional organisation which has its sights set on the international stage';[50] and in South Africa in the 1970s. Similarly, the Macmillan group, owned by the German company Holtzbrinck, includes Pan Macmillan South Africa and Australia, and has countless other offices engaged in the worldwide distribution of mainly textbook titles and academic and reference works, and also of literary fiction in a variety of languages.

The more literature associable with specific national or ethnic identities enters the market, the more the market, despite increasing concentration and globalization, can make the claims to inclusivity and universality that justify its particular form of dominance. Expanding markets for literatures in English have depended on the incorporation of a plurality of identities for global export. Paul Jay's statement that 'English literature is increasingly postnational'[51] needs to be tempered by awareness of the market that this postnationality serves. If 'contemporary writing is produced in a postnational, global flow of deterritorialized cultural products appropriated, translated, and recirculated worldwide,' as Jay states, that 'flow' is not untapped, but is instead checked by observable hierarchies.[52] While it may be true that the organization of the study of literature around national divisions is increasingly outmoded, and that attention to the cross-border traffic in texts and their contents is the better path for future literary scholarship, it remains the case that the expansion of the market for English literatures has been mostly an Anglo-American phenomenon. Products from a plurality of locales are incorporated into the central metropolitan locations of New York and (decreasingly) London. Despite the undoubted prominence of works by writers not simplistically identifiable as Anglo-American, the locus of production and consumption that drives the trade, and hence the economic beneficiaries of its operations, remains centered in the Anglo-American metropolizes. It doesn't help that much critical scholarship originates in those same metropolitan locations; this is the new 'international division of labour' that Biodun Jeyifo identifies.[53] It is for all of these reasons that one might be forgiven for thinking that the distinction between 'World' literature and 'Western' literature has never been more tenuous.[54]

The kind of postcolonial writing most often picked up for global distribution has certain characteristics. It is typically novels, currently the best selling literary genre. Writing in European languages, and especially in English, is privileged. As Gordon Graham argues, 'the unacknowledged tide that has carried the corporations into many lands is the speed with which the English language has increased its dominance as the world's main commercial language.' Successful firms 'are either based in countries where English is the native language, or have taken deliberate decisions to move out of their own language cultures.'[55] In 2003 Graham noted that five times more books are translated from English into other languages than vice versa. He claims that in order for 'foreigners' to be read within the Anglo-American market they either have to write in English, or win the Nobel Prize, which is seemingly the only evaluative guarantee that one's work will be translated.[56] UNESCO states that 50 per cent of all translation is from English into other languages, and that only 6 per cent of translation is into English,[57] though these figures mean less when one considers that there are simply more books published in English to begin with, and that the more books published in English the lower the rate of translation into English will seem.[58]

A more salient statistic may be, in this case, the amount of English literary fiction that is read *in English* across the globe. Indeed some of my own rationale for referring to an Anglo-American marketplace rather than a Euro-American one stems from the general dominance of English. This is in line with Pascale Casanova's recent concession that in moving from literary internationalism to commercial globalization, major European publishing centres like Paris are losing ground to a more 'polycentric,' pluralistic literary field which is nonetheless increasingly organized around London and New York, in part due to the commercial triumph of the English language.[59] Though major transnational media firms like Bertelsmann may be headquartered in Europe, their publishing companies release a great deal of material in English, which is more and more the global vernacular of literary fiction despite the fact that it is not the world's dominant first language. Eva Hemmungs Wirtén's explanation is convincing: 'English is the vernacular of the world because power is assigned in the interstices between linguistic supremacy *and* control of the industries that capitalize on content, information, knowledge, or other assets of intellectual property *in that language.*'[60]

In addition, a growing consensus holds that celebrated postcolonial writers are most often those who are *literary* in a way recognizable to cosmopolitan audiences accustomed to what Timothy Brennan identifies as the 'complexities and subtleties' of a very specific kind of 'great art.'[61] In Casanova's terms, the pole that dominates 'world literary space,' which has to be reached to achieve literary consecration, defines itself in opposition to those underdeveloped literary worlds still 'dependent on political – typically national – authorities.' Various kinds of formalism, for example, seem to be privileged over realism 'in all its forms and denominations – neonaturalist, picturesque, proletarian, socialist.'[62] Moreover, if literary writing that addresses the politics of specifically Third World nations has become its own niche in the Anglo-American market, in part because readers want to be educated to a certain degree about 'other' realities – so that political material becomes eminently marketable – the texts that fulfil that interest most often accord with a broadly anti-imperialist political liberalism. This is, as Brennan writes, a liberalism 'that openly and consciously seeks to throw off what it considers to be the clichés of the postwar rhetoric of third-world embattlement.'[63] It often entails 'a harsh questioning of radical decolonization theory; a dismissive or parodic attitude towards the project of national culture; a manipulation of imperial imagery and local legend as a means of politicising "current events"; and a declaration of cultural "hybridity".'[64]

Brennan's characterization of cosmopolitanism as '*local* while denying its local character' is similar to Masao Miyoshi's discussion of what he calls the 'TNC class,' made up of the employees of transnational corporations in their guise as efficient managers of 'global production and consumption, hence of world culture itself.' Miyoshi describes that class as presumably 'clear of national and ethnic blinders,' but 'not free of a new version of "ideologyless" ideology,' the ideology of cultural management.[65] Much of Miyoshi's argument about the role that academics should play in articulating an opposition to the 'TNC class' relies on analogies he makes between it and academic professionals themselves, who are also 'frequent fliers and globe-trotters,' addicted to a sanitizing discourse of pluralism and an identity politics which is, in his view, a form of collaboration with the processes of transnational capitalism.[66] This increasingly common reading of the general parameters of cosmopolitanism – its liberalism, pluralism, and seeming congruity with multinational capitalism – is echoed in Arif Dirlik's picture of postcolonial literature as a feature of capitalist accumulation in the culture industries, and as part of the way the metropolitan university asserts control of its many peripheries. As I discussed previously, Dirlik and others tend to claim that the distinguishing features of celebrated postcolonial writing coincide with the concerns of metropolitan critics in general, concerns which encourage an adherence to a largely inadequate or utopian politics of hybridity and postnationality. In turn it is no great surprise that metropolitan critics and postcolonial authors alike have tended to negotiate positions that recognize, deflect, or interrogate their own complicity in this general situation.

To review, several things characterize the postcolonial literature that achieves the greatest success in the current market: it is English-language fiction; it is relatively 'sophisticated' or 'complex' and often anti-realist; it is politically liberal and suspicious of nationalism; it uses a language of exile, hybridity, and 'mongrel' subjectivity. What is the function of writers' biographies in additionally ensuring their success within the market? Celebrated postcolonial writers are typically situated in relation to a number of underdeveloped locales, such that what Brennan calls the 'banners' of geographical affiliation are always in sight: 'Being from "there" in this sense is primarily a kind of literary passport that identifies the artist as being from a region of underdevelopment and pain.'[67] Writers like Rushdie are made to 'present their own "Third World" identities as a mark of distinction in a world supposedly exempt from national belonging.'[68] In fact these writers in part succeed because of their ostensible attachment to specific locations. In effect the trumpeted 'complexity' of successful postcolonial literary production is a sign of a '[l]iterary sophistication [...] doubly authoritative because it is proof of overcoming *that* to join *this*.'[69] That said, just as postcolonial literatures emerge in relation to the expansive demands of an ever more global trade in literary texts, any focus on biographical specificity and local 'identity' in the promotion of postcolonial writers is also related to more wide-scale trends in the industry's general positioning of authors. I turn now to a fuller description of these trends, and to an account of what impact they should have on the existing historical narrative that documents the emergence of the market-dependent author.

Authorship incorporated, authorship erased

Writers' desire for personal renown has probably always existed, and many certainly sought fame before an expansive form of market celebrity was an option. Likewise, as a promotional technique public exposure of authorial personae is not a particularly recent development; its initial acceleration can be traced to the mass-circulation consumer magazine and the human-interest journalism that arose in the late nineteenth century. What has changed is the overall commercial structure of the literary field, toward the multinational organization I have just outlined, and with it the possibilities for authorial self-articulation. Our narrative of the material history of authorship needs to evolve in tandem with such changes in order to recognize an altered series of interconnected spheres of authorial anxiety and self-articulation. How exactly should these changes be registered?

Pierre Bourdieu's own authorial crisis helps me begin to answer this question. In drawing distinctions between the restricted and extended subfields of the literary marketplace – in brief, between the mass market and its more elite counterpart – it is Bourdieu's sociology of the literary field which scholars tend to reference. Yet in the postscript to his most recent articulation of this sociology, published in 1992 as *Les règles de l'art* and in English translation in 1996, he emphasizes the increasing obsolescence of his own pioneering work on authorship in a way that actually clarifies its central implications. Before the publication of *The Rules of Art,* in line with the history I trace above, Bourdieu had claimed influentially that the rise of a market that made it possible for authors to make a living by writing was accompanied by an ideology of separation from market concerns. That split had seemed like a generative assumption of the majority of Bourdieu's work on the literary field, defining one aspect of his approach to cultural consumption in general. For example, in *The Field of Cultural Production* he writes of the 'charismatic' ideology of romantic authorship as a complex process of authorial creation based on 'suppressing the question of what authorizes the author.'[70] That ideology contributes to the field of restricted production, which exists only anxiously within a larger marketplace reliant on large-scale production as a means of capitalist accumulation.[71] In a related way, one of the assumptions of the body of *The Rules of Art* is that the idea of the artist as autonomous from the economic sphere is inseparably linked to the rise of a commercial culture that allowed artists to make a living producing art.[72] Bourdieu's analysis of the development of a belief in artistic autonomy is, then, more or less a debunking of the notion of artistic disinterest, or an attempt to show that those who try to separate themselves from socio-economics are, by the very gesture of separation, in fact delimited and determined by them.

That said, in the postscript to *The Rules of Art* Bourdieu emphasizes the inadequacy of precisely the generative opposition on which his work to date had been based, an opposition said to be in the ascendant position since at least the nineteenth century in France, and coincident with the romantic periods in many Western cultures. Within the contemporary market, Bourdieu argues, the old division between elite and mass production is 'threatening to disappear, since the logic of commercial production tends more and more to assert itself over avant-garde production (notably in the case of literature, through the constraints of the book market)' (345). He laments that the dominant holders of power in the society, whom he typically places in opposition to the 'dominated portion of the dominant class' that makes up the cultural field, have a new stranglehold 'over the instruments of circulation – and of consecration.' In effect, then, 'the boundary has never been so blurred between the experimental work and the *bestseller*' (347). Thus the values that attach to the supposedly split realities of 'merchandise' and 'signification' no longer remain even 'relatively independent of each other' (141). The priorities of Escarpit's 'cultured circuit' are eminently marketable within their own niche. Experimentation sells. Highbrow, middlebrow, and lowbrow categories are collapsed. The very nature of the contemporary publishing industry makes claims to an authenticity defined by separation from the market a near impossibility.

In turn, in the same postscript, as a marked response to the situation he laments, in what I consider a moment of authorial crisis, Bourdieu promotes the very autonomy his *oeuvre* to date had seemed to question so consistently and rigorously. He claims that if intellectuals are going to continue to have a role in public, political life, it will be due to their belief in their own autonomy. Indeed the power of intellectual intervention in the political sphere will depend upon general acceptance of the 'relative' autonomy of the intellectual fields of art, science, and literature, and upon social validation of the values of disinterestedness and expertise associated with them (340). In John Guillory's words, Bourdieu suggests that 'the space cleared by the refusal of market demand is precisely the space in which social determinations can be explored without wholly acceding to market demand.'[73] Distance and engagement are not opposing forces. Instead the best purpose of any socially-sanctioned distance is precisely a form of expert engagement. It is this sanctioned role that is said to be undermined within the current culture industries.

What I want to emphasize is the degree to which Bourdieu's attempt to revive the position of autonomy within the literary field arises from an explicitly political motivation. This encapsulates in large part the locus of my own investigation. The role Bourdieu promotes for artistic or critical autonomy from the economic sphere of the extended marketplace is a legitimized, disinterested and objective form of political engagement. In turn, that political engagement should operate within the market on the principle of its autonomy from market economics.

Otherwise, for example, his own consistently Marxist politics can be stripped of any objectivity and branded mere ideology or marketable resistance by those charged with the tasks of assessment and consecration. So the argument that symbolic goods have two realities, one as 'merchandise' and the other as 'signification' – an argument Bourdieu outlined in his own early work only in order to undermine it – is the very argument *The Rules of Art*'s postscript sets out to prop up. Finally, and in the name of specific political realities, faith in authors' ability to resist market colonization is something to maintain. He pits himself in opposition to the dominant economics of the market in much the way the romantic or avant-garde artists he once studied had done. Under the new conditions of multinational capital, in order to continue his own explorations and critiques of the many social and economic determinants of cultural production, Bourdieu *must* oppose the increasingly ruthless demands of the market, much though he had historicized the same gesture time and again in his own past work.

In that sense the postscript is neither a radical departure from his earlier work nor a statement of its irrelevance. Instead by turning in upon itself it performs a clear articulation and exemplification of the often neglected implications of his previous theories. In line with the seeming paradox recurrent in all his work, autonomy is never autonomous, since intellectuals such as Bourdieu can only achieve the position by debunking it and by pointing out that it does not have to equal any 'transcendental illusion' (341). It is up to them to situate and historicize their own autonomy, which is equivalent to tracing the historical emergence of the social and economic conditions which make it possible. This situating and historicizing is of course precisely what Bourdieu had long been devoted to. Autonomy only makes sense at all when one recognizes the paradoxical – or, better, dialectical – character of its emergence, and grants that the issue of its status is eternally relevant, because it 'must reckon with obstacles and powers which are ceaselessly renewed' (343). The fight is not yet won. Bourdieu's autonomous gesture is a small part of an ongoing struggle, and it is articulated in full knowledge of this fact. As in all of Bourdieu's work, the value of autonomy can never be absolutely determined, and can never exist in some inherent opposition to the social and the economic, since on the contrary those are the things that always condition and delimit it.

The only way to preserve autonomy is to fight for it, much though to fight for it is to seemingly descend from it by dirtying one's hands with the everyday mess of political work. Here, Bourdieu wants to celebrate the space of emergence of autonomy – a privileged space, he admits – because it is where the most expedient instruments of reason are manufactured and made workable. In this spirit he pleads for the creation of a 'veritable *Internationale of intellectuals,* committed to defending the autonomy of the universes of cultural production, or, to parody a language now out of fashion, *the ownership by cultural producers of their instruments of production and circulation* (and hence of evaluation and consecration)' (344). The publishing company Bourdieu started in 1996 and ran from his university office, *Raisons d'agir* (Reasons to Act), continues to take up this 'out of fashion' challenge now, producing inexpensive works that often register specific concerns about media concentration and multinational capitalism, such as Serge Halimi's *Les nouveaux chiens de garde* (1997; 2005) and Bourdieu's own *Contre-feux: Propos pour servir à la résistance contre l'invasion néo-libérale* (1998).

By his own account, part of what Bourdieu aimed to overcome with *Raisons d'agir* was the fact that authors and other artists were more than ever fundamentally divorced from the processes of their works' production and dissemination. One of the major features of the process of concentration in the publishing industry, or one area where change has been exacerbated by corporatization, is the trajectory of authors' careers, and in turn the way they understand what they do. Many of the most important developments in publishing in recent years have involved the status and positioning of authors. For example, the 'blockbuster' phenomenon means that a dwindling number of 'star' authors receive an increasing percentage of a given firm's available dollars in the form of lucrative advances and royalties. In addition, any integrity ostensibly involved in the traditional relationship between the 'leisured' writer and the 'gentleman' publisher has been put into question as agents have taken on more central roles in authors' careers. It is agents who negotiate with publishers and arrange subsidiary and ancillary rights for works' adaptation and republication in the available formats of transnational media synergy, in effect auctioning each iteration of a given title off to the highest bidder, making the publisher a mere guarantor of a book's effective distribution and profitability within the market.

Moreover, part of the aggressive marketing of certain titles, necessary in order for book divisions to remain competitive within transnational media firms, entails an emphasis on the connections between the book in question and its biographical author. The author's name and attached personae have become key focal points for the marketing of literary texts, such that one could argue that the current industry brands literature more by authorship than by other aspects of or ways of approaching a given work's meaning. The popularity of authorial branding is in part attributable to the development of commercial media that facilitate the expansion and proliferation of the many ways in which a book might be promoted. Publishers have realized the effectiveness and cheapness of forms of publicity – Joe Moran lists 'magazine and newspaper features and television and radio appearances'[74] – which focus on authors. In this way the status of authorship as a promotional sign relates to industry massification, commodification, and the proliferation of what Andrew Wernick identifies as the 'consumer reportage on one or another branch of the culture industry' that ties literature to specifically 'ad-carrying media.'[75]

Wernick suggests an analogy between the author 'as a kind of sign' and brand names in general: 'Brand-names developed out of patents, at first as a way to lay title (against stealers and forgers) to the personal ownership of the formula, invention or design embodied in a product.'[76] The promotion of authors provides such a means of laying title, of attaching the personal to what might appear otherwise: 'Promotion requires "authors" through whom to address consumers *from the heart of the product*, even where the craft mode it implies is wholly absent.'[77] Within a fragmented market defined by the proliferation of choices, selling specific identities to distinct consumers facilitates the process of consumption. In Gardiner's words, 'new technologies conspire with cultural practices to disguise the systematized commodification of literary production and suggest customization and direct appeal.'[78] Individual authorial identities are part of this disguise, as, for example, bookstore chains rely on author appearances, book signings, and book clubs to encourage people to be self-conscious about their status as book buyers, or about their participation in a literary culture. John Cawelti made a similar point as long ago as 1977, claiming that in a commodity culture where the writer relies on the sales of her work, and author-reader relationships are mediated through newspapers, radio, and television, 'the only way in which the general public can be present to a writer [...] is through the mechanism of celebrity.'[79] Thus the figure of the author becomes an increasingly important marker of differentiation, a way of concealing mass production in individuation. In that sense, if a pull between industry conglomeration and market fragmentation has defined publishing in recent years, something analogous has happened within the sphere of authorship. The expanding market's proliferating possibilities for promotional co-optation of the author as brand is disguised by the individual personal appeal of the writer's unique subjectivity.

Meanwhile, while aspects of their work have been professionalized, such that they can become members of various associations and organizations, for literary authors perhaps more than others there is no sense in which they are pure professionals or even regular workers. Authors' conditions of employment are notably unusual. As James L. West points out, authors do not face qualifying exams or certification, and they have little formal training, no licensing system, and 'few clearly identified goals.'[80] Instead their position is inherently ambiguous and vague. What has been professionalized, though, is the publishing industry that frames what they do. Whereas once the functions of printing, binding, typesetting, and bookselling were united in one firm or even one individual, each of these tasks has been gradually parceled out, while new roles – marketer, editor, agent – have been introduced. The publisher's task is basically to organize the various subcontracted activities necessary to turn texts into books. It is for these reasons that West claims that throughout the last century writing for the literary market 'has been more nearly a craft, a cottage industry.' The author assembles 'literary piecework' that an agent-middleman presents to a publisher on his behalf, and the publisher then turns that work into 'saleable goods' through the services of others.[81]

Such professionalization and disaggregation within the publishing industry has influenced the way authors understand their own labour. Much though they are cognizant of the fact that their works reach a disparate series of niche readerships through the intervention of various industry professionals – mostly, the agent and editor – they are allowed to remain substantially ignorant of the many processes essential to bringing their books to the market. They are one small part of a vast and complex machine, yet at the same time their personae as authors are crucial to the promotional circuit necessary to a book's success within the market.

Put simply, the author is as irrelevant to the realities of production as he is essential to the mediated and fragmenting hyperrealities of promotion. Rephrasing Barthes' famous quip that the birth of the critic follows upon the death of the author, Wernick writes: 'The birth of the author, as an imaged Name for the "originator" of a text, has meant the death of authorship as an authentic activity.' The rise of the author as 'a promotional subject' has contributed to the crisis in authorship that makes impossible 'that self-possessed command over authoring which has provided an ideological cover for the transformed relation of authorship to the market that itself brought the modern elevation of authorship about.'[82]

This promotional vortex is not unrelated to poststructuralism's anti-authorial theses. Instead one of the most crippling features of Barthes' formulation of the 'death of the author' is actually the way it helps to strip authors of the forms of agency they already experience as somehow unavailable to them. In that sense there is in fact a unique accord between Barthes' brand of anti-authorial discourse and the implications of the proliferation of authorial identities as promotional signs. In both theory and the market the text is only the author's in a minimal way.[83]

In turn, as was true of the romantic-era's professional author-cum-genius creator, economy and subjectivity also tend to merge here, as writers express anxiety about the fact that the accelerated proliferation of their own personae is in fact a kind of ruse. In Bourdieu's terms, artists of all kinds are now:

> more than ever tributaries of the whole accompaniment of commentaries and commentators who contribute directly to the production of the work of art by their reflection on an art which often itself contains a reflection on art, and on artistic effort which always encompasses an artist's work on himself.[84]

Self-reflexivity involves writers incorporating into their aesthetic arsenals various kinds of meta-commentary: on the act of writing itself, on the status of literature within culture at large, and on their own careers as authors, especially as they recognize themselves as 'tributaries' in a vast field of cultural exchanges that operates substantially outside of whatever sphere they can be said to control. It is in acknowledgement of this absence of agency that Salman Rushdie speaks of an 'I' who is witness to his own irrelevance in the epigraph to this chapter: 'I feel as if I have been concealed behind a *false self*, as if a shadow has become substance while I have been relegated to the shadows.' Images that only 'shadow' the author's self, constructed as his texts circulate to unpredictable, impersonal, volatile audiences, appear to the world as the substance of that 'I'; they relegate some truer person which the actual 'I' would have us recognize to a shadowy nothing beyond our apprehension. In this light, when Barthes promotes the proliferation of interpretations brought about by 'the death of the author' he also effectively denies authors some ability to defend their works against certain readings they might find problematic, or even, as in Rushdie's case, against political factions' appropriation or denigration of their very identities as writers.

Joe Moran's pioneering study of 'star authors' in recent American fiction basically interprets writers' participation in the market in terms of the distinctions developed during the romantic period: 'celebrity in the United States has been conferred on authors who have the potential to be commercially successful and penetrate into mainstream media, but are also perceived as in some sense culturally "authoritative" – in other words, they occupy a contested area [...] between the restricted and extended subfields.'[85] Moran's posited 'contested area' seems to be one in which authors achieve authority through the articulation of a critique of the 'extended' literary field. However, as occupants of the restricted field, many authors express their awareness of the way it is actually constrained by the same parameters that hold within the extended field of textual production for commodity consumption. In the words of a critic who recently argued that the era of literary celebrity is over, 'the specific articulation of the private authorial genius versus the mass marketplace is no longer possible,' in large part because there is no longer a 'clear elite field' of coterie, family-owned, or 'gentleman' publishers combining critical and market viability.[86] That elite field is instead a recognized marketing niche within an expanded global marketplace that is run by a transnational class of professionals. Part of any current authorial crisis stems from the fact that distancing oneself from material concerns is no longer a viable option. If an author's attempt at self-definition does manifest itself as hints of nostalgia for an autonomous past, that nostalgia rapidly gives way to a will to be reconciled with a global market for cultural products that is dominated by concentration within transnational media firms.

I focus at some length on Bourdieu's postscript to emphasize precisely this: while never entirely impossible, appeals to the position of authorial autonomy are always made within conditions of strain, and then subject to near immediate stress or erasure. When they occur they are mediated by a further self-conscious awareness of the forms of scrutiny that any such position has faced. It is in this sense that the mechanisms of literary consecration have been thoroughly demystified. One cannot talk euphemistically about books or their authors in a way that insists on their romantic separation from basic economics. In James English's view, authors, journalists, and even academics can now only express 'amused complicity' in the face of the commercial success and popular appeal of literary fiction. All gestures of refusal seem dated when they involve maintaining the position of the 'prophetic-subversive,' insisting upon one's ability to avoid submission to the rules of the game.[87] As experience indicates, were someone like Martin Amis to express too great an interest in the outcome of prize adjudications, or in the size of his next advance, those few brave souls who might still dare to call him 'crass' would likely be subject to near immediate ironic destabilization and mockery. Salman Rushdie's case, which I turn to at length in the next chapter, would seem to support this general point as well, as he has rarely tried to separate himself from the interconnected cultural and economic forms of capital available to the celebrity literary author. Far from subscribing to the doctrine of refusal once assumed by the likes of Jean Paul Sartre and John Berger, Rushdie has actively courted the particular kind of public attention that comes with winning a literary prize. His televised anger at not winning the Booker for *Shame* (1983) is suitably infamous. As an event it also exemplified the intertwining of the restricted and extended subfields of the cultural market, as the ceremony for an elite literary award became material for London media and celebrity gossip mills, and as the famous writer's event performance encouraged further sales of his 'serious' fiction.

Rushdie's example returns me, though, to the special case of postcolonial authors. I have tried to emphasize that as a field of production the politicized niche of postcolonial literature is characterized by its own unique assumptions and practices. Timothy Brennan has gone to considerable lengths to identify these characteristics, arguing that 'a *politics* of names and faces' is 'the calling card' or authorization of a 'new cosmopolitan' literature.[88] Those writing from or about the developing world, and situating their narratives within an often violent political history, are expected to act as interpreters of locations they are connected to through personal biography: 'authors ranging from Brazil to South Asia,' he writes, 'exist not as individuals but as elements in an intertextual coterie that chooses them as much as they choose it.'[89]

My contention has been that such demands are made in part because the niche marketing that some associate with the promotion of exoticism is also the publishing industry's response to proliferating possibilities for accessing segmented markets of readers on a global scale. Writers become representatives of their purported societies, 'cultures,' nationalities, or subnationalities, transformed into all too singular embodiments of lengthy histories they can hardly hope to encompass. This happens not because writers are the market's passive dupes, but instead because of the historical development of and then convergence between the market position of postcolonial literatures and the market function of signatured authorship. The tendency within the globalized literary marketplace to manipulate and market the distinctions between biographical authors overlaps with the tendency within the postcolonial field of production to privilege work that can be identified with a specific geographical struggle or political history. This aspect of the field is itself a form of nostalgia for what David Simpson has called, in another context, 'the imagined lost world of metaphysical and epistemological assurance.'[90] The condition of postcoloniality that makes such a world 'lost' to begin with simultaneously creates panicked appeals to its continued desirability. What has been otherwise discredited can be resurrected as pastiche, to paraphrase Simpson.[91] In this sense, a plurality of identities circulating within the Anglo-American publishing industry is not a simple matter for celebration.[92]

Ultimately, cultural consecration or demystification takes on a decidedly different resonance when the author in question is part of a politicized incursion of writers from the periphery into the solid tradition of British literary canonicity. For example, Amitav Ghosh's withdrawal from the Commonwealth Writers Prize in 2001 was not done ironically, and nor was it based in any denial of the inevitable commercialization or consecration of literary production. His motivation was instead his objection that the category of 'commonwealth literature' applies a disputed historical formulation to contemporary writing, trapping it in a category it often critiques, while simultaneously excluding the multitude of non-English writing that comes out of the so-called Commonwealth nations. In a letter to the *Times of India* explaining his decision, Ghosh states that as far as he can tell his nominated novel *The Glass Palace* 'is eligible [...] partly because it was written in English and partly because I happen to belong to a region that was once conquered and ruled by imperial Britain. Of the many reasons why a book's merits may be recognised, these seem to be the least persuasive.'[93] His remarks indicate his effort to assert an authorial will in relation to the work in question, since *The Glass Palace* itself implicates and reimagines the kind of monolithic history of imperial conquest that the 'commonwealth' categorization leaves untouched. Moreover, far from rejecting the commercial implications of the prize system, Ghosh publicized his own politically motivated refusal in a way that carefully courted public interest. After disseminating his official rejection of the prize nomination with his letter to the *Times* he went on to include the same material on his website (www.amitavghosh.com), where it was posted in tandem with a series of letters that others wrote in support of his decision, and with links to media coverage of the entire episode. Here, an act of political refusal becomes a gateway to authorial self-definition and to career development and promotion.

In a related way, while compelling questions about Rushdie's desire for acclaim and market share have mostly not come from any faith in an inherent distinction between what is valuable and what is saleable, that doesn't mean that such challenges have simply not existed. Instead, in ways I describe in Chapter 3, challenges to Rushdie's persona and *oeuvre* have merely arisen from different sources, as within the field of postcolonial production as a whole the rituals that consecrate literary value are constantly beset by a series of ethical and political critiques. In Rushdie's case those critiques have been potent enough to solicit his own attempts to register and counter them.

Predicting Huggan's general analysis of the postcolonial field, Aijaz Ahmad's understanding of Third World literature emphasizes its definition by the 'grids of accumulation, interpretation and relocation which are governed from the metropolitan countries,' where it is 'available to the metropolitan university to examine, explicate, categorize, classify, and judge as to its worthiness for inclusion within its curriculum and canon.'[94] It 'comes to us not directly or autonomously'; instead a given work faces the metropolitan mechanisms of consecration, and is only then 'first designated a Third World text, levelled into an archive of other such texts, and then globally redistributed with that aura attached to it.'[95] Circularly, Third World literature simply *is* that set of texts that is available for and has managed to make it beyond some more specific locality, while still having attached to it, always, the aura of its transcended origin. In accordance with what I have identified as postcolonialism's touristic logic, Ahmad argues further that Third World literature's definitive lack of autonomous circulation is countered by 'other kinds of cultural productivities.' These are the 'entire linguistic complexes as yet unassimilated into grids of print and translation.' They are necessarily vague and difficult to identify, but they are at least 'not archival but local and tentative,' and, in contrast to the compromised writings that are celebrated as Third World literature, they arise from histories that are 'more variegated and prolix, more complexly and viscerally felt.'[96]

It would be difficult to prove the existence of an inherent ethical distinction between the global marketplace for English-language literature and some smaller circuit determined by its locality, or, for that matter, between a locally-attuned critical practice and a metropolitan field of consecration. Still, despite the complex nature of the organization of the field and of the distribution of its audiences, and despite the fact that its parameters are continually subject to serious scrutiny by all of its participants, in Ahmad's analysis successful writers – Rushdie chief among them – are associated with the negative characteristics of the 'unmoored' and 'unbelonging' global literary marketplace, while more local vernacular figures maintain a position of prestige that is dependent on their lack of access to the same sphere. It is thus somewhat odd that Ahmad claims that it is in celebrating the creative individual's ability to transcend local attachment – as a primary 'condition of true understanding' – that the market for Third World texts is a space for the perpetuation of a romantic tradition.[97] It seems to me that it is actually in championing the authenticity of the incorruptible, or untheorizable, or autonomously-constituted nature of the local (especially vernacular) writer that postcolonialism can claim its romantic inheritance in this case. Indeed it is the continued existence of *this* romanticism – one defined in relation to the politics of global capital, as the market is itself politically constituted – that presents some challenge to the total demystification of authorship's autonomous positioning.

If in the influential and privileged romantic model authentic success is actually equivalent to economic failure and destitution, in its postcolonial version the ultimate position of mystified esteem may belong to those who never offer their localized texts to the global field of print capitalism to begin with. Or, if within the general literary field the romantic author-function has been entirely discredited, it has nevertheless managed to retain some continued life for certain audiences situated in the postcolonial sphere. In those instances where writers do seek to attain some measure of self-authorization, where autonomy continues to posses some small (if discredited and destabilized) purchase or appeal, this often derives from the desirability of negotiating a position in relation to the burdens of precisely this kind of incorporation. In fact the weight of many self-conscious gestures lies here, as writers respond to the idea that there is some essential fault involved in making one's persona available for consumer access within a globalized industry. Where they are denied any claim to one kind of autonomy, they seek to negotiate another.

*

In sum, no contemporary author could easily continue a romantic tradition of opposition to commodification, expressing a privileged elite disdain for material motivations. The economic conditions that prevail within the literary marketplace are a concern in part *because* negotiating any separation from them is rarely possible. In line with an overall demystification of the literary field, appeals to authorial autonomy occur only in attenuated ways that at once support and challenge the idea of the writer's distinction or self-awareness. Contributing to any overall attenuation is the way postcolonial authors' relation to the marketplace has been politicized. For them what often matters is the way their work is situated within a global market that has developed niche audiences for specific forms of postcolonial expression. The political ramifications of the global culture industry are constantly in sight. Joe Moran recognizes that writers have often turned to the theme of 'loss of control and agency' as a direct response to a dual erasure – in theory and in the market – of the author's ownership over his own work.[98] He also recognizes that the fiction that results is not mere solipsism. He summarizes its concerns admirably:

> These texts often provide a productive way of dealing with anxieties about the survival of authorship as a meaningful activity in an age when ideas and images are often corporately owned, and the dangers of being trapped in a persona which assumes simplistic connections between writer and work.[99]

My own point is that this process is complicated yet again when the authors involved are situated within the politicized niche of post-colonial literary production, and when from that position they attempt to confirm their own roles as agents fit to authorize their works. They do not seek to separate themselves from the commercial or economic spheres – the basis of those 'corporately owned' images – but rather to interact with various forms of politicized interpretation and reception that are imbricated with transnational culture and capital. In ways I describe throughout these pages, ignoring the political implications of the niche marketing of postcolonial literature leads us away from this important emergent trope of authorial self-consciousness: the trope of self-authorization through awareness of the political uses or appropriations of one's works.

As the literary field's producers and participants become increasingly aware of processes of concentration and fragmentation in the publishing industry, and as writers are marketed to appeal to specific subject positions or as representatives of particular political locales, they have frequently used their works not to suggest their distance from the material or the political, but to register precisely the connections between the two, beneficial or otherwise. In their texts narratives of all kinds are already commodities; there is little space of separation from the market, but there is a continual engagement with its boundaries and implications, and with its many diverse and often conflicting audiences. As Bourdieu's watershed postscript to *The Rules of Art* implies, there is no divide between political concerns and global capital's cultural interests. After all, his self-consciously constituted '*Internationale of intellectuals*,' evoked only through 'parody[ing] a language now out of fashion,' would exist in specific opposition to the cosmopolitan managers of transnational media, managers who have been served by and have helped facilitate the rise of postcolonial literatures in English. Transnational capitalism's relationship to cultural production is fundamentally political. It may be that the unique market positions of the writers I discuss have made them particularly sensitive to this fact, as well as defensive about it.

Part II

3
Salman Rushdie's 'Unbelonging': Authorship and 'The East'

Recently there has been a burgeoning of interest in the interconnected symbolic and material economies that arise given emerging global markets for cultural goods. Two studies are particularly compelling attempts to encourage conversation about the relevance of this topic to literary study. Though neither book focuses exclusively on the subject, at various points their respective authors diagnose the current literary marketplace and the global mechanisms of evaluation and consecration that attend it. They make unusually comparable arguments about the specific way a text's locality relates to its entry into a newly dominant global field.

In *The Economy of Prestige*, James English argues that within the global market for symbolic goods prestige depends on 'strategies of subnational and extra-national articulation.' Success comes to those who are willing and able 'to take up positions of doubled and redoubled advantage: positions of local prestige bringing them global prestige of the sort that reaffirms and reinforces their local standing.'[1] While authors may be dependent on the appearance of local content and applicability, ultimate esteem only accrues to texts that are 'world-readable,' and only the most consumable forms of subnationality make a text 'eligible' for global acclaim.[2] In *The World Republic of Letters*, first published in 1999 as *Le republique mondiale des lettres*, Pascale Casanova states that the world literary system has typically granted acclaim to those who construct themselves as willing inhabitants of the 'autonomous pole' centering global literary discourse. Their access to this space results from a willing absenting of themselves from national imperatives, and an embrace of the aesthetics of international modernism, which is characterized by 'a specific form of recognition that owes nothing to political fiat, interest, or prejudice.'[3] More recently, though, in line with the developments I outlined earlier, the system has been subject to some significant changes, since, with the development of transnational media corporations and their multinationalism-cum-multiculturalism, there emerges a world literature that actually 'mimics' the style of international modernism.[4] Today's industry involves the promotion of a kind of book that is given 'the label "world fiction"' and then specifically 'aimed at an international market.' This literature is not legitimately autonomous but instead only appears to be so; it is modernity's 'composite measure.'[5] In fact what is left of the real 'autonomous pole' is threatened by the commercial system that accommodates this discredited 'appearance' of modernism, in which the local writer enters the global field not to access the more legitimate cultural capital attached to modernist aesthetics, but out of a desire to achieve global celebrity. In this vein, echoing Bourdieu and Valery Larbaud at once, Casanova contrasts an idealized 'intellectual International' – 'a small, cosmopolitan, enlightened society' that features 'the free circulation of great works of avant-garde literature from all over the world' – with a new, 'denationalized' commercialism that uses the language of the avant-garde to sell products.[6]

In reading a text's success in the current global market as the result of a kind of agentless domination, in which the logic of the field reduces the products that circulate within it to 'world-readability' or to commercialized 'composites' of modernism, English and Casanova each offer a description of the system that is a form of resignation about its ostensible authority. Below, I will use the case of Salman Rushdie – by all means, the most consecrated, commercially successful, and 'denationalized' postcolonial writer – to argue that while the idea of a 'composite' autonomous pole of world literary production certainly exists, it is far from being a dominant and homogenous monolith. Its autonomy is instead an idea, one that is used to shore up the interests of those who choose to value it, but which can also be challenged by alternative conceptions of autonomy that offer other possibilities for the evaluation and attribution of prestige. Though London and New York are currently the centers of the international trade, they do not necessarily annex, by way of celebration, a world literature that emerges from national or subnational locations only in order to more successfully abandon them. Nor do they successfully reduce 'foreign' texts to global comprehensibility, much though they might try. The 'world-readability' or universalizability of a given work is not inherent in it or essential to its position in the world system. It is instead the result of a series of actual or imagined reading practices that can also be challenged and opposed, in some cases by the very texts that achieve global acclaim. In other words, texts are 'world-readable' when some 'world-readability' is read into them. One could convincingly emphasize the 'local-readability' of the same consecrated world texts, or the way they oppose what is necessary for the global acclaim they have nonetheless achieved, or, indeed, the relevance of locally-inflected debates and issues to the very way that any denationalized sphere of acclaim gets constructed.

This is precisely what I aim to do throughout Part II, by emphasizing that qualms about postcolonial authorial autonomy arise from what are often highly localized circumstances of individual authors' struggles with the politics and positioning that constrain their careers. As autonomy always involves establishing the possibility of maintaining distance from something, that something changes depending on the circumstances of the author who makes a claim to it, and thus the very nature of the distance signaled by the term 'autonomous' changes with it. What does Rushdie think he needs to establish or show in order to justify his own career success? To what set of interests does he need to oppose himself?

In answering these questions, the interrelation between two of the many narratives elements in his 2001 novel *Fury* is of particular interest: its quasi-autobiographical story of Malik Soyinka, a lapsed English academic turned New York-based content creator for the culture industries; and its account of a national liberation struggle knowingly based on the real political turmoil taking place in Fiji in 1999–2000 and receiving considerable coverage in the US media at the time of the book's composition. After falling in love with a woman who has a personal connection to the region Malik uses the crisis as material for his work. In turn, despite his own lack of specific political commitment, the region's combatants take up Malik's stories as iconic political totems. As he has before, Rushdie emphasizes that even the most revolutionary political struggle can be integrated fitfully into an international market for cultural commodities that have an appealingly political *frisson* and orientation, and that these same commodities can in turn be caught up in very real political struggles. But *Fury*'s interest in the circulation of political narratives is additionally coloured by paranoia about texts being available for forms of appropriation that may have no relation to the intentions of any author. In fact in *Fury* art's politicization is synonymous with the absence of its attachment to any functioning creator-figure who can authorize its meanings. In making this case about authorship, politics, and what is identified as 'the industry of culture,'[7] Rushdie attempts to constrain the way his career experiences can be understood.

He does this in a way that is paradoxical, though, and that is articulated self-consciously, as is true in the other cases I discuss after Rushdie's; the pursuit of self-authorization tends to be fraught with antinomies, given that it derives its meaning and force from the same field of production with which it takes issue. But is to want to be extricated from a particular political milieu or debate, even though it might be said to have given your work a market or made it critically relevant, in fact to be inevitably and eternally determined by it? Recognizing that authors seek autonomy in relation to specific situations and circumstances need not be akin to claiming that whatever self-exemption they appeal to is finally delimited by what it attempts to oppose. Instead, through a consideration of some aspects of Rushdie's case, what I wonder here is whether it is absolutely impossible to ever simply oppose the circumstances of one's career as a writer. What I emphasize is a tension between self-articulation and its market constraints; this is a productive tension that shouldn't be sidelined by resignation about the commercial dominance of any denationalized, depoliticized, easily consumable world literature.

There is a residual language of disgust in reviews of Rushdie's work, especially when the subject of conversation is the author's fame, wealth, or celebrity status. While at one time commercial success might have prevented a writer from receiving considerable critical attention, Rushdie's own work has been more taught, more studied, and more celebrated than that of any other postcolonial author. Yet his career trajectory, from relatively local notoriety in London to celebrification as a global icon, shows that the position of the postcolonial writer can still be compromised by mainstream success or financial viability, not because of faith in a form of artistic genius to which economic recompense is irrelevant, but instead due to the politics of the global market for English-language literary fiction.

Fury responds to the anxieties of an author whose works have consistently been the most tantalizing political commodities for various consumer groups, from postcolonial critics in Anglo-American universities to religious leaders in the Islamic world. The critique Malik tries to offer in his own narratives is not generally of commodification, but specifically of the lack of authorial control granted him as a major producer of texts for a global market for world culture. As Rai claims about the contest over Vina Apsara's death in *The Ground Beneath Her Feet* (1999), debates about culture within the industry of the global popular are never just economic, dealing with 'audience share or advertising revenue.' The effort to separate legitimate cultural production from its large-scale version is outdated. Instead, as Rai claims, 'Meaning itself is the prize,'[8] and that meaning is significantly political. In this vein, *Fury* registers Malik's anxiety about the impossibility of determining the political significance of his own works. Self-consciously, though, Rushdie avoids entirely crediting Malik's laments about his own lack of power over his situation. Indeed doing so is an aspect of what I read as Rushdie's two-part maneuver that responds to his own reception. He uses Malik's experiences to admit complicity in building the trajectory of his own career, while still managing to challenge those forces that are most responsible for the worst of what Malik suffers, and that are ultimately related to Rushdie's own celebrification and demonization.

*

In the first part of this book I argued that the publishing of literary fiction has become increasingly global in structure. It now involves agents for a series of prominent 'lead' authors making deals for global distribution with publishers that are situated within transnational corporations or conglomerates. These operate through numerous dispersed branch offices, are often headquartered in New York, and deploy media synergy to promote most effectively the products they create and the creators they represent. The development of serious literary fiction as a popular marketing category has been an integral part of this process, accompanied and encouraged by the increasing presence of writers of nominally non-European origins, often from formerly colonized nations, writing in English for a largely Anglo-American marketplace.

The literature championed by postcolonial scholarship develops largely out of this matrix, and Rushdie is one of its definitive authors. In fact his career has flourished in tandem with the market presence of literary fiction and of writing by authors from formerly colonized nations. Initially operating primarily within the London literary milieu, he has progressively moved into a more global position, in a way that makes his career as a whole uniquely analogous to the literary marketplace I take to be increasingly defined by the processes of transnational corporate concentration.

It was the events that were quickly known as 'the Rushdie affair' that catapulted Rushdie into an unimaginable stratosphere of public prominence. Forced into hiding after the Ayatollah Khomeini declared the official fatwa, Rushdie was nonetheless subject to endless scrutiny by interested literary journalists and gossip columnists alike. Finding his way into ever more print, he 'vanished into the front page,' as Martin

Amis famously quipped.[9] But Rushdie was a major figure before the late 1980s. Though his first novel *Grimus* (1979) sold a dismal 800 copies in hardcover, from *Midnight's Children*, published in 1980 by Jonathan Cape, a premier London outlet for literary fiction, Rushdie was one of the industry's major figures. The initial printing of *Midnight's Children* in England was a modest 1,750 copies, but it went on to sell in the tens of thousands in hardcover in the UK and the US.[10] Winning the Booker Prize in 1981 significantly boosted its sales and the novel was continually reprinted. *Shame* (1983), also Booker-nominated, followed a similar trajectory, selling even more initial copies in hardcover and appearing as a Vintage trade paperback. With three novels behind him, in 1983 Rushdie earned a place on the first incarnation of *Granta*'s prestigious 'Best of Young British Novelists' list. Beyond the directly commercial sphere, Rushdie's focus on problems of nationality and postcoloniality in South Asia, and in particular his open critiques of the political programs of the region's several new national formations, guaranteed his consistent presence within that pantheon of celebrated 'empire writes back' authors of special interest to the emerging field of postcolonial literary studies.

Thus, living in London and writing about South Asia for an audience of English-language readers, Rushdie was an unusually celebrated and successful writer from an early stage in his career. Until the mid-1980s his works were sold to publishers in London and New York separately, with their main market and first appearance in London. However by the time of the publication of *The Satanic Verses* (1988) it became difficult to locate Rushdie primarily within a London milieu. In 1987 he 'released' his English agent Deborah Rogers and his editor Liz Calder, who had moved to Bloomsbury Press and was expected to bring Rushdie's next book with her. *The Jaguar Smile* (1987), his most avowedly leftist work, was the first Rushdie title for which she did not act as editor. Instead he hired maverick New York agent Andrew Wylie, who is also known as 'the Jackal,' a sure sign that he was a major player in the literary market, and also that he hoped to secure a large advance for his next novel, *The Satanic Verses*. In fact in order to 'establish the book's value in the marketplace,'[11] *The Satanic Verses* was sold to publishers in Germany and Italy before it found a place in England and the US. Two publishers, Knopf and Viking-Penguin, were eventually contending for the manuscript, driving advances up and piquing the interest of industry insiders. Through the combined appeal of the amount of the offered advance (US$850,000) and the international reach of Penguin's many branch offices (including India), Viking eventually won publication rights. The novel was released in September 1988. Censorship and bans followed throughout the Muslim world and included Pakistan, Saudi Arabia, Egypt, Indonesia and South Africa. It still circulated in those areas, though covertly: photocopies of offensive sections appeared within Muslim communities, often for purposes of critique, and pirate editions were common.[12]

The novel's opponents established a link between Rushdie and the US, though he continued to live with police protection in England. In Karachi they stormed the US Information Center, and burned the US flag alongside dummies made in Rushdie's likeness.[13] Though not the connection his enemies intended, in terms of his career as an author the association was not unwarranted. Rather than appearing first in the London market through Victor Gollancz, Jonathan Cape, or Bloomsbury, for example, *The Satanic Verses* and most of Rushdie's subsequent works have been released by dominant international publishers like Viking-Penguin. Penguin had itself been moving toward a New York base since purchasing Viking in 1975. Chief executive Peter Mayer, who negotiated *The Satanic Verses* deal, had moved to New York in 1987 and conceded that 'the HQ of Penguin was wherever he was.'[14] Although Rushdie stayed in London throughout the period of the fatwa, and though attention to his plight and to his literary work continued in that city, from that time the process of publishing his books originated in New York with his agent there, from which location they were then released and reviewed wherever his publishers had their many branch offices. The publisher of choice was either Viking-Penguin, owned by Pearson since 1971, or Vintage, a Random House imprint under Bertelsmann. Finally and most recently, like Malik Soyinka, Rushdie left London behind to move to New York himself. He resides there now.

In turn, even irrespective of *The Satanic Verses* fatwa, Rushdie's iconic status has been at the heart of some considerable controversies. His persona has been perennially celebrated and denounced, and his literary offerings are subject to near constant debate and reevaluation. Indira Gandhi launched a lawsuit to combat the way she was represented in *Midnight's Children*, and the book was subsequently banned in several Indian states. *Shame* faced similar legal challenges and was banned in Pakistan due to its less than sympathetic portraits of Zia-ul-Haq, and of Zulfikar Ali Bhutto and his daughter Benazir, who appears in its pages as 'the Virgin Ironpants.' In this way, years before his virtual imprisonment in his London apartment, accusations of offence and attempts at censorship drew more attention to Rushdie and his career, solidifying his position as an author of marketable commodities with a certain political *frisson*. Indeed the more famous and celebrated he has become the more his authorial image and his texts have been subject to interpretive appropriation, held up by various politicized factions as representative of either laudable or abhorrent political positions. His writing was and still is, for example, called a deracinated betrayal of a cultural heritage and, alternatively, a triumphant celebration of mongrel subjectivity and freedom from the constraints of tradition. As Graham Huggan writes, like V.S. Naipaul, Rushdie has been 'subjected to a vigorous, at times vindictive, politics of labelling, where conspicuously indefinite terms such as "cosmopolitan", "migrant", "postcolonial" and "Third World writer" have been appropriated, deployed and renegotiated in the continuing effort to stake out territory in wide-ranging cultural debates.'[15]

Does Rushdie belie the realities of the migrant condition with his metaphorical terminology of 'border crossing' and exile, a language he willingly deploys despite his thoroughly privileged life in the Anglo-American metropoles? Answering this question, noting that Rushdie 'stands foremost among those [...] who have been elevated by global media-markets and metropolitan academies as the preeminent interpreters of postcolonial realities to postmodern audiences,' Revathi Krishnaswamy claims that the author's works are key to the process through which 'words such as "diaspora" and "exile" are being emptied of their histories of pain and suffering and are being deployed promiscuously to designate a wide array of cross-cultural phenomena.'[16] Krishnaswamy's moral gesture, distinguishing Rushdie's brand of 'voluntary self-exile' from a more legitimate 'forced' version[17] – establishing what Rob Nixon has called 'the ratio of violence to choice in the prompting of [a writer's] departure'[18] – is one often made by those concerned about his uniquely celebrated position within both postcolonial literary critical circles and the mainstream marketplace.

Indeed Rushdie's name has been ubiquitous in debates about the special status of Indian Writing in English (IWE) within the broader field, a status thought to perpetuate and justify an attendant lack of attention to South Asia's abundant vernacular writings. In introducing an anthology of Indian writing Amit Chaudhuri claims that Rushdie's example has become 'a key to the way Indian writing is supposed to be read and produced [...] Rushdie both being the godhead from which Indian writing in English has reportedly sprung, revivified, and a convenient shorthand for that writing.'[19] Rushdie's style, characterized by its abundance, its non-linearity, its incorporation of magical elements, and its references to an Indian epic tradition, has become 'emblematic of a non-Western mode of discourse,' at once postcolonial and 'inescapably Indian.'[20] When India celebrated its independence in 1997 it was the global prominence of its English-language writers that news broadcasts throughout the world claimed as the surest sign of the country's cultural wealth and general status. Rushdie's solid position within the mainstream of Anglo-American fiction is often taken as representative of the privileging of IWE within the global marketplace more generally, evident in things like Arundhati Roy's 1997 Booker Prize (the first for a writer still resident in India), Naipaul's 2001 Nobel Prize, and the hugely successful International Festival of Indian Literature held in Delhi in 2002.

There are a variety of reasons why English-language writers from South Asia, and in particular from India, seem to have produced an ideally cosmopolitan writing. Recent patterns of South Asian immigration have been characterized by the metropolitan movements of a relatively prosperous middle class of educated professionals who are thought to be fairly happily deterritorialized. Authors emerging from this matrix are thought to combine social privilege with subversion: writing in English, they are available for consecration as embodying a national or supranational voice, unmoored from the more 'minor' perspectives[21] identified with vernacular regional writing; they are willing to separate politics and aesthetics in the appropriate manner, to act as interpreters of the lands they have left behind, and to deploy a 'semantics of subalternity' attractive to Anglo-American readers.[22] It in this spirit that Leela Gandhi claims that 'the figure of the new/postcolonial Indian English novelist is in a deliciously "win-win" situation,' speaking from 'an enviable position' of simultaneous privilege and dissent, articulating a special kind of subversion that comes with social status.[23] It is Rushdie who normally stands as the paradigmatic figure of this privileged simultaneity.

Reflecting on media coverage of the literature festival in Delhi in 2002, Bishnupriya Ghosh describes a 'yawning chasm' between those she calls 'cosmopolitical South Asian writers' and others who continue to reside in South Asia and write in the vernacular languages.[24] A powerful hierarchy of political legitimacy has developed around precisely this divide: Naipaul safely occupies the bad end of the order of things, a figure like Kannada author U.R. Ananthamurthy sits somewhat comfortably at the sanctioned opposite pole, and 'cosmopolitical' figures like Rushdie and Ghosh are positioned variously in between. As his career has developed Rushdie has inched dangerously closer to Naipaul's position, much to his own chagrin.

As Ghosh carefully notes, the postcolonial literary field is significantly more heteronymous than belief in any 'chasm' would suggest.
The success of some cosmopolitan writers has depended upon their
willing participation in a 'fetishistic localism,' for example, while
others have attained success precisely by 'dismantling the elite "global
Indian" subject.'[25] Widely read by diasporic South Asian communities
and within South Asia as well, especially after the opening of
HarperCollins and Penguin offices in Mumbai, IWE has audiences that
read vernacular writing as well, and that do not necessarily applaud all
those features associated with a more global or 'cosmopolitical' writing.
In fact the way that even IWE itself becomes associated with a particular set of characteristics, and the way Rushdie becomes IWE's author-
icon *par excellence* – so that he can be said to have 'put India on the
literary map,' for example, while new South Asian writers are called
'midnight's children' or 'midnight's grandchildren' – are situations
that have never gone unchallenged. The constitution of the field of
IWE is constantly beset by debate and criticism, and the most vociferous politicization of its market position comes from 'within,' emitting
from that same group of relatively privileged metropolitan elites
thought to make the field itself operative.

Yet much though the notion of an unbridgeable divide between local
undiscovered legitimacy and global compromised acclaim is a problematic one, it nonetheless arises from identifiable sources, and is often put
to work in the service of specific and even understandable interests. For
example, as I will continue to argue in the chapters that follow, constru-
ing the market's global or local versions as embodying one set of characteristics or another is something writers often do in order to police
their own relative successes and failures. Rushdie's situation makes an
excellent general case. Far from indifferently ignoring the politicization
of IWE, or of his own work as the most obvious (and obviously marketed) exemplar of that writing, in recent years he has mounted a full-
scale self-defensive attack against the sources, nature, and implications
of the charges he has faced. His anxious self-positioning is most apparent in his opposition to what he blithely calls 'the East.' This is a highly
expedient category with an expansive set of features that serves to
encompass all those audiences who have rejected his status and output.
It is deployed in ways that might surprise readers otherwise accustomed
to thinking of Rushdie as a figure fully committed to post-nationality
and deterritorialization.

For example, when the Indian authorities refused his requests for
locations to shoot the film version of *Midnight's Children* – a move mir-

rored by the Sri Lankan government soon after – Rushdie's response, in introducing the published screenplay, was to add their denials to a long history of discord between himself and 'the East,' claiming he had never recovered from the 'terrible blow' of India's opposition or indifference to his work. His language is interesting: 'That *Midnight's Children* should have been rejected so arbitrarily, with such utter indifference, by the land about which it had been written with all my love and skill, was a terrible blow.'[26] Rushdie fashions himself as a writer with nothing but love for the land of the novel's setting, a land to which he further connects himself by claiming that he wrote *Midnight's Children* to begin with as a way of representing and memorializing his own childhood in Bombay. According to Rushdie, in response that beloved 'land' – and not simply the government, or one part of the vast bureaucracy that makes such decisions – rejects his work both entirely and 'arbitrarily,' and in doing so rejects the author's love.

This posturing establishes a fairly stark opposition between the author and the entirety of South Asia, one further encouraged as Rushdie generally poses as a beleaguered writer, claiming that the very act of publishing the screenplay of his finally unmade film is one of defiance against what he clearly views as political censorship. He goes on to state that 'the rejection of *Midnight's Children* changes something profound in my relationship with the East. Something broke, and I'm not sure it can be mended.'[27] Looking at the sort of debates about Rushdie's work described above, as the author is situated in a number of privileged spaces defined variously by language use, 'voluntary self-exile,' and metropolitan location, suggests, though, that Rushdie's oppositional gesture is ultimately prestaged by the same criticism he wants to challenge. 'The East' had, after all, already broken with him, having long produced those audiences that critically interrogated the conditions allowing him his distinct success.

Moreover, Rushdie had made the same distinguishing gesture on numerous occasions that significantly preceded his anger over not being able to film *Midnight's Children*, such that his posture of opposition to 'the East' has become a kind of definitive gesture, a refrain most clearly useful in discrediting aspects of his own reception. As early as *Shame* he wrote: 'I tell myself this will be a novel of leavetaking, my last words on the East from which, many years ago, I began to come loose.'[28] In a more recent article he claims there has been a 'deep rift' between himself and India since the country became the first to ban *The Satanic Verses*, declaring him 'persona non grata' and barring him from many events and locations, including the Nehru Centre in London, and the 1997 celebrations at the Indian consulate in New York.[29]

In 1997 an issue of the *New Yorker* celebrated the 50-year anniversary of India's independence. Devoted to India's current geopolitical position and cultural output, it ran Rushdie's by now infamous article on the state of literature in India, in which he announced that Indian prose writing in English:

> is proving to be a stronger and more important body of work than most of what has been produced in the eighteen 'recognized' languages of India, the so-called 'vernacular languages' [...] this new, and still burgeoning 'Indo-Anglian' literature represents perhaps the most valuable contribution India has yet made to the world of books.[30]

This is a remarkably self-congratulatory statement; it appears near the beginning of a piece that is as a whole rife with both outright and more guarded forms of self-justification. After stating the superiority of Indo-Anglian writing to the many vernacular literatures, for example, Rushdie goes on to note that '[f]or some Indian critics, English-language Indian writing will never be more than a postcolonial anomaly – the bastard child of Empire, sired on India by the departing British.'[31] He claims that criticism levied at Indo-Anglian literature comes solely from Indians – though often ones 'who are themselves members of the college-educated, English-speaking élite' – and then carefully notes all of the characteristics attributed to this writing by those 'Indian critical assaults':

> Its practitioners are denigrated for being too upper-middle-class; for lacking diversity in their choices of themes and techniques; for being less popular in India than outside India; for possessing inflated reputations on account of the international power of the English language, and of the ability of Western critics and publishers to impose their cultural standards of the East; for living, in many cases, outside India; for being deracinated to the point where their work lacks the spiritual dimension essential for a 'true' understanding of the soul of India; for being insufficiently grounded in the ancient literary traditions of India; for being the literary equivalent of MTV culture, or of globalizing Coca-Colonization; even, I'm sorry to report, for suffering from a condition that one sprightly recent commentator [...] calls 'Rushdie-itis...a condition that has claimed Rushdie himself in his later works.'

No specific critique of Rushdie's prominence or success can match his own self-conscious list of objections to work like his. Rather than engaging with or answering any of these criticisms, though, Rushdie's form of rejection of such attacks is to lament a 'cheapening of artistic response,' as well as the fact that 'so few of these criticisms are literary [...] they do not deal with language, voice, psychological or social insight, imagination, or talent [...] they have to do with class, power, and belief.'[32]

This piece on the merits of Indian writing since independence, which focuses significantly more attention on the hostile *reception* of Indo-Anglian writing than it does on the sort of aesthetic evaluation Rushdie claims to want to trumpet instead, makes a gesture equivalent to his more recent sad hostility about what he construes as the deliberate suppression of the film version of *Midnight's Children*. Rushdie clearly distances himself from what he specifically identifies as an Indian or South Asian – hence 'regional' or 'minor' – critical tendency. To use Casanova's terms, he rejects a heteronymous national or regional tradition aligned with the land of his birth, in favour of appealing to a specifically autonomous aesthetic lineage apparently distinct from 'class, power, and belief.' This is in fact Rushdie's exemplary gesture of authorial self-construction: namely, his claim to want to finally turn his back on all those varied approaches to literary production that are interested in anything other than the somewhat mystified artistry and 'talent' at play in the work itself.

*

Fury is an instance of Rushdie devoting a sustained fictional work to this same gesture, but its negotiation with whatever autonomy might be accorded to its author is significantly less self-assured than either of the two non-fiction pieces I have just described. *Fury*'s main character is a celebrity intellectual and 'retired historian of ideas' who has recently moved to New York City (3). Malik has left his wife and son in London for a world that is a promise of respite from his rage about his family life, but also a provocation to his furious contempt for much of contemporary culture. Strolling through the streets of the city in the novel's early pages, Malik's thoughts indicate some of this contempt:

> In all of India, China, Africa, and much of the southern American continent, those who had the leisure and wallet for fashion – or more simply, in the poorer latitudes, for the mere acquisition of

things – would have killed for the street merchandise of Manhattan, as also for the cast-off clothing and soft furnishings to be found in the opulent thrift stores.

He continues, 'America insulted the rest of the planet [...] by treating such bounty with the shoulder-shrugging casualness of the inequitably wealthy' (6). While such sentiments can be read as Rushdie's attempt to mediate the charges of venality levied at his own recent exploits, the structural inequality Malik notices is not something from which he then sets out to separate himself. Instead his life has been, and continues to be, defined by a serious entanglement in consumer culture and the media that markets it. Giving up a job at Cambridge in the late 1980s, Malik was commissioned by the BBC to develop a series of history-of-philosophy programs for television, thus moving him from a stable academic job to the more fragmented, piecemeal, and haphazard work of producing creative content for television, and eventually for the internet. The cultural content Malik creates for *The Adventures of Little Brain* is based on popularized versions of the thought of important European philosophers. He thus becomes an author of thoroughly middlebrow products: educational texts designed for mass consumption.

Malik's show is a sensation, benefiting from what the narrator speaks of as the 'industry of culture' which, since the 1970s, has come to 'replace that of ideology, becoming "primary" in the way that economics used to be.' That industry is said to have spawned 'a whole new *nomenklatura* of cultural commissars, a new breed of apparatchiks engaged in great ministries of definition, exclusion, revision, and persecution' (24). Malik first notices Mila Milo, the young woman who goes on to market the narratives he creates in New York, because, like many other teenage girls, she models herself on Little Brain, Malik's own celebrated character.

Little Brain is a representative cultural product, involved in a history that has made culture's products 'primary' rather than representational. She is 'first a doll, later a puppet, then an animated cartoon, and afterward an actress, or, at various other times, a talk-show host, gymnast, ballerina, or supermodel, in a Little Brain outfit' (96). She is also a symbol of Malik's impotence when faced with the power of critical and market reception. This impotence is suggested by her very name, which connotes her intelligence and inquisitiveness but also, importantly, her autonomy as an entity productive of ideas and subjectivities for a mass audience. Malik is only her creator in the most minimal sense, and the industry of culture guarantees that she will endlessly proliferate. Authorial control of the meanings attached to her proliferating texts is limited at best: 'She had outgrown her creator,' and is no longer a 'simulacrum' but somehow real, much to Malik's dismay. She eventually even passes out of his hands completely and into the control of a 'concept group' at the BBC called the Little Brain Trust (97). Malik is merely one more person struggling to keep abreast of the significance that people like Mila Milo attach to Little Brain's existence, and failing miserably. 'This creature of his own imagining,' we are told, 'born of his best self and purest endeavor, was turning before his eyes into the kind of monster of tawdry celebrity he most profoundly abhorred' (98).

The novel's plot and its various metafictional layers are complicated and require some elucidation here. In coming to New York Malik partially flees his own renown and the inescapable presence of Little Brain in his life. Still, New York offers no relief. Malik meets a woman named Neela Mahendra, a recognizable stand-in for the book's real-life dedicatee, Padma Lakshmi, Rushdie's future wife and the force that presumably drew him to the US. Neela is a television producer involved in the nationalist political struggle of a South Pacific nation called Lilliput-Blefuscu, a transparent stand-in for Fiji. Her family are Indo-Lilliputians ('Indo-Lillies'), her ancestors Indian indentured labourers brought to the islands in the 1890s. Their fight is with the indigenous 'Elbee' (L.B./Lilliput-Blefuscu) community over constitutional rights to the land they have worked for four generations (157–8). Neela's interest in this struggle has a profound impact on Malik's creative life. With encouragement from Mila Milo, he begins to create a new set of characters with a market value intimately tied to the politically-inflected narrative he imagines for them. Mila Milo even convinces Malik to sell these characters and their surrounding narrative to her internet company, guaranteeing him creative control while her company markets his cultural product in cyberspace. Malik's experience with such marketing has obviously been traumatic, and Mila urges him to embrace the demise of myths of singular authority and creative genius, urging him to 'be a little more flexible,' since 'the whole concept of ownership as far as ideas is so different now, it's so much more cooperative' (178).

These two events – meeting Neela, and starting a new creative project – are not unrelated. Indeed in creating his new narrative Malik's influences are the set of events taking place in Lilliput-Blefuscu, and his urge to represent the traumas entailed in his previous experiences as creator of *The Adventures of Little Brain*. Malik is said to create each new character by imagining its 'back-story,' a framework which the narrator describes as a 'fictional beast capable of constant metamorphosis, which fed on every scrap it could find: its creator's personal history, scraps of gossip, deep learning, current affairs, high and low culture, and the most nourishing diet of all – namely, the past' (190). Malik's creative process thus ensures that the contents of his eminently marketable narratives are built on the tribulations of his own personal life, as well as on contemporary politics. In fact the new story's main figure, an 'amoral cyberneticist' called Akasz Kronos, described as 'an artist,' and '[t]he most dangerous man in the world' (146), is based on Malik himself, just as Malik is a figure for Rushdie.

While Malik elaborates the story of *The Puppet Kings* (as he titles the new set of stories he creates), the 'real' political conflict in Lilliput-Blefuscu rages on. Neela and Malik attend an Indo-Lilly parade and demonstration in New York, run by Babur, leader of the FRM/'Fremen' (the Filbistani Resistance Movement), waving the flag of his proposed 'Republic of Filbistan,' where 'Filb' stands for 'Free Indian Lilliput-Blefuscu.' Meanwhile a coup is occurring in the embattled nation. An indigenous Elbee called Skyresh Bolgolam is working to reverse the reforms in favour of Indo-Lillies made in a new constitution, recently implemented by liberal president Golbasto Gue. The 'back-story' of *The Puppet Kings* is given in this context. Akasz Kronos creates a puppet race to respond to the 'terminal crisis' of his civilization. He then sells his puppets to the leader of Baburia, a nation made up of 'two small mountain-islands.' As Malik's *Puppet Kings* narrative emerges, it becomes clear that it directly references the political situation in Lilliput-Blefuscu, which we have already recognized as itself a stand-in for Fiji. Each of Kronos's puppets is based on a figure in Malik's life, including a Goddess of Victory puppet, modeled on Kronos's love Zameen (in turn modeled on Neela, said to be modeled on Padma). There is even a Dollmaker puppet, Kronos embodying himself in his creation and adding another level to *Fury*'s metafictional layers, since Rushdie clearly figures himself in Malik, Malik in Kronos, and Kronos in the Dollmaker puppet.

Fittingly, the Puppet Kings break free of Kronos' control, as the Dollmaker plots with the other puppets until they learn to overthrow the 'Prime Directive' of Kronos' program, which should guarantee that only he has ultimate control over the puppets' actions. The puppets then stage a revolution, plotting to live in Baburia not as workers but as equals to the native Baburians. The action of *The Puppet Kings* begins there, and is presented in instalments through Mila Milo's web company and read by millions throughout the world.

Mila Milo's Puppet Kings website thrives globally, settling 'production, distribution, and marketing agreements with key players – Mattel, Amazon, Sony, Columbia, Banana Republic' (214). Malik is trapped again in a media world, talking to journalists about his narratives, a procedure described as 'an unnerving, hollowing kind of work, during which he could hear himself sounding false, knowing also that a second layer of falsehood would be added by the journalists' responses to his words' (217). The PlanetGalileo.com website, which sells merchandise of all kinds, guarantees that Malik's narratives are ripe for every form of commercialization: 'Click on the links for more PK [Puppet Kings] info or on the icons below for answers to 101 FAQs, access to interactivities, and to see the wide range of *PK merchandise available* for INSTANT shipping NOW. All major credit cards accepted' (168). Malik's narrative, in short, 'proliferated into this many-armed, multimedia beast' (190), and he is further implicated in the commercial culture he once hoped to flee, cast like Kronos, who is, after all, modeled on himself, in the role of greedy artist in search of ever more lucre.

These two worlds – the political life of the Indo-Lillies, and the cultural industry of PlanetGalileo.com – already intertwined, only become further enmeshed. The fictional narrative of *The Puppet Kings*, partly derived from the energy of the conflict in Lilliput-Blefuscu, becomes directly implicated in the region's future political life. In Mildendo, capital of Lilliput-Blefuscu, toy stores are raided, masked men making off with just-imported supplies of Kronosian Cyborg masks and costumes. The FRM, it turns out, identify with the plight of the Puppet Kings, 'whose inalienable right to be treated as equals – as fully moral and sentient beings – was denied by Mogol the Baburian [king of Babur]' (226). Such identification is entirely natural, of course, given that Malik modeled the Peekay (PK/Puppet King) Revolution while inspired by the FRM's own. The slogan of the Peekay Revolution is 'Let the Fittest Survive,' and T-shirts bearing those words begin to appear around New York. As with Little Brain, again Malik's characters 'began to burst out of their cages and take to the streets. From around the world came news of their images, grown gigantic, standing many stories high on city walls' (225). Malik begins, horrified, to witness the 'intervention of the living dolls from the imaginary planet Galileo-1 in the public affairs of the actually existing earth' (226). 'Real life had started obeying the dictates of fiction,' the narrator observes, 'providing precisely the raw material he needed to transmute through the alchemy of his reborn art' (170).

In sum, then, Malik's own art, and in turn that art's reception, are deeply reliant on the dissolution of barriers between the categories of the real and the fictional, the actual and the simulation, human beings and their fictional representations. That dissolution also confuses the boundaries between political movements and the cultural products from which they derive energy, or to which they make reference, in disseminating information about the merits of their given cause.

*

With this basic outline in mind, reference to *The Jaguar Smile* becomes appropriate, as one of *Fury*'s companion texts. Both works draw attention to the process through which images and their origins can become radically separate, as cultural texts are used to sell or promote political ideologies. Indeed Rushdie seems to use his earlier experiences in Nicaragua as a means of imagining the process through which cultural products like Malik's web-based narratives are endowed with additional political weight. When Rushdie was writing *The Jaguar Smile* in 1986–7, Nicaragua's Sandinista revolutionaries were being vilified in the mainstream Western press as pro-Soviet communists. The Reagan administration had in fact started an infamous war by proxy against the rebel leftwing leaders by financially and militarily supporting the Contra militia; the media coverage of the Sandinistan cause merely supported the administration's prerogative. Rushdie became a sponsor of the Nicaragua Solidarity Campaign, then active in London, and visited the country in July 1986 not as a neutral observer but as the guest of an organization suggestively called the Sandinista Association of Cultural Workers (ASTC). The ASTC brought sympathetic writers and artists to the country to see the revolution from the inside. Rushdie's visit to Nicaragua happened just after the International Court of Justice in the Hague had ruled that US aid to the Contras, whom Rushdie calls 'the counter-revolutionary arm the CIA had invented, assembled, organized and armed,'[33] was in violation of international law. As Rushdie notes, '[t]he situation was surreal: the country that was in fact acting illegally, that was the outlaw, was hurling such epithets as *totalitarian, tyrannous* and *Stalinist* at the elected government of a country that hadn't broken any laws at all; the bandit was posing as the sheriff' (40). The Sandinistas were painfully aware of the power of those 'hurling [...] epithets,' and of the general role that the Western media was playing in negatively interpreting their revolutionary political program. The ASTC knew bringing cultural workers to Nicaragua could help put a positive spin on the country's new political leadership. It seems appropriate, then, to suggest that the Sandinistas were strategically deploying sympathizers like Rushdie in an effort to encourage positive interpretations of their struggle.

A major focus of *The Jaguar Smile* became, in turn, Rushdie's argument with the Sandinistas' willingness to control the media within Nicaragua and censor information unsympathetic to their movement. A related feature of Rushdie's account is its focus on the prominence of the political iconography of a 'martyr-culture' throughout the country (19). That iconography is central to Nicaragua's landscape as Rushdie depicts it. He recounts: 'Of the ten earliest leaders of the Frente Sandinista de Liberación Nacional, nine had been killed before Somoza fell. Their faces, painted in the Sandinista colours of red and black, stared gigantically down on the Plaza de la Revolucion' (18). Similar visuals are one ubiquitous part of the country's internal communications system.

A good example is Sandino's hat, the representative icon of the Revolution's 'most famous ghost,' Augusto César Sandino (21). Indeed at the headquarters of the biggest trade union in Nicaragua, the CST (Central Sandinista de Trabajadores), Lenin and Marx flank Sandino's hat in a powerful triptych that acts to associate the Sandinista cause with the revolutionary history of socialist politics and cultural production. The proliferation of such images serves a direct political purpose as a locus of revolutionary meaning. During the turmoil of the 1920s and 30s Sandino contested the US-backed conservative politics of both Adolfo Díaz and the first Somoza, hiding in the mountains with his resistance fighters until he was betrayed after finally negotiating a peace deal. The image of Sandino's hat, typically obscuring his face, became central to the Sandinistas' political aesthetic, evoking a form of stark opposition to conservative politics in Central America. Though Sandino was not a socialist, the Sandinistas turned his death into a kind of martyrdom as an aid to their ongoing effort to construct the kind of historical narrative of local resistance that would justify their own struggle.

Rushdie reveals the stories behind several other prominent political icons in the course of the book, discussing figures like Julio Buitrago and Carlos Fonseca. He typically points to these figures, explaining their histories and how they came to such prominence in the Nicaraguan imagination, in order to show that the omnipresent iconography that is meant to represent them carries the weight of the recent political past. It is through this very public form of culture that they attempt to contest the meaning-making power of the rightwing broadcast press throughout Central America, which reached viewers and listeners in Nicaragua itself and influenced international news coverage of the Sandinista government.[34] In Rushdie's depiction, the very real political struggle in Nicaragua thus has key cultural correlates, since its success depends at least in part on the Sandinistas' ability to contest rival narratives both locally and internationally.

When Rushdie visits Frente Sandinista de Liberació n Nacional leader Daniel Ortega at home he notes that his children appear in 'Masters of the Universe' T-shirts, 'featuring the eternal battle of He-Man and Skeletor.' Rushdie reminds his readers of the 'omnipresence of US culture' (51) in the country:

> In Nicaragua, there were old Jack Nicholson movies on the television, Coca-Cola did great business, the people listened to Madonna on the radio, singing about *living in a material world / and I am a material girl*; baseball was a national obsession [...]. In the old Somoza days, when the newspapers were censored, they would print photographs of Marilyn Monroe and other Hollywood movie stars in place of the banned articles. (36–7)

Around the time of Rushdie's visit Ortega himself was touring the US, making appearances on various talk shows, actively trying to constrain the interpretations of the Sandinista revolution that were being encouraged by the Western media. Ortega was attempting to use the tools of his opponents against them. Yet Rushdie's interest in Ortega's talk show tour makes the political leader's compromised position, as someone reliant on the US media culture he ultimately despised, into another instance of the necessary but troubled alliance that captivates him throughout *The Jaguar Smile*: the alliance between the Sandinistan political project and the media available for its local and international promotion.

In sum, throughout *The Jaguar Smile* Rushdie's focus is the Sandinistas' political iconography, coupled with their contentious control of media resources within the country, as a counter to the power of the US-backed rightwing media that sought to influence public perception of the revolution. The decoration of public spaces with slogans and images of revolutionary heroes, and Ortega's manipulation of the mechanisms of promotion available in the American media, are two sides of the same coin. The book that Rushdie produced is itself caught up in the struggle, since *The Jaguar Smile* was possible due to the Sandinistas' interest in controlling public perception of their cause, resulting in the ASTC bringing largely sympathetic writers to the country. It did not hurt that Rushdie was a considerably famous author who would have little trouble selling a book manuscript about his trip, and whose published work would enter the market accompanied by reviews, interviews, and potentially even televised appearances. Published in 1987, the book that most emphasizes Rushdie's adherence to a leftist political tradition in fact coincided with his turn toward New York, Andrew Wylie, and a more aggressive investment in his own career, an investment that just preceded the global dissemination of *The Satanic Verses* and the political crisis that attended it.

*

Rushdie's decision to set *Fury*'s loosely fictional liberation struggle in a nation meant as a stand-in for Fiji has considerable interest in relation to *The Jaguar Smile*. The revolution orchestrated by the Sandinistas has a political valence not entirely unlike Fiji's recent volatility. The Fiji Labour Party, endorsed by a significant portion of the Indo-Fijian population, came to power in May 1999, making Mahendra Pal Chaudhry, a prominent socialist and trade unionist, the first Indo-Fijian Prime Minister. Many welcomed his 'Rainbow Coalition' as a positive move toward breaking down the boundaries between so-called 'ethnic' Fijians and Indo-Fijians. However, some ethnic Fijians opposed the new government on the grounds that Fiji should always be run for and controlled by other Fijians; in 2000 they actually took control of the government through violent means, encouraging some Indo-Fijians to organize their own countering protests.[35] This coup and counter-coup roughly form the set of events that *Fury* references. They were anticipated by a similar coup in 1987, which saw an elected coalition government deposed by a militia made up of rightwing supporters of a state run by and for ethnic Fijians alone. Scholars have linked that 1987 coup to American and Australian anti-communist interests, which perceived the Fiji Labour Party, then part of the elected coalition, as a leftwing group that welcomed links to the Soviet Union and other communist states.

During the events of 2000 debates raged over which segment of Fiji's population controlled the majority of the nation's resources. On the one hand, ethnic Fijians and their sympathizers have tended to position the Indo-Fijians as orchestrating a reversal of fortune, taking the dominant position in the nation's economy and leaving a large number of indigenous Fijians unemployed and disenfranchised. On the other hand, another set of interests notes the way ethnic Fijians have engaged in the cultural performance of their ethnicity to gain a privileged position in the region's political and economic life. This privilege extends back to the time when the Fijians were themselves fairly contented subjects of the British Empire, spared the specific work to which other colonial peoples were subject because Indian labourers were indentured instead. Indentured labour arrived in Fiji to begin with in order to allow for the maintenance of the traditional Fijian way of life and the system of chiefs set up to administer the colony.[36] Despite the ethnically mixed history of the area, which has involved migrations of populations from throughout Polynesia, as well as from India and China, the Fijians have maintained their specific connection to the land through the marketing of a distinct national identity for the purposes of both national politics and global tourism.

In particular, as Andrew Ross points out, the Fijians have presented their culture as a 'lifestyle trade commodity' within the niche of eco-tourism, in a way that specifically avoids reference to the region's significant political strife, multiculturalism, and the majority population of Indo-Fijians.[37] The construction of this form of attachment to the land can take on decidedly racist overtones, as evidenced by an address presented to a conference of women at the UN in June 2000, in which Taina Woodward lends support to the coup by claiming that 'Fijians' (as opposed to 'Fiji citizens') are a communalist and peace-loving people who welcomed the Indo-Fijians as 'visitors,' but cannot accept their 'take over' of the homes and government rightly belonging to the people indigenous to the land.[38] Woodward's language references the prominent local stereotype of the Indian as greedy capitalist: in Fiji they are simply taking advantage of a 'bargain' negotiated with the former British colonial administration, outstaying their welcome and failing to integrate sufficiently into the Fijian way of life.[39]

The Indo-Fijians thus faced and continue to face a significant challenge in bringing their concerns to the attention of the media and into the consciousness of those who might visit the region as tourists. In *Fury* Neela explains her region's media image as a hindrance to political progress, claiming that people in the West consider Lilliput-Blefuscu 'a South Sea paradise, a place for honeymoons and other trysts' (63). Malik also later attempts to ingratiate himself to Babur through reference to the Puppet Kings web company, claiming it can help him reach 'a mass global audience' in order to 'win hearts and minds' (244). Indeed the FRM's appropriation of the Puppet Kings narrative and its staging of various media events are active responses to the necessity of formulating a presence that can counter the more powerful images prevalent within their specific national milieu and more internationally.

Now, in contrast to his largely sympathetic portrait of the necessities behind the Sandinistan revolution, Rushdie represents the FRM political program with considerable ambiguity, and as orchestrated and controlled by an increasingly authoritarian and violent man. In many ways Rushdie relies quite heavily on the actual events taking place in Fiji in early 2000, events he wrote about himself in the *New York Times* around the time of *Fury*'s composition. Many commentators have read the opposition to Indo-Fijian inroads into government office as a conflict artificially racialized by indigenous Fijians unwilling to acknowledge the flaws in their own leadership.[40] In *Fury*, though, instead of complicating the notion that the agitation against Chaudhry's government was a fight for power between two races, and instead of any focus on the leftist political orientation many attributed to the newly elected 'Rainbow Coalition,' Rushdie has Neela insist that the ethnic Elbees staged their coup in reaction to the threat that the 'Big Endia-wallahs' who espouse 'free-market mercantilism, and profit mentality' might take over the country (158). Neela's views, though those of an Indo-Lilly, exist in significant discord with most accounts of Fiji's ethnic politics, as she rather sympathetically suggests that the indigenous Elbees fear the capitalist mercantilism, and not some leftist labour-orientation, urged by the new coalition politics. In contrast to his stance on Nicaragua, then, and when the conflict involves a population of Indo-Fijians, not to mention a large number of more recent Gujarati immigrants, Rushdie adopts a divided voice, representing a more ambiguous position toward the uprising in which Babur and his compatriots are engaged.

In *Fury*'s final pages, as Malik pursues Neela to Lilliput-Blefuscu, where she is concluding her documentary with an insider's view of the FRM counter coup, Malik's fictional narrative and the 'real' world of the FRM struggle clash head on. Babur appears in a Kronos/Dollmaker costume, going by the name of Commander Akasz (227). All the Fremen wear masks of characters from *The Puppet Kings*. Having originally modeled Akasz on himself, when Malik arrives in Mildendo he notes that 'the dominant image in Lilliput-Blefuscu – a country close to civil war [...] was, as he had known it must be, a close likeness of himself' (239). He is in a 'Theatre of Masks' where 'the original, the man with no mask, was perceived as the mask's imitator: the creation was real while the creator was the counterfeit!' (239). Neela's face, too, is concealed beneath a Zameen mask, 'an imitation of itself' (243). 'Lilliput-Blefuscu had reinvented itself in his image,' we read, '[i]ts streets were his biography, patrolled by figments of his imagination and altered versions of people he had known' (246). Thus, his fictional creations, directly drawn from the political struggles of contemporary life, suffer not the fate of irrelevance or passing fashion, but rather influence and inspire the political struggles for national sovereignty so common to the latter half of the twentieth century and the early years of the twenty-first. Or, said differently, and in reference to Nicaragua, Malik's experiences dramatize the extent to which political life has a fictional, cultural valence, as political movements adopt styles derived from the resources of the culture industries.

The Jaguar Smile suggests that, much like Lilliput-Blefuscu, through Rushdie's eyes Nicaragua is a landscape that exemplifies the relationship between politics and cultural iconography. Liberation movements thrive on the narratives of cultural resistance that they create and appropriate; they feed, creatively, on what Malik's narratives also need: 'personal history, scraps of gossip, deep learning, current affairs, high and low culture, and the most nourishing diet of all [...] the past' (190). Though one text is apparently fact and the other fiction, *The Jaguar Smile* mirrors the later book's interest in the relationship between liberationist political movements and the power of the celebrated image. In *The Jaguar Smile* the Sandinistas and the Western media are engaged in a struggle over who gets to control political mythmaking. Every icon and every narrative can be appropriated and transmitted as a political message. In *Fury*, alternatively, while the struggle is still over the making of meaning, it takes place between a producer of cultural goods and the larger audience of receivers who do with his works what they will. In either case, as narratives take on a variety of iconic significances, the importance of their origins is radically upset. But *Fury* performs an important departure. What is the relationship between Rushdie's career development, his take on the Nicaraguan political struggle's media implications, and the representation of the activities of the Indo-Lillies, or Indo-Fijians, in *Fury*? Answering this question is a way to begin to understand the nature of the self-conscious authorial self-articulation in which *Fury* is ultimately engaged.

*

The Jaguar Smile is invested in championing the meaning-making practices of the Sandinistas, and pays so much attention to the culture industries in order to explain the disadvantaged position of the Nicaraguan revolutionaries. In contrast *Fury* makes no attempt to justify or explain the political program of the FRM, but rather emphasizes the way revolutionary movements can be seamlessly incorporated into global popular culture like the Puppet Kings web phenomenon, as well as how revolutionary movements in turn appropriate that global culture in ways cultural producers may never have imagined. Like the FRM, the revolutionaries in *The Jaguar Smile* go into battle in disguise: 'Sandinista guerrillas often went into action wearing masks of pink mesh with simple faces painted on them,' we are told (25). Whereas in *The Jaguar Smile* Rushdie sees resistance fighters taking on masks of peasant anonymity, and finds the heroes of the revolution all across the landscape that the Sandinistas seek to control, in *Fury* what Rushdie sees in Lilliput-Blefuscu's political iconography (through Malik's eyes, seeing himself in Babur's Kronos costume) is *his own face*.

Malik mourns that he cannot control the dissemination and impact of the narratives that make up *The Puppet Kings*. He cannot decide to what movements they lend a voice, or to what purposes they are put. The price of involvement in the creation of culture – especially culture of obvious political relevance – is the potential for dangerous appropriations and the entanglement of one's works with real violence. Whereas *The Jaguar Smile* applauded the efforts of the Sandinistas to control the meaning of their struggle, in *Fury* Malik views the adoption of his stories and images by the FRM with considerable horror, despite the fact that he used Lilliput-Blefuscu's politics in the creation of his Puppet Kings narratives to begin with. Malik has already seen Little Brain lent to the world of high fashion and global popular culture, and he thematizes this experience in *The Puppet Kings* by making Kronos incapable of controlling the Puppetmaster cyborg and his kin. The subsequent reintegration of those narratives into the world produces his anxiety about the way the meaning they take on erases not just his intentions but, as the novel's frequent reference to masks suggest, his very identity. This is the most significant point of difference between the two treatments. If *The Jaguar Smile* sees contemporary political movements necessarily drawing on the resources of media, and participating in the conscious creation of a historically situated iconography, in *Fury* those movements instead pose a direct challenge to the personal rights of one individual.

The difference is in part produced by Rushdie's understandable fascination with the contentious status of his own authorial persona. In fact in terms of Rushdie's career the FRM and their brutal leader –

certainly no Daniel Ortega – resemble no one so much as the fundamentalists who enacted, in Rushdie's oft-expressed view, a politicized appropriation of *The Satanic Verses* that is analogous to what the FRM do to Malik's works. Much of the logic of *Fury* surely derives from the cultural politics of the Rushdie affair, which, as a number of critics have noted, made Roland Barthes' pronouncements about the 'death of the author' all too literal. Martine Hennard Dutheil de la Rochère notes that the fate of *The Satanic Verses* as a novel 'exemplifies the process of commodification, which appropriates objects and restructures their meaning according to the imperatives of political opportunism or consumerist logic.' If *Fury* amply demonstrates Rushdie's belief that ideas have real effects in the world, and his interest in what Dutheil de la Rochère calls 'the interplay between fact and fiction, reality and imagination, the world and word,' it also shows what *The Satanic Verses* controversy suggested – simply put, 'that the agency of writing escapes the control of the author and exceeds his intentions.'[41]

In this sense *Fury* recenters the question of authorship by depicting the intending author's marginalization. This recentering process is one that Rushdie initiated after the fatwa made it necessary for him to affirm his authorial intentions, despite having written a novel that questions the idea of origins at every turn. 'In Good Faith,' one of Rushdie's passionate defenses of *The Satanic Verses*, is full of statements like 'we must return for a moment to the actually existing book,' 'decontextualization has created a complete reversal of meaning,' and 'the original intentions of *The Satanic Verses* have been so thoroughly scrambled by events as to be lost for ever.'[42] A major problem with a credo like Roland Barthes' is the way it denies the author precisely such attempts to enact what Séan Burke refers to as an author's specific political power 'to distance himself from the attribution of erroneous, blasphemous or criminal motives.'[43]

That said, understanding *Fury* also requires acknowledging Rushdie's recent conflict with what he constructs as a dominantly South Asian tendency to politicize his authorship and to critique the figure of Rushdie as the embodiment of IWE's privileged market position. This is part of what makes it necessary for him to reflect and refract the reception of *The Satanic Verses* in *Fury*. True to Rushdie's recently restated alienation from 'the East,' there is uncharacteristically little of South Asia in the novel. There is, however, that dictatorial FRM revolutionary, a descendent of the indentured labourers whose experiences offer one version of the authentic migrancy that Rushdie has been accused of mining for his universal metaphorics of 'border crossing' and 'mongrel' subjectivity. As the most scorned manipulator of Malik's works for very real political ends, Babur stands in for the more problematic aspects of Rushdie's reception. Rushdie has himself said, in relation to the fatwa, that in attempting to portray an 'objective reality' he 'became its subject,'[44] thus witnessing an alternative self going around as Rushdie, but in the image of the devil, and fearing that 'my other may succeed in obliterating me.'[45] Malik has the same fear that Babur, in the guise of Akasz, may obliterate him. So while it is the first of Rushdie's major novels to abandon South Asia as subject and setting, the book is in fact haunted by 'the East' to which the author is irreparably bound by the mutually-constituted forces of political fiat and industry positioning. Said differently, since for Rushdie what constrains his authorship are forms of reception that he tends to castigate as not fitting with his own celebration of 'unbelonging,'[46] insofar as they emanate from what he associates with 'the East,' there is no straightforward turn away from the South Asian milieu toward some narcissistic solipsism.

As I have said, Babur is one of the politicized subalterns to whom Rushdie opposes himself in rejecting 'the East,' and it is ultimately in relation to him and his movement that we can understand Malik's (and Rushdie's) opposition to his own situation. It is not the case that *Fury* completely credits Malik's tendency toward rage and self-pity. To engage in too vocal a lament about his situation is to deny that he actually benefits from his troubled circumstances by using them as fictional material in further products available for wide-scale distribution and promotion. Malik certainly complains that he lacks the agency to either access or be responsible for those mechanisms that control what his creations have been made to do. His desire to have some say in how he is perceived manifests itself in narratives that emphasize his own lack of power or sway. He asserts his presence by revealing his own absence or, more correctly, by revealing the many ways his seeming presence masks a deeper, more significant absence. His authorship is exaggerated in ways that he doesn't want it to be, but also delimited in precisely those cases when he thinks it should have force. But part of what *Fury* does is query to what extent authors are victims of the current culture industry's ceaseless circulations and mass deceptions. Malik is never beyond blame. He derives his texts from political materials and he uses his work to reference his own biography in a way that can only encourage the collapsing of distinctions between self and text. In this way *Fury* indicates the author's concurrent complicity in and retreat from the world of global celebrification.

Indeed in depicting Malik's agonized form of literary labour, emerging in circumstances of globally-extended cultural production, and in turn how that labour influences his subsequent creations, Rushdie registers his own complicity in constructing the political functionality of his texts. If there is any self-absolution going on in the novel it is precisely in the way Rushdie uses Malik's case to admit some blame for the situation so described.

Still, while Rushdie never fully credits Malik's tendency to lament the fate of his works, he does imply that ultimately the author should not be held accountable for any essential confusion between the text at issue and the body of the writer who created it and is under threat because of it. In this way, the major source of trouble in *Fury* is actually the process of celebrification, much though Rushdie has clearly been involved in the construction and diffusion of his own celebrated image.[47] The word 'celebrity,' appearing repeatedly in the novel, was not widely available as a predicate noun until relatively recently. Once a synonym for 'pomp,' used to indicate 'observance of rites and ceremonies,' it later came to describe a position of fame or public renown ('Salman Rushdie's deserved celebrity'). It could finally stand in for an individual ('Salman Rushdie is a deserving celebrity') only in the second part of the nineteenth century, during the time of Mark Twain and Charles Dickens, which Daniel J. Boorstin deemed the 'Graphic Revolution.'[48] Joe Moran contends that it was during this period, a time of tremendous growth in marketing culture in general, that American newspapers and magazines marketed writers by encouraging them 'to work in journalistic, reportorial forms which implicitly connected writing and personality and which appeared in close proximity with more direct attempts to manufacture a persona through news, reviews, interviews and photographs.'[49] The British case was not dissimilar. With the collapse of the monopoly that the circulating libraries had over the consumption of fiction, author-based marketing techniques began to take on their current ubiquity, and the availability of anonymity or pseudonymity as authorial postures gradually eroded in turn. As Leah Price argues, signatured authorship then became more important and entrenched, while advertisements and gimmicks (including 'autographed photographs, illustrated interviews, [and] house tours') violated distinctions between public and private, between the text as an entity and the flesh of the author who composed it.[50]

Rushdie's negotiation with 'celebrity' and its implications signals his desire to reckon with his own position within a marketplace laden with values about the status of literary culture relative to the general economy. *Fury* is certainly Rushdie's most obviously autobiographical novel, making basic fictional material out of his having left his third wife and their son to move to New York and start a relationship with his future wife Padma Lakshmi, a Miss Universe contestant and model half his age. This aspect of the text encourages the common complaint that it is an exercise in solipsistic self-fashioning, a calculated effort at self-construction and defense designed to deflect the public criticism of Rushdie's private life. Amitava Kumar's review accuses Rushdie of the grossest self-regard, claiming the book's major theme is success or stardom, in his view the one thing that Rushdie 'really cares about.'[51] He contends that the book's protagonist is entirely complicit in everything he seems to critique, and that its political narrative is undermined by Rushdie's 'zeal for self-glorification' and by his fundamental inability to sympathetically approach those unlike him in social stature, education, or class. Kumar sees Rushdie's own work in *Fury*'s description of the fiction written by character Jack Rhinehart: 'lucrative profiles of the super-powerful, super-famous, and super-rich.'[52] Many voiced similar criticisms.[53]

However, while the book is self-referential and solipsistic, as Kumar and others note, it is self-defensive about something other than the author's lifestyle choices. I have tried to show that *Fury*'s subject is not so much Rushdie's biography as it is public interest in the author's personal circumstances. It confronts the way that the celebrification of literary authors has as an operative feature this marked collapsing of distinctions between the private self and the public text, such that the novel's more interesting solipsism is actually its paranoia about the author's personal status within a literary marketplace that simultaneously celebrates, consecrates, and derides him. Predicting Kumar's critique of its 'zeal for self-glorification,' the novel tells its readers that it is not a mere biography in a mask. It is not a straightforward attempt on the part of the author to constrain his image in the eyes of an increasingly critical public, a public put off by his seeming willingness to make himself a popular spectacle and pursue an Americanized dream of global popularity. Rather, *Fury* self-consciously parades its biographical masking. It is about the *process* of writing veiled memoirs, as Malik interprets his own career through the narratives he creates. What is true of *The Puppet Kings* is true of *Fury*: both are about lives making their way into fictions and fiction making its way, all too viscerally, back into the world where meaning is made. It is then entirely appropriate, given the fate of Malik's own narratives, that critical reception of *Fury* almost universally read the text as the product of Rushdie's self-obsessed solipsism.

The book is less about Rushdie's life, and more about 'Rushdie' as brand name, as paratext, and as icon. It concerns the very process through which 'Rushdie' then turns his 'back-story,' a story defined by the contentious politicization of literary works, into yet another book, available for more scrutiny and critique. This makes a major burden of the text establishing the value of some serviceable distinction between 'Rushdie' (author of literature), Rushdie™ (the celebrated icon, the lionized figure), and Rushdie (the person).

Malik's constant response to being a global icon and celebrity is discontent, and he feels he has little control over the procedures that implicate him in what he disavows. He certainly doesn't desire the status that has accrued to him. Instead his prominence is a major problem for him, while he continues to find few things more pleasurable than time spent with his rather nerdy collection of handmade dolls, indulging his creative storytelling instincts. Authorship comes to him as a natural talent and a serious compulsion, but being celebrated for it remains a kind of imposition, especially because it makes his persona and his texts available for circulation within a system that he is actually quite horrified to find himself caught up in. In other words, Malik has a power, largely deriving from artistic drive and talent, which he seems to feel should allow him to fictionalize and manipulate contemporary politics, as well as his own personal experiences, without facing the specific repercussions that he does in the course of the novel. His desire is to be able to draw from the political scene, to use his genius to transmute its violence into text, without having his own image subject to reintegration back into the real-world of tumultuous political struggle.

So while *Fury* does not entirely absolve Malik of any accountability for his position within the market, it still dramatizes its operations as outside of the writer's specific sphere of interest or desire. Malik wants to matter as an author of his text's meaning, but not, it seems, as an author-*figure* lionized by the global media and transnational culture industries; this is the status for which Rushdie has himself received such significant criticism, and which makes him available for general scrutiny to begin with. Indeed this is where Malik and Rushdie most converge. Is it true that Rushdie is without agency, having no say in how his texts go out into the world and reach their many readers? In the case of *The Satanic Verses*, Rushdie may have made a number of major decisions that affected what unfolded after the novel's publication. For example, might it be true that his insistence that his publishers go ahead with a paperback version added fuel to his opponents' fire? Did it sanction their sense that Rushdie lacked sensitivity about the violence that ensued, caring more to adhere unflinchingly to the principle of the writer's ultimate freedom, an adherence which in this case had the additional benefit of being lucrative? However these questions are answered, admitting some complicity in the situation he laments does not mean that the writer accepts the postcolonial author's total fate. It may be Malik's willful decision to engage with the political realities of particular locales that has made his works available for certain forms of political appropriation, in a process he might have then predicted. Still, ultimately, he does not approve of the real-world impact that his works have had, especially as that impact extends to public interest in the writer himself; he cannot control it, and nor does he feel he should have to.

Rushdie's traveller's account of a recent trip to India, depicted as an opportunity to heal the rift between him and his homeland, solidifies a connection between Malik and his author in this respect. After detailing the various barriers to his acting as an average citizen, such as access restrictions and bodyguards, his emphasis becomes his desire 'to bore India into submission,' to be uninteresting to the average person in a way that celebrities rarely are.[54] 'People – journalists, policemen, friends, strangers – all write scripts for me, and I get trapped inside those fantasies,' he writes. In his own script, though, 'the problems I've faced are gradually overcome, and I resume the ordinary literary life that is all I've ever wanted.'[55] Once physically there at long last, Rushdie comes to realize that the country is not so obsessed with his presence as he had thought (or been led to believe), and as he begins to think that the burden of *The Satanic Verses* fatwa can finally be cast off, he celebrates. If media coverage states 'Oh, there's a novelist in town to go to a dinner? What's his name? Rushdie? So what?' Rushdie thinks that's all the better. In fact he describes his euphoria about passing into irrelevance as 'an event of immense emotional impact, exceeding in force even the tumultuous reception of *Midnight's Children* almost twenty years ago.'[56] *Fury* shares this same language, depicting a beleaguered writer who wants to stop living in a scenario he did not create for himself, because it causes problems that challenge his right to authorize his own texts and, more importantly, his own life. Rushdie states his commitment to going unnoticed, and it is only then that he is reconciled with this place he calls 'the East.'

In Part I, I argued that as the marketing of biographical authors becomes more pronounced as a mode of differentiation within the marketplace, the proliferation of texts in their critical and market contexts threatens to make authorial control over meaning insignificant, all the while making certain authors central to the literary landscape. With *Fury* Rushdie suggests that this simultaneous undermining of the author-function and celebrification of the author-figure is also what permits his demonization – quite literally, here, his transmutation into a devilish masked man he attempts to remain distinct from. Like Malik's, Rushdie's works have an obvious political relevance that makes them available for contentious debate. His material is controversial and has proven to be offensive to some audiences. He uses his own experiences in his writing and as such makes that material available for commentary and market appropriation. In *Fury* he grants this, and still wonders why this must have anything to do with him becoming a celebrated individual. Why must he be lionized in such a way that everything from basic criticism to threats of violence are directed at his person, while opposition to his work routinely has to do with his own ostensible personal venality, or abandonment of South Asia, or deracinated love for the Anglo-American metropoles? In line with Casanova's theorization of the 'autonomous pole,' it is his unrelenting connection to a particular locale – whether he is said to romanticize it, market it, or abandon it – that has been, he thinks, a uniting feature of the most vociferous forms of politicization of his work. What Rushdie opposes in rejecting 'the East' is, thus, the way he feels he has been personally, viscerally, even bodily implicated in a whole series of real-world struggles that he would prefer have little to do with the actual nature or meaning of his literary works. Again, the problem is his elevation to the status of icon (Rushdie™), and the related privileging of hostile attention to his person (Rushdie), over any consideration of the techniques and concerns that could be properly associated with a more functional authorship.

In the end, though, diagnosing this problem involves tensions that may be irresolvable: any autonomous sphere only makes sense in relation to the distinctly local heteronomy of political forces (and vice versa, as I'll argue in my next chapter); Rushdie writes a transparently autobiographical work that critiques public interest in his life; he takes leave from 'the East,' again, but by having it haunt every page, as one representative ideologue threatens the author's life and identity; he appeals to an aesthetic realm, where the creator can simply go about his work unbothered and unknown, despite his willing contribution to his own celebrity stature. Finally, though I wrote above that the author's admission to some complicity in creating his own peril does not disallow any critique of his own contested position, I think the more accurate claim is that in Rushdie's case admitting guilt and deflecting criticism are part of the same maneuver. Self-implication is meant to grant more legitimate force to his opposition to what he takes to be his targeting by the Baburs of the world.

4
Locating J.M. Coetzee

Both Salman Rushdie and J.M. Coetzee are interested in the implications of dissolving barriers between the private and the public, both are strident critics of censorship, and both perceive themselves as having been victims of political forms of literary valuation. Yet these initial similarities should not obscure the differences in the nature of the pressures they have faced. These pressures have produced unique forms of authorial self-articulation, or disparate routes to the same desire to claim some absent self-authorization. Rushdie is much more a literary celebrity than Coetzee, or, at least, Rushdie's persona is that of someone who has tended to embrace his celebrity lifestyle, while Coetzee's belongs to a more uncompromising, private, somber person who retreats from the limelight and refuses opportunities for self-promotion and display. Rushdie's self-construction in *Fury* turns on his own iconic celebrification as a paradigmatic author of 'the East.' He dramatizes his access to some innocence in the production of that status, but he does not deny the political efficacy or relevance of fiction, and he admits to some complicity in the making of his own authorial crisis. His claim to innocence occurs in tandem and tension with his admission of guilt.

In contrast, in a set of narratives that offer possibilities for various kinds of confessional self-implication, Coetzee subjects the very terminology of guilt and innocence to radical scrutiny. Indeed this is in large part his way of participating in the market for postcolonial narratives. In *The Master of Petersburg* (1994) there is no strict separation between the private interior self and the public sphere for Fyodor Dostoevsky, and some knowledge of this is what causes him to lament and to experience an anxiety that actually brings about the act of writing itself. For Coetzee, too, the personal reticence of his public authorial persona exists in tension with the way introspection and self-critique feature as recurring modes in his texts. These very modes are countered yet again, though, since in terms that specifically encompass what he takes to be his critics' position, his recent novels, including *The Master of Petersburg*, *Disgrace* (1999), and *Elizabeth Costello* (2003), dramatize the naivety of any censorious audience that believes in the viability of self-awareness in confessions of guilt.

In part because of this very tendency to undermine the status of any narrative representation of self-awareness, writing about Coetzee's authorial self-consciousness is a tricky enterprise. It is made additionally challenging by the way Coetzee positions the demand for sincere self-implication within an insistent binary that prestages my own approach. This binary contrasts an ideal sphere of literary valuation and a mode of reception politicized by the material conditions of apartheid South Africa. It recurs throughout his *oeuvre*, especially as a feature of his remarkable attentiveness to writers' self-constructing appropriations of other author-figures, which is often articulated as a critique of any tendency to interpret literature in a way that is consistent not with a writer's sense of his own art, but instead with the interpreter's existing interest in a specific notion of *how* art signifies and takes on value. Coetzee makes this distinction in delineating two options for understanding T.S. Eliot, for example. On the one hand, he states, one can read Eliot sympathetically and on his own terms, accepting his claim to the 'transcendental-poetic' significance of literary work; or, on the other hand, one can instead attempt to place him in the sort of socio-cultural matrix that the writing 'itself' seeks to challenge.[1] My own argument will be that these options carefully mirror another distinction that Coetzee draws, this time between his hostile local public and a more sympathetic global audience, so that what I claim – namely, that attention to Coetzee's conflicted market positioning clarifies some of what is at stake in the binaries he posits – becomes, in his terms, precisely the kind of imposition of a set of socio-cultural concerns meant to disallow any autotelic definition of the 'transcendental-poetic.' My materialist reading of Coetzee's investment in a whole series of interconnected polarities – the local versus the global, the ethical versus the political, the socio-cultural versus the 'transcendental-poetic' – puts me in a tug-of-war with the writer himself. It is by emphasizing the inadequacy of many of the dualities he constructs, and by discussing the specific market circumstances that have given them part

of their resonance, that I plan to avoid the trap Coetzee has set for
me.

*

Before the official fatwa was issued against him, but after the instiga-
tion of an initial furor over *The Satanic Verses*, Rushdie was invited to
speak at a book week organized by the *Weekly Mail*, South Africa's independent grassroots newspaper. Both the newspaper and the Congress
of South African Writers (CSAW) sponsored his invitation, but local
Islamic groups protested, threatening violence against him, and as a
consequence the invitation was withdrawn. Nadine Gordimer and
Coetzee had been scheduled to sit on the panel with Rushdie, and they
each appeared despite his forced absence. Gordimer, a member of the
CSAW, spoke in support of its decision, on the grounds that, given the
apartheid political climate, respect for the political will of minority
groups was of primary importance. Coetzee maintained, alternatively,
that the censorship of Rushdie reminded him quite precisely of the
Afrikaner church's opposition to what it censoriously defined as blas-
phemy and irreligion of all sorts.[2] He spoke of what Ian Glenn calls
'the alarming willingness of the new order to follow the practices and
logic of the old.'[3] Coetzee's views on the censoring of Rushdie –
his opposition to the silencing of writers regardless of their positions
vis-à-vis majority or minority group status – positioned him in firm
opposition to the radical sentiment of the time, as embodied in the
CSAW's position. That opposition to more radical political opinion was
one with which he had become increasingly associated. Indeed what
he expressed that day predicts his subsequent formulation of a more
consistent position on the place of writers in relation to the demands
of political realities and social necessities. Coetzee himself has faced
those demands since the inception of his career, so in formulating his
own stance he has responded not just to the political climate of
apartheid South Africa, but also to the impact that climate has had on
his own career development and reception.

Censorship and embargo were common fates for books in South
Africa under apartheid, but Coetzee's novels were not held back by this
kind of institutional constraint. The censorship board did consider *In
the Heart of the Country* (1977) before passing it, though; the chair's
report called it 'a difficult, obscure, multileveled work that will be read
only by intellectuals,' and concluded that the 'likely reader' would not
locate 'reality' or any explicit message within its pages.[4] Perhaps

because it was not clearly set in South Africa but an ambiguous 'outpost of empire,' as the jacket blurb stated, when *Waiting for the Barbarians* (1980) was studied it also passed. In the censor's words, the novel's content was 'of world-wide significance, not particularized.' He added: 'Though the book has considerable literary merit, it quite lacks popular appeal. The likely readership will be limited largely to the intelligentsia, the discriminating minority.'[5]

So in a climate of institutional censorship Coetzee's novels circulated more freely than others; they were allowed the chance to be designated 'universal' for a more global readership served by multinational publishers precisely because they did not offend local censors.[6] As Coetzee himself has said, in this case somewhat apologetically, 'my books have been too indirect in their approach, too rarefied, to be considered a threat to the order.'[7] However, being largely immune to censorship did not mean Coetzee was given permission to act as an autonomous artist, somehow apart from the realm of the political. In fact the opposite may be true. In his own view what he faced in lieu of institutional scrutiny is the hostile attention of the very intellectual community the official censorship board designated the 'likely' readers of his works.

Coetzee's first novel, *Dusklands*, was published in 1974 by a small South African firm called Ravan Press, founded in 1972 as an outlet for the progressive research conducted by the Study Project on Christianity in Apartheid Society. It quickly became 'the best-known outlet for aspirant black writers,'[8] especially through *Staffrider*, its influential Black Consciousness periodical. Ravan's focus was revisionist social history that was Marxist or dissident in orientation, and that emphasized 'the impact of socio-economic forces on the lives of ordinary people.'[9] Initial publication of Rick Turner's influential *The Eye of the Needle* (1972), followed by other titles within the New History of Southern Africa Series, and by conference volumes based on the leftist History Workshop at the University of Witwatersand, all established their credentials within the larger sphere of locally-owned, anti-state, anti-apartheid, alternative publishing. This particular niche was itself part of the prolix and multilingual publishing landscape in South Africa; local pro-state firms catered to their own portion of the reading public, and multinationals that were comparably liberal and enlightened also staked their claims, especially to a relatively prosperous English-speaking middle class readership.

Among South Africa's roughly 40 million inhabitants only 400,000 people are book buyers, while 12–15 per cent of the population has been deemed functionally illiterate.[10] Only a small portion of the population is mainly English speaking, and Eve Horwitz Gray identifies 'an ever-decreasing circle' after the end of apartheid, through which a mainly white industry targets a similarly constituted white middle class reading public.[11] Local literary writers unwilling to settle for this limited audience have been mostly dependent on international markets for success. Coetzee's career is indicative, as through his initial contract with Ravan he quickly found his footing within a wider industry. Glenn Moss, managing director at Ravan from 1988, states that *Dusklands* was picked up by the press only after many others turned it down, answering to what he calls the 'strait-jacket of com-mercialism.'[12] Given the novel's success Coetzee was able to secure a contract with the British firm Secker & Warburg for his next book, *In the Heart of the Country.* He then negotiated with Secker & Warburg to guarantee South African rights to Ravan, an arrangement in place for several of his subsequent titles, which are now distributed in South Africa and North America by Random House or its Vintage imprint. Ravan cofounder Peter Randall states: 'It was painful to know that as a small publisher we could not compete with international houses to retain authors for whom we had taken the initial risks.'[13]

In common with almost all locally-owned anti-apartheid presses, Ravan was subsumed by a larger multinational company soon after the demise of the regime it existed to oppose, becoming a part of Hodder & Stoughton Educational South Africa, and then of Macmillan in 2000.[14] If there was a viable anti-state industry under apartheid, those who sought to succeed in that market could only do so given the conditions of apartheid they wanted to see eradicated. When those conditions were alleviated, so was the need for the local alternative industry. In Guy Berger's terms, the alternative press in South Africa became a casu-alty of true democracy.[15] In addition to a general sense of 'political exhaustion,' Dick Cloete notes as a cause of this process the 'dispersal of intellectuals and activists' out of the realm of alternative media and into the state bureaucracy.[16]

Unlike Ravan, multinational firms then and now functioned less as outlets for new South African writers and more as distributors of already recognized brand name figures. It is in this capacity that they played an important role in South African literary development, helping to establish a cadre of internationally famous writers, and becoming particularly important allies for those otherwise silenced by local censors or forced to live in exile.[17] They helped launch the careers of those that Michael Chapman calls 'mainstream internationals,' writers like Coetzee, Gordimer, and André Brink, who have been marketed as the country's 'premier literary spokespersons.'[18]

It is not surprising that a significant portion of the local readership for the works that appeared in this context made stringent political demands of writers. Broadly, those deserving of attention and praise should have a clear anti-apartheid message; they should share with Ravan's revisionist historians a commitment to empiricism and documentary realism; and they should write in a style accessible to as wide an audience as possible.[19] In part these demands were a correlate to the volatility of the South African political situation in the 1970s and 80s. In Coetzee's case, *Dusklands* was published before the events of Soweto that significantly changed the country's political climate, but after militant labour and student movements and the promotion of Black Consciousness had all gained significant ground. After 1976 the government elaborated a program of 'stabilization' to counter its rapidly diminishing international credibility, as well as the 'growing tempo of armed struggle and internal insurrection.'[20] The 1980s were the time of the 'ultimate excesses of Afrikaner Nationalist preference,'[21] when radicalism of all kinds faced intense countering tactics, to which it responded in kind. Thus it was just as Coetzee's market presence was beginning to be established that local writers were confronting an increasing necessity for explicit political commitments.

Yet while this precise form of pressure was undeniably produced within the context of a local political struggle with immense energy and resolve, it was not unrelated to a sphere of action and communication that extended beyond South Africa's borders. Those who enjoyed the special privilege of accessing markets outside of South Africa were, as a consequence of preeminence, particularly subject to the most virulent demands for political engagement and responsibility. They were thought to be responsible for expressing the political goals of the anti-apartheid movement, and for doing so in stark terms. In Chapman's words, this arose from the fact that their 'local subject matter and preoccupations [were] received more widely abroad than at home and, at home, by relatively few "literary" readers.' They had to be 'more than artists, even less than artists, and as the text of the South African problem impinged on the texts of their books, they had to get out of the study and appear on public platforms as special cases of the political seer.'[22]

The conditions of apartheid meant that this set of 'mainstream internationals' was asked to take on the role of 'spokespersons' when addressing their disparate but connected readerships. First, there was a local progressive audience that valued political commitment in its writers to an unusual degree, but for understandable reasons; and second, there was a global literary marketplace that sought insight into the local conditions of life in South Africa, a place with a literary output then typically defined in terms of apartheid political violence. The political demands made by the one audience were inseparable from authors' unique access to the other. As I emphasized in previous chapters, though such distinctions are by no means entirely invalid, there is a danger in giving too much weight to any tendency to unduly polarize the local literary market and the global cultural sphere often construed as situating the world's localities. The South African case is not different. What I want to note, though, is a common perception – one shared by Coetzee, as I will show – of a broad separation between an international audience that distinguished his work as particularly worthy of praise and reward, and a community of interest convinced that his novels betrayed the necessary connection between the local anti-apartheid struggle and fictional practice. There is a further related tendency in reception of Coetzee's work, and in scholarly assessment of that reception, to align these respective reading publics with disparate literary critical traditions, so that the politicization of Coetzee's *oeuvre* is read as a conflict between two critical tendencies, one more often Marxist in orientation, and the other poststructuralist. Stated succinctly, the configuration of the postcolonial field experienced by Coetzee, as a globally accredited mainstream South African writer, has entailed some faith in a fairly rigid divide between these two available publics: a local South African literary community made up of *citizen-activists*, and a larger global market of typically apolitical *consumers* of products with themes reliant upon, but not overly invested in, specific political objectives.

A paradigmatic initial example is Gordimer's review of *The Life and Times of Michael K* (1983), which appeared in the *New York Review of Books* (*NYRB*) rather than a local South African paper.[23] Her criticisms of the book – that it 'denies the energy of the will to resist evil' and contains 'a revulsion against all political and revolutionary solutions'[24] – contain significant authority on the requisite politics. She belongs to that locally politicized South African readership but is also one of the white 'mainstream internationals' with ready access to a wider sphere. While praising the novel's literary merits, she cautions that Coetzee's frequent use of allegory reads like a 'desire to hold himself clear of events and their daily, grubby, tragic consequences,' and calls his earlier work the 'North Pole to which the agitprop of agonized black writers [...] was the South.'[25] She also consciously treats her piece as an education for readers of the *NYRB*, which is the most widely read source of literary book reviews in the English-speaking world, especially in North America. For example, she informs them that Michael K is more than he seems, that his experience allegorically represents 'in 1984 [...] hundreds and thousands of black people in South African squatter towns and "resettlement" camps.'[26] Assuming her readers lack awareness of the specificities of South African life, in an act of intervention she sets herself the task of providing the missing context that would be available to Coetzee's fellow South Africans. Her comments on the book are meant to prevent readers of the *NYRB* from otherwise accepting it as a vaguely allegorical rumination on the nature of human suffering or the search for a secure home. She places herself in the camp of those who would reject the ostensible universals of a purportedly non-localized cosmopolitan writing. This is in marked opposition to the statements of the several censors who screened and passed Coetzee's early work, such as Rita Scholtz, who wrote in her report on *Michael K* itself that it should not be restricted in any way specifically because its readers would experience it not as political fiction but as 'a work of art.'[27]

Of course many of Coetzee's readers would claim strict adherence to neither of these positions, just as there are instances of praise for his fictional work within South Africa, and opposition to it by others who have no readily identifiable attachment to the region. In all cases, whether they are situated within South Africa or otherwise, reading communities are divided along lines of race and class as well as along lines of political commitment. Of interest here is simply the way a more politicized readership becomes associated with the local sphere of action and engagement, while a readership more willing to separate fiction from the strict dictates of a specific kind of political literature is situated within a global consumer sphere. In understanding the particular forms of political fiat and judgement that Coetzee's own work identifies as part of the author's experience, it is these more characteristic turns in his embattled reception that are most relevant.

In Coetzee's experience the criticism he has faced within South Africa has entailed a preference for the realist novel, especially social realism or Lukácsian critical realism. As Gordimer's review of *Michael K* indicates, writers like Coetzee have been thought to perform, as Chapman puts it, 'an endless deferral of moral consequence which, in the agonised society, can merely provoke the impatience of those for whom reality is less an elusive signifier, more a crack on the head by a police truncheon.'[28] Continuing a 'critical orthodoxy' initiated by Michael Vaughan in 1982, Chapman's own work on Coetzee is both representative and 'recuperatory.'[29] He has been highly critical of the poststructuralist tendencies in Coetzee's writing, and wary of the kind of reception Coetzee has most often received outside of South Africa, best embodied in the work of Teresa Dovey. Her 1988 study of Coetzee's 'Lacanian allegories,' the first monograph on his fiction, appeared just as the Department of Literary Theory at the University of South Africa held a two-day seminar on *Foe* (1986), Coetzee's most self-consciously academic novel, and one that reads now as a kind of cookie-cutter introduction to the major tendencies of postmodern literature and thought.[30] Chapman condemns the conference, especially its embrace of poststructuralist challenges to the transparency of history, as entirely inappropriate 'in a country like ours, where history [...] is likely to manifest itself, concretely, as low wages or the police cell.'[31] Leftist thinkers like himself, he says, are concerned about 'how easily Coetzee's "deconstructions" can be appropriated by institutions of higher education, how remote they must seem to the *arché* and *telos* of black South African history.'[32]

For her own part, Dovey has been one of Coetzee's most vocal defenders. In introducing the first bibliography of his works in 1990, she summarized some of the dominant tendencies in the reception of his fiction, claiming it had been most potently constrained by 'discourses which [...] revolve around the central problematic of writing and resistance,' or the question of political relevance.[33] Her own work has emphasized the importance of allegory and psychoanalysis in interpreting Coetzee's fiction, so it is not surprising that she is a harsh judge of what she sees as 'vulgar' Marxist approaches, summarily dismissed here as the 'obsessive demand for one's writing to be politically relevant.' In fact she negates concerns about Coetzee's specific agency and social privilege by claiming 'with a writer like Coetzee, personal biography does not, indeed, seem very important.'[34] Also, rather than granting the legitimacy of the localizing critical practice of writers like Vaughan and Gordimer, she reconceptualizes the nature of the divide between Coetzee's 'two publics' by linking Marxist approaches to a center-periphery binary and a resulting culturalist bias. She claims that South African critics have been resistant to psychoanalytic or poststructuralist engagements with fiction not so much for reasons of political urgency, but in a 'desire to avoid contamination from European or North American centres of learning, and to speak one's "own" language [...] the natural response of the periphery to the metropolitan centre.'[35] More recently, but in a similar vein, in terms Coetzee would by all means endorse, Louise Bethlehem has opposed the tendency of South African literary critics to believe that 'writing provides a supposedly unmediated access to the real,' and that 'the transparent rendering of South African life is a type of "resistance".'[36] Citing Coetzee's critical reception as a 'useful point of entry for examining how a shared instrumentalist conception of language unites critics of South African literature in English,' instead of granting some sympathetic authority to political necessity Bethlehem attributes this instrumentalist thinking to epistemological fear of the 'arbitrariness of signification.'[37]

These are merely a few representative cases. As I have stated, there is no monolithic South African critical apparatus that universally condemns the sort of project Coetzee has been engaged in. Nor is it true that only South African critics took on the task of assessing his fiction in political terms. What purposes do the standard polarities serve, then? Most obviously, their construction is a feature of the politicization of the work of writing in South Africa, as critics work to discredit the approaches they associate with their opposition. Thus much work on Coetzee has been built upon a stated desire to justify the claims of one or the other side in an ongoing polemical battle, and a will to dismantle these same polarized positions has also been the premise for an extensive variety of critical work. To cite just one prominent example, in both his full-length study of Coetzee and a more recent debate with Benita Parry, David Attwell consciously bridges what he understands as the divide between the two camps.[38] The world of Coetzee criticism suffers from what Attwell calls an 'oversimplified polarization' between 'those registering the claims of political resistance and historical representation (who agree that Coetzee has little to offer) and [...] those responsive to postmodernism and poststructuralism.' He suggests that from the early- to mid-1980s, as the first significant body of critical work on Coetzee was built up, there was a consensus that he offered a portrayal of the 'breakup of the dominating, rationalist subject of colonialism,' but 'neither an analysis of the play of historical forces nor a moral anchor in the search for a humane response to colonialism and apartheid.'[39] Attwell claims to do away with this binary by arguing that Coetzee's work explores precisely the fields of experience and aesthetics in which it is caught up, illuminating the tensions that arise given overlapping spheres of text, politics, and history in South Africa.

In this light it has not been any absolute distinction between the local and the global, or the individual consumer and the social citizen, or poststructuralist writing and a literature responsive to Marxism, that has earned Coetzee his position within the market, but rather his ability to construct these pole positions in a way that forces readers to debate their relative credibility and purchase. Perhaps counter-intuitively, then, their codification is best seen as an aspect of a significant interrelation between the local and global fields. It would have been difficult for any reading of Coetzee to avoid confronting the pull of South African political strife, nor did many seek to. Where any critics local to South Africa might have been unsatisfied with Coetzee's work for political reasons, for example, those less obviously embroiled in the local field have been known to praise him for the political impetus that local critics thought lacking. None could claim that Coetzee avoided political questions entirely, since the very fact that he offered critics in general the chance to discuss South African politics, and the possible relationships between politics and aesthetics, was what gave him his presence within the global literary field. Indeed, as Ian Glenn claims, whether within South Africa or abroad, those interested in Coetzee's work have been typically obsessed with 'determining his political allegiances,'[40] so much so that any scholars interested in the way the relationship between aesthetics and politics has been understood and debated since World War II would be well served by turning their attention to the substantial body of critical work produced in response to his fiction.

To return briefly to Pascale Casanova's work, in some ways apartheid South Africa was exemplary of what she identifies as typical of the world literary system. It was a 'deprived literary space'; a national struggle continued to dominate cultural production, but the local field was sophisticated enough to have evolved its own contending autonomous and heteronomous poles. Coetzee's 2003 Nobel Prize win could be said to have finally confirmed his safe 'extra-territorial' positioning, as the prize itself exists in order to develop standards of universality.[41] From its early championing of writers from nations defined by their 'neutrality,' to its later support for literary 'idealism,' to its privileging of works 'whose national character was neither too pronounced nor too much insisted upon,' the prize committee has consistently defined literary excellence as 'incompatible with what might be called cultural nationalism.'[42] In granting this special distinction to Coetzee's work, something the international literati long expected to happen, the committee noted that his concern with the 'values and conduct' that result from apartheid enters his work not as national narrative but to suggest that such problems 'could arise anywhere.' According to the judges his themes are decidedly non-localized: he is 'ruthless in his criticism of the cruel rationalism and cosmetic morality of Western civilization'; his work is about 'weakness and defeat.'[43]

As I have already suggested, these universalizing claims needn't be read as the only available approach to Coetzee's work, or even as the most authoritative or consecrated one. Much though Coetzee has sought to avoid lending his accredited literary voice to any straightforward anti-apartheid statement, insisting instead on some special autonomy for aesthetics, he has nevertheless clearly benefited from critical and market interest in literary writing coming out of apartheid South Africa, and he has sought to comment in his own ambiguous way on the South African political scene. While varieties of national form such as critical realism or oral modes might be a hindrance to world consecration, as Casanova argues, the author's refracted engagement with his own locality is certainly not, as Coetzee's own success proves.

Moreover, if literature concerned with political violence, postcoloniality, and nation-formation has stable niche positioning within the global market for literary fiction, and if South Africa's 'mainstream internationals' have found considerable success within such a niche, critics working outside of South Africa have nonetheless had to confront what Ian Glenn calls 'local suspicion' and uneasiness about these writers' work when trying to justify their profound interest in 'these particular South African goods.'[44] In discussing Rushdie's career I stressed the way that any notion of an 'autonomous pole' takes on relevance in relation to the heteronomy of local forces. Attention to Coetzee's case reveals the same interrelation, while also clarifying how local demands can be premised upon the author's access to a larger sphere, in this case as 'spokesperson,' 'mainstream international,' or privileged, white, middle class writer.

*

It is Coetzee himself for whom delineating the characteristics of the local and global fields has proven most generative, not least because trapping his readers in a series of unending debates has fostered his career and encouraged his canonization. More important for my purposes, though, is the fact that despite the complexities of the relationships between local markets and global ones, and between politicized critics and poststructuralist ones – Rita Scholtz, David Attwell, and Nadine Gordimer are all part of the South African intelligentsia, after all – Coetzee has perpetuated the idea that he has been subject to a uniquely local form of political scrutiny. In general he has done much to encourage the delineation of two critical publics for his work, understood as espousing distinct and opposed sets of political demands and related aesthetic expectations; these occupy pole positions he tends to name 'ethics' and 'politics.' As early as 1986, in an interview with Dick Penner, he claimed that one of his publics was based in the US, and one in South Africa, the latter 'very heavily influenced by Marxism, by general Third World thinking.'[45] More recently he described this as 'a radical intelligentsia, mainly black' within South Africa, and a white liberal intelligentsia outside it.[46] In interview with David Attwell in 1992 he attributes some of the success of his writing abroad to a metropolitan taste for the exotic, catered to and provoked by the entertainment industry; he speaks of idealism as a 'crime of a sort in South Africa today,' and claims that talk about writers in South Africa leads to claims about what they *'ought* to be writing,' often sliding into polemics.[47] He has also identified with Mario Vargas Llosa's statement that literature is a 'living, systematic, inevitable contradiction of all that exists'; it stands against what Coetzee calls, with much relevance for what follows, 'both the bureaucrat-censor in the hire of the tyranny, and [...] the revolutionary scheming to enroll the writer in the grand army of the revolution.'[48]

Coetzee's postapartheid fiction perfects this long-standing polarizing tendency. *The Master of Petersburg, Disgrace,* and *Elizabeth Costello* all suggest that the scrutiny to which Coetzee has been subject has entailed a demand for specific kinds of political commitment and sincerity. Each posits figural connections between legal structures of judgement and the politicization of the work of writing in South Africa, and critiques the ostensible appropriation of the writer's voice for political purposes. My suggestion is that each can also be read as a defensive commentary on the perceived constraints of South Africa's local cultural climate and the effects of those constraints on Coetzee's career as a whole. By aligning the local demands made upon his writing with a system of judgement, and linking public scrutiny to the restrictive receptive apparatus that puts his own work on trial to assess its worth as either a local or a global product, Coetzee credits what another set of critics have embraced in his work. He figures his own experiences in his fiction in a way that gives one specific segment of his readership the tools with which to read his novels, past and present, in a way that sanctions their own tendency to applaud it (or, perhaps, any other postcolonial literature) as political *to a point,* but as ultimately and rightly critical of the more strident politics of critical realism. Rather than registering the concerns of his critics by altering his narrative strategies, he creates narratives infused with an authorial self-consciousness that at once incorporates, diffuses, or dispels their views. His works are in this way permeated by his involvement in a significant contest over definitions of literature's value, and this struggle has everything to do with South Africa's political history. They are definitively local even as they attempt to lay claim to something else.

Indeed, Coetzee's repeated return to the subject of the position of the writer within South Africa is part of an ongoing effort to undermine a definition of the literary that he wants to discredit as produced within a narrowly national and myopic South African sphere. It is this construct of the politicized local public that the novels I discuss here set out to further codify. While admitting that its modes of thought have contributed to whatever limited self-scrutiny he might claim to engage in, he always deconstructs the possibility of any honest self-scrutiny as well, in a way that tends to justify his own position, albeit ambiguously. Indeed the insistence on ambiguity is an essential part of Coetzee's brand of self-justification. In Elizabeth Costello's case, for example, insisting on a necessary space of ambiguity and ethical indecision becomes something that only a more distanced global sphere can accommodate. In contrast to the political pole as Coetzee constructs it, the ethical pole, which he maps onto non-localized literary production, can actually make room for what is opposed to it. As someone who occupies it, Coetzee willingly recognizes the ambiguity of the pull between ethics and politics, and constantly questions the very relevance and legitimacy of the individual introspection and self-critique he is, on the surface, engaged in. Ultimately, attaining the ethical pole is actually about the denial of the will to decide between ethics and politics; in contrast, in Coetzee's terms, the political position has no room for anything but itself.

*

The Master of Petersburg imagines Fyodor Dostoevsky as a beleaguered author caught in a series of conflicts: one with Russia's bureaucratic police state, one with a leader of its revolutionary opposition, and another with his own authorial self.[49] As someone devoted to aesthetics in a time of political turmoil, he is plagued by his conscience, but in a way that is compounded by a further self-conscious inability to trust his own feelings of guilt. It is set in the eponymous Russian city in late 1869 and depicts the infamous real-life Nechaev episode, in which the People's Vengeance, a powerful faction within a wider revolutionary movement sweeping Russia, murdered one of their own. Dostoevsky heard about the episode while exiled in Dresden and, troubled by it, incorporated a veiled version of it into *The Devils* (1871–2). Coetzee's book makes the event more personal to the Russian novelist by turning the murdered student into his own stepson, Pavel, who in reality survived his father. Dostoevsky returns to Petersburg to solve the mystery of Pavel's death. After initial investigation he discovers that his stepson was connected with Nechaev, the nihilist-anarchist leader of the group and the mastermind behind its design to overthrow the state. Pavel's possessions, held for the majority of the novel by a police investigator called Maximov, include a list of people the People's Vengeance has plans to assassinate.

These possessions also include a story the boy wrote, but never published. It is a thinly disguised depiction of the current political situation and involves the Russian people dramatically overthrowing the country's landowning class, precisely the kind of committed fiction Coetzee perceives his critics to have demanded from him. In part, Fyodor objects to this unpublished, privately owned story being used as evidence against his son, because he sees such a fiction as existing in the realm of abstraction, as a private utterance unfit to circulate in the public domain. He asks, 'Do you really intend to construe this as evidence against my son – a story, a fantasy, written in the privacy of his room?' (42). More centrally, though, he is reluctant to admit that even published work, no matter how ostensibly political, can be used as evidence of a person's actual thoughts or beliefs, or in a legal context as proof in the passing of any kind of judgement. Instead literary expression is the manifestation of an imaginative life that cannot be definitively linked to a specific subjectivity belonging to a punishable individual. Properly understanding it requires inhabiting all perspectives at once: 'reading is being the arm and being the axe *and* being the skull; reading is giving yourself up, not holding yourself at a distance and jeering' (47). To Fyodor all of Pavel's papers should be returned to him, including his letters, his diary, and this story, because they are private in just this sense of being irrelevant to the state's singular political prerogative. He negotiates with Maximov to achieve this end.

Fyodor's belief in the inaccessibility of the truth of any subjectivity is wedded to the problem of the nature of confession. In *The Devils*, in a chapter expunged from some editions of the book, a man called Stavrogin visits the monk Tikhon and confesses to having committed an unspecified crime. Tikhon then questions Stavrogin's motives for confessing, which leads him to attempt to confess his real motives for his initial act of confession, and so on. Before writing *The Master of Petersburg*, Coetzee outlined some of its major concerns in his own scholarly work on Dostoevsky's novel. He argues that, due to the nature of human consciousness, 'the self cannot tell the truth of itself to itself and come to rest without the possibility of self-deception. True confession does not come from the sterile monologue of the self or from the dialogue of the self with its own self-doubt, but [...] from faith and grace.' He refers specifically to the Tikhon episode as a 'skeptical interrogation of the confessional impulse.'[50]

In *The Master of Petersburg*, whose last chapter is also titled 'Stavrogin,' those convinced of the honesty of their own expressions of political commitment certainly face a similar Dostoevskian skepticism. For example, Fyodor understands Nechaev's role in political life in a way that strips the young revolutionary of any claims to self-awareness. In his own younger years Dostoevsky was attracted to socialism and Fourierism, but he was shaken by experiencing four years in a Siberian labour camp, after which he claimed that the ideal of freedom from political tyranny had little relevance to the Russian peasants he lived with there. It was partly as a result of this disillusionment that Dostoevsky wrote *The Devils*, thereby expressing his sense that an 'evil spirit' was 'taking over the minds of a rising generation of half-educated Russian youth.'[51] In a similar way, Fyodor repeatedly denies that the realm of politics is anything other than one particular manifestation of metaphysics, in which a universal 'evil spirit' manifests itself in Nechaev. In this way Nechaev is refused the political will and initiative he so ardently claims to possess.

Coetzee delineates Fyodor's tendency to make the political somehow supernatural and metaphysical in direct opposition to Maximov's search for concrete meaning in Pavel's story. Maximov admits to being 'dull and earthbound' (47), and claims it is no help to Russia to go around talking about privacy and fiction, or discussing ideas 'as if [they] had arms and legs' (44). Insisting on the impossibility of ever accessing the sincere political beliefs of any subject does not help the state convict those they perceive as criminals. In this way Maximov, the novel's representative of state power, is depicted as sharing a language with Nechaev himself, his ostensible archenemy. In fact interspersed with his repeated visits to Maximov are Fyodor's conversations with Nechaev's people, part of an effort to attach meaning to Pavel's death by discovering its real cause. Katri, a member of the People's Vengeance, thinks the police killed Pavel, but Fyodor comes to suspect it was Nechaev, thus establishing a structural connection between the authorities and their opposition, both groups being obviously willing to commit murder to support their political goal of 'helping Russia.' More important, in exchange for answers to his queries about Pavel, Nechaev wants Fyodor to write in support of his movement, to denounce what happened to his own son and 'tell the truth' through the underground media, since what Nechaev calls 'our shameful Russian press' will never tell it (103). Like Maximov, Nechaev has no patience for 'clever talk,' and claims it is something he plans to get rid of when he attains the power he seeks (104). Fyodor's task would be to write and attach his name to what is likely to be a falsified account of what happened to Pavel, to be printed with a small illegal hand press. He is challenged in the most political terms: 'Isn't it time you tried to *share* the existence of the oppressed instead of sitting at home and writing about them and counting your money?' (186).

Nechaev wants to use the statement as a catalyst for change, as an authorization of the position of the radical element, but to write it Fyodor is certain he would have to abandon every principle he holds as an author. Like Maximov, Nechaev insists on simplicity, on everything worth saying being reduced to a page, asking, 'why should some people sit around in luxury reading books when other people can't read at all?' (199). 'History is made in the streets,' he says, 'And don't tell me I am talking *thoughts* right now. That is just another clever debating trick' (200). Nechaev's most cherished divide is the one between talk and action, and intellectuals are merely people who have learned to think so much that they can no longer act (199). In fact he hardly cares who Fyodor is, really, claiming, 'A crowd isn't interested in fine points of authorship' (200). Yet as a man seeking political power he is obviously willing to deploy the aura of Fyodor's authorial persona when its specific cultural capital will serve his purpose. What he wants is the recognizable power of Fyodor's writing; he wants the product of a skilled author, a speech act in the strongest sense. Perhaps paranoid, Fyodor begins to see Pavel's death itself as part of a plot, imagining that all along Nechaev's goal was to corner him and appropriate his voice as an author to use in support of his revolutionary cause (203).

Nechaev's distrust of those who can turn the language of action into just another language, another way of articulating 'thoughts,' is the same distrust proponents of critical realism have directed at Coetzee's use of poststructuralist methods to depict South African political quandaries. This is one part of the self-implication involved in Coetzee's construction of Fyodor. Another is that just as he imagines Nechaev was willing to murder to appropriate the voice of a famous author, Fyodor begins to feel he sells his own life and the lives of those around him for a profit. He recognizes and admits that he is involved in an economy that requires him to seek profit in stories of people's trauma. However he is also at pains to maintain the crucial distinction between his own activities and those of Nechaev and Maximov. Just as Maximov uses Pavel's story as proof he was guilty of conspiring against the government, Nechaev wants to use Fyodor's narrative powers to convince the public that the People's Vengeance should run the county, thus heralding a coup. Both rely on a literature of simplicity, one that speaks an everyday language and purports to tell a truth about the society with which it is concerned. Again, Coetzee links Nechaev with the voice of the very authorities he wants to overthrow. Fyodor, in opposition, sees his writing as the only imaginable purpose of his 'life inside Russia, or with Russia inside me, and whatever Russia means.' He subjects himself to self-scrutiny for precisely that reason. Life, he tells his landlady and lover, is 'a price or a currency [...] something I pay with in order to write' (221–2).

The result is hardly a positive one; to him it seems 'A life without honour; treachery without limit; confession without end' (222). Any accessible 'real' experience is not something that his work expresses or manifests. Instead the opposite is true, since the process of writing subsumes and in a sense forever obscures the subjectivity that acts to produce the work, so that writing only produces an endless deferral of a mode of expression that could access the truth: hence, 'confession without end.' Writing becomes in essence a process of withholding information about the self through apparent confessional revelation. Such a necessary deferral means that the author's own subjectivity is the inevitable and imperfect subject of all of his writing. This is no source of pride for Fyodor, but rather encouragement for his ongoing, irresolvable scrutiny of the sincerity of his own intentions as an author.

*

In writing about Dostoevsky's work Coetzee claims that its themes are self-delusion and the inadequacy of models of public discourse that believe in sincerity of expression. Fyodor believes that the latter can only arise 'from faith and grace,' neither of which can be found in 1860s Russia, or in Coetzee's South Africa, which are instead places of *disgrace*, best met with a critical skepticism.

Disgrace has proven to be a galvanizing piece of literature.[52] It was a major market success, it earned Coetzee his second Booker Prize and the Commonwealth Writers Prize, and its critical reception was nothing short of frenzied. Its objectives are as vast as this reception suggests. While offering a veritable 'state of the nation' address about postapartheid South Africa, it raises deliberately provocative questions about continued racial strife, the ongoing prevalence of violent crime, and the nature of the reconciliation process meant to usher in a healed nation. Protagonist David Lurie is an old-world, obsolete holdover in the postapartheid nation. He teaches romantic literature, is writing an opera about Byron, and lives in Cape Town and Grahamstown, areas comprising the old British Cape Colony. His Cape Town University College has become Cape Technical University, in a rationalization process not unlike what was taking place at Coetzee's own university in the latter half of the 1990s,[53] and he teaches communications now instead of English. When he attends a rehearsal for the play his student lover is acting in, it seems to him the worst of art after apartheid. It is the product of a nation reborn, its only concern a forced catharsis through which all the old prejudices are brought into the open and 'washed away in gales of laughter' (23). If *Disgrace* belongs to this same general field of postapartheid writing, it stubbornly defies any similar cathartic pull with a narrative of abysmal doubts about how new the current South Africa situation actually is.

Though a number of early reviews called *Disgrace* Coetzee's most straightforward work, critics soon noted that its surface realism is deceptive, and that Lurie's story broadly allegorizes the Truth and Reconciliation Commission (TRC) and its role in postapartheid nation-building. Established after the election of the African National Congress, with the passing of the Promotion of National Unity and Reconciliation Act in 1995, the TRC entailed the granting of general amnesty to human rights abusers who agreed to the 'full disclosure' or confession of their crimes. People seeking amnesty had to admit their guilt in a formal setting, and they also had to prepare themselves for invasive attention from the media and wider public, which was often the greater challenge.[54]

The first half of *Disgrace* tells of Lurie's brief affair with a young student. She is less than fully willing to engage with him sexually and eventually files a formal complaint, and he is brought before a university committee designated to make recommendations about how he might best be 'punished' for his behaviour. Facing his colleagues, he is willing to admit to the affair but refuses to express the contrition in which his auditors seem much more interested. Through this initial narrative the novel evokes several specific aspects of what the TRC was designed to do, and of how its results were dramatized for the public. Though victims of apartheid violence might benefit from receiving a contrite apology, soliciting actual personal remorse could never be designated an official part of the commission's work, given that, as Sue Kossew points out, 'it was deemed too difficult to measure its sincerity.'⁵⁵ That said, as the TRC process involved both the formal commission and the mediated public dissemination of its procedures, those engaged in any confession were viewed most favourably when they were publicly and visibly contrite about what they were admitting to. Lurie's case becomes publicized through the media as a 'scandal,' much like what happened to those who agreed to confess publicly for the TRC and make themselves available to media scrutiny in order to receive official pardon. Like Fyodor, what seems to offend Lurie most is this annihilation of his private life by public derision, and he explains to his daughter that private life is what the public craves: 'Prurience is respectable, prurience and sentiment. They wanted a spectacle: breast-beating, remorse, tears if possible' (66). His reference to crying in public evokes televised images of apartheid's stalwarts in tears, as they sought to attain some amnesty through their confessions in pursuit of a kind of secular grace.

In crediting the terminology of 'reconciliation' the TRC relied on general acceptance of what Richard A. Wilson calls a 'religious-redemptive vision' that 'stressed public confession by victims'; it 'created meaning for suffering through a narrative of sacrifice for liberation [that] encouraged the forsaking of revenge.'⁵⁶ Like the group of colleagues that Lurie faces, the TRC was not a legal body but rather a 'forum.' Through it people were invited to speak about their experiences, not with an end to some official judgement or punishment, but precisely in order to avoid such sentencing. Rebuilding a newly democratic South Africa relied on appeals to such redemption and social reconciliation. It also required a notable structural dependence on religious institutions; many TRC events were held in churches, which became 'a fountainhead of symbolism' and the social-institutional infrastructure through which people told their stories.⁵⁷

Disgrace is run through with the same religious overtones: the book's title suggests as much, and after Lurie admits his guilt, but refuses to repent, he is exiled to a kind of limbo on his daughter Lucy's farm. In general Lurie's denunciation of his own tribunal's demands shares something with charges that the success of the TRC was too much premised on the religious connotations of its confessional approach, entailing a troubling conflation of the spheres of religion and the law, of 'catharsis with contrition.'[58] Lurie says: 'I pleaded guilty, a secular plea. That plea should suffice. [...] Repentance belongs to another world, to another universe of discourse' (58). He refuses the spectacle of public sincerity on the grounds that he will not express a contrition he does not feel. He will admit to his wrongdoing but will not repent, and he is not prepared, as a colleague suggests, to 'acknowledge [his] fault in a public manner' (58).

Thus, in constructing Lurie's case so that it shares this figural terrain with the TRC, Coetzee evokes the demands for sincerity in public expression of guilt or regret that were often lamented as missing from the formal TRC process, but which remained relevant to its mediated public versions. By suggesting that personal guilt is after all not a matter of public spectacle but of inner knowledge, if even that, and that the statement of it is somehow insincere to begin with in that it asks that someone retrospectively regret past actions, *Disgrace* questions the faith the overall TRC process ostensibly had in the sincerity of its participants. In addition, in a way completely in line with Dostoevsky's purported 'skeptical interrogation of the confessional impulse,' the novel also evokes more general questions about the status of public or publicized truth. The terms of Lurie's opposition to his tribunal's demands align him with Fyodor in this way, and overlap with what I cited earlier as Coetzee's support for Dostoevsky's consistent challenge to the truth value of confession. Recall Coetzee's words on this subject: 'the self cannot tell the truth of itself to itself and come to rest without the possibility of self-deception. True confession does not come from the sterile monologue of the self or from the dialogue of the self with its self-doubt, but...from faith and grace.'[59]

So, while Lurie's experiences broadly allegorize the TRC's procedures, such that he might be read as a stand-in for some general guilty subject constructed and then absolved through a prevalent discourse of reconciliation, my own sense is that he is also a figure designed to continue Coetzee's combative attention to forms of scrutiny quite specifically related to his own career. The novel's engagement with the TRC is imbricated with Coetzee's ongoing authorial self-construction, as what is elaborated in *The Master of Petersburg* is carried over into a work that takes up a disparate set of contexts but in surprisingly similar terms. Lurie's audience, which includes his peers on the university committee tasked with judging him, as well as the larger public that soon gets wind of his case, makes demands akin to the ones Coetzee sees himself as having been subject to, and which he has a notable interest in destabilizing. Namely, the demand for sincerity within the constraints of public confession, as critiqued within the novel, figures what Coetzee thinks he has himself faced from those who consecrate critical realism as the only appropriately political form of response to South Africa's situation. As he has said, support for such realism 'hinges, when you test it, on a naïve criterion of the writer's sincerity,'[60] and taking it as proof of a writer's worth within the literary sphere requires the assumption that its deployment expresses his own deeply held, entirely sincere political commitments. Otherwise it is an easy enough ruse, an effort to achieve consecration by appealing to some political viability.

The second part of *Disgrace* takes place mostly at Lucy's farm, and it is there that a second major political issue emerges: that of black land reclamation, and the 'one settler, one bullet' ideology that pervades the thinking of some opponents to the continued settler presence of Afrikaners after the demise of official apartheid. It is on the farm that Lucy and her father are subject to a horrific attack by three black men, and Lucy is raped and becomes pregnant. The attack is depicted as part of a larger spate of crimes against whites that the authorities are unwilling or unable to prevent. The rape echoes Lurie's own abuse of Melanie and is in general not unrelated to the novel's earlier concern with some of the limitations of the TRC. Indeed the book's two parts are carefully though ambiguously intertwined. Grant Farred has unequivocally criticized what he sees as the accommodationist tendencies of the ANC as the country's dominant black political party, writing that 'By adopting a policy of national reconciliation, the ANC [African National Congress] implicitly requires that its black citizenry forget [...] or only selectively recall instances of the apartheid state's repression and exploitation.' He criticizes the TRC in similar terms, stating that it does nothing to remedy what is to his mind the biggest continuing problem the country faces: 'the real hegemony, white property'.[61] Farred himself uses a religious language, akin to the one that Coetzee associates with contemporary South African politics throughout *Disgrace*, to critique white 'self-assurance' and confidence. As a guarantee of sincerity, or an assurance that things have really changed, Farred wants white South Africans to accept their 'culpability [...] a condition containing the possibility of reparation to that nation's black citizenry.'[62]

Farred is in good company. Many have noted that the TRC process did little to rectify 'an uncomfortable legacy of seemingly apolitical crime and vigilantism,' by some accounts the product of 'apartheid's legacy [...] evident in extensive poverty, educational deprivation, and a warped criminal justice system.'[63] The feeling of fear that generally exists around Lucy's farm is a product of these conditions; the new nation continues to be rife with criminality and violence, and people like Lucy are afraid to point to blacks as participants in wrongdoing. In contrasting the experiences of Lucy and her father, all involving male violence against women, the novel constructs a South African politics that is premised upon a series of reversals: the crimes of David Lurie, a white man raised in an old country, are fodder for public spectacle, while the crimes of black youth are carefully hidden by the victim herself. The opposite would have once been the case, as Lucy claims: 'what happened to me is a purely private matter. In another time, in another place it might be held to be a public matter. But in this place, at this time, it is not. It is my business, mine alone' (112).

Lucy's response to this situation is to adhere to a necessary and warranted self-abasement or 'disgrace' in the promotion of emotional and psychological reconciliation. Her decision to abandon her land and marry into the family of her black neighbour and former employee is the ultimate expression of this necessary sacrifice. In contrast, Lurie relates crime against whites to issues of ownership and the risk associated with having possessions, using the phrase 'war reparations' (176) to define what happens on Lucy's farm and during the eventual pillaging of his own house. 'Not human evil,' he thinks, 'just a vast circulatory system, to whose workings pity and terror are irrelevant' (98). Lucy's approach to recovering from the attack is to take it on as a necessary burden, a sacrifice made for crimes committed by her own race in turn, and as the price she has to pay for refusing to leave her farm. A more public language of material recompense becomes central to Lucy's understanding of her private trauma. In contrast, while her father is aware of the kind of history that might justify thinking of Lucy's victimization as a material necessity, his understanding of this kind of logic is nonetheless an ironic and often contemptuous one. Lucy's body and her property are items in 'a vast circulatory system.' 'That is how one must see life in the country: in its schematic aspect,' he tells himself, 'Cars, shoes, women too. There must be some niche in the system for women and what happens to them' (98). The robbery that takes place at his own house is similarly understood as 'another incident in the great campaign of redistribution' (176).

This instrumentalist understanding of the motivation for crime, or indeed for human behaviour in general, is subject to criticism in a number of ways within the novel as a whole. For example, it is a mode of analysis implicated in the general narrative of economic rationalization that is changing the structure of Lurie's university, turning Lurie's sexual abuse case into a media spectacle, and making the public sphere a place for what Attwell calls 'an exercise in Foucauldian power intent on destroying the concept of a private life.'[64] Still, when Lurie himself relays the tenets of this way of thinking with significant irony, he does so only within the confines of the narrative's *style indirect libre*, which ensures that he is both a focalizing perspective and himself implicitly ironized by the distance between author and narrator.

That is, in the first part of the book the reader is left with some room to wonder if we are meant to admire Lurie's refusal to perform for the public in the desired way, and his denial of the judicial-religious language of his own hearing process, or if we are instead meant to banish him to the hell he has entered because he will not participate in the requisite staging of some sentimentalized contrition. This ambiguity carefully mirrors Coetzee's own seemingly polarized critical reception, so that it can be said that he uses Lurie not to implicate himself in something untoward, but to register an impasse between those who appreciate the discursive questions he tends to ask (as posed, for example, to the TRC's judicial-religious language), and those who might, for example, wish him willing to participate sincerely and openly in the long-awaited construction of a postapartheid national culture. Rather than engaging in some full self-implication, Coetzee shows the extent to which his self-construction might be informed by the debates that have defined his own reception; he performs this admission only while constructing the terms of the same debates in a way that seems designed to coerce the reader into acceptance of his position. In a related way, in the book's second part, and in a mode characteristic of Coetzee's method, skepticism toward an expedient materialist position is articulated through a double movement: first we encounter an ironic portrayal of the position based on material recompense, and then we face a further ironic undermining of that same initial skepticism, as it is associated with Lurie's compromised perspective. In a way that is highly relevant to *Elizabeth Costello*, as I will soon discuss, *Disgrace* ironizes the voice that is itself so prone to political skepticism, thus undermining the potential clarity of expression that might obtain for any political will or perspective. Any claim to a position in relation to the best path for South Africa's future can only be illegitimate, or have the limited legitimacy of Coetzee's classic form of recognition, which is always actually at heart a denial or destabilization.

*

In sum, like *The Master of Petersburg*, *Disgrace* suggests that political revolutions can potentially turn into complex reversals of old inequities:

the religious language of the established church prevails, criminals go unpunished, and one population accepts a 'disgrace' it comes to feel it deserves. This is hardly a fair assessment of contemporary South Africa, and nor does it represent the only possible way of understanding the context of the TRC,[65] but the impetus behind it is clearer when one considers the specificity of Coetzee's desire to respond to aspects of his own milieu. *Disgrace* takes up two major features of the postapartheid South African landscape: the will toward peace and reconciliation codified by the TRC, and the idea that material recompense, if not total economic restructuring, might be a more effective remedy to continued strife within the emerging democracy. The former is presented in a way that challenges its reliance on a faulty assumption of transparency, but the latter is no untroubled alternative. My contention is that these two political interventions are actually also a means through which Coetzee undertakes authorial self-articulation, such that *Disgrace* challenges Coetzee's politicized reception on the basis of its presumed naïve faith in realism's expression of authentic political faith, as well as on the grounds of its commitment to any politics premised on a basic materialist or instrumentalist understanding of human motivation and behaviour.

How are these respective critiques of political sincerity and of the discourse of materiality related? For Coetzee, both are premised on a reductive approach to human desire, whether manifest as faith in a straightforward form of sincere self-understanding and self-expression, or as a politics premised upon animalized needs, desires, and their fulfilment, where there is simply violence and its rebuff, or crime and retribution. This relationship is clarified in *Elizabeth Costello*,[66] which in fact takes up the issue of economic rationalization in a way that lends credibility to Lurie's reluctance to accept his daughter's submission to the notion of material retribution.

It is a book that could not exist if Coetzee did not have the career that he does, since it is an academic novel devoted to the adventures of the eponymous author, as well as a testament to the proliferating possibilities for subsidiary or auxiliary rights for what writers produce, made up largely of previously published pieces that were themselves often originally given as lectures.[67] By their very nature the various chapters already respond to Coetzee's fame, as they were delivered in instances when, by virtue of his status, he was called upon to share his thoughts on topics not always directly related to what he takes to be his task as a writer. As the views she articulates in her talks are recounted through a distanced narrator, at times focalized by her son's perspective and at times by her own, there is no absolute identification between Coetzee and Costello. She is in part a self-reflexive creation that puts ironic distance between Coetzee's own speaking voice or opinions on subjects like 'The Novel Today,' and the fictional utterances of an imagined female novelist and the other people she encounters. Moreover, some of the situations in which Costello expresses her views are debates with other thinkers – her conversations with Emmanuel Egudu in 'The Novel in Africa' chapter, for example – so that Coetzee destabilizes any single perspective in a way completely in line with the challenge that *The Master of Petersburg* and *Disgrace* pose to those who believe in the absolute sincerity of any statement or the value of holding to one unquestionable political position.

Yet that challenge is the substance of the book. It is made in relation to the demands of an audience in general, and specifically the demands of a critical and interested audience who are placed in a position to judge and who demand certain commitments from Costello. In this sense Costello and Coetzee are in fact quite aligned. She is a famous writer and a sought after speaker, and hails from a settler-colonial country, in this case Australia rather than South Africa. More important, the book's overall method, which is one of distanced, skeptical observation of stated perspectives, and of self-conscious avoidance of statements of belief, largely accords with the overall contents of the talks Costello gives and the subsequent discussions she has about them with others. Costello in fact embodies many of the qualities Coetzee sees as essential to literary work. This part of her characterization finds its most thorough articulation in the chapters concerned with 'the lives of animals.'[68]

In a series of talks and debates Costello expresses her views on animal rights. She is herself a vegetarian and opposes the tendency of scholars of animal psychology to sanction the abusive treatment of animals by insisting on the ways they are unlike humans. Yet she does not offer any explicit program for proper behaviour in relation to animals; she merely offers up a series of ideas with no active correlate. 'I have never been much interested in proscriptions,' she says (82). Such is shown to be the only possible conclusion given her interest in and description of Wolfgang Köhler's experiments on apes, which she imagines as an influence on Kafka's 'Report to an Academy,' in which an ape stands upright, fully-clothed, and tells an audience about his transformation from the ways of the ape to those of human beings. She accuses Köhler of propelling apes from 'the purity of speculation (Why do men behave like this?) [...] towards lower, practical, instrumental reason (How does one use this to get that?)' (73). He does this by including in all of his experiments the banana as bait. That is, whatever tendencies the ape might have to some other way of thinking are subsumed by the necessity of simple survival – 'an appetite that needs to be satisfied' (73) – which demands a reasoned, pragmatic approach to problems and their solutions. This compulsion is said also to lead '*away* from ethics and metaphysics towards the humbler reaches of practical reason' (74).

Recall that a common reading of Kafka's 'Report to an Academy' is a postcolonial one, which sees Kafka's story of the process through which an ape assumes human characteristics and addresses a human audience as an articulation of his own minority position in relation to the German-speaking community in Prague, German being the language in which he wrote his major works.[69] This reading can extend to suggest that Kafka, responding to the dominance of empire in the early twentieth century, set out to explore the issue of colonial mimicry in general, in which the subject population emulates the traits of the dominant one in order to receive favour. Regardless, a representative status can certainly be granted to this particular ape, and Coetzee may evoke Kafka to acknowledge a shared complexity of relationship with issues of empire and language, both speaking and writing in a colonizing language but neither being in any straightforward way willing members of the colonizing culture. More importantly, in referring to 'Report to an Academy' Coetzee evokes the ape as author and public speaker, since in the context of the original delivery of 'The Lives of Animals' Coetzee is addressing an audience, speaking about a fictional woman addressing an audience, who in turn speaks about an ape doing the same. Here in a public speech it seems that Costello seeks a representative status for Köhler's ape just as Kafka sought one for his. So while Köhler's ape is subjugated and forced to answer the demands of reality rather than pursue the concerns of metaphysics, she herself is that ape, subjected to her own audience's demand that her talk lead to some specific material prescription. In turn, for Coetzee as the speaker behind Costello, the ape in Köhler's work is also the writer or critic faced with an intolerable material reality and given little choice but to respond.

In this light Coetzee's setup of Costello's address refracts *Disgrace*'s ambiguous presentation of the argument that material redress might best prevent criminality, and might recompense those who suffered apartheid's violence. In both cases, a position that aims at rectifying material differences is necessary, not ideal. Metaphysics and speculative ethics would dominate in ideal conditions, and the ape would not be constantly forced to confront his very real material hunger. In the past Coetzee has been reluctant to suggest that one could choose between ethics and politics, claiming: 'the last thing I want to do is to *defiantly* embrace the ethical as against the political [...]. I neither claim nor fail to claim that there can be a third position.'[70] Here something similar happens, as Costello seems to embrace the metaphysical realm, while that very embrace requires its denial, since to adhere to anything with conviction or certainty is, according to the logic of the text, the opposite of metaphysics. This position of complete refusal of political commitment or even of the very utterance of an assurance of any kind is further articulated, and then complicated again, as it must be to hold weight, in the novel's remaining chapters.

In 'At the Gate' Coetzee imagines Costello passing into the afterlife in a dreamscape that resembles a number of Kafka's parables or allegories. Specifically, he draws from or conflates two pieces: 'Before the Law,' in which the protagonist confronts a gatekeeper figure in a similarly dreamlike place, and an early scene of courtroom interrogation in *The Trial*, in which K faces the judges at the bench for the first time. In a sense, though, the world Costello encounters *is* literature, all too familiar to her and eerily reminiscent of countless scenes in known works. She wonders if it is a writer's specific hell, 'a purgatory of clichés' (206). When Costello arrives at this gate to what appears to be heaven or at least some desirable other world, upon speaking to the guard or 'featureless functionary' there she finds she cannot pass through before preparing a 'statement of belief' (194). Earlier I noted that in defending Rushdie's right to speak in South Africa Coetzee drew parallels between Rushdie's opponents and the Afrikaner church. I also argued that in *Disgrace* he critiques the TRC as a judicial-religious experience disguised as secular politics. Here, for Costello, this critique achieves the status of pastiche, as the writer is forced to utter statements of commitment before gaining access to what appears to be a version of heaven. Initially, in terms redolent of Coetzee's own self-defenses, Costello resists the imperative of belief. 'It is not my profession to believe,' she tells the man at the gate, 'just to write. Not my business. I do imitations, as Aristotle would have said' (194). She is nonetheless forced to reluctantly write and rewrite her statement of belief, and to appear before a bench of judges called 'the board' in order to defend herself.

Through this allegorical structure of trial and self-defense Coetzee admits his own writing is the product of defensiveness, emerging from his desire to articulate a position that will allow him to attain literary sanction without wholesale capitulation to the demands of his critics. The statement Costello pens in fact comments on, or is homologous to, the book as a whole, as a reflection on the very nature of belief, and as an articulation of her final resistance to simple political positions that offer obvious lessons for living or prescriptions on behaviour. She writes, 'I am a writer, a trader in fictions [...]. I maintain beliefs only provisionally: fixed beliefs would stand in my way' (195). She requests exemption, in light of her profession, from the rule that all petitioners should hold at least one belief. Before the board she attempts to explain what a writer is. She begins by calling herself, after Czeslaw Milosz, a 'dictation secretary,' claiming: 'It is not for me to interrogate, to judge what is given me. I merely write down the words and then test them, test their soundness, to make sure I have heard right' (199). This is Costello's 'ideal self,' striving to put aside opinions and prejudices 'while the word which it is her function to conduct passes through her' (200).

The judges subject her to a kind of questioning that mirrors time and again Coetzee's sense of his position as a writer under conditions of apartheid. They have no tolerance for allegory, and respond badly when she tries to deploy that mode to impress them (218). When she is unable to claim that her statements are forms of sincere self-expression – when they ask if she speaks for herself, she answers, 'Yes. No, emphatically no. Yes and no. Both' (221) – they titter and then laugh outright. Facing Costello as an Australian, the judges evoke the Tasmanians, and wonder if she is 'bankrupt of conscience' (204). Doesn't she care about them and their plight? 'Violations of innocent children. The extermination of whole peoples. What does she think about such matters?' (202–3). She thinks to herself that the trial is more about the extermination of the Tasmanians than it is about her position as a writer; it has to do with 'the question of historical guilt' (203). In addition, in discussing her trials with another more experienced petitioner she is told that these statements of belief are known locally as 'confessions' (212), and that her stubbornness is seen as a sign of privilege. Her 'Unbelief – entertaining all possibilities, floating between opposites,' is said to be the mark of a leisured life, whereas most people *must* believe, and must choose (213). She also gives Costello the key that links the world of this text to that of *Disgrace*: she warns her that the point is not real belief, deeply held in the heart of one's self, but its performance, the appearance of belief: 'They may say they demand belief, but in practice they will be satisfied with passion'

(213). 'Show them you feel and they will be satisfied,' she says (214). 'I do not give shows,' is Costello's response. 'I'm not an entertainer.' She will not articulate unopposed beliefs, and connects a willingness to do so to a degraded entertainment that has nothing to do with the inflated literary status she assigns to herself.

Ultimately Costello's fate is undetermined. She is left rambling to the 'functionary' at the gate about 'the special problems of a writer, the special fidelities' (224), because, of course, the writer *believes* in not believing, has faith in being faithless, and has thus particular, situated and important *fidelities* of her own, ones that should allow her at least some version of access to the realm of sanction and beneficence, or some claim to the warm glow of general acceptance. Indeed as the novel ends it is clear that the only form of grace she will ever achieve is her own recognition that ultimately even an adherence to metaphysics or a denial of all certainties implies a level of conviction. She does, after all, believe, but not with conviction, and not in belief.

*

I conclude by summarizing and restating the overall implications of my approach to Coetzee's career and fictions. In the South African case, the local field of literary production develops its demands in relation to the access that some of its participants have to a larger global sphere. The whole world of meaning and value that arises as a product of the workings of this complex system only does so as a result of tension and struggle. The meaning of the global literary marketplace is *made*, such that whatever significance accrues to the various inside-outside, local-global, citizen-consumer polarities does so as a product of an ongoing struggle over the nature and value of literary pursuit and production. The positions one assumes bare the residue of these many conflicts, so that they are only incompletely absolute and polarized at any moment in their articulation. Coetzee's case is dramatic proof. His understanding of the sphere that he associates with speculative ethics is in part informed by, or made resonant because of, his simultaneous positioning within a local South African milieu and a larger global one. In his recent fiction the metaphysical or ethical sphere is mapped onto the global literary field in the same 'complex set of overlays' that he identifies when writing about Gordimer's use of Turgenev's paratextual authorial image.[71] In other words, one of Coetzee's characteristic figural gestures – that is, his embrace (via denial) of the ethical position over the political one, in part by undermining the pressing necessities that require the making of any such decision – derives meaning from the existence and functioning of the material sphere of authorship within a literary marketplace that circulates the products of South Africa's political conflict.

It only seems ironic that in the postapartheid era, when demands for a committed literature have quietened,[72] and when a wide-scale anti-apartheid publishing culture has been subsumed by multinationals like Macmillan and Random House, Coetzee has consistently returned to a reductive binary between a writer's ethics and the political scene. This very return is what constitutes Coetzee's recent work as emerging from a form of authorial anxiety that fosters various self-defensive gestures. If we understand the postapartheid era as one defined by attempts to recuperate and understand the past, so that the prominence of the TRC can be said to be based essentially in the appeal of the question 'Who were you during the decades of apartheid?',[73] it is entirely natural that Coetzee would mount an elaborate, often metaphorical, always refracted defense of those aspects of his work that have been judged worthy of praise. In its own way, each of the novels I have discussed attempts to answer the 'Who were you?' question Shuan Irlam claims as the new South African obsession. Or, more correctly, and in deference to the paratexts that define authorship, they answer, 'Who were you perceived to be, and why aren't those perceptions authoritative?'

Costello's confrontation with the board, those given the task of judging her worth before allowing her to achieve a kind of grace, is just this kind of answer. It is a defense of Coetzee's own commitment to a refusal of the constraints of political allegiance, and ultimately a validation of the concerns of that part of his audience – often aligned with an Anglo-American or global marketplace – less worried about the local necessities of South African political realities. Through it Coetzee clearly displays his awareness of the arguments of those who have pitted themselves against him, all the while seeking to validate the views of those who sanctioned his career to begin with. In this sense, what is staged as a more universal and speculative consideration of the autonomy of the artist, is just as much a pointed critique of the literary politics that constrain Coetzee's reception as an author of narratives vaguely connected to his South African background.

Again, justifying something ostensibly universal is a profoundly local and particular activity, and *Elizabeth Costello* carries on a process of self-justification initiated in Coetzee's earlier novels. Its fascination with the concept of grace is clear in Coetzee's earlier ruminations on Dostoevsky's career, in which the Russian novelist is recuperated as an author who questioned the legitimacy of all statements of sincere politics as manifestations of a naïve belief in a state of 'faith and grace' patently non-existent in the actual world. Then, in *Disgrace*, post-apartheid South Africa is said to require a similar investment in the reality of human sincerity and self-awareness, and to demand its citizens be subject to a public gaze possessed by faith in confession, guilt, and reconciliation. In general, within each of these works the expression of local concerns is consistently challenged as supremely ill-conceived, as insufficiently knowing, and as reliant on the very systems of judgement and perception critics might claim to want to challenge. Thus Maximov is linked to Nechaev, both demanding a kind of critical realism that Fyodor cannot abide, and both subjecting him to intense scrutiny and judging him lacking in the requisite commitment to political realities. Thus in *Disgrace* the TRC as an expression of the politics of the new South Africa is compared to the judicial-religious discourse inherited from the old regime, applied through different means but with equal vigour; that discourse insists that people be available for forms of public scrutiny that entail an adherence to unreasonable standards of private belief, which is in any case, again, something ultimately inaccessible to the public's gaze. Thus the grace that Elizabeth Costello pursues is ultimately a state in which the dictates of material reality can be ignored, where ethical rumination is possible and does not involve the neglect of a history of necessities and the demands of economic rationality.

These conditions are precisely those that do not exist within the discursive field, in part formed by a specific cultural marketplace, that Coetzee's fiction registers as true to the author's experience. Costello's desired state accords much more with the characteristics attributable to some unopposed global literary field, such as the one that the Nobel Prize judges imagined in distinguishing Coetzee's own work. Within it, the exploration of political materials does not require strict adherence to specific positions expressed through realistic literary modes. It does not require the patina of political commitment, but rather allows for an exploration of the limitations of precisely such demands and of the modes of consciousness that let them take hold. For Coetzee, what prevents this state of grace from emerging is that set of local concerns that seem to require that the literary work return to earth and answer the major political questions that it raises *en route* to selling itself to the global market for English-language literature.

5
Zulfikar Ghose and Cosmopolitan Authentication

'The Portuguese when they discovered Brazil thought it was India. They had simply lost their way, as I may have mine.'[1]

'What is so human about novelists is that they never give up hoping that their next book will make them very rich.'[2]

Attention to Zulfikar Ghose routinely involves commentary on his refusal to make the focus of his writing any locale that can be readily identified with his own authentic or authenticating background as a person from South Asia. He has not avoided South Asian settings entirely. *The Murder of Aziz Khan* (1967) is a plainly realist novel set in Pakistan, and Ghose's early poetry and his autobiographical *Confessions of a Native-Alien* (1965) notably deal with his early life in South Asia and the perils of incorporation into a new culture. In this sense Feroza Jussawalla and Reed Way Dasenbrock's claim that Ghose has entirely ignored the experience of exile or immigration is not quite true,[3] and nor is it the case that his early work refuses to idealize the land of his birth. In fact *Confessions of a Native-Alien* offers South Asian material in a way that accommodates Western readers, teaching them about the geography and culture of both Sailkot and Bombay. It also approaches childhood with considerable nostalgia, though this is filtered through some wariness about the violence associated with claims to a secure national identity, perhaps inevitable given his material is British India in the 1940s. It was with the 1970s Incredible Brazilian trilogy (hereafter the Brazilian trilogy), made up of *The Native* (1972), *The Beautiful Empire* (1975), and *A Different World* (1978), that Ghose significantly left South Asian topics behind. In fact he shifted his fictional attention to South America, writing novels that fall into the broad category of magic realism, making him literary fiction's only Pakistani-Anglo-American author working with South America's most noted literary genre.

Very little critical work concerning Ghose has ever been undertaken, and he has been especially neglected since the early 1990s. Indeed *The Triple Mirror of the Self* (1992) marks something of a turning point in his career, after which he moved completely out of the literary mainstream and into a smaller regional community of South Asian writers and publishers, taking up a position beneath the radar of any sustained critical attention. *Veronica and the Góngora Passion* (1998) was released by TSAR Publications, a Toronto-based company that publishes *Exile* magazine and the *Toronto Review of Contemporary Writing Abroad* (formerly the *Toronto South Asian Review*), both of which have also carried Ghose's stories and essays. Part of his move into this smaller regional market has to do with the fact that *The Triple Mirror of the Self* only sold a few hundred copies and was, as Ghose has said, 'a huge commercial loss for the publisher [Bloomsbury].'[4] In fact the manuscript was turned down by close to 20 American publishers, 'one editor making the remarkable statement that it was too good to be published.'[5] Since 1992 Ghose has written two more novels that both have what he calls 'a South Asian background,' neither of which has found a publisher. These manuscripts do not treat South Asian material in any straightforward fashion, though. In Ghose's words, *Rajistan, Texas* 'is set in Houston which in the novel appears to have become inhabited entirely by Indians'; the other work is 'set at a date a few hundred years in the future when much of the planet is under water, only two major countries are left, India and Brazil.'[6] In any case, these works have naturally not been attractive prospects for major multinational firms with quick access to information about authors' past sales.

Throughout this book I have argued that a prominent aspect of the marketing of contemporary literary fiction is the situating of postcolonial authors and their works within clearly differentiated political locales, and that what Timothy Brennan calls the 'banners' of geographical affiliation are always in sight in journalistic and critical treatments of postcolonial writers. For Salman Rushdie, Derek Walcott, and J.M. Coetzee, some coincidence between their biographical regional origins and their literary material has been an important aspect of their career development and reception. They may have benefited from this coincidence in broad terms, but they have also faced specific challenges based on it, and have responded to those challenges in their works in turn. An interesting test, then, for an exploration of the effects of the requirement of some geographical authentication is the career of someone like Zulfikar Ghose, whose works tend to undermine, or at least confuse, all reference to securely bounded regional origins. The purpose of this chapter is to consider the fictional configurations of reading and authorship that are of service to a writer who critiques the dominant postcolonial field from a marginal position, rather than simply negotiating a more comfortable ascendance within an always politicized mainstream.

My focus is *The Triple Mirror of the Self*, which is in three parts.[7] The first is made up of the narrative of a man named Urim, who has taken up residence in a village called Suxavat, a place familiar to readers of Ghose's work who are accustomed to his South American settings. Urim tells the tale of Suxavat and its destruction at the hands of an Interior Ministry in pursuit of gold. He is one of the few survivors. In the novel's second part, the set of notebooks in which Urim records his tale – the Urim manuscript – passes into the hands of Jonathan Pons, an American academic who is featured in Urim's story, but who insists he was never with Urim in South America and that his presence in Urim's narrative is entirely fictional. Pons' research into the 'origins' of the manuscript, facilitated by a grant designed to aid in the completion of a work left unfinished by the 'death of its author' (119), moves us backwards in time, in pursuit of Urim's past. Pons eventually finds that before travelling to South America Urim lived a life in exile. He was an American poet and academic he calls Zinalco Shimomura, after a stint as an immigrant to England, during which time he fell in with a bohemian crowd where he was known as Shimmers. And, before arriving in England, Pons claims, Urim was Roshan Karim, a boy growing up as a Punjabi Muslim in British India during the period just before independence. Roshan's story makes up the novel's third part.

The overall narrative is further complicated by questions about how the Urim manuscript fell into the hands of the 'the renowned master of Latin American realism,' Valentin Sadaba, who then gives it to Pons (101). We are also left to wonder why Urim wrote Pons into his narrative, how much Pons' editorial prerogative controls what we learn about the narrator of the Urim manuscript, and whether or not the entire last section of the novel, detailing Roshan's (Urim's) early life in South Asia, was penned by Pons himself. Presumably assembled by Pons after careful research and editing, the contingent texts that make up the novel's three parts rather carefully map Zulfikar Ghose's own personal journey, moving from India to England to the

US. They also map his fictional tendencies, present in the Urim manuscript's South American setting and its depiction of the geopolitical violence, encouraged by capitalist accumulation, which leads to Suxavat's destruction.

With the background of Ghose's career in mind, and with particular reference to the extensive critical commentary on his refusal of an easy political categorization or originary national affiliation, *The Triple Mirror of the Self* reads as a thorough theorization of two interconnecting aspects of postcolonial authorship: first, the way biographical authenticity and specificity determine modes of reception of postcolonial literary texts; and second, the attendant constraints on the way those texts circulate in Anglo-American markets in general. Ghose's theorization of the place of postcolonial literature in the current marketplace is of course entirely interested. In fact he depicts the relationship between postcolonial textual production and Anglo-American reception in a way that emphasizes or even explains how the parameters of that relationship exclude his own works. In turn he goes to considerable lengths to distance himself from the cosmopolitan function of postcolonial literature, as sanctioned by the Anglo-American market, and uses his novel to stage his rejection of the role of Third World writer and the expectation that he will act as an interpreter of an authenticated location. *The Triple Mirror of the Self* shows how the political liberalism that, in Brennan's words, 'openly and consciously seeks to throw off what it considers to be the clichés of the postwar rhetoric of third-world embattlement,'[8] can relate to an emphasis on biographical authenticity. That is, while critiquing the kind of authenticating geographical specificity that might sanction his career, Ghose also links the power of that specific form of authentication to a larger literary sphere in which a cosmopolitan audience is said to look upon political struggles through a surface tokenism that masks considerable detachment, operating as though, in Ghose's words, 'the only thing that mattered was some sociological connection in a simple prose that could be consumed by the buying public eager to have its trite preconceptions affirmed.'[9]

Specifically, through his characterization of Jonathan Pons and his relationship to the Urim manuscript, Ghose makes the attachment of significant value to a brand of biographical authenticity a prerequisite for Anglo-American cosmopolitanism. As a cosmopolitan intellectual, Pons is depicted as more committed to the politics of postcolonial identities than to concern about the geopolitical violence of late capitalism, as his major interest in the Urim manuscript is a systematic tracing of the origins of its author. The process of tracing those origins entirely ignores the manuscript's critique of the value attached to authenticity, its positing of a link between authenticity and real geopolitical violence, and its overall concern with the incursion of late capitalism into South America's geopolitical landscape. To clarify further, I think *The Triple Mirror of the Self* theorizes an Anglo-American market for postcolonial writing in at least two ways. First, the novel significantly explores the search for origins as a process figuratively connected to real political violence, since within the novel both texts and individuals are incorporated into national authorizing or authenticating narratives only through violent circumstances. Second, in exploring the fate of a manuscript of unknown origins as it circulates across continents – a manuscript which takes the realities of political violence as its subject – the novel critiques the process through which academic readers and literary critics, figured through Jonathan Pons, use the political as a form of cultural capital, while assuming that the most important thing about a narrative is the specific way it connects to a writer's origins.

*

In *Structures of Negation*, the only book-length study of Ghose's work, Chelva Kanaganayakam applauds him for being brave enough 'to forsake what could have been a comfortable niche among post-colonial writers.'[10] In a review of *The Triple Mirror of the Self*, Dasenbrock calls Ghose 'one of the most unusual writers in English today,' and explicitly relates his oddity to the fact that 'the setting of his fiction over the past twenty years has been none of the places where he has resided, but rather South America.'[11] Introducing the 1989 issue of *Review of Contemporary Fiction* that featured Milan Kundera and Ghose, Jussawalla and Dasenbrock emphasize his outsider status even more, claiming he 'evades most of our accepted ways of talking about and grouping contemporary literature,' while his work has 'steadily moved away from typical concerns and themes of contemporary South Asian writing in English or of Commonwealth writing in general.'[12] They note the haphazard placement of Ghose's works on library shelves – they appear with South Asian literature in English, English literature, American literature, and even adolescent or popular fiction – as evidence of his evasion of standard categories, and as a sure sign that the relevant literary institutions cannot effectively decide into which niche such a writer should be placed.

Granted, some of Ghose's difficulties in establishing a successful career are arguably the product of fictional tendencies too obscure or experimental for the mainstream market. His early novel *Crump's Terms* (1975) was finished in 1968 but unpublished for eight years, rejected by his usual publisher Macmillan and a number of others. However, Macmillan recognized the commercial potential of the Brazilian trilogy and agreed to take *Crump's Terms* with that, in the hopes that the success of the trilogy would encourage an interest in the earlier novel. *Crump's Terms* is far from mainstream reading, nor is *Hulme's Investigations into the Bogart Script* (1981), which met a similar fate before finally being accepted by Curbstone, a small Texas press.[13] Ghose has never been exclusively represented by one publisher. In recent years, after the more popular success of the Brazilian trilogy, and the publication of a number of other South American novels, first in England by Macmillan or Bloomsbury, and then in New York by Overlook Press, Harper & Row, and Viking, amongst others, his recent collection of short stories, *Veronica and the Góngora Passion* (1998), was released in Canada by TSAR Publications, as mentioned above. So Ghose, when writing less experimental or obscure prose, has not had trouble finding a number of publishers and at least a modest international audience interested in his work. In fact, as Dasenbrock claims, the usual South American setting of his works has been an attraction to some readers. His books have been put out by some major publishers and translated into many languages, including French, Dutch, and Portuguese, and marketers have often drawn attention to his chosen fictional landscapes with book covers emphasizing the exotic appeal of the Amazon or the intrigue of South American political violence.

Still, he has never won a literary award, and, as Kanaganayakam notes, as an author he 'continues to remain relatively unknown in academic circles, hardly discussed in literary journals, and only tenuously linked to Commonwealth, British, and American writing.'[14] There has been little effort, in other words, to incorporate Ghose's work into a canon of literature relevant to postcolonial scholarship, and it is his lack of attention to South Asian themes that is the recurring concern of the few literary academics and journalists who have paid attention to his work. It is not his occasional obscurity but rather his South American settings that have, as Dasenbrock argues, 'played a part in that fiction's not receiving the degree of serious attention it deserves.'[15] In interview Dasenbrock and Jussawalla thus suggest to Ghose that in terms of the 'degree of awareness' of his work he has suffered from 'the law that everything should fit a nice, neat national category.' Ghose responds: 'my books don't sell, and I receive very little serious critical attention. It is very rare for a reviewer to remark upon the quality of my prose or to reveal a comprehension of the imaginative structure of my work.'[16]

The few existing attempts to incorporate Ghose into the postcolonial canon have also been markedly constrained by the need to respond to the question of Ghose's refusal of his authenticating South Asian origins. One approach to recuperating Ghose's work for literary study is the insistence that though it may seem otherwise, in fact his books do draw heavily on personal experience. Kanaganayakam claims, for example, that Ghose's background is not absent from his fiction, and that in fact his work is in search of 'a new poetics for the literature of the native-alien experience.'[17] It is, in Kanaganayakam's view, not Ghose but the reader who is at fault for failing to recognize the interdependence of Ghose's fictions and his 'biographical circumstances,' as she is deceived by their seeming distance from one another. According to this view, it is not the case that Ghose's works are simply not related to his own background, or that they eschew all reference to the author's biography in favour of total absorption in another world or culture. In fact their representation of South America is often more iconic than literal, more allegorical than strictly representational. In interview with Ghose, M.G. Vassanji tells him: 'your South America is a certain fused, dreamlike place: names of cities are mentioned only passingly, countries are not distinguished, and the spoken language is uniform [...] it could be any place.'[18] Ghose has himself claimed that he does not write about any 'particular culture,' neither South America nor South Asia.[19]

In this vein, some have also noted that it is entirely appropriate that Ghose's fiction registers what Kanaganayakam calls 'the irreversibility of the predicament of exile.' Unlike those Commonwealth or post-colonial writers who have dealt with the problems of identity and exile 'by recreating in their art a realistic or sentimentalized version of the land of their birth,' since the early 1970s Ghose's work has instead insisted on its own deracination, and has suggested the homelessness that is after all characteristic of Ghose's life.[20] Ghose was born in Sailkot, in what was then British India but became Pakistan, and moved to Bombay at a young age, where, as he points out in *Confessions of a Native Alien*, his father changed their Muslim last name Ghaus to the more Hindu Ghose in order to ensure the family would blend into the urban environment of Bombay.[21] His very name thus embodies one of the early fractures of his identity: his separation from his Muslim origins but also his outsider position within Hindu culture. Ghose has claimed that he felt neither Indian nor Pakistani but in between, a situation that was no doubt exacerbated when his family immigrated to England. In *Confessions of a Native-Alien* Ghose constructs himself as a 'Native-Alien' both in England and in the Indo-Pakistan of his early life. He calls himself an 'Indo-Pakistani born before Pakistan existed, moved to Bombay, then England,' and describes the layers of his early identity as the 'schizophrenic theme of much of my thinking.'[22] His claim of a tenuous identity is a critique of the more essentialized appeals to nationalist location behind the fracturing of India and Pakistan, as the political reality that made his own early life so complex and often violent. He did not settle in England; after starting his career as a writer Ghose moved to the US, where he has taught at the University of Texas since the 1960s.

A reading of Ghose's career that emphasizes the coincidence between his life in exile and his rootless fictions is supported by comments Ghose himself has made. In interview with Kanaganayakam he claims that in his early writing life he thought his works contained nothing of him, that he was merely 'pursuing some compulsion of the imagination.'[23] Yet he began to realize that even in those works furthest from his experience he was writing about himself in some way. About the Brazilian trilogy, set entirely in South America and dependent on its political history and culture, he says: 'I was talking about the idea of place. The attraction of self to a certain landscape. Certain images in [the Brazilian trilogy] have to do with memories of having been to particular parts of Brazil, but one can say that I was unconsciously trying to create the idea of the human soul seeing a glimpse from time to time of paradise and longing to be there.'[24] These sentiments are echoed in his interview with Vassanji, in which he denies any real connection between South Asia and Brazil in the trilogy, but then claims that 'there are a good many images, especially of landscapes, where there is a sort of montage effect in my mind: I've only got to look hard at the superimposed Brazilian landscape and I can see an Indian landscape showing through it.'[25]

Yet, in the same interview with Vassanji, in which he admits there are parallels between his fictional rendering of South America and his early life in South Asia, he also emphasizes a more critical stance, opposing any suggestion that his origins are a relevant subject for discussion in relation to his fiction, and indeed confronting some of the market orthodoxies of postcolonial literature head on. 'Home is in my mind, my imagination,' he claims. 'Home is the English language and what I can do with it and what I can read in it.' Rather than reiterating the standard challenge to English as a dominant language, he evokes his habitation in a language and a world of fictions first and foremost. He even romanticizes England, claiming it will always be his home, as the place where he began to be a writer, 'or began emerging as a writer and being recognized as a writer.' In 1986, though he had been living in the US for many years already, England was still where his books were first published, as he also points out. He directly attacks the tendency to 'put a work into a nationalist category because of its content,' calling it 'naïve,' and insisting that the 'best works of the second half of the twentieth century have not come from a particular background.'[26] He claims that the writing itself is the space in which he develops, and that his writing is in many ways the content of his experience: 'If I spend a year writing a novel and, finishing it, start another one, my only "real experience" has been that I have written a novel.' Appealing to an ostensibly more legitimate Pakistani or South Asian past would be, Ghose suggests, a pose, and as such his appeal to an authentic national location would be a sign of the inauthentic in his self-presentation and fictional work. After all, such an appeal is not an option first and foremost because Ghose was not brought up as a religious Muslim and he does not recognize himself as in any way Pakistani: 'I did not have the heritage I am supposed to be guilty of having broken with,' he states.[27] In conversation with Jussawalla and Dasenbrock, in facing continual questions about why he rarely writes about the immigrant condition, and why he resists South Asia as a setting, his tone becomes quite hostile: 'I'm not multi-cultural, I'm British. I'm really more Anglo-Saxon than the Anglo-Saxons. I cannot speak my native Punjabi or Urdu or Hindustani because I have been uprooted from India for three-quarters of my life now.'[28] This hostility appears continually in Ghose's critical non-fiction, and manifests itself as a critique of any tendency to locate literary value in 'some indigenous source,' which he associates with an Anglo-American capitalist cultural market that he claims exploits 'the cultural relations between the West and the recently liberated countries.'[29]

In short, as Kanaganayakam points outs, Ghose only 'ostensibly' establishes 'a binary construct in which empirical and imaginative realities occupy separate and often mutually exclusive worlds.' Those opposed realities in fact exist in a tension, and for Ghose they often come together in the guise of a critique of what Kanaganayakam calls the presence of 'post-colonial experience' – an experience with a concrete material reality attached first and foremost to a specific national identity – as a 'legitimizing feature in literature.'[30] That is, those writers who can be identified with a specific geopolitical location that is broadly postcolonial, or who fit into the niche of what Ghose has called 'that hideous bureaucratic invention, Third World Literature,' will be expected to speak to the politics of that location very specifically.[31] Ghose's tendency to focus on an aesthetic tradition and literary impetus should be read as an attempt to distinguish himself from this market niche and its usual legitimations. His repeated insistence in his critical non-fiction that writers should espouse no particular '-ism' popular with a current audience,[32] while evidently combatively dedicated to a troubled aesthetic ideology, takes on a different valence when read in this light. It can be interpreted as an explicit and rather pained reaction to his own racialization at the hands of his critical public. Thus, most recently, Ghose has lamented that 'when people read Conrad or Nabokov, they don't talk about some specific identity of the authors but of the aesthetics of their work whereas with my work, I've never read a single word about the quality of my prose but the question often turns up of the apparent confounding of South American and South Asian settings.'[33]

In sum, there are two tendencies in critical approaches to Ghose's work, and they appear in critical appraisals, as well as in his own self-construction in interviews and in his autobiographical works. Both approaches are significantly based on the question of Ghose's refusal to appeal to his South Asian ethnicity for the sake of establishing a successful career within the niche of postcolonial literature – a niche in which those authors situated within a political location clearly aligned to their fictional concerns most often find success. One tendency involves an insistence that there is in fact a significant parallel between Ghose's life and his fictions, given that his experience has been defined by exile, and that he has never felt a specific attachment – definable, for example, through language, religion, or a clear nationality – to any South Asian location. In this reading, his literary works, though set in South America, figure that landscape through Ghose's own early childhood in British India and, more importantly, thematize what Kanaganayakam calls a 'new poetics for the literature of the native-alien experience.'[34] The other tendency involves a radical separation of Ghose's life from his art, and an insistence on the irrelevance of the former to the latter. This tendency is supported by the lack of specificity in Ghose's rendering of South America, and is best embodied in Ghose's own self-constructing privileging of the realm of fiction, his insistence that his writing is more often about the experience of making fictions than it is about any specific place identifiable on a map.

*

As is clear from the conversations and approaches outlined above, the very fact that Ghose has attempted to distance himself from an authenticating South Asian past has ironically guaranteed that precisely that attempt has become the interpretative obsession of his readers and critics, schooled to expect a specific conjuncture of life and art, the absence of which forms a critical impasse that has impeded the range of approaches to Ghose's work, and indeed, as he readily recognizes, his success as a novelist. It is fair to highlight the antimony which will by now be obvious: Ghose's works are situated in a field overwhelmed by considerations of biographical authorship precisely because they call those considerations into question at every turn. Criticism of his work is defined by attention to a perceived lack. Ghose's career gives credence, in practice, to Séan Burke's distrust of the anti-authorial tendencies of much contemporary literary scholarship: 'the theory of authorial absence,' he writes, 'no more signaled a disengagement with issues of authorship than iconoclasm attests to the dwindling of the icons.'[35] Whereas Burke evokes the absence (or presence) of the author as a subject of continued interest to academic critics, in Ghose's case the situation is almost reversed: while as an author he consistently absents his biographical self from his fiction, his doing so seems to require that critics draw him back in. This is an irony that is not lost on Ghose. I noted earlier that in *The Triple Mirror of the Self* Jonathan Pons can 'complete' Urim's manuscript because he receives a grant to work on a text left unfinished by the death of its author. Urim's lack of authorial agency (we assume he perished somewhere in South America) is what permits Pons' use of his text, and that use is resolutely determined by the question of Urim's authorial identity. Thus Pons' relationship with the Urim manuscript, a manuscript that critiques the notion of geographic or national authenticity, as I will show, rather carefully mirrors the relationship Ghose's critics have with his works, consistently drawing the author in just as he attempts to leave himself out.

  We know from the beginning of *The Triple Mirror of the Self* that Urim is an outsider, 'not a native of this region' (9), in the interior of South America. Those local to Suxavat call him Urim after the Urimba, an 'immigrant tree,' and much of his account of life there is made up of observations about the behaviour of the local residents. Suxavat is between countries, claimed on occasion by 'Brazil, Peru and Colombia [...] raising obscure legal issues at The Hague' (3). The people who live there are unconcerned about establishing a particular nationality. The region is said to be partly inhabited by descendants of nineteenth-century *seringueros*, rubber tappers who travelled so far from the economic centers that they stopped trying to get back. It is thus a consciously marginal, peripheral place full of outcasts, the children of self-exiles from the harsh economic life of the region and its focus on commodities like rubber and gold. Urim arrived in Suxavat with Tambour, a former gold-miner who struck it rich but left his wealth behind in favor of burying himself in the jungle. The land is said to possess a certain slowness, allowing for 'a wonderful serenity of mind that saw no purpose in the sort of deliberate haste characteristic of societies that measured time as a unit of money' (47). In short it has somehow managed to escape dependence on the general world economic order. It is a kind of oasis from standard economic and political structures, or from modernity in general.

However, though Suxavat is not rooted in a particular nation or any recognizable modernity, and is presented as a kind of oasis, it is notably not a primal paradise fit for tourist consumption, and the rituals of its inhabitants are thoroughly corrupt and mediated, referencing no significant collective memory of obvious origins. Early in the narrative people from a neighbouring village come looking for new young brides, and Urim views the performances with ironic distance. Suxavat's monkey-dancers, for example, perform something '*suggesting* a raid on an enemy,' that 'was all an *artful rendering* of a former reality, for such tribal warfare had long ceased in the region' (9, my emphasis). All their actions are said to happen 'as if' they embodied some reality, and their expressions are 'feigned' (9). The actual bride ceremony, performed by the markedly charlatan Nebbola, another foreigner in exile, is described in similar terms, and is said to be 'made up of memories so remote that their recurrence as fragmentary images seemed comical':

> The effect was rather like watching Japanese youths performing a rock concert with all the physical gestures of British or American pop stars or coming across on a sidewalk in Los Angeles tall, blue-eyed Americans in orange-coloured robes chanting the praises of Krishna, each group appropriating an alien tribal practice with a sincerity so genuine it is sad to behold. (16)

Indeed Urim speculates that Nebbola's invented ceremonies likely recreate something he had seen 'in a television documentary about a remote people' (17).

The people of Suxavat are thought to welcome invented rituals because there are none they know from immediate memory or through a community of shared origins. The residents of Suxavat are rather a hodgepodge of individuals, or the descendants of individuals, who have fled from a culture they have deemed corrupt or dissatisfying. They are like Tambour, for example, who has escaped from the town of Xurupá, a bulldozed 'sea of mud' that used to be a rain forest but was demolished to establish a gold-mining operation, and who claims, setting out to kill a jaguar, 'I'll go native with a spear' (61). Tambour's use of a phrase like 'I'll go native' suggests Ghose's wariness about the tendency to romanticize the 'native,' authentic, or untouched culture that might be thought to exist in the jungles of South America. Similarly, when Urim originally decides to travel to the interior with Pons, from Natal to Xurupá, it is after Pons evokes with little self-consciousness a clichéd language of the search for a new 'frontier' to explain his wish to visit the mining town. Urim claims to have followed Pons out of a desire to remove himself more thoroughly 'from the source of [his] original flight' (38), the basis of which is at this point unknown. It is in Xurupá that Urim first meets Tambour, who tells him about Suxavat, saying, 'God knows whose land it is to claim.' Urim's response is ironic: 'Ah, the simple life, I remarked [...] the old romantic nostalgia for a bucolic sort of paradise' (54).[36]

Over the course of Urim's narrative, Suxavat turns from a seeming political utopia to a place savaged by the ceaseless movement of capital into the interior of the continent. This transition is clearly familiar from Ghose's other fictions, which have, since *The Murder of Aziz Khan,* consistently formed what W.H. New calls 'a continuing analysis of power: of its workings, and of its basis in the economics of ownership and desire.'[37] Men from the non-descript Interior Ministry appear and tell the people of Suxavat that they want to offer them 'relocation' so they can possess their land. The men from the Ministry link the land's 'value' to its 'potential for development,' and insist that Suxavat has no such value and that the people there should simply give it up for a better place. The people naturally refuse, only to have a specifically violent nationality imposed upon them. They are in fact murderously incorporated into the modern national system and exchange economy, which dictates here that the lives of the people in the region are less valuable than the gold that can be mined there.

When the village is destroyed we can conclude that its absence of authenticity, something which might have been represented by concrete rituals with a clear relation to communal memory, or a clear sense of tribal identity, does not make its destruction any less tragic. While negating any posited authentic origin, Ghose makes such a collective past unnecessary to the kind of communally-based opposition to global capitalism that people find in Suxavat. Clearly, that is, Urim's manuscript, while critiquing authenticity, does not suggest this critique requires abandoning an oppositional stance toward capitalist incursions into South America's interior. Thus, again, Ghose's work distinguishes itself from what Ella Shohat calls the 'celebration of syncretism and hybridity' within a dominant variety of postcolonial literature and criticism, a celebration that comes with no replacement for the located authenticity it often denies. Shohat claims that this celebration, 'if not articulated in conjunction with questions of hegemony and neo-colonial power relations,' risks 'appearing to sanctify the *fait accompli* of colonial violence.'[38] The conjunction she recommends is precisely the one Urim articulates. Put differently, Ghose refuses to make what Sheldon Pollock calls 'the single, desperate choice' between cosmopolitanism and vernacularization, between 'a national vernacularity dressed in the frayed period costume of violent revanchism and bent on preserving difference at all costs and [...] a clear-cutting, stripmining multinational cosmopolitanism that is bent, at all costs, on eliminating it.'[39] Refusing to recognize the pressure to choose between such 'desperate' options is what Pollock identifies as the only proper response to the paradoxes of modernity.[40] Ghose's work is precisely this kind of refusal.

Suxavat is also a place recognizable from Ghose's earlier fiction, which often involves characters who dream of a paradise that is ultimately false, but worth imagining, and who are caught up in the movement of modernity's political power and capital. In fact the Urim section of the novel acts as an obvious pastiche of Ghose's own *oeuvre*.[41] In Aamer Hussein's review of the novel, he describes Urim's narrative as 'parodying the pretensions of a would-be Anglophone magical realist, replete with felines, reptiles, sexual rituals and nubile native maidens.'[42] In the novel itself, when Valentin Sadaba gives Pons the manuscript he comments that it 'could well be one more sad attempt by an Englishman to emulate the Latin storytellers' (116), a clear allusion to the fact that Ghose's own South American novels are most often read as magic realist, in exactly the 'Latin' tradition Sadaba evokes.

Around the time when he was writing *The Triple Mirror of the Self*, Ghose said of an earlier novel: 'You could take *A New History of Torments* [1982] and change all the Spanish names to Indian names, substitute the Himalayas and the Ganges for the Andes and the Amazon, but the novel itself would not alter [in] the slightest.' He also said that in *A New History of Torments* (hereafter *Torments*), 'the setting has nothing whatsoever to do with anything,' and that in writing it he had entered 'a phase of pure invention.'[43] In *Torments* the vagueness of the South American location is a part of the plot, and standard clichés about the mysteries of the continent's interior regions are ruthlessly satirized. Jonathan Pons and his cosmopolitanism, which I will turn to below, are predicted here in the representation of the jungle adventures of Jason and Bob. Jason, whose name and quest evoke the myth of the Golden Fleece, is the son of a prominent South American tobacco plantation owner, sent away to school in England when his care passes into the hands of his father's brother-in-law, Mark Kessel. Jason later visits the region with Bob, a friend from school who travels to South America with considerable curiosity and the eyes of a tourist. He always carries a notebook to record impressions of 'local customs,' while Jason similarly sees his fellow countrymen 'as members of a remote tribe.'[44] The boys set out to do fieldwork for an article they hope to publish in their school's 'anthro mag' to impress their professor (158), and Mark Kessel, Jason's scheming uncle, sends them to what he believes will be their deaths by encouraging them to follow the directions on a complicated map said to lead to El Dorado, a paradise untouched since the time of the Incas. An inheritance is at stake in Kessel's deceit, and he seems convinced that the 'jungle would devour them in two days' (162).

When Jason and Bob first begin their journey, where they want to find a 'savage' simplicity they instead encounter a people thoroughly familiar with their anthropological-cum-tourist mentality, and consistently knowledgeable about the less 'savage' culture that the two think they are leaving behind. For example, in one village, while carrying out their 'probing investigations into the life of the savage,' they are surprised to overhear a radio playing a popular American song (176). As a partial result of their essential ignorance of the basic landscape of the Amazon they are exploring, they face considerable problems. After being swindled by a ruthless conman who manipulates their pretensions to anthropological legitimacy, Bob is nearly claimed by dysentery and goes home to England to recover. Jason bravely carries on, entering a world he wants to believe 'somehow more real than that served by jet liners' (192). However, the more he sees the less he believes in his original notion of the 'Indian' in a 'natural state,' calling the idea 'sentimental rubbish' (199). The further into the interior he travels the more disappointed he is with each encounter with the tribal culture he was once so intrigued by. All the stereotypes of a clichéd jungle narrative are ironically present, shown as preposterous in their existence side-by-side with the incursion of corporate development capital into the South American landscape. Thus, after a companion Jason meets along the way is devoured by cannibals, and he flees from a tribe of man-hating women, he stumbles through the forest practically dead, only to find himself suddenly emerging at the other side to arrive at a well-kept, functioning farm (226).

The location he reaches accords with the map. Thus, the land he sought, and that was sought before him by Mark Kessel, turns out to be thoroughly manmade. It is not El Dorado but instead land belonging to Oyarzún, a landowner descended from a Spanish colonialist (249), and thus one who might be considered a destroyer of South America's old world. The paradise of El Dorado is replaced by a manmade paradise made possible only by Oyarzún's extreme wealth and political privilege. The golden sheep of the myth of the Golden Fleece is even present in the form of a pastiche, a manmade symbol of human acquisitiveness and greed: Oyarzún has had a sheep sculpture made from Mark Kessel's golden Lincoln Continental. Even this paradise is ultimately impermanent. By the novel's end Oyarzún and Kessel are both dead at the hands of political radicals in search of the golden Lincoln, and, without the extensive labour and careful maintenance needed to preserve the illusion of paradise Oyarzún's land is quickly subsumed by the South American jungle in which it is, after everything, still situated. Kanaganayakam claims that *Torments* is a novel that 'looks at man not as a social animal, not as one whose actions govern and are governed by social life, but as one who is driven by destructive and uncontrollable instincts, but is nevertheless condemned to search unceasingly for a lost paradise, for a satisfying vision of reality' (150). This summation represents much of what Ghose's fiction attempts to achieve, and the lost paradise to which Kanaganayakam refers is shown to be dependent on myths of authenticity that *Torments* constantly questions.

Similarly, in Suxavat most of Urim's story involves his fascination with a young girl named Horuxtla, whom he continually relates to the 'virgin forest' of the region and the seeming purity it embodies. His metaphors are dominantly colonial, and he sees the girl as a land to be conquered, though he cannot bring himself to do it. Despite his descent into the interior of South America, seemingly the furthest he could go 'from the source of [his] original flight' (38), he cannot escape the pressure of desire, which is figured as a desire for possession of a secure contentment through contact with something of absolute, unadulterated value. When Urim finds out that Horuxtla is not the innocent that he imagines, he claims that 'really, there were no illusions in this world, no fantastic appearances, no reality that was magical, only bits of action, each succeeding one a piece of knowledge so terrible that we could only bear it as reality by imposing upon the visible surface the disguise of metaphor' (50). She is the last fantasy in which he engages, and the value of her purity is tarnished beyond repair by her exposure to others' desires. He says of her fellow villagers: 'They took her being for granted. They possessed her and were possessed by her. The world they inhabited was their communal property [...]. I, the creator in my secret mind of a poetry to her beauty, must remain excluded' (62).

In other words, due to his status as an outsider and exile in a world he can idealize precisely because he does not belong to it (and, recall, no one else does either), Urim sees himself as excluded from the fulfilment of his desire for true possession. His longing for belonging of a kind, manifest here as sexual desire, is not a response to a need for geographical location, but an expression of a deeper problem he experiences in being alive, and that he imagines the residents of Suxavat experience as well. Urim is self-conscious about the fact that his idealization of Horuxtla involves a large measure of self-deceit, and he is also aware of the links between his own desire for possession and the events that propel the destruction of the village in which he found a partial sanctuary.

However, despite Urim's wish to escape in some final way his quest for a source of absolute value, and despite his scorn for all pretence to authenticity, he is finally bound once again to what he sought to question, this time by Jonathan Pons, who is within the frame of the novel the mediator between Urim's narrative and the world. Because the Urim manuscript as a whole is a pastiche of Ghose's fictional tendencies, Jonathan Pons' treatment of it makes him a clear figure for Ghose's critical reception in general.

*

It is never clear why Urim includes Jonathan Pons in his narrative, though it does make it more likely that the narrative would one day fall into Pons' hands, and that it would therefore be subject to inter-pretive scrutiny. It is in Natal, upon first arriving in South America, that Urim claims to have met Jonathan Pons for the first time. However, the way Urim depicts their first meeting hints that Pons may be a reflection of or a figure for someone else, a distorted version of some other person, and thus Urim's fictional recreation. He recalls being in a hotel lobby and catching a glimpse of Pons, 'seeing his face reflected back from one wall and almost merging with my own profile on another' (35). He recalls that Pons was travelling on 'some founda-tion grant,' something 'anthropological,' but he also recalls thinking Pons 'a hedonist rather than a scholar' (35). They engage in typical tourist activities, on Pons' suggestion, visiting some churches and the marketplace. Terms Urim characteristically uses to describe the baroque churches they see include 'neglect,' 'moth-eaten' and 'tumor-ous,' and the marketplace fares no better. The handicrafts they find there are 'primitive' – they hazily gesture toward a remembered past they cannot embody (36). Urim thus finds no value in them, but merely appeases Pons and amuses himself by going along. It is Pons who thinks these activities central to his visit, to his experience of the local culture.

But Pons is characterized throughout as the consummate cosmopol-itan, and his position is defined by a series of ambiguities. He is intro-duced as a narrator in the book's second section, where he describes his own research and how he came to possess the Urim manuscript, and appends a number of texts that he acquires in investigating its prove-nance. Always a dilettante, having received five separate grants in seven years he uses the money to do next to nothing. For example, before pursuing research into the origins of the Urim manuscript, he claims that the transfer of his mental energy is thankfully easy, since his work on his current project, which involved him spanning the globe for many months, had not yet made its way from his 'mental notes' to his laptop computer, which he nonetheless carries every-where. 'I was a superior scholar for knowing what scholarship not to attempt,' he claims (118). In fact he only takes on research that requires travel, and it is in Peru, atop Machu Picchu, that he meets Valentin Sadaba, from whom he eventually receives the manuscript. Sadaba claims not to have read the entire manuscript, and thus does not know that Pons figures in it. For Sadaba the coincidence – and 'Coincidences don't happen but to advance some plot' (116) – is merely running into an American intellectual who can make some-thing of the manuscript. It is then able to circulate across continents, like Pons himself, and like the gold being unearthed in Xurupá, in pursuit of which Suxavat was demolished.

Before giving him the manuscript Sadaba introduces Pons to his life in Peru, in a section of the novel that articulates numerous elisions between economic and cultural capitals. In fact the only approximation of a real religious experience in the novel involves Pons' exposure to a shrine made of gold and lit with candles, which suggests the ritual worship of gold as a source of wealth and a center of value. This form of worship, the worship of a commodity with a value defined through the culture at large, but which is in turn used to value other commodities, obviously has pernicious effects, as Urim's text witnesses. When Sadaba meets Pons to give him the manuscript it is in a decrepit area of town at the 'Banco Real.' Pons wonders, 'What could he want to get from a bank? Gold?' (109). In truth it is the Urim manuscript, but having Pons speculate that it might be gold links economic and literary value as cultural constructions, a linkage that carries specific weight given that the Urim manuscript itself concerns the way a national government, in the guise of its Interior Ministry, unearths gold at the cost of turning Xurupá and Suxavat into veritable wastelands. In other words, the exchange that takes place at the 'Banco Real' makes the manuscript and the cultural logic it critiques – in this case, gold as a standard of value – more or less analogous. What Urim's text purports to express is undermined by the system in which it has to circulate.

Making the site of Pons' acquisition of the manuscript the 'Banco Real' predicts the way Pons uses the manuscript for purposes the narrative it contains would condemn. It also predicts Pons' treatment of the Urim manuscript as a means of access to further personal wealth by way of research grants. The 'Banco Real' has a significant fictional precedent in Ghose's 1986 novel, *Figures of Enchantment*, the focus of which is the fictions that the dispossessed and underprivileged create for themselves in order to survive. Like *Torments*, while sympathizing with the impetus behind the creation of imaginary value, *Figures of Enchantment* shows that each fiction or figure in which a given character invests is reliant on some myth of authenticity, some appeal to an ultimate source of meaning, value, and contentment (what one might find at the 'Banco Real'), which Ghose finally depicts as dangerous fictions that are above all impossible to realize.

At the novel's opening we are introduced to Gamboa, a Bureau of Statistics employee in an unidentified South American country ruled by a repressive dictatorship and its massive bureaucracy. Through his characterization of Gamboa, Ghose draws parallels between statistical calculations or 'figures' and the dreams of a better life that obsess the poor, since his mental 'figures,' left on small scraps of paper around his office, involve financial calculations of imagined wealth. A major part of Gamboa's fantasy is a picture, kept in his cubicle at work, of an island from a tourist brochure where he thinks he will find a better life, 'a brightness elsewhere, a landscape which was daily comforting,'[45] not unlike the life Urim and Tambour seek in Suxavat. After being denied an expected promotion, Gamboa sympathizes with anti-government movements and gets picked up as a communist during a rally he attends on a lunch break. Instead of killing him, due to 'the captain's cruel idea of a sporting chance' (36), Gamboa is dropped on a deserted island that might be thought to resemble the one in his fantasies.

It turns out to be the opposite of paradise, and all those who live there dream instead of returning to the mainland (127). The island, Santa Barbara, is the location of a nitrate extraction operation. Its inhabitants were set up there by the government for that specific purpose, we learn, and all goods coming into the island are sold to residents by the main-land chemicals company that employs them. They are thus perpetually in debt to their employers, as well as underpaid (114). Their desire for return to the mainland, like Gamboa's fantasies about future wealth and an island paradise, are thus shown to be the products of present circum-stances, responses to dissatisfactions stemming from social, political, and economic inequalities. Throughout *Figures of Enchantment* the poor are depicted as constantly creating and indulging in fictions of enchantment that compensate for present ills in this way. These figures are the product of perpetual dissatisfaction, and while they help the characters get through life, they also keep them from engaging in a collective politics that might orchestrate a more thorough change to the political situation. After all it is only when Gamboa is forced to stop imagining what his life would be like after a promotion that he begins to align himself with anti-government movements. Other sources of imaginative investment include the lottery, and a soap opera called *Joanna's Sacrifice*, which Gamboa's daughter, as a single mother working at a grocery store, and then as a hotel chambermaid, watches every week without fail.

Dreams of future wealth are the most common fantasies for the char-acters in *Figures of Enchantment*, but there is no sense in which money itself is a stable value. Instead the government is shown to be in thrall to foreign banks and lending agencies, and the wages of underpaid employ-ees are tied to this situation. The value of the local currency is radically contingent and arbitrary, much like the value or status of the dreams of the novel's characters, which change in accord with their circumstances.

In fact the novel is full of characters who either attempt to attribute false value to objects or ideas in order to further their own goals, or who fall prey to such characters. Young Federico, encouraged by the prevalence and mainstream legitimacy of the lottery within his city, takes up gambling at an early age, and on his first trip to a gaming house is robbed by a confidence man who convinces his victims of his sincerity while wooing them with images of riches. Local merchant Popayan, whose shop is set up in Nuevo Soho, which is a bohemian site of alternative value early in the novel, is another sort of confidence man, selling objects in his general store and pawn shop that are actually useless, but to which he attributes false value through trickery. We observe him wondering how to alter a common print, 'wondering how best he could treat the paper,' to give it a value it does not have, 'to make it look older in order to pass it off as a rare print to sell to a collector' (62).

Popayan's creation of false value is further linked to banking and currency, since over the course of the novel Nuevo Soho is stripped of all alternative force and turned into a banking nexus. While 'banking executives busied themselves with currency deals, international loans and the export trade,' Popayan sells his property and turns to financial fictions rather than cultural ones, spending his days 'pouring over certificates of deposit and accounts of his investment in stocks and bonds' (181). He also tricks Federico without much difficulty, selling him a cape and amulet, insisting they will make his dreams come true. And it seems to work: Federico finds the beautiful woman and rich house he desires, or at least he convinces himself as much, though what comes of achieving his fantasy is a life as a male prostitute. Ernesto Vivado, who introduces him to the life of prostitution, is a 'dealer in sensations,' a man thoroughly of the postmodern economy, or a 'middleman of other people's dreams,' as he calls himself (105). His jobs include finding extras and exotic locales for Hollywood, and arranging trips into Amazonia and Disney World for rich Brazilians (105).

The novel as a whole thus depicts each of its characters – Vivado, Popayan, Federico, Gamboa and his daughter – as either engaged in the creation of fictions that promote their own economic or political goals, or in thrall to a variety of culturally defined fictions, either of wealth or of an earthly paradise that will bring true happiness. More importantly, the novel shows how these fictions depend on contingent values that have no stable origin or absolute source, like a nation's currency. What makes each of their figures or fabulations possible, but also ultimately fruitless, is the appeal to any of a series of myths of authentic origins or stable value. It is this pursuit of authenticity and a stable system of value that reappears in *The Triple Mirror of the Self*, in the way Pons engages with the manuscript he acquires at the 'Banco Real.'

Pons does nothing with the manuscript, naturally, until there is a grant available to work with it. As already mentioned, he locates a foundation in Nebraska that offers research grants 'to persons who undertook the completion of a work left incomplete by the untimely death of its author' (119). The presence of a few blank notebooks amidst the pile leads him to conclude that the work is unfinished, and after reading the text through he titles it 'The Burial of the Self,' the title of the first section of the actual novel in which we encountered it to begin with. The text thus exists for the reader, since Pons is our intermediary editor, only because of the presence of his cosmopolitan class. Pons initially speculates that Sadaba himself penned the manuscript, especially as it contains a critique of South American political violence and the triumph of repressive dictatorships. Sadaba is a harsh critic of American cultural imperialism and economic power of all kinds. In fact he is denied a visa by the US State Department after being invited to attend a conference in New York, where intellectuals 'invite celebrities from South America and Eastern Europe and then, with sublime masochism, submit themselves to ferocious abuse from the visitors for America's "cultural imperialism"' (115). Pons attempts to distance himself from what Sadaba detests. In accordance with the sort of cosmopolitanism that is '*local* while denying its local character,'[46] Pons claims he is not a representative of the 'American intellectual establishment,' but he is evidently a cosmopolitan version of precisely that. Sadaba addresses him as such, claiming 'Your tragedy is that you see the world only as your investment.'

Pons was never in Natal or Xurupá, stating 'I simply do not travel to destinations to which I cannot fly first class,' but he recognizes himself in Urim's representation: 'Urim was thinking of *me* when he invented that person. What is more, he was thinking of me *maliciously*' (120). It is because he recognizes himself that he manages to piece together the 'real' identity of its author. He decides the narrative was written by a man he calls Zinalco Shimomura, who arrived at his university in Arizona 'the year [he] spent doing a comparative study of theatre productions of Shakespeare in London, Corneille in Paris and Sophocles in Athens' (122). Pons' investigation into Urim's origins leads him to friends of Shimomura's living in London, and through them he accesses other texts, published and unpublished, written by the author of the Urim manuscript in the past. One of these is an unfinished fragment titled 'You,' published in an obscure journal. That fragment is included in the novel's second section, becoming part of its collection of assembled evidence about Urim's early life, filtered and reconstructed by Jonathan Pons. He is also given 'the English notebooks,' which reveal part of Shimomura's past as an immigrant to England from South Asia.[47]

Pons uses all of these materials, finally, to gloss the obscurities of Urim's text. Urim's initial narrative is haunted by something, memories of the life that he left behind, but that creep to the surface of his thoughts at moments of crisis that we do not at first understand. These thoughts beneath the surface of Urim's story hint at the complicated history that Pons later unravels. The appearance of references to an indistinct past is marked by negation, by a refusal to make certain pronouncements or narrate a discernible history. 'I will say nothing of the history of passions which may well be the sum of a confusion of dreams with their conversion of dull events into marvellous fictions' (6), he writes. And, when the men in their overalls arrive to decimate Suxavat, Urim claims 'they had now come to possess the land by the method used by earlier invaders in the Americas, by exterminating the inhabitants rooted there' (85). In listening to the gunfire Urim remembers General Dyer, our first clue that he knows something of India, probably through fairly direct experience. It is the trauma of the slaughter in Suxavat that evokes Dyer for him: 'there was a continuous firing of a succession of guns, producing in my mind the image of a crowd of people forced into a small clearing and massacred' (87). He experiences that moment,

> as if a terrible past had begun to heave out of that jungle's darkness, giving me the impression that I stood upon layers of centuries which were projecting fragmented mirror images of one another [...] it seemed that another time, another bloody past with its history of murders, reflected its images from the shattered mirror of the present. (87–8)

Furthermore, after fleeing the destruction in Suxavat, he spends his final days with Horuxtla, numb even to her presence by the extent of his trauma. In the last moments of his narrative, and seemingly the last moments of his consciousness, he stares at the Andes and says her name, before concluding: 'There was no Horuxtla. The name echoing in my brain was not *Horuxtla*. Staring at the high peaks, in a land of origins, the sound I heard was *The Hindu Kush*' (97). He thus sees in the

Andes the Hindu Kush, substituting one landscape for another just at the moment when he has seemingly had enough of life, and meaning has been vacated from all ostensibly authentic places of respite. These references to General Dyer and the Hindu Kush prompt aspects of Pons' inquiry into the narrator's past, and contribute to the originary story he finally attaches to Urim and his previous British and American incarnations.

That originary story makes up the third and last section of the novel, which Pons titles 'The Origins of Self,' depicting Roshan Karim in South Asia. Just at the end of the second section, before Roshan is introduced, Pons writes:

> I realized that I must concern myself only with that language which would rediscover, oh, not some miserable truth which is but a paltry thing, but the precise detail embedded in the florid, passionate, miraculous and infinitely elusive figures that haunt memory, to reinvent the idea itself or reality after discovering that reality, poor thing, has no existence at all. (194)

So, after assembling numerous texts collected from a variety of sources, all attesting to Urim's past, the manuscript's 'elusive figures' are no more clear to him than when he began his research. Pons resolves to 'reinvent' a reality that might provide a fitting gloss for Urim's text. That reality, instead of being 'some miserable truth,' is Pons' attempt to find 'precise detail' that could explain Urim's obscurities. Those details are what make up Roshan's story. The story of Roshan's (or Urim's) early life in South Asia is thus not as concrete or realist as it seems upon first reading, and its status as a text of 'origins' has to be questioned. It is instead written by a man who hardly knew its supposed subject, and who instead reinvents a possible past based on present evidence.

Through Pons' reconstruction, Roshan's experience is of a culture in conflict, of life in Bombay during the time of the Quit India movement and World War II, on the approach to independence. Political violence becomes more and more prominent, and the narrative references General Dyer and the Amritsar massacre, as well as the Hindu Kush, thus finding ostensible sources for the buried memories and more difficult references in the Urim manuscript. The world Pons imagines for Roshan is thus thematically consistent with the Urim manuscript, a conceit that allows us to imagine they are of the same authorship, conforming to our expectations about how authored texts relate both to one another and to a distinct biography. Pons constructs a past that would be specifically worthy of an author of literature. The most obvious influence in the telling of Roshan's story is in fact James Joyce's *Portrait of the Artist as a Young Man* (1916), a narrative that constructs the plausible early experiences of someone with an artistic and specifically literary sensibility. As Roshan grows up he develops an interest in language, in poetic mimicry, in women, and in the nation and his separation from it. The early sexual experiences of Roshan and his friends make up the majority of the narrative; their depiction acts as a farcical, though often tragic, commentary on a larger narrative of religious divisions and sectarian violence. For example, one scene entails Roshan gleefully masturbating in his Hindu friend's kitchen in an attempt to desecrate his parents' presumed fear of Muslim impurity.

Roshan's story, told in third person, closely mirrors the general narrative of, as well as several specific incidents in, Ghose's autobiographical *Confessions of a Native-Alien*. Yet, if Ghose is here reincorporating his early text, marketed in the 1960s as plainly autobiographical, he distances himself from what might have been a straightforward story of his ostensible origins told to appease those critics who have called for one. The South Asian material is presented here instead as Pons' own imaginative reconstruction of the early life of the subject of his research, the presumably dead author of the Urim manuscript. Though Roshan's story shares specific incidents with *Confessions of a Native-Alien*, by constructing Pons as relaying what he imagines to be the life of an author he hardly knew, Ghose implicates his earlier narrative in the cultural logic of cosmopolitanism that Pons embodies. Here, that logic implies a specific understanding of authorship in relation to nationality, and finds the birth of an author's sensibility in a childhood landscape viewed with nostalgia. In other words, *The Triple Mirror of the Self* takes up the vaunted return to South Asia only to suggest that it is not the product of a mind legitimately engaged in a consideration of a specific authenticating past. Instead, that return is made to seem the fantasy of an elite cosmopolitan class that justifies its jet-setting privilege by collecting information about what is foreign to it in order to make itself more representative of the world. It can only do so when the status of the authentic, that which authorizes the legitimacy of the effort, is unquestioned, or at the very least left with considerable integrity.

At the end of 'The Origins of the Self,' Roshan takes a train trip with his father into the mountains. The Hindu Kush is figured in these final pages as embodying everything the novel as a whole explores and exposes. First, it is a geographical feature that Ghose associates with his childhood and remembers with fondness in *Confessions of a Native-Alien*. As I note above, Ghose has later claimed, in numerous contexts, that it and other aspects of South Asia's geography could be substituted for countless other mountain ranges or features of any landscape to the same effect, the specificity of its location having no significant meaning. In Urim's narrative the Hindu Kush is seen in the Andes and heard in the name 'Horuxtla,' just as General Dyer is seen in the brutal annihilation of the villagers in Suxavat, in a way that collapses the distinctions between South Asia and South America. Here, the Kush reappears in Pons' fictional recreation of the life of a teenage boy whose experiences might represent the origins of the author of the Urim manuscript. In the description of Roshan's initial vision of the Hindu Kush, the narrative is in second person:

> There! your father says. The Hindu Kush. The great crown of mountain peaks lit up golden in the morning sun on the head of India that no human hand can reach. And the invaders, so pompous in their concert of conquest, when they come here all they can ever conquer is illusion. But you looking at the Hindu Kush or at your father's dream of it aware of the unbearable beauty of white snow on white ice reinventing your father among glittering peaks so as not to suffer alone in your afterlife *the curse of your beginning* no longer not yet 7 but all the ages you must be before your body becomes a drop of moisture frozen in one of the tiny cracks in the ice alone in *this land of origins* this crunched up vertically thrusting land of suggestive distortions in *exile even in your first moment* from which there is never an emancipation could you come to an inch of the wall of ice and crack its surface like a geologist certain there must be an important *fossil* in the rock-face that *crucial missing link* deposited in the ice smashing wildly and shouting in the unechoing ice-bound valleys But you But you But you. (343, my emphases)

The passage's obscurities actually elucidate much of what the novel as a whole has to say about the dangerous appeal of the pursuit of authenticity. The Hindu Kush appears as both a marker of absolute origins, as its walls form a surface of light that reflects Roshan's image of himself, and the impossibility of those origins. The mountain range is seemingly self-contained, pure and unadulterated, because it cannot be possessed, even by 'the successive empires' that could 'own it only on maps [...] the invaders, so pompous in their concert of conquest, when they come here all they can ever conquer is illusion.' Thus even the image of permanence is an illusion, and the illusion of absolute possession through conquest, like Urim's image of Horuxtla, is a facade. Similarly, the reflection Roshan sees of his own image can be demolished. In fact, it is the very pursuit of that 'crucial missing link' or connection to 'this land of origins' – the same phrase used to evoke the Amazon landscape at the end of Urim's narrative – that leads to a despair that marks the futility of the effort: 'smashing wildly and shouting in the unechoing ice-bound valleys But you But you But you' (343).

Pons is like that geologist in pursuit of an 'important fossil,' or the 'crucial missing link.' What Pons is missing is the biography that will explain how a narrative came to be and who authored a text. Like Jason in *Torments*, like Gamboa in *Figures of Enchantment*, Pons wants to crack the surface of an originary story that will explain everything, and Roshan wants the ice face of the Hindu Kush to reflect an image of himself. But that image is subject to destruction at every turn, and necessarily so, since a lack of willingness to question the image is what leads to violence in the novel itself. This is true in British India, where distinctions based on the authenticity of origins lead to religious violence; and it is true in Suxavat, where the Interior Ministry's insistence that the land belong to a specific nation, and be subject to the greed of its government, leads to its destruction.

Most importantly, if the 'Origins of the Self' section of the novel is Pons' reconstruction of a past life that Urim might have lived, this passage concerning the Hindu Kush, written in the second person, signifies Ghose's intrusion into Pons' reconstruction. By intruding in this way Ghose directly confronts, through Pons, a critical community whose existence his novel has posited and theorized, and declares his agency in the authoring of his own texts. He interrupts Pons' attempt to establish Urim's origins in order to question the validity of Pons' procedure. Thus, this passage on the Hindu Kush, appearing at the very end of Roshan's story and indeed at the end of the novel as a whole, shares a logic, or, more exactly, metonymically suggests, what *The Triple Mirror of the Self* attempts in response to Ghose's experience as an author in general.

That is, on the one hand Ghose's novel encourages the radical separation between the author's lives and his fictions by, for example, ruthlessly critiquing Pons' tendency to link the two, by rewriting the content of the autobiographical *Confessions of a Native-Alien* as the imagined construction of an academic, and by making the collapsibility of national geographies a theme in itself. On the other hand, the irony that has in many ways plagued Ghose's career, in which the further he goes to insist on the distinction between his material and South Asia, the more often South Asia reappears in the imaginations of critics, is precisely the irony the text explores. In the most obvious way, the structure of the novel is analogous to Ghose's own career, and more so than any of his previous works. As such it suggests that the author's works do in fact reflect the trajectory of his life in exile, since despite our awareness of Pons as an intermediary, or perhaps because the story he tells is so convincing, it is hard to ignore the relationship between Roshan's past and the kind of narrative that Urim writes. Furthermore, as I have tried to show, in numerous ways understanding the specificity of the novel's meaning depends on a fairly sound understanding of Ghose's position within the literary marketplace and how that position has been critically received.

In his position as an American intellectual with the capital to live a cosmopolitan lifestyle, Jonathan Pons is the guarantor of the cultural status of the Urim narrative, a narrative that is a pastiche of Ghose's South American *oeuvre*. Ghose thus figures his own narratives as significantly authorized by an Anglo-American cosmopolitan class, and as circulating across continents in a way which privileges that class as the one in the position to sanction cultural texts and make decisions about their importance and about how they should be valued and scrutinized. Urim's text figures Ghose's own works, and in turn Pons figures those who have read them in specifically biographical terms. In other words, and more exactly, one of the primary functions of *The Triple Mirror of the Self* is an interrogation of the status of the cosmopolitan as consumer and interpreter of the local for a global cultural field. In accordance with what Urim identifies as Pons' anthropological vision, the cosmopolitan seeks an authenticating myth to legitimize his project, the absence of which leads him to piece together evidence and finally create a myth of his own.

In Pons, Ghose has created a character whose cosmopolitan existence privileges the locality of South Asian ethnicity as a legitimating factor in the study of a text, a text which must then provide what Ghose has called 'a flattering mirror image of oneself to a certain group.'[48] The novel's primary target is Pons, but also what Pons desires and then constructs: the originary story of Roshan Karim. Roshan's story, derived from Ghose's own early work and indeed his autobiography, stands in for the kind of postcolonial cosmopolitan writing my own project has been consistently concerned with. It is a kind of writing that Ghose obviously rejects, and that has been summarized – by Timothy Brennan, again – as expressing,

> the contradictory topoi of exile and nation [...] fused in a lament for the necessary and regrettable insistence of nation-forming, in which the writer proclaims his identity with a country whose artificiality and exclusiveness have driven him into a kind of exile – a simultaneous recognition of nationhood and an exile from it.[49]

It is precisely such a national origin that Ghose explored, often through 'lament,' in some of his earlier works, and most notably in *Confessions of the Native-Alien*. In *The Triple Mirror of the Self* that same ambiguous nostalgia is the structure of understanding that Pons attempts to impose on the Urim manuscript through his reconstruction of the life of its author.

In conflict with Pons, within the Urim manuscript and in turn within *The Triple Mirror of the Self* as a whole, Ghose questions the tendency to posit an original identification with the nation that is then renounced, or to engage in a form of national identification that is suitable for sale to a literary culture that is schooled in cosmopolitanism, and of which Pons is representative. Ghose's work suggests that Pons' privileged position in relation to the locations he visits is analogous to the relationship that obtains in the literary marketplace, between the Anglo-American readers of literary fiction and the material represented for them by the Third World or postcolonial cosmopolitans who are aligned with specified national locales as interpreters, whether as residents or in exile. By imagining Jonathan Pons as a cosmopolitan anthropologist, Ghose expresses his own desire to separate himself from the position seemingly demanded of him by the market: the position of interpreter of a supposedly 'authentic' culture for a market of interested readers, who, like Brennan's cosmopolitans, search for the 'unique expression of the non-Western' in order to construct their own identities as part of a global embrace that is not local or Western, but instead suitable for export as properly international and encompassing.

A question raised throughout Ghose's *oeuvre*, and specifically in *Torments* and *Figures of Enchantment*, is the question of the relationship between authenticity and value, which relates to the larger question of the position of the postcolonial writer in the literary marketplace. In essence *The Triple Mirror of the Self* is a meditation on the conditions that guarantee the exclusion of its author from mainstream success as a sanctioned postcolonial writer. Ghose's representation of the market is an interested response to his own career experiences, and a reaction to the way certain modes of valuing texts have constrained his success. For example, Ghose's depiction of the centrality of questions of biography in reception of postcolonial texts by no means accords with the supposed dominant orthodoxy of anti-authorialism in literary studies. Such anti-authorial perspectives simply do not exist in Ghose's experience of the market for postcolonial literatures, nor do they much influence the way that literature is received by critics and academics, though Ghose might wish otherwise. In *The Triple Mirror of the Self*, instead, Anglo-American reception of postcolonial texts entails a turn toward the touristic consciousness I posited in Part I, or toward an obsession with the authenticity of representation, authenticity as sanctioned by biographical detail, which leads critics to ignore other sources of literary value that might legitimate more attention to work like Ghose's.

Conclusion

Postcolonial literature, once theorized as Third World literature, perhaps soon to be recategorized again as global literatures, or as the literatures of globalization, has had an important role to play in fostering market expansion in the publishing industry. Much of my study has been premised on this argument, yet its terms suggest a larger sphere of influence and dissemination than reality warrants. Over the past few decades literary fiction has become a viable, recognized marketing niche, and the incorporation of postcolonial writers has been an important part of its global entrenchment. Still, it continues to command nothing like the market share of mass-market romance fiction, or Japanese manga, or textbooks for those learning English.[1] Very few regular readers read literary fiction and an even smaller number read postcolonial literature. Those who do thus belong to a relatively specialized field, one that is not divided up into groups of corrupt cosmopolitan consumers and authentic engaged global citizens, or of canny producers and dehistoricizing, exoticizing readers. Or, more correctly, if they are so divided, scholars interested in the materiality of the postcolonial field have not yet completed the kind of research that would prove as much.

My sense is that even the most dedicated empirical observation, undertaken through extensive ethnographic surveying of readers, publishers, editors, authors, reviewers, and agents, for example, would reveal that the field of postcolonial production is actually one whose members function through habitual, ritualized kinds of self-conscious positioning. This seems a natural enough facet of postcolonial literary scholarship in particular, given the challenges it has faced since its (also always contested) moment of emergence. From its terminology, to its origins and purposes, to its major political priorities and implications, the field's development has been attended by a series of accusations and countering critiques. Part of what demands careful self-conscious navigation – and this is something else I suspect further research would confirm – is the politicization of its relationship to global capitalism. From this there emerges an accompanying set of concerns: about imbalances between the northern metropolitan locations and their peripheral 'others'; about the compromises involved in incorporation into the culture industries of late capitalism; and about how local cultural production interconnects with or maintains some separate integrity from the global, as it is variously read as what is triumphantly 'unassimilated,'[2] or as a glocalized market fetish, or as abandoned in the embrace of modernist autonomy. It is this politicization that I have wanted to keep in view by emphasizing the touristic conscience through which the field's producers and consumers work to distinguish their practices from others who belong to the same broad network.

Until the time when these speculative statements about the field's constitutive features – its politicized relationship to global capitalism, and its participants' tendency toward self-consciousness – might give way to concrete empirical research, which would itself be inevitably challenged by the necessary caveats to empiricism's claims, one thing that we do have for assessment are the figures of readership and authorship perceivably deployed by producers working within the postcoloniality industry. My own interest has been in identifying some of these figures and thinking about why they exist and take the shape that they do.

In part, self-consciousness about socio-cultural identity and positioning has become an essential, expected feature of contemporary culture, extending well beyond the postcolonial field. We all undertake routine, requisite forms of self-conscious articulation, whether to self-authenticate, self-implicate, or self-celebrate, because we are suspicious that others will otherwise do it for us, or, more likely, because they have done so already. This is what David Simpson critiques as the inevitable 'exaltation' involved in situating oneself. It is 'a protest against an overwhelming sense of impotence,' as is certainly evident in the texts I have discussed.[3] Is the problem that, as Simpson claims, we stress attachment, allegiance, and alliance, just as we become more certain that there is nothing absolutely secure on which to premise our insistence?[4] What determines the nature of this protest for postcolonial writers in particular? That is, more specifically, how and why does the postcolonial intellectual – a category that includes literature professors and arts journalists as well as poets and novelists – self-consciously fantasize and construct the processes through which his or her own texts are consumed?

The Triple Mirror of the Self highlights, as a problem, that the association between a biographized author and a particular region can be an excessive burden within the postcoloniality industry. Despite the accepted critical truisms about the author's death, postcolonial writers are undoubtedly attached to their texts, and in ways they do not necessarily sanction. This attachment is in part a requirement of the cosmopolitan function of the literature the industry traffics in. That said, my attention to authorial self-construction, by way of recuperating authors for interpretation of their texts, comes with no necessary theoretical imperative to respect the general relevance of authorial intentionality to literary study. Instead I have wanted my readings to be less about celebrating intentionality, and more about the signs of authors' questing after a modicum of agency, however imperfect and delusional their results might be. The politics of the field of postcolonial production, as they attend the career development of many authors, inspire and delimit this questing, and also make their way into the literary works I have discussed, whether as theme, technique, or figural residue. Ghose is one example, as he uses his work to critique the marketplace through which his literature passes, by critiquing how the range of that passage is restricted by certain features of the circuit of communication. Paradoxically, recognizing the power and persuasiveness of this aspect of his novel requires substantial engagement with Ghose's biography and reception, exactly those subjects whose centrality *The Triple Mirror of the Self* laments.

Ghose's scathing characterization of cosmopolitan Jonathan Pons is also part of what Brennan promotes as an '"economics" of the cultural intellectual,' which he calls 'the most consequential field of action' for the future of globalization studies.[5] Assembling this kind of economics is an immense task, and one that my own work only begins to develop.

One of the encompassing intentions of the present study has been to encourage more analyses of the relationships between literature, politics, and economics, and therefore more interaction between humanities and social sciences approaches to cultural production. While these linkages may be common in cultural economics, communications studies, or print culture studies, it is only recently that literary scholars, and in particular scholars of postcolonial literature, have turned their attention to the specific interconnections between the content of literary work and the circuits through which texts pass as they are produced and received. Understanding and historicizing the market position of writers like Ghose, Walcott, or Coetzee signals the influence the current prominence of postcolonial writing should have on the material history of literary authorship. Attention to the politicized niche of postcolonial literature suggests that postcolonial authorial anxiety – and the specific forms of self-consciousness it gives rise to – departs from any straightforward fear of market colonization. All the works I have discussed here are exercises in self-authorization, designed to register the writer's awareness of the political uses or appropriations of his works, appropriations that are intimately related to the market function of postcolonial literatures. In a way that is perhaps uniquely relevant to postcolonial authors, commercialization and politicization are intimately connected. Indeed, as I state at the end of Part I, the career histories of the authors I have studied are evidence that transnational capitalism's relationship to cultural production is a political one.

There is very little that might accord with any putative authenticity left in the world, and literary scholars need not be, in Miyoshi's words, merely 'recognizing the different subject positions from different regions and diverse backgrounds.' Plurality is 'a given of human life,' he claims; it should be analyzed rather than trumpeted, especially when diversity and difference are often the products of inequalities we should be proposing ways to erase.[6] Critiquing a politics of authenticity, as both Zulfikar Ghose and Miyoshi do, is not equivalent to critiquing any association between writers and their texts. The problem is that the association between an author and a national authenticity is often an excessive burden within specifically postcolonial literatures, taken on as a partial requirement of the cosmopolitan function of those literatures. The fitful solution, at least for some writers, is the unique form of responsive authorial agency I've taken account of here.

Notes

Introduction

1 Jerome McGann, *The Textual Condition* (Princeton: Princeton University Press, 1991); D.F. McKenzie, *Bibliography and the Sociology of Texts* (London: British Library, 1986).

2 Gerard Genette, *Paratexts: Thresholds of Interpretation*, trans. Jane E. Lewin (Cambridge: Cambridge University Press, 1997).

3 Robert Darnton, 'What is the History of Books?' *Proceedings of the American Academy of Arts and Sciences* 3.3 (1982), 67.

4 A model based on the concept of a field of cultural production is elaborated in Pierre Bourdieu, *The Field of Cultural Production*, ed. Randal Johnson (Cambridge: Polity Press, 1993) and Pierre Bourdieu, *The Rules of Art: Genesis and Structure of the Literary Field*, trans. Susan Emanuel (Stanford: Stanford University Press, 1996); the field of postcolonial production is characterized and theorized in Graham Huggan, *The Postcolonial Exotic: Marketing the Margins* (London: Routledge, 2001).

5 Derek Walcott, 'The Fortunate Traveller,' in *The Fortunate Traveller* (New York: Farrar, Straus and Giroux, 1982), 96.

6 I adopt the phrase 'the market reader' from Wendy Waring's pioneering article on the marketing of postcolonial texts: 'Is This Your Book? Wrapping Postcolonial Fiction for the Global Market,' *Canadian Review of Comparative Literature* 22 (1995), 455–65.

7 Benita Parry, 'Directions and Dead Ends in Postcolonial Studies,' in *Relocating Postcolonialism*, eds. David Theo Goldberg and Ato Quayson (Oxford: Blackwell Publishers, 2002), 71.

8 E. San Juan Jr., *Beyond Postcolonial Theory* (New York: St. Martin's Press, 1998), 13.

9 Biodun Jeyifo, 'For Chinua Achebe: The Resilience and the Predicament of Obierika,' in *Chinua Achebe: A Celebration*, eds. Kirsten Holst Petersen and Anna Rutherford (Oxford: Heinemann, 1990), 53–4.

10 W.K. Wimsatt and Monroe C. Beardsley, 'The Intentional Fallacy,' in *The Verbal Icon: Studies in the Meaning of Poetry* (Lexington: University of Kentucky Press, 1954), 3.

11 Roland Barthes, 'The Death of the Author,' in *Image-Music-Text*, ed. and trans. Stephen Heath (London: Fontana, 1977), 142–8.

12 Séan Burke, *The Death and Return of the Author: Criticism and Subjectivity in Barthes, Foucault and Derrida* (Edinburgh: Edinburgh University Press, 1992), 157.

13 Juliet Gardiner, 'Recuperating the Author: Consuming Fictions of the 1990s,' *PBSA* 94 (2000), 257.

14 Ibid., 274.

Chapter 1   The Industry of Postcoloniality

1   Walcott, 'The Fortunate Traveller,' 89–90. Subsequent page references appear in the body of the text.
2   Huggan, *Postcolonial Exotic*, 4. Subsequent page references appear in the body of the text.
3   Some of Huggan's ideas about exoticism also appear in his earlier work on tourism; cf. Patrick Holland and Graham Huggan, *Tourists with Typewriters: Critical Reflections on Contemporary Travel Writing* (Ann Arbor: University of Michigan Press, 1998).
4   Dean MacCannell, *The Tourist: A New Theory of the Leisure Class* (New York: Schocken Books, 1976), 107. cf. Jonathan Culler, 'The Semiotics of Tourism,' in *Framing the Sign: Criticism and Its Institutions* (Norman: University of Oklahoma Press, 1988), 156.
5   Goffman characterizes 'front regions' as 'where a particular performance is or may be in progress,' whereas 'back regions' are 'where action occurs that is related to the performance but inconsistent with the appearance fostered by the performance' (*The Presentation of Self in Everyday Life* [New York: Doubleday Anchor, 1959], 134). The spatial distinction between the kitchen and the seating area in a restaurant is perhaps the most straightforward example. Goffman's broad interest is 'impression management' as a general aspect of everyday social interaction, and he does not distinguish the tourism industry from other service sector businesses. However it is interesting that his identification of the *metaphorically* theatrical or performative aspects of business practice anticipated the formation of an *intentionally* theatrical 'experience economy' that tourism is often taken to embody. Many businesses now create consumer spaces like stages, with employees engaged in performing elaborate acts designed to make consumers believe in their own participation, including staged access to the once hidden 'back regions.' So, for example, a restaurant seating area might be positioned such that diners can see what goes on in *a* kitchen, typically a cleaned-up stage version of the actual kitchen where most of the food is prepared and cooked. On tourism as the experience economy's apotheosis, see Jeremy Rifkin, *The Age of Access: The New Culture of Hypercapitalism, Where All of Life is a Paid-For Experience* (New York: Putnam, 2000), for whom it is 'much more like staged commercial entertainment than cultural visitation' (149); and John Urry, *Consuming Places* (London: Routledge, 1995), who argues that the history of tourism proves that capitalism existed in 'disorganized' forms – dependent largely on the consumption of images rather than on the production of concrete items – long before the postmodern era. Urry interprets the late capitalist economy as one in which 'tourism's specificity dissolves,' as it finally epitomizes the entire way 'contemporary social and cultural experience' is organized (148). I return to the subject of tourism's exemplarity below.
6   MacCannell, *Tourist*, 94.
7   cf. James Buzard, *The Beaten Track: European Tourism, Literature, and the Ways to Culture, 1800–1918* (Oxford: Oxford University Press, 1993), who

notes that during the industry's development the tourist was often *defined* by his inability to access what is 'authentic,' something then 'represented as a fugitive essence, hounded into hiding by encroaching modernity' (10).

8 MacCannell, *Tourist*, 94, 102.

9 Culler, 'The Semiotics of Tourism,' 164.

10 Huggan's language of condemnation compares well with Crystal Bartolovich's resolute claim that the Third World has been transformed, quite literally, into 'a battery of (highly regulated) objects for metropolitan consumption,' and that such commodification is an 'ineluctable consequence of the globality of contemporary capitalism' and its celebration of specific 'culturalisms' that detach objects from their material sources (Introduction, *Marxism, Modernity and Postcolonial Studies*, eds. Crystal Bartolovich and Neil Lazarus [Cambridge: Cambridge University Press, 2002], 14). That language is further exaggerated in the work of Tobias A. Wachinger, Huggan's former student, who states that the new writing promoted by postcolonial critics as coming from a 'space in between' the West and its former colonies is in fact 'subject to a powerful machinery of consumption [...] a particular apparatus of control' that 'reduces' all literature to the position of fetishized commodity (*Posing In-between: Postcolonial Englishness and the Commodification of Hybridity* [Frankfurt am Main: Peter Lang, 2003], 12).

11 Arif Dirlik, 'The Postcolonial Aura: Third World Criticism in the Age of Global Capitalism,' *Critical Inquiry* 20 (1994), 356, 331; Aijaz Ahmad, 'The Politics of Literary Postcoloniality,' in *Contemporary Postcolonial Theory: A Reader*, ed. Padmini Mongia (London: Arnold, 1996), 276. For further scrutiny of the complicity of postcolonial scholarship with global capitalism and its cultural offshoot, postmodernism, see, for example, San Juan Jr., *Beyond Postcolonial Theory*; Benita Parry, 'Directions and Dead Ends in Postcolonial Studies,' in *Relocating Postcolonialism*, eds. David Theo Goldberg and Ato Quayson (Oxford: Blackwell Publishers, 2002), 66–81; and Ella Shohat, 'Notes on the "Post-Colonial",' in *Contemporary Postcolonial Theory: A Reader*, ed. Padmini Mongia (London: Arnold, 1996), 321–34. Masao Miyoshi's 1993 statement is a good synthesis: 'The current academic preoccupation with "postcoloniality" and multiculturalism looks suspiciously like another alibi to conceal the actuality of global politics. [...] colonialism is even more active now in the form of transnational corporatism' ('A Borderless World? From Colonialism to Transnationalism and the Decline of the Nation-State,' *Critical Inquiry* 19 [1993], 728.)

12 Simon Gikandi, 'Globalization and the Claims of Postcoloniality,' in *Anglophone Literatures and Global Culture*, eds. Susie O'Brien and Imre Szeman, spec. issue of *South Atlantic Quarterly* 100 (2001), 646.

13 Robert J.C. Young, *Postcolonialism: an Historical Introduction* (Oxford: Blackwell, 2001), is the most notable effort. The phrase 'the historical legacy of Marxist critique' (6) is his. He also suggests that the troubled term 'postcolonialism' be jettisoned in favour of what he views as the more accurate 'tricontinentalism.' While it may seem like wishful thinking to annex for postcolonial study a uniquely 'radical political genealogy' (131), Young's term would likely prove useful in distinguishing between what has been read as irreconcilable tendencies in postcolonial literary practice.

14 Timothy Brennan, 'From development to globalization: postcolonial studies and globalization theory,' in *The Cambridge Companion to Postcolonial Literary Studies*, ed. Neil Lazarus (Cambridge: Cambridge University Press, 2004), 133.

15 Timothy Brennan, *At Home in the World: Cosmopolitanism Now* (Cambridge: Harvard University Press, 1997), 105.

16 Culler, 'The Semiotics of Tourism,' 161.

17 Ulf Hannerz, 'Cosmopolitans and Locals in World Culture,' in *Global Culture: Nationalism, Globalization and Modernity*, ed. Mike Featherstone (London: Sage, 1990), 237–41.

18 James Buzard, *Disorienting Fiction: the Autoethnographic Work of Nineteenth-Century British Novels* (Princeton: Princeton University Press, 2005), 8.

19 James Clifford argues that ethnography sought to make itself a science of observation in part through the establishment of 'a privileged allegorical register' claiming authority over other available ways of making meaning out of experience ('Ethnographic Allegory,' in *Writing Culture: The Poetics and Politics of Ethnography*, eds. James Clifford and George E. Marcus [Berkeley: University of California Press, 1986], 103).

20 James Clifford, *The Predicament of Culture: Twentieth-Century Ethnography, Literature, and Art* (Cambridge: Harvard University Press, 1988), 9.

21 Renato Rosaldo, *Culture and Truth: The Remaking of Social Analysis* (Boston: Beacon Press, 1989), 82.

22 In fact it is likely that the category of the global market reader is so abstract that it can only be deployed rhetorically, producing results that will be distant from the empirical validity so crucial to most book history methodology. A few empirical studies of reading practices of relevance to the postcolonial field do exist. Given that a key 'other' to academic readers is audiences for popular culture, it is not surprising that these have been subject to the most sustained attention, or that studies of their habits are considered part of a general field now called 'the ethnography of reading.' See, for example, Radhika Parameswaran, 'Western Romance Fiction as English-Language Media in Postcolonial India,' *Journal of Communication* 49 (1999), 84–105; Jyoti Puri, 'Reading Romance Novels in Postcolonial India,' *Gender & Society* 11 (1997), 434–52; and Wendy Griswold, *Bearing Witness: Readers, Writers, and the Novel in Nigeria* (Princeton: Princeton University Press, 2000). These studies aim at an understanding of discrete and carefully delimited 'cultures' of reading. Janice Radway's classic study of romance reading is paradigmatic (*Reading the Romance: Women, Patriarchy, and Popular Literature*, 2nd edn. [Chapel Hill: University of North Carolina Press], 1991). In it the practices of a group of small-town middle class women are surveyed, contextualized, and finally explained. Readers' responses to survey questions are not simply reported; rather they are also interpreted for an academic audience, in a way that shows what these non-academic readers do not understand about their own experiences. In this case, the claim is that their repetitive reading of mass-market romance responds to their need for a nurturing emotional sustenance denied them as subjugated members of a fundamentally patriarchal culture. Radway's involvement in the culture of romance reading is always that of an insider-outsider. She spends time with her subjects and gains their confidence, but she is not herself a romance reader. She also adheres to the feminism that the surveyed readers intuit only in part, and imperfectly.

23 Culler, 'The Semiotics of Tourism,' 158.
24 Ibid.
25 Derek Walcott, 'What the Twilight Says: An Overture,' in *Dream on Monkey Mountain and Other Plays* (New York: Farrar, Straus and Giroux, 1970), 7–8. Further page references appear in the body of the text.
26 See Ian Gregory Strachan, *Paradise and Plantation: Tourism and Culture in the Anglophone Caribbean* (Charlottesville: University of Virginia Press, 2002), 199, for a critique of Walcott's positioning of the peasant or the fisherman as the 'new Adam.'
27 Timothy Brennan, *Salman Rushdie and the Third World: Myths of the Nation* (New York: St. Martin's Press, 1989). cf. Timothy Brennan, 'Cosmopolitans and Celebrities,' *Race and Class* 31 (1989), 1–19.
28 Paul Breslin, *Nobody's Nation: Reading Derek Walcott* (Chicago: University of Chicago Press, 2001), 21.
29 Bruce King, *Derek Walcott: A Caribbean Life* (Oxford: Oxford University Press, 2000), 281.
30 Breslin, *Nobody's Nation*, 39.
31 King, *Derek Walcott*, 277.
32 Paula Burnett, *Derek Walcott: Politics and Poetics* (Gainesville: University Press of Florida, 2001), 318.
33 Qtd. in ibid., 7.
34 Breslin, *Nobody's Nation*, 42–3.
35 King, *Derek Walcott*, 407.
36 Ibid.
37 Breslin, *Nobody's Nation*, 41.
38 Stewart Brown, Introduction, *The Art of Derek Walcott*, ed. Stewart Brown (Bridgend, Wales: Seren Books, 1991), 7.
39 Walcott, 'What the Twilight Says,' 39. cf. Burnett, *Derek Walcott*, 177.
40 King, *Derek Walcott*, 385.
41 Derek Walcott, 'The Fortunate Traveller,' *London Magazine* (November 1981), 5–12.
42 Burnett, *Derek Walcott*, 178.
43 Walcott has claimed that his own early plays 'flared from a mind drenched in an Elizabeth literature,' including Webster's works ('What the Twilight Says,' 11).
44 Burnett, *Derek Walcott*, 195.
45 Ibid., 197.
46 Ibid., 201.
47 Ibid., 205. In an interview with Burnett in 1988 Walcott said, 'if tyrants read, really read, they wouldn't do what they did, because too much would be revealed, too much would touch them. I think we read now the way tyrants read: we read for information. We don't read to be touched' (Ibid., 314).
48 In fact it is a major trope for many key cosmopolitan writers, perhaps most notably V.S. Naipaul, who has claimed to feel like an exotic alien 'to those among whom he was born,' but also to a reading audience 'that is not composed of members of his own culture' (Roger Célestin, *From Cannibals to Radicals: Figures and Limits of Exoticism* [Minneapolis: University of Minnesota Press, 1996], 177). If a writer constantly states his alienation

from all available affiliations, can he be said to have an 'own culture' at all? For Célestin, Naipaul renounces what is 'primitive' and constantly deexoticizes the so-called Third World because it is the presumed integrity of some 'primitive' culture that keeps him from fully ascending to the status of the 'romantic writer' figure he most admires (199). He cannot detach no matter how much he might desire to. Naipaul embraces 'the West' because it offers him the chance to be free of responsibility. At 'home' he cannot escape concern because he cannot escape 'an affiliation that cannot accommodate a denial of the historical predicament of that area of the planet' (212). cf. Rob Nixon, *London calling: V.S. Naipaul, Postcolonial Mandarin* (Oxford: Oxford University Press, 1992).

49 John Thieme, *Derek Walcott* (Manchester: Manchester University Press, 1999), 199.
50 Burnett, *Derek Walcott*, 176.
51 Ibid., 206.
52 John Urry, *The Tourist Gaze: Leisure and Travel in Contemporary Societies* (London: Sage, 1990), 100–2.
53 Clifford, *Predicament of Culture*, 4.
54 Buzard, *Beaten Track*, 335–7.
55 Blake Morrison, 'Beach Poets,' *London Review of Books* (16 September –6 October 1982), 16.
56 Helen Vendler, 'Poet of Two Worlds,' *New York Review of Books* (4 March 1982), 23.
57 Ibid., 26.

Chapter 2   Postcolonial Writers and the Global Literary Marketplace

1 Salman Rushdie, 'In Good Faith,' in *Imaginary Homelands: Essays and Criticism 1981–1991* (London: Granta Books, 1991), 405.
2 R. Jackson Wilson, *Figures of Speech: American Writers and the Literary Marketplace, from Benjamin Franklin to Emily Dickinson* (New York: Knopf, 1989), 4.
3 Michael Newbury, *Figuring Authorship in Antebellum America* (Stanford: Stanford University Press, 1997), 5.
4 Michael T. Gilmore, *American Romanticism and the Marketplace* (Chicago: University of Chicago Press, 1985), 1. For general discussion of an ostensible 'reading revolution' see, for example, Robert Darnton, 'First Steps Toward a History of Reading,' in *The Kiss of Lamourette: Reflections in Cultural History* (New York: W.W. Norton, 1990), 154–87. For one take on a later, fuller 'explosion' of mass literacy see, for example, Janice Radway, *A Feeling for Books: The Book-of-the-Month Club, Literary Taste, and Middle-Class Desire* (Chapel Hill: University of North Carolina Press, 1997).
5 Martha Woodmansee, 'The Genius and the Copyright: Economic and Legal Conditions of the Emergence of the "Author",' *Eighteenth-Century Studies* 17 (1984), 427.
6 Ibid., 446.
7 Ibid., 426.

8 Peter Jaszi and Martha Woodmansee, Introduction, *The Construction of Authorship: Textual Appropriation in Law and Literature*, eds. Woodmansee and Jaszi (Durham: Duke University Press, 1994), 3.

9 Séan Burke, 'Reconstructing the Author,' Introduction, *Authorship: From Plato to Postmodern*, ed. Séan Burke (Edinburgh: Edinburgh University Press, 1995), xviii.

10 Mark Rose, *Authors and Owners: The Invention of Copyright* (Cambridge: Harvard University Press, 1993), 6.

11 Ibid., 13.

12 Wilson, *Figures of Speech*, 9.

13 Donald E. Pease, 'Author,' in *Authorship: From Plato to Postmodern*, ed. Séan Burke (Edinburgh: Edinburgh University Press, 1995), 268.

14 Raymond Williams, *The Long Revolution* (London: Chatto & Windus, 1961). On the modern history of the relationship between aesthetics and utility, cf. Terry Eagleton, *The Ideology of the Aesthetic* (Oxford: Basil Blackwell, 1990), and Janet Wolff, *Aesthetics and the Sociology of Art* (London: Allen & Unwin, 1983).

15 Séan Burke, 'The Biographical Imperative,' *Essays in Criticism* 52 (2002), 195.

16 Wimsatt and Beardsley, 'The Intentional Fallacy,' 12; my emphasis.

17 Pease, 'Author,' 270.

18 Eva Hemmungs Wirtén, *Global Infatuation: Explorations in Transnational Publishing and Texts: the Case of Harlequin Enterprises and Sweden* (Uppsala: Section for Sociology of Literature at the Department of Literature, Uppsala University, 1998). Transediting can be thought of as the way glocalization works in the publishing world, as an original text is edited and altered to appeal to a variety of localities that would be less receptive to it otherwise.

19 Ben Bagdikian, *The New Media Monopoly* (Boston: Beacon Press, 2004), 3–4.

20 Herbert I. Schiller, *Culture, Inc.: The Corporate Takeover of Public Expression* (Oxford: Oxford University Press, 1989), 36–7.

21 Ben Bagdikian, *The Media Monopoly*, 6th edn. (Boston: Beacon Press, 2000), 126; Eva Hemmungs Wirtén, *No Trespassing: Authorship, Intellectual Property Rights, and the Boundaries of Globalization* (Toronto: University of Toronto Press, 2004), 85.

22 Ibid., 87.

23 Richard J. Barnet and John Cavanagh, *Global Dreams: Imperial Corporations and the New World Order* (New York: Simon & Schuster, 1994), 69.

24 For recent general accounts of the process of media concentration in the publishing industry, not cited in the body of this chapter, see Beth Luey, 'The Impact of Consolidation and Internationalization,' in *The Structure of International Publishing in the 1990s*, eds. Beth Luey and Fred Kobrak (New Brunswick, NJ: Transaction Publishers, 1992), 1–22; Douglas Gomery, 'The Book Publishing Industry,' in *Who Owns the Media? Competition and Concentration in the Mass Media Industry*, 3rd edn., eds. Douglas Gomery and Benjamin M. Compaine (Mahwah, NJ: Lawrence Erlbaum Associates, 2000), 61–145. For stringent commentary on the same, in addition to Bagdikian, see, for example, Mark Crispin Miller, 'The Publishing Industry,' in *Conglomerates and the Media*, eds. Patricia Aufderheide et al. (New York: New Press, 1997), 107–33; Ted Solotaroff, 'The Literary-Industrial Complex,' *New*

Republic (8 June 1987), 28–45; Leo Bogart, *Commercial Culture: The Media System and the Public Interest* (New York: Oxford University Press, 1995). Laura J. Miller attempts to keep up with the breathless pace of changes in ownership patterns ('Major Publishers with North American Holdings,' 1 August 2006 <http://people.brandeis.edu/~lamiller/publishers.html>).

25 Gordon Graham, 'Multinational Publishing,' in *International Book Publishing: An Encyclopedia*, eds. Philip G. Altbach and Edith S. Hushino (New York: Garland, 1995), 243–6.
26 Ibid., 244.
27 Jason Epstein, *Book Business: Publishing Past, Present, and Future* (New York: W.W. Norton, 2001), 4.
28 Ibid., 12–13.
29 Ibid., 13, 26.
30 Schiller, *Culture, Inc.*, 32.
31 Randall Stevenson, 'A Golden Age? Readers, Authors, and the Book Trade,' in *Oxford English Literary History*, Vol. 12, *1960–2000: The Last of England?* (Oxford: Oxford University Press, 2004), 129–30.
32 Ibid., 149.
33 Elizabeth Long, 'The Cultural Meaning of Concentration in Publishing,' in *The Structure of International Publishing in the 1990s*, eds. Beth Luey and Fred Kobrak (New Brunswick, NJ: Transaction Publishers, 1992), 99.
34 Ibid., 94.
35 Rowland Lorimer and Eleanor O'Donnell, 'Globalization and International-ization in Publishing,' *Canadian Journal of Communications* 17 (1992), 494.
36 Ibid., 500.
37 *Books in Print 2003–2004*, Vol. 8, *Authors S–Z / Publishers & Indexes* (New Providence, NJ: Bowker, 2003), vii.
38 Bagdikian, *Media Monopoly*, 19.
39 Ibid.
40 André Schiffrin, 'The Corporatization of Publishing,' *The Nation* (3 June 1996), 32.
41 Long, 'Cultural Meaning,' 98.
42 Robert Escarpit, *Sociology of Literature*, 2nd edn., trans. Ernest Pick (London: Frank Cass, 1971), 59.
43 Richard Todd, *Consuming Fictions: The Booker Prize and Fiction in Britain Today* (London: Bloomsbury, 1996), 13–14. In the UK, Terry Maher had much to do with these developments. Todd (123–4) notes that Maher's Pentos company acquired Dillon's in 1977 and turned it from a university bookshop into a major retailer of a wide variety of books. Rival chain Waterstone & Co. Ltd., later Waterstone's, founded in 1982 and run by W.H. Smith from 1989, eventually took over Dillon's. When Pentos collapsed in 1995 there were approximately 150 Dillon's branches in the UK; and in 1996 there were 103 branches of Waterstone's in the UK and Ireland. cf. Maher's *Against My Better Judgment: Adventures in the City and in the Book Trade* (London: Sinclair-Stevenson, 1994), his own account of the role of Dillon's in changing English publishing and in destabilizing the Net Book Agreement, an industry standard that regulated cover prices in the English book trade until 1995, forbidding price reductions by retailers.

44 Juliet Gardiner, 'Reformulating the Reader: Internet bookselling and its impact on the construction of reading practices,' *Changing English* 9 (2002), 162–3.
45 Barnet and Cavanagh, *Global Dreams*, 79.
46 'In Full Colour: Cultural Diversity in Book Publishing Today,' ed. Danuta Kean, supplement, *The Bookseller* (12 March 2004), 3.
47 Ibid., 5.
48 Ibid., 7.
49 Ibid., 10.
50 'Penguin to set up new publishing venture in Ireland,' 1 August 2006 <http://www.penguin.ie/static/cs/uk/503/pressrelease/penguin_ireland.pdf>.
51 Paul Jay, 'Beyond Discipline? Globalization and the Future of English,' in *Globalizing Literary Studies*, ed. Giles Gunn, spec. issue of *PMLA* 116 (2001), 33.
52 Ibid., 41.
53 Biodun Jeyifo, 'On Eurocentric Critical Theory: Some Paradigms from the Texts and Sub-Texts of Post-Colonial Writing,' in *After Europe: Critical Theory and Post-Colonial Writing*, eds. Stephen Slemon and Helen Tiffin (Sydney: Dangaroo Press, 1992), 107. It is worth noting that scholarship on the history of the book has largely reflected this division. Having paid ample attention to North American and Western European histories, it is only beginning to turn to colonial and postcolonial topics (Mary Hammond and Robert Fraser, 'Conference Report I: The Colonial and Postcolonial History of the Book,' *SHARP News* 13.2 [2004], 1–2).
54 Harald Weinrich, 'Chamisso, Chamisso Authors, and Globalization,' *PMLA* 119 (2004), 1344.
55 Graham, 'Multinational Publishing,' 247.
56 Gordon Graham, 'Press File,' *LOGOS* 14 (2003), 166.
57 *Index Translationum*, UNESCO, 1 August 2006 <http://www.unesco.org/culture/xtrans/html_eng/index6.shtml>, and cited in Anthony Pym, 'Two principles, one probable paradox and a humble suggestion, all concerning percentages of translation and non-translation into various languages, particularly English,' 1 August 2006 <http://www.fut.es/~apym/on-line/rates/rates.html>, par. 1.
58 Ibid., par. 10.
59 Pascale Casanova, *The World Republic of Letters* (Cambridge: Harvard University Press, 2004), 164.
60 Wirtén, *No Trespassing*, 54.
61 Brennan, *Salman Rushdie*, 36–7.
62 Casanova, *World Republic of Letters*, 108, 197.
63 Brennan, *At Home in the World*, 39–40.
64 Brennan, 'Cosmopolitans and Celebrities,' 7.
65 Miyoshi, 'Borderless World?' 742.
66 Ibid., 750. Slavoj Žižek similarly states: 'the privileged *empty point of universality* from which one is able to appreciate (and depreciate) properly other particular cultures [...] is the very form of asserting one's own superiority,' since what appears to be 'the hybrid coexistence of diverse cultural life-worlds' is in fact 'the form of appearance of its opposite, of the massive presence of capitalism as *universal* world system' ('Multiculturalism, Or, the Cultural Logic of Multinational Capitalism,' *New Left Review*

os 225 [1997], 46). It is worth noting that each of these positions is significantly predicted by *The Communist Manifesto*'s claim that 'The bourgeoisie has through its exploitation of the world market given a cosmopolitan character to production and consumption in every country. [...] From the numerous national and local literatures, there arises a world literature' (Karl Marx and Friedrich Engels, *The Communist Manifesto*, trans. Samuel Moore [London: Penguin Classics, 1985], 83–4). cf. Erich Auerbach's lament that 'man will have to accustom himself to existence in a standardized world, to a single literary culture, only a few literary languages, and perhaps even a single literary language' ('Philology and *Weltliteratur*,' *Centennial Review* 13 [1969], 3).

67 Brennan, *At Home in the World*, 38.
68 Brennan, 'Cosmopolitans and Celebrities,' 2.
69 Brennan, *At Home in the World*, 38.
70 Bourdieu, *Field of Cultural Production*, 76.
71 Ibid., 39.
72 Pierre Bourdieu, *The Rules of Art: Genesis and Structure of the Literary Field*, trans. Susan Emanuel (Stanford: Stanford University Press, 1996). Page references appear in the body of the text.
73 John Guillory, 'Bourdieu's Refusal,' in *Pierre Bourdieu: Fieldwork in Culture*, eds. Nicholas Brown and Imre Szeman (Lanham, MD: Rowman & Littlefield, 2000), 37.
74 Joe Moran, *Star Authors: Literary Celebrity in America* (London: Pluto Press, 2000), 37.
75 Andrew Wernick, 'Authorship and the Supplement of Promotion,' in *What is an Author?* eds. Maurice Biriotti and Nicola Miller (Manchester: Manchester University Press, 1993), 90–1.
76 Ibid., 93.
77 Ibid., 95; my emphasis.
78 Gardiner, 'Recuperating the Author,' 270.
79 John Cawelti, 'The Writer as a Celebrity: Some Aspects of American Literature as Popular Culture,' *Studies in American Fiction* 5 (1977), 165.
80 James L. West, *American Authors and the Literary Marketplace since 1900* (Philadelphia: University of Pennsylvania Press, 1988), 12.
81 Ibid., 20.
82 Wernick, 'Authorship,' 102.
83 cf. Moran, *Star Authors*, 58.
84 Bourdieu, *Rules of Art*, 170.
85 Moran, *Star Authors*, 6.
86 Loren Glass, *Authors Inc.: Literary Celebrity in the Modern United States, 1880–1980* (New York: New York University Press, 2004), 27, 180.
87 James F. English, *The Economy of Prestige: Prizes, Awards, and the Circulation of Cultural Value* (Cambridge: Harvard University Press, 2005), 220–2.
88 Brennan, *At Home in the World*, 200.
89 Ibid., 203.
90 David Simpson, *Situatedness, or, Why We Keep Saying Where We're Coming From* (Durham: Duke University Press, 2000), 217.
91 Ibid., 11.
92 cf. Miyoshi, 'A Borderless World?' 751.

93   Qtd. in Rebecca Allison, 'Novelist quits "imperial" Commonwealth contest,' *The Guardian* (22 March 2001), 5.
94   Aijaz Ahmad, *In Theory: Classes, Nations, Literatures* (London: Verso, 1992), 44, 80.
95   Ibid., 45.
96   Ibid., 81.
97   Ibid., 36–7.
98   Moran, *Star Authors*, 68–9.
99   Ibid., 70.

Chapter 3   Salman Rushdie's 'Unbelonging': Authorship and 'The East'

1   English, *Economy of Prestige*, 312.
2   Ibid., 320.
3   Casanova, *World Republic of Letters*, 12.
4   Ibid., 169.
5   Ibid., 171.
6   Ibid., 172.
7   Salman Rushdie, *Fury* (Toronto: Vintage, 2002), 24. Subsequent page references appear in the body of the text.
8   Salman Rushdie, *The Ground Beneath Her Feet* (Toronto: Vintage, 1999), 482.
9   Qtd. in Brian Stewart, '*The Magazine* Interview: Salman Rushdie,' in *Salman Rushdie Interviews: A Sourcebook of his Ideas*, ed. Pradyumna S. Chauhan (Westport, CT: Greenwood Press, 2001), 292.
10 W.J. Weatherby, *Salman Rushdie: Sentenced to Death* (New York: Carroll & Graff, 1990), 42.
11 Ian Hamilton, 'The First Life of Salman Rushdie,' *New Yorker* (25 December 1995 & 1 January 1996), 112.
12 Weatherby, *Salman Rushdie*, 79.
13 Ibid., 150.
14 Eric de Bellaigue, *British Book Publishing as a Business since the 1960s* (London: The British Library, 2004), 53.
15 Huggan, *Postcolonial Exotic*, 85.
16 Revathi Krishnaswamy, 'Mythologies of Migrancy: Postcolonialism, Postmodernism, and the Political of (Dis)location,' *Ariel* 26 (1995), 128.
17 Ibid., 134.
18 Rob Nixon, 'London Calling: V.S. Naipaul and the License of Exile,' *South Atlantic Quarterly* 87 (1988), 7.
19 Amit Chaudhuri, 'The Construction of the Indian Novel in English,' Introduction, *The Picador Book of Modern Indian Literature*, ed. Amit Chaudhuri (London: Picador, 2001), xxiv.
20 Ibid., xxv.
21 Ahmad, *In Theory*, 75. cf. Vikram Chandra, who has critiqued, defensively, what he identifies as the conflation of 'regional' writing with freedom from the taint of ideology or Western influence, calling it a 'search for saints' ('The Cult of Authenticity,' *Boston Review* 25 [February/March 2000], 1 August 2006 <http://bostonreview.net/BR25.1/chandra.html>, par. 36).

He points out that 'on Indian campuses' IWE is often referred to as *'bhasa* writing': *'Bhasa* is literally "language," and therefore Indo-Anglian writing is non-language writing. Indo-Anglian writers, then, are writers from nowhere ['pan Indian or, worse, cosmopolitan'] who write in a non-language' (par. 25).

22 Krishnaswamy, 'Mythologies of Migrancy,' 129, 139.

23 Leela Gandhi, 'Indo-Anglian Fiction: Writing India, Elite Aesthetics, and the Rise of the "Stephanian" Novel,' *Australian Humanities Review* 8 (1997–98), 1 August 2006 <http://www.lib.latrobe.edu.au/AHR/archive/>, par. 18.

24 Bishnupriya Ghosh, *When Borne Across: Literary Cosmopolitics in the Contemporary Indian Novel* (New Brunswick, NJ: Rutgers University Press, 2004), 3.

25 Ibid., 61, 58.

26 Salman Rushdie, Introduction, *The Screenplay of* Midnight's Children (London: Vintage, 1999), 10.

27 Ibid., 1, 12.

28 Salman Rushdie, *Shame* (London: Picador, 1984), 28.

29 Salman Rushdie, 'A Dream of Glorious Return,' in *Step Across This Line: Collected Nonfiction 1992–2002* (New York: Random House, 2002), 181.

30 Salman Rushdie, 'Damme, This is the Oriental Scene for You!' *New Yorker* (23 & 30 June 1997), 50.

31 Ibid., 52.

32 Ibid., 54.

33 Salman Rushdie, *The Jaguar Smile: A Nicaraguan Journey* (New York: Viking, 1987), 13. Subsequent page references appear in the body of the text.

34 In particular, media outlets in Honduras and Costa Rica have been linked to anti-Sandinista, pro-contra funding sources in the US, including the CIA (see, for example, Angharad N. Valdivia, 'The U.S. Intervention in Nicaragua and Other Latin American Media,' in *Revolution and Counterrevolution in Nicaragua*, ed. Thomas W. Walker [Boulder, CO: Westview Press, 1990], 352).

35 For accounts of these developments see Brij V. Lal and Michael Pretes, eds., *Coup: Reflections on the Political Crisis in Fiji* (Canberra, Australia: Pandanus Books, 2001), and Satendra P. Nandan, *Fiji: Paradise in Pieces*, comp. and ed. Anthony Mason (Bedford Park, Australia: Centre for Research in the New Literatures in English, 2000).

36 Victor Lal, *Fiji, Coups in Paradise: Race, Politics and Military Intervention* (London: Zed Books, 1990), 13.

37 Andrew Ross, 'Cultural Preservation in the Polynesia of the Latter-Day Saints,' in *The Chicago Gangster Theory of Life: Nature's Debt to Society* (London: Verso, 1994), 90.

38 Taina Woodward, 'On Being Fijian,' in *Coup: Reflections on the Political Crisis in Fiji*, eds. Brij V. Lal and Michael Pretes (Canberra, Australia: Pandanus Books, 2001), 49.

39 Ibid., 50.

40 See, for example, Sanjay Ramesh, 'The Race Bandwagon,' in *Coup: Reflections on the Political Crisis in Fiji*, eds. Brij V. Lal and Michael Pretes (Canberra, Australia: Pandanus Books, 2001), 125.

41 Martine Hennard Dutheil de la Rochère, *Origin and Originality in Rushdie's Fiction* (Bern: Peter Lang, 1999), 217.

42 Rushdie, 'In Good Faith,' 395, 402, 403.

43 Séan Burke, 'Ideologies and Authorship,' in *Authorship: From Plato to Postmodern*, ed. Séan Burke (Edinburgh: Edinburgh University Press, 1995), 219.

44 Rushdie, 'In Good Faith,' 404.

45 Ibid., 406.

46 Ahmad, *In Theory*, 157.

47 His 1999 collaboration with U2, resulting in the real-world production of the eponymous hit song from *The Ground Beneath Her Feet* – lyrics by Rushdie, music by Bono – is one example. His cameo appearance in *Bridget Jones's Diary* (2001) is another.

48 Daniel J. Boorstin, *The Image: a Guide to Pseudo-Events in America* (New York: Harper & Row, 1961), 57.

49 Joe Moran, *Star Authors*, 22.

50 Leah Price, 'From Ghostwriter to Typewriter: Delegating Authority at Fin de Siècle,' in *The Faces of Anonymity: Anonymous and Pseudonymous Publication from the Sixteenth to the Twentieth Century*, ed. Robert J. Griffin (New York: Palgrave, 2003), 214.

51 Amitava Kumar, 'The Bend in their Rivers,' rev. of *Fury*, by Salman Rushdie, and *Half a Life*, by V.S. Naipaul, *The Nation* (26 November 2001), 34.

52 Ibid., 35.

53 cf. the following reviews: Boyd Tonkin, 'Fury! The Savaging of Salman Rushdie,' *The Independent* (7 September 2001), 1; John Leonard, 'Puppet Show,' *New York Review of Books* (4 October 2001), 35–7; Bharat Tandon, 'Confusion in the doll's house,' *TLS* (7 September 2001), 4–5. On the turn against Rushdie see John Sutherland, 'Suddenly, Rushdie's a second division dud,' *The Guardian* (3 September 2001), 5.

54 Rushdie, 'A Dream of Glorious Return,' 190.

55 Ibid., 191.

56 Ibid., 206–7.

Chapter 4   Locating J.M. Coetzee

1 J.M. Coetzee, 'What is a Classic? A Lecture,' in *Stranger Shores: Essays 1986–1999* (London: Secker & Warburg, 2001), 1–19. cf., in the same volume, 'Gordimer and Turgenev' (268–83) and 'Translating Kafka' (88–103).

2 In Coetzee's own brief comments on the Rushdie affair, he calls it 'a badge of honor to have been acted against punitively,' one that he has never achieved, 'nor, to be frank, merited' (J.M. Coetzee, *Doubling the Point: Essays and Interviews*, ed. David Attwell [Cambridge: Harvard University Press, 1992], 298).

3 Ian Glenn, 'Nadine Gordimer, J.M. Coetzee, and the Politics of Interpretation,' *South Atlantic Quarterly* 93 (1994), 30.

4 Qtd. in Peter D. McDonald, '"Not Undesirable": J.M. Coetzee and the Burdens of Censorship,' in *Re-constructing the Book: Literary Texts in Transmission*, eds. Maureen Bell et al. (Burlington, VT: Ashgate, 2001), 180.

5 Qtd. in Peter D. McDonald, 'The Writer, the Critic, and the Censor: J.M. Coetzee and the Question of Literature,' *Book History* 7 (2004), 290.

6   McDonald, '"Not Undesirable",' provides an excellent brief history of literary censorship under apartheid, emphasizing the gradual liberalization of
the activities of the boards. For more on South African literature and censorship see J.M. Coetzee, 'Emerging from Censorship,' and 'The Work of the
Censor: Censorship in South Africa,' in his *Giving Offence: Essays on
Censorship* (Chicago: University of Chicago Press, 1996), 34–47, and
185–203; and Nadine Gordimer, *What Happened to* Burger's Daughter, *Or
How South African Censorship Works* (Emmarentia, South Africa: Taurus,
1980).

7   Coetzee, *Doubling the Point*, 298.

8   Phaswane Mpe and Monica Seeber, 'The Politics of Book Publishing in
South Africa: a Critical Overview,' in *The Politics of Publishing in South Africa*,
eds. Nicholas Evans and Monica Seeber (London: Holger Ehling Publishing,
2000), 25–6.

9   Albert Grundlingh, 'Publishing the Past: Ravan Press and Historical
Writing,' in *Ravan: Twenty-Five Years (1972–1997)*, ed. G.E. de Villiers
(Randburg, South Africa: Ravan Press, 1997), 27.

10   Nicholas Combrinck and Maggie Davey, 'We Will Publish What You Deem
to be Great: A Dialogue about Trade Publishing and Its Readers in South
Africa,' in *The Politics of Publishing in South Africa*, eds. Nicholas Evans and
Monica Seeber (London: Holger Ehling Publishing, 2000), 227.

11   Eve Horwitz Gray, 'The sad ironies of South African publishing today,' *Logos*
7 (1996), 262.

12   Glenn Moss, 'The life and changing times of an independent publisher in
South Africa,' *Logos* 4 (1993), 144.

13   Peter Randall, 'The beginnings of Ravan Press: a memoir,' in *Ravan: Twenty-
Five Years (1972–1997)*, ed. G.E. de Villiers (Randburg, South Africa: Ravan
Press, 1997), 9.

14   Mpe and Seeber, 'The Politics of Book Publishing in South Africa,' 26.

15   Guy Berger, 'Publishing for the People: The Alternative Press 1980–1999,' in
The Politics of Publishing in South Africa, eds. Nicholas Evans and Monica
Seeber (London: Holger Ehling Publishing, 2000), 87.

16   Dick Cloete, 'Alternative Publishing in South Africa in the 1970s and
1980s,' in *The Politics of Publishing in South Africa*, eds. Nicholas Evans and
Monica Seeber (London: Holger Ehling Publishing, 2000), 68.

17   Mpe and Seeber, 'The Politics of Book Publishing in South Africa,' 35.

18   Michael Chapman, *Southern African Literatures* (London: Longman, 1996),
385.

19   David Attwell, 'The Problem of History in the Fiction of J.M. Coetzee,' in
Rendering Things Visible: Essays on South African Literary Culture, ed. Martin
Trump (Athens: Ohio University Press, 1990), 102.

20   Alf Stadler, *The Political Economy of Modern South Africa* (London: Croom
Helm, 1987), 96.

21   David Philip and Mike Kantey, 'South Africa,' in *International Book
Publishing: An Encyclopedia*, eds. Philip G. Altbach and Edith S. Hushino
(New York: Garland Publishing, Inc., 1995), 419.

22   Chapman, *Southern African Literatures*, 385–6. cf. Glenn, 'Nadine Gordimer,'
who states things perhaps too starkly: 'South African dealers in symbolic
capital or cultural goods in an international market during the past thirty

years increasingly had to have an antiapartheid record, had to have the sanction of black political organizations' (18).

23 Nadine Gordimer, 'The Idea of Gardening,' rev. of *The Life and Times of Michael K*, by J.M. Coetzee, in *Critical Essays on J.M. Coetzee*, ed. Sue Kossew (New York: G.K. Hall, 1998), 139–44. Rpt. from *New York Review of Books* (2 February 1984), 3, 6. Page references are from the 1998 volume.
24 Ibid., 143.
25 Ibid., 139.
26 Ibid., 141.
27 Qtd. in McDonald, 'The Writer, the Critic, and the Censor,' 291.
28 Chapman, *Southern African Literatures*, 389.
29 Louise Bethlehem, '"A Primary Need as Strong as Hunger": The Rhetoric of Urgency in South African Literary Culture under Apartheid,' *Poetics Today* 22 (2001), 376.
30 Teresa Dovey, *The Novels of J.M. Coetzee: Lacanian Allegories* (Craighall, South Africa: Ad. Donker, 1988). Papers from the *Foe* conference are assembled in *Foe*, ed. Marianne de Jong, spec. issue of the *Journal of Literary Studies* 5 (1989).
31 Michael Chapman, 'The writing of politics and the politics of writing: on reading Dovey on reading Lacan on reading Coetzee on reading...(?),' *Journal of Literary Studies* 4 (1988), 327.
32 Ibid., 334.
33 Teresa Dovey, Introduction, *J.M. Coetzee: A Bibliography*, comps. Kevin Goddard and John Read (Grahamstown, South Africa: National English Literary Museum, 1990), 1.
34 Ibid., 2, 12.
35 Ibid., 5.
36 Bethlehem, '"A Primary Need",' 366.
37 Ibid., 375, 368.
38 David Attwell, *J.M. Coetzee: South Africa and the Politics of Writing* (Los Angeles: University of California Press, 1993); both Benita Parry, 'Speech and Silence in the fictions of J.M. Coetzee' (149–65) and David Attwell, '"Dialogue" and "fulfilment" in J.M. Coetzee's *Age of Iron*' (166–79) appear in *Writing South Africa: Literature, Apartheid, and Democracy, 1970–1995*, eds. Derek Attridge and Rosemary Jolly (Cambridge: Cambridge University Press, 1998).
39 Attwell, *J.M. Coetzee*, 1–2.
40 Glenn, 'Nadine Gordimer,' 11.
41 Casanova, *World Republic of Letters*, 148.
42 Ibid., 149.
43 Qtd. in Alan Riding, 'Coetzee, Writer of Apartheid as Bleak Mirror, Wins Nobel,' *New York Times* (3 October 2003), A1.
44 Glenn, 'Nadine Gordimer,' 13–14.
45 Qtd. in Dovey, Introduction, 6.
46 Coetzee, 'Gordimer and Turgenev,' 272.
47 Coetzee, *Doubling the Point*, 202–3, 145, 339.
48 Coetzee, 'Emerging from Censorship,' 46.
49 J.M. Coetzee, *The Master of Petersburg* (London: Minerva, 1995). Page references appear in the body of the text.

50 J.M. Coetzee, 'Confession and Double Thoughts: Tolstoy, Rousseau, Dostoevsky (1985),' in *Doubling the Point: Essays and Interviews*, ed. David Attwell (Cambridge: Harvard University Press, 1992), 291, 288.
51 J.M. Coetzee, 'Dostoevsky: *The Miraculous Years*,' in *Stranger Shores: Essays 1986–1999* (London: Secker & Warburg, 2001), 141.
52 J.M. Coetzee, *Disgrace* (London: Vintage, 2000). Page references appear in the body of the text.
53 Mark Sanders, 'Disgrace,' in *J.M. Coetzee's* Disgrace, ed. Derek Attridge, spec. issue of *interventions* 4 (2002), 365–6.
54 Heather Deegan, *The Politics of the New South Africa: Apartheid and After* (London: Longman, 2001), 137–9.
55 Sue Kossew, 'The Politics of Shame and Redemption in J.M. Coetzee's *Disgrace*,' *Research-in-African-Literatures* 34 (2003), 159.
56 Richard A. Wilson, *The Politics of Truth and Reconciliation in South Africa: Legitimizing the Post-Apartheid State* (Cambridge: Cambridge University Press, 2001), xix.
57 Ibid., 131.
58 Isidore Diala, 'Nadine Gordimer, J.M. Coetzee, and André Brink: Guilt, Expiation and the Reconciliation Process in Post-Apartheid South Africa,' *Journal of Modern Literature* 25 (2001–2), 57.
59 Coetzee, 'Confession and Double Thoughts,' 291.
60 Coetzee, *Doubling the Point*, 338–9.
61 Grant Farred, 'Bulletproof Settlers: The Politics of Offense in the New South Africa,' in *Whiteness: a Critical Reader*, ed. Mike Hill (New York: New York University Press, 1997), 64–5.
62 Ibid., 67. Grant Farred has also written on Coetzee and on *Disgrace*, mainly in negative terms. See 'The Mundanacity of Violence: Living in a State of Disgrace,' in *J.M. Coetzee's* Disgrace, ed. Derek Attridge, spec. issue of *interventions* 4 (2002), 352–62, and 'Back to the borderlines: thinking race *Disgrace*fully,' in *Symposium on* Disgrace, eds. Leon de Kock and Deirdre Byrne, spec. issue of *scrutiny2* 7 (2002), 16–19.
63 David Attwell and Barbara Harlow, Introduction, *South African Fiction After Apartheid*, eds. David Attwell and Barbara Harlow, spec. issue of *Modern Fiction Studies* 46 (2000), 2–3.
64 Attwell, '"Dialogue" and "fulfilment",' 338.
65 For a more utopian assessment of the importance of the commission see Rosemary Jolly, 'Desiring Good(s) in the Face of Marginalized Subjects: South Africa's Truth and Reconciliation Commission in a Global Context,' in *Anglophone Literatures and Global Culture*, eds. Susie O'Brien and Imre Szeman, spec. issue of *South Atlantic Quarterly* 100 (2001), 693–715.
66 J.M. Coetzee, *Elizabeth Costello* (London: Secker & Warburg, 2003). Page references appear in the body of the text.
67 For example, its first chapter is based on J.M. Coetzee, 'What is Realism?' *Salmagundi* 114–115 (1997), 60–81, acknowledged there as first delivered as the Ben Belitt Lecture at Bennington College in 1996. It or a similar piece was also given as the Dawson Scott Memorial Lecture at PEN's International Writers Day in 1996. It was thus composed for a listening audience, and instead of directly addressing the question of the nature of realism Coetzee complicates matters by telling a story about a character named Elizabeth

Costello who is invited to a similar speaking engagement and gives a talk called 'What is Realism?' Other chapters derive from similar circumstances.

68 Coetzee first delivered both of these chapters, 'The Lives of Animals' and 'The Poets and the Animals,' as talks in the late 1990s. cf. J.M. Coetzee, *The Lives of Animals* (Princeton: Princeton University Press, 1999).
69 Gilles Deleuze and Félix Guattari. *Kafka: Toward a Minor Literature*, trans. Dana Polan (Minneapolis: University of Minnesota Press, 1986).
70 Coetzee, *Doubling the Point*, 200.
71 Coetzee, 'Gordimer and Turgenev,' 280.
72 Graham Peachey, 'The post-apartheid sublime: rediscovering the extraordinary,' in *Writing South Africa: Literature, Apartheid, and Democracy, 1970–1995*, eds. Derek Attridge and Rosemary Jolly (Cambridge: Cambridge University Press, 1998), 57. cf. Njabulo S. Ndebele, *South African Literature and Culture: Rediscovery of the Ordinary* (Manchester: Manchester University Press, 1994).
73 Shaun Irlam, 'Unraveling the Rainbow: the Remission of Nation in Post-Apartheid Literature,' in *After the Thrill is Gone: A Decade of Post-Apartheid South Africa*, eds. Rita Barnard and Grant Farred, spec. issue of *South Atlantic Quarterly* 103 (2004), 712.

Chapter 5   Zulfikar Ghose and Cosmopolitan Authentication

1 Zulfikar Ghose, in interview. See Chelva Kanaganayakam, 'Zulfikar Ghose: An Interview,' *Twentieth Century Literature* 32 (1986), 180.
2 Zulfikar Ghose, *The Fiction of Reality* (London: Macmillan, 1983), 76.
3 Feroza Jussawalla and Reed Way Dasenbrock, Introduction (108–9), and 'A Conversation with Zulfikar Ghose' (140–53), in *Milan Kundera / Zulfikar Ghose*, spec. issue of *Review of Contemporary Fiction* 9.2 (1989).
4 Personal interview with Zulfikar Ghose, 25 January 2004, unpublished.
5 Ibid.
6 Ibid.
7 Zulfikar Ghose, *The Triple Mirror of the Self* (London: Bloomsbury, 1992). Page references appear in the body of the text.
8 Brennan, *At Home in the World*, 39–40.
9 Personal interview.
10 Chelva Kanaganayakam, *Structures of Negation: the Writings of Zulfikar Ghose* (Toronto: University of Toronto Press, 1993), 5.
11 Reed Way Dasenbrock, rev. of *The Triple Mirror of the Self*, by Zulfikar Ghose, *World Literature Today* 66 (1992), 785.
12 Jussawalla and Dasenbrock, Introduction, 108.
13 Kanaganayakam, *Structures of Negation*, 172–7.
14 Kanaganayakam, 'Zulfikar Ghose,' 169.
15 Dasenbrock, rev. of *The Triple Mirror of the Self*, 785.
16 Jussawalla and Dasenbrock, 'Conversation with Zulfikar Ghose,' 148.
17 Kanaganayakam, 'Zulfikar Ghose,' 169.
18 M.G. Vassanji, 'A Conversation with Zulfikar Ghose,' *Toronto South Asian Review* 4.3 (1986), 19.

19 Jussawalla and Dasenbrock, 'Conversation with Zulfikar Ghose,' 144.
20 Kanaganayakam, 'Zulfikar Ghose,' 171.
21 Zulfikar Ghose, *Confessions of a Native-Alien* (London: Routledge & Kegan Paul, 1965), 2.
22 Ibid., 1–2.
23 Kanaganayakam, 'Zulfikar Ghose,' 178.
24 Ibid., 179.
25 Vassanji, 'Conversation with Zulfikar Ghose,' 21.
26 Ibid., 17–18.
27 Ibid., 20.
28 Jussawalla and Dasenbrock, 'Conversation with Zulfikar Ghose,' 146.
29 Zulfikar Ghose, *The Art of Creating Fiction* (London: MacMillan, 1991), 154.
30 Kanaganayakam, *Structures of Negation*, 3–4.
31 Zulfikar Ghose, 'Orwell and I,' *Toronto Review of Contemporary Writing Abroad* 19.3 (2001), 17.
32 See, for example, Ghose, *Art of Creating Fiction*, 35, 44.
33 Personal interview. cf. Ghose, 'Orwell and I,' for additional commentary on the categories through which those given a Third World label are allowed to participate in the literary marketplace. Ghose speculates that for a writer like Orwell an Indian birth is considered a mere accident, while for him it is the defining feature of his participation in literary culture. Even if he had moved to India as a small child, Ghose speculates, he would 'remain where the English placed me soon after I began to publish in London – somewhere just outside their peripheral vision where they occasionally see a blur that sometimes appears to have an interesting definition but remains a blur' (15). He notes, for example, his inclusion in early anthologies of Commonwealth poetry, and attributes this to his having been born in Pakistan and available for filling a niche that few others could at the time (19).
34 Kanaganayakam, 'Zulfikar Ghose,' 169.
35 Burke, *Death and Return*, xvi.
36 Later in the novel, Pons recounts a story told by Shimomura's wife in a letter to a friend, in which she and her husband get lost in the Arizona desert and end up in a village called Kailost (notably, an anagram for Sailkot). They witness a 'tortoise dance' put on by the 'Indians' who live there. Mokhwa Jaghès, a village elder, must more or less force the participants to remember their parts, which they seem to be otherwise making up as they go along. The performance is comically inept and ends in a brawl, to which Mokhwa says, 'Nothing comes back of the past, ceremony is dead in us' (147). In addition, the Sailkot / Kailost confusion shares something with the fact that Shimomura sees a Gujarati village girl in Isabel, and she a South American in him.
37 W.H. New, 'Ghose, Zulfikar,' in *Contemporary Novelists*, 5th edn., ed. Lesley Henderson (Chicago: St. James Press, 1991), 358.
38 Shohat, 'Notes on the "Post-Colonial",' 330.
39 Sheldon Pollock, 'Cosmopolitan and Vernacular in History,' in *Cosmopolitanism*, eds. Carol A. Breckenridge et al. (Durham: Duke University Press, 2002), 17.
40 Ibid., 47.

41 Ghose commented on nationality and belonging in an interview in 1991, in a way that additionally evokes Suxavat. He calls nations myths or fantasies produced by 'years of propaganda by the airlines,' and argues that 'the idea of a fantasy home that perhaps all people possess is the idea of that alternative life in which we are somehow better and happier, it is perhaps a rehearsal of the other life that we might want to choose as a permanent abode' (Bruce Meyer, 'An Interview with Zulfikar Ghose,' in *Selected Poems*, by Zulfikar Ghose [Karachi: Oxford University Press, 1991], 101). The actuality of place is less important than one's desire for another life, and individuals are attracted to the specifics of nationality out of a desire for that 'fantasy home,' a desire that is easily manipulated.

42 Aamer Hussein, 'In various incarnations,' *TLS* (20 March 1992), 20.

43 Qtd. in Kanaganayakam, *Structures of Negation*, 138.

44 Zulfikar Ghose, *A New History of Torments* (New York: Holt, Rinehart & Winston, 1982), 157. Subsequent page references appear in the body of the text.

45 Zulfikar Ghose, *Figures of Enchantment* (New York: Harper & Row, 1986), 5. Subsequent page references appear in the body of the text.

46 Timothy Brennan, 'Cosmo-Theory,' in *Anglophone Literatures and Global Culture*, eds. Susie O'Brien and Imre Szeman, spec. issue of *South Atlantic Quarterly* 100 (2001): 660.

47 Along the way, Shimomura marries the Peruvian Isabel Valdivieso. Pons is obviously hostile to Isabel, calling her one of the 'new species of highly motivated and politically aggressive female professors' (137). He characterizes her as a woman plagued by origins that she constantly tries to elude or escape. Isabel's father is said to have served as Minister of the Interior in Peru – a mirror for the Interior Ministry in Urim's narrative – and she distances herself from his political brutality by losing herself in America and the American dream. Even her overly green lawn is unnatural in the desert of the Southwest (151). Her pursuit of a 'normal' American life and a successful suburban existence is said to have disappointed her husband. She travels to Peru with her daughter, attempting to orchestrate a definitive break with her past, but is killed in a case of mistaken identity, the car she was travelling in having been previously reserved for a conservative presidential candidate. There is irony in her death, as her conflicted relationship with her past and her father's brutalities, precisely what she was seeking distance from in visiting Peru, finds her eventually figured as a stand-in for her conservative father, a potentially legitimate target of terrorist rage (178). Pons tells her tale as an explanation for Shimomura's flight to South America and subsequent residence in Suxavat as Urim. His approach to her story emphasizes what he sees as the dangers of attempting to definitively leave one's past behind. Isabel's story is in many ways a literalization of the idea that a person's origins author her subsequent life, despite her efforts to ensure otherwise.

48 Ghose, *Art of Creating Fiction*, 155.

49 Brennan, *Salman Rushdie*, 26.

Conclusion

1 A decline in US readership for the 'literature' category is in fact lamented in a recent and much publicized study: *Reading at Risk: a Survey of Literary Reading in America* (Washington: National Endowment for the Arts, 2004).
2 Ahmad, *In Theory*, 81.
3 Simpson, *Situatedness*, 197.
4 Ibid., 217.
5 Brennan, 'From development to globalization,' 138.
6 Miyoshi, 'Borderless World?' 751.

Select Bibliography

Ahmad, Aijaz. *In Theory: Classes, Nations, Literatures*. London: Verso, 1992.

Altbach, Philip G., and Edith S. Hushino, eds. *International Book Publishing: An Encyclopedia*. New York: Garland Publishing, Inc., 1995.

Attridge, Derek, and Rosemary Jolly, eds. *Writing South Africa: Literature, Apartheid, and Democracy, 1970–1995*. Cambridge: Cambridge University Press, 1998.

Attwell, David. *J.M. Coetzee: South Africa and the Politics of Writing*. Los Angeles: University of California Press, 1993.

——, and Barbara Harlow, eds. *South African Fiction After Apartheid*. Spec. issue of *Modern Fiction Studies* 46 (2000).

Bagdikian, Ben. *The Media Monopoly*. 6th edn. Boston: Beacon Press, 2000.

——. *The New Media Monopoly*. Boston: Beacon Press, 2004.

Barnard, Rita, and Grant Farred, eds. *After the Thrill is Gone: A Decade of Post-Apartheid South Africa*. Spec. issue of *South Atlantic Quarterly* 103 (2004).

Barnet, Richard J., and John Cavanagh. *Global Dreams: Imperial Corporations and the New World Order*. New York: Simon & Schuster, 1994.

Barthes, Roland. *Image-Music-Text*. ed. and trans. Stephen Heath. London: Fontana, 1977.

Bell, Maureen, et al., eds. *Re-constructing the Book: Literary Texts in Transmission*. Burlington, VT: Ashgate, 2001.

Biriotti, Maurice, and Nicola Miller, eds. *What is an Author?* Manchester: Manchester University Press, 1993.

Bogart, Leo. *Commercial Culture: The Media System and the Public Interest*. New York: Oxford University Press, 1995.

Boorstin, Daniel J. *The Image: a Guide to Pseudo-Events in America*. New York: Harper & Row, 1961.

Bourdieu, Pierre. *The Field of Cultural Production*. ed. Randal Johnson. Cambridge: Polity Press, 1993.

——. *The Rules of Art: Genesis and Structure of the Literary Field*. trans. Susan Emanuel. Stanford: Stanford University Press, 1996.

Breckenridge, Carol A., et al., eds. *Cosmopolitanism*. Durham: Duke University Press, 2002.

Brennan, Timothy. *At Home in the World: Cosmopolitanism Now*. Cambridge: Harvard University Press, 1997.

——. *Salman Rushdie and the Third World: Myths of the Nation*. New York: St. Martin's Press, 1989.

Breslin, Paul. *Nobody's Nation: Reading Derek Walcott*. Chicago: University of Chicago Press, 2001.

Brown, Stewart, ed. *The Art of Derek Walcott*. Bridgend, Wales: Seren Books, 1991.

Burke, Séan. *The Death and Return of the Author: Criticism and Subjectivity in Barthes, Foucault and Derrida*. Edinburgh: Edinburgh University Press, 1992.

——, ed. *Authorship: From Plato to Postmodern*. Edinburgh: Edinburgh University Press, 1995.

Burnett, Paula. *Derek Walcott: Politics and Poetics*. Gainesville: University Press of Florida, 2001.

Casanova, Pascale. *The World Republic of Letters*. Cambridge: Harvard University Press, 2004.

Célestin, Roger. *From Cannibals to Radicals: Figures and Limits of Exoticism*. Minneapolis: University of Minnesota Press, 1996.

Chapman, Michael. *Southern African Literatures*. London: Longman, 1996.

Chaudhuri, Amit, ed. *The Picador Book of Modern Indian Literature*. London: Picador, 2001.

Clifford, James. *The Predicament of Culture: Twentieth-Century Ethnography, Literature, and Art*. Cambridge: Harvard University Press, 1988.

Coetzee, J.M. *Disgrace*. London: Vintage, 2000.

——. *Doubling the Point: Essays and Interviews*. ed. David Attwell. Cambridge: Harvard University Press, 1992.

——. *Elizabeth Costello*. London: Secker & Warburg, 2003.

——. *Giving Offence: Essays on Censorship*. Chicago: University of Chicago Press, 1996.

——. *The Master of Petersburg*. London: Minerva, 1995.

——. *Stranger Shores: Essays 1986–1999*. London: Secker & Warburg, 2001.

Darnton, Robert. 'What is the History of Books?' *Proceedings of the American Academy of Arts and Sciences* 3.3 (1982): 65–83.

de Bellaigue, Eric. *British Book Publishing as a Business since the 1960s*. London: The British Library, 2004.

Deegan, Heather. *The Politics of the New South Africa: Apartheid and After*. London: Longman, 2001.

de Villiers, G.E., ed. *Ravan: Twenty-Five Years (1972–1997)*. Randburg, South Africa: Ravan Press, 1997.

Dirlik, Arif. 'The Postcolonial Aura: Third World Criticism in the Age of Global Capitalism.' *Critical Inquiry* 20 (1994): 328–56.

Eagleton, Terry. *The Ideology of the Aesthetic*. Oxford: Basil Blackwell, 1990.

English, James F. *The Economy of Prestige: Prizes, Awards, and the Circulation of Cultural Value*. Cambridge: Harvard University Press, 2005.

Epstein, Jason. *Book Business: Publishing Past, Present, and Future*. New York: W.W. Norton, 2001.

Escarpit, Robert. *Sociology of Literature*. 2nd edn. trans. Ernest Pick. London: Frank Cass, 1971.

Evans, Nicholas, and Monica Seeber, eds. *The Politics of Publishing in South Africa*. London: Holger Ehling Publishing, 2000.

Featherstone, Mike, ed. *Global Culture: Nationalism, Globalization and Modernity*. London: Sage, 1990.

Gardiner, Juliet. 'Recuperating the Author: Consuming Fictions of the 1990s.' *PBSA* 94 (2000): 255–74.

Genette, Gerard. *Paratexts: Thresholds of Interpretation*. trans. Jane E. Lewin. Cambridge: Cambridge University Press, 1997.

Ghose, Zulfikar. *The Art of Creating Fiction*. London: Macmillan, 1991.

——. *Confessions of a Native-Alien*. London: Routledge & Kegan Paul, 1965.

——. *The Fiction of Reality*. London: Macmillan, 1983.

——. *Figures of Enchantment*. New York: Harper & Row, 1986.

——. *A New History of Torments*. New York: Holt, Rinehart & Winston, 1982.

———. *The Triple Mirror of the Self*. London: Bloomsbury, 1992.

Ghosh, Bishnupriya. *When Borne Across: Literary Cosmopolitics in the Contemporary Indian Novel*. New Brunswick, NJ: Rutgers University Press, 2004.

Gilmore, Michael T. *American Romanticism and the Marketplace*. Chicago: University of Chicago Press, 1985.

Glass, Loren. *Authors Inc.: Literary Celebrity in the Modern United States, 1880–1980*. New York: New York University Press, 2004.

Glenn, Ian. 'Nadine Gordimer, J.M. Coetzee, and the Politics of Interpretation.' *South Atlantic Quarterly* 93 (1994): 11–32.

Goffman, Erving. *The Presentation of Self in Everyday Life*. New York: Doubleday Anchor, 1959.

Goldberg, David Theo, and Ato Quayson, eds. *Relocating Postcolonialism*. Oxford: Blackwell Publishers, 2002.

Gomery, Douglas, and Benjamin M. Compaine, eds. *Who Owns the Media? Competition and Concentration in the Mass Media Industry*. 3rd edn. Mahwah, NJ: Lawrence Erlbaum Associates, 2000.

Gunn, Giles, ed. *Globalizing Literary Studies*. Spec. issue of *PMLA* 116 (2001).

Huggan, Graham. *The Postcolonial Exotic: Marketing the Margins*. London: Routledge, 2001.

'In Full Colour: Cultural Diversity in Book Publishing Today.' ed. Danuta Kean. *The Bookseller* 12 March 2004: Supplement.

Jaszi, Peter, and Martha Woodmansee, eds. *The Construction of Authorship: Textual Appropriation in Law and Literature*. Durham: Duke University Press, 1994.

Jeyifo, Biodun. 'For Chinua Achebe: The Resilience and the Predicament of Obierika.' In *Chinua Achebe: A Celebration*. eds. Kirsten Holst Petersen and Anna Rutherford. Oxford: Heinemann, 1990. 51–70.

Jussawalla, Feroza, and Reed Way Dasenbrock, eds. *Milan Kundera / Zulfikar Ghose*. Spec. Issue of *Review of Contemporary Fiction* 9.2 (1989).

Kanaganayakam, Chelva. *Structures of Negation: the Writings of Zulfikar Ghose*. Toronto: University of Toronto Press, 1993.

King, Bruce. *Derek Walcott: A Caribbean Life*. Oxford: Oxford University Press, 2000.

Kossew, Sue, ed. *Critical Essays on J.M. Coetzee*. New York: G.K. Hall, 1998.

Krishnaswamy, Revathi. 'Mythologies of Migrancy: Postcolonialism, Post-modernism, and the Political of (Dis)location.' *Ariel* 26 (1995): 125–46.

Luey, Beth, and Fred Kobrak, eds. *The Structure of International Publishing in the 1990s*. New Brunswick, NJ: Transaction Publishers, 1992.

McDonald, Peter D. 'The Writer, the Critic, and the Censor: J.M. Coetzee and the Question of Literature.' *Book History* 7 (2004): 285–302.

McGann, Jerome. *The Textual Condition*. Princeton: Princeton University Press, 1991.

McKenzie, D.F. *Bibliography and the Sociology of Texts*. London: British Library, 1986.

Miyoshi, Masao. 'A Borderless World? From Colonialism to Transnationalism and the Decline of the Nation-State.' *Critical Inquiry* 19 (1993): 726–51.

Mongia, Padmini, ed. *Contemporary Postcolonial Theory: A Reader*. London: Arnold, 1996.

Moran, Joe. *Star Authors: Literary Celebrity in America*. London: Pluto Press, 2000.

Newbury, Michael. *Figuring Authorship in Antebellum America*. Stanford: Stanford University Press, 1997.

Nixon, Rob. *London calling: V.S. Naipaul, Postcolonial Mandarin*. Oxford: Oxford University Press, 1992.

O'Brien, Susie, and Imre Szeman, eds. *Anglophone Literatures and Global Culture*. Spec. issue of *South Atlantic Quarterly* 100 (2001).

Rifkin, Jeremy. *The Age of Access: The New Culture of Hypercapitalism, Where All of Life is a Paid-For Experience*. New York: Putnam, 2000.

Rose, Mark. *Authors and Owners: The Invention of Copyright*. Cambridge: Harvard University Press, 1993.

Rushdie, Salman. 'Damme, This is the Oriental Scene for You!' *New Yorker* 23 & 30 June 1997: 50–61.

——. *Fury*. Toronto: Vintage, 2002.

——. *The Ground Beneath Her Feet*. Toronto: Vintage, 1999.

——. *Imaginary Homelands: Essays and Criticism 1981–1991*. London: Granta Books, 1991.

——. *The Jaguar Smile: A Nicaraguan Journey*. New York: Viking, 1987.

——. *The Screenplay of* Midnight's Children. London, Vintage: 1999.

——. *Shame*. London: Picador, 1984.

——. *Step Across This Line: Collected Nonfiction 1992–2002*. New York: Random House, 2002.

San Juan Jr., E. *Beyond Postcolonial Theory*. New York: St. Martin's Press, 1998.

Schiller, Herbert I. *Culture, Inc.: The Corporate Takeover of Public Expression*. Oxford: Oxford University Press, 1989.

Simpson, David. *Situatedness, or, Why We Keep Saying Where We're Coming From*. Durham: Duke University Press, 2000.

Stadler, Alf. *The Political Economy of Modern South Africa*. London: Croom Helm, 1987.

Stevenson, Randall. *Oxford English Literary History*. Vol. 12, *1960–2000: The Last of England?* Oxford: Oxford University Press, 2004.

Strachan, Ian Gregory. *Paradise and Plantation: Tourism and Culture in the Anglophone Caribbean*. Charlottesville: University of Virginia Press, 2002.

Thieme, John. *Derek Walcott*. Manchester: Manchester University Press, 1999.

Todd, Richard. *Consuming Fictions: The Booker Prize and Fiction in Britain Today*. London: Bloomsbury, 1996.

Urry, John. *Consuming Places*. London: Routledge, 1995.

——. *The Tourist Gaze: Leisure and Travel in Contemporary Societies*. London: Sage, 1990.

Walcott, Derek. *Dream on Monkey Mountain and Other Plays*. New York: Farrar, Straus and Giroux, 1970.

——. *The Fortunate Traveller*. New York: Farrar, Straus and Giroux, 1982.

Weatherby, W.J. *Salman Rushdie: Sentenced to Death*. New York: Carroll & Graff, 1990.

West, James L. *American Authors and the Literary Marketplace since 1900*. Philadelphia: University of Pennsylvania Press, 1988.

Williams, Raymond. *The Long Revolution*. London: Chatto & Windus, 1961.

Wilson, R. Jackson. *Figures of Speech: American Writers and the Literary Marketplace, from Benjamin Franklin to Emily Dickinson*. New York: Knopf, 1989.

Wilson, Richard A. *The Politics of Truth and Reconciliation in South Africa: Legitimizing the Post-Apartheid State*. Cambridge: Cambridge University Press, 2001.

Wirtén, Eva Hemmungs. *No Trespassing: Authorship, Intellectual Property Rights, and the Boundaries of Globalization*. Toronto: University of Toronto Press, 2004.

Woodmansee, Martha. 'The Genius and the Copyright: Economic and Legal Conditions of the Emergence of the "Author".' *Eighteenth-Century Studies* 17 (1984): 425–48.

Young, Robert J.C. *Postcolonialism: An Historical Introduction*. Oxford: Blackwell, 2001.

Žižek, Slavoj. 'Multiculturalism, Or, the Cultural Logic of Multinational Capitalism.' *New Left Review* os 225 (1997): 28–51.

Index

Achebe, Chinua, 35
aestheticism, 8–9, 15–17, 34–7, 39–40,
    79–80, 87, 91, 110, 121–4, 153
    and the professionalization of
        authorship, 45–8, 184n14
Ahmad, Aijaz, 19, 21, 72–3
Alfred A. Knopf, 50, 84
Amis, Martin, 70, 84
Ananthamurthy, U.R., 87
anthropology, 27, 158, 161, 171–2
anti-authorialism, 11–12, 44, 48,
    67–8, 104, 154, 173, 176
Arts Council of England, 56–7
authenticity
    and autonomy from market
        economics, 72–3, 157, 177
    and folk culture, 27–31, 156, 161
    and tourism, 18–22, 40–3
    and writers' biographies, 4, 147–8,
        154, 169–73, 177
authorship
    biographization of, 11, 61, 65–8,
        70–1, 106–10, 145, 154, 176–7
    contemporary conceptions of, 3–4,
        48–9, 61–75
    and copyright law, 46–8
    professionalization of, 45–7, 54, 67,
        106
    romantic conceptions of, 4, 45–8,
        62

barcodes, 52
Barthes, Roland, 11–12, 67–9, 104
    see also anti-authorialism
BBC, 31, 55, 57, 92–3
Berger, John, 70
Bertelsmann, 25, 49, 50, 56, 59, 85
Bloomsbury, 84, 85, 145, 149
Booker Prize, 70, 84, 87, 129
book history, *see* history of the book
    and print culture studies
Bookseller, 55, 56–7
bookstores, 52, 54–6, 66, 185n43

Bourdieu, Pierre
    and autonomous authorship, 2–4,
        62–5
    The Field of Cultural Production, 3,
        62
    and media concentration, 63, 65,
        75
    The Rules of Art, 62–5, 69–70
Brathwaite, Edward Kamau, 41
Brennan, Timothy, 22, 31, 59–61, 70,
    145, 147, 172, 176
Brink, André, 116

Calder, Liz, 84
capitalism
    cultural, 42, 80, 148, 162
    and cultural production, 3, 16,
        19–21, 175, 177, 180n10,
        180n11, 186n66
    experiential, 179n5
    and guilt, 5–7, 17, 21–2, 25, 34–8,
        110, 112–13, 132–3, 140
    and the publishing industry, 45,
        49–54, 56–61, 175–7, 184n24
    and violence, 147–8, 156–7, 159
Casanova, Pascale, 59–60, 79–81, 110,
    122–3
censorship
    and J.M. Coetzee's career, 114–15,
        119, 190n2, 191n6
    and media concentration, 52
    and Salman Rushdie's career, 85–6,
        89, 190n2
Cerf, Bennett, 50
Chandra, Vikram, 58, 188n21
Chaterjee, Upamanyu, 58
Coetzee, J.M.
    career development and reception,
        9–10, 112–25
    and censorship, 114–15, 119,
        190n2, 191n6
    Disgrace, 9, 113, 124, 129–40, 143
    Dusklands, 115, 116–17

203